"*The Double* begins by intriguing us, procee
engage, and ultimately manages to disturb

JOSÉ
SARAMAGO

Winner of the Nobel Prize for Literature

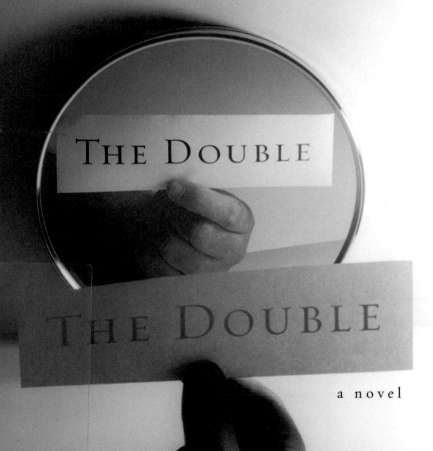

THE DOUBLE

THE DOUBLE

a novel

PRAISE FOR THE DOUBLE

"A wonderfully twisted meditation on identity and individuality. *The Double* succeeds in probing that human core we think we know until a master artist forces us to reconsider."

—*The Boston Globe*

"Saramago's...garrulous omniscient narrator—droll, delightful, persnickety, philosophical, always second-guessing—actually steals the book from the story's two carbon-copy protagonists....A last little twist, delivered in a final paragraph of a mere two pages, is delicious."—*Entertainment Weekly*

"In the end, it is this quest for his double that lifts Tertuliano out of his apathy as Saramago's observations, in small bursts, lift themselves up in startling truth and beauty."

—*San Francisco Chronicle*

"The water is deep but clear, and the face you see in it may be your own."   —*The News & Observer* (Raleigh, NC)

"There is a cheerful, whimsical quality to this book...It seems the Nobel-winning novelist was dancing with his own double an ebullient gremlin who wanted to write a moral potboiler."

—*The Baltimore Sun*

"*The Double* becomes a taut, surprising ride toward inevitable destruction. A shattering conclusion." —*Minneapolis Star Tribune*

"Think *Catcher in the Rye* meets *The Twilight Zone.* In an age when human cloning is feasible, *The Double* turns out to be more than just a fable. It's a sly warning." —*Fort Worth Star-Telegram*

"[An] inventive tale."   —*The Philadelphia Inquirer*

"Saramago posits questions of identity with relentless dark humor." —*Bookmarks*

"The plot is full of surprising, clever twists...and though the premise and series of events described are out of the ordinary (if not totally surreal), the story is convincing. That's because the author is in total control of his narrative." —*Milwaukee Journal Sentinel*

"[A] gripping plot, sprinkled with bitter humor and subtle irony." —*Political Affairs*

"Saramago is at his literary best....A testament to the unusual talents of both the novelist and the translator."—*Deseret News*

PRAISE FOR THE CAVE

"Nothing about *The Cave* feels like the work of either an old man of 80 or a world-famous author playing it safe...It is yet another triumph, albeit a typically melancholy one, for Portugal's, or even the world's, greatest living novelist. Read it—or just look straight ahead, turning neither to the left nor to the right, and imagine that literature is what's on the bestseller list." —*The Washington Post Book World*

"Saramago is arguably the greatest writer of our time....He has the power to throw a dazzling flash of lightning on his subjects, an eerily and impossibly prolonged moment of clarity that illuminates details beyond the power of sunshine to reveal. A genuinely brilliant novel." —*Chicago Tribune*

"One expects nothing less than another masterpiece from a remarkable writer who really may be, as many readers (including this one) believe, the greatest living novelist."—*The Boston Globe*

JOSÉ SARAMAGO

THE DOUBLE

Translated from the Portuguese by
Margaret Jull Costa

A HARVEST BOOK
HARCOURT, INC.

Orlando   Austin   New York   San Diego   Toronto   London

For information about permission to reproduce selections from this book,
write to Permissions, Houghton Mifflin Harcourt Publishing Company,
215 Park Avenue South, New York, New York 10003.

www.HarcourtBooks.com

This is a translation of *O Homem Duplicado*.

The Library of Congress has cataloged the hardcover edition as follows:
Saramago, José.
[Homem duplicado. English]
The double/José Saramago; translated from the Portuguese
by Margaret Jull Costa.—1st U.S. ed.
p. cm.
I. Costa, Margaret Jull. II. Title.
PQ9281.A66H6613 2004
869.3'42—dc22   2004009224
ISBN-13: 978-0151-01040-0   ISBN-10: 0-15-101040-4
ISBN-13: 978-0156-03258-2 (pbk.)   ISBN-10: 0-15-603258-9 (pbk.)

Text set in Centaur MT
Designed by Linda Lockowitz

Printed in the United States of America

First Harvest edition 2005
DOC 10 9 8 7 6 5 4

For Pilar, until the last moment
For Ray-Güde Mertin
For Pepa Sánchez-Manjavacas

Chaos is merely order waiting to be deciphered.

—*The Book of Contraries*

I believe in my conscience I intercept many a thought
which heaven intended for another man.

—LAURENCE STERNE,
The Life and Opinions of Tristram Shandy

THE MAN WHO HAS JUST COME INTO THE SHOP TO RENT A video bears on his identity card a most unusual name, a name with a classical flavor that time has staled, neither more nor less than Tertuliano Máximo Afonso. The Máximo and the Afonso, which are in more common usage, he can just about tolerate, depending, of course, on the mood he's in, but the Tertuliano weighs on him like a gravestone and has done ever since he first realized that the wretched name lent itself to being spoken in an ironic, potentially offensive tone. He is a history teacher at a secondary school, and a colleague had suggested the video to him with the warning, It's not exactly a masterpiece of cinema, but it might keep you amused for an hour and a half. Tertuliano Máximo Afonso is greatly in need of stimuli to distract him, he lives alone and gets bored, or, to speak with the clinical exactitude that the present day requires, he has succumbed to the temporary weakness of spirit ordinarily known as depression. To get a clear idea of his situation, suffice it to say that he was married but can no longer remember what led him into matrimony, that he is divorced and cannot now bring himself to ponder the reasons for the separation. On the other hand, while the ill-fated union produced no children who are now demanding to be handed, gratis, the world on a silver platter, he has, for some time, viewed sweet History, the serious, educational subject which he had felt called upon to teach and which could have been a soothing refuge for him, as a chore without meaning and a beginning without an end. For those of a nostalgic temperament, who tend to be fragile and somewhat inflexible, living alone is the harshest of punishments, but, it must be said, such a situation, however painful, only rarely develops into a cataclysmic drama of the kind to make the skin prick and the hair stand on end. What one mostly sees, indeed it hardly comes as a surprise anymore, are people patiently submitting to solitude's meticulous scrutiny, recent public examples, though not particularly well known and two of whom even met with a happy ending, being the portrait painter whom we only ever knew by his first initial, the GP who returned from exile to die in the arms of the beloved fatherland, the proofreader who drove out a truth in order to plant a lie in its place, the lowly clerk in the Central Registry Office who made off with certain death certificates, all of these, either by chance or coincidence, were members of the male sex, but none of them had the misfortune to be called Tertuliano, and this was doubtless an inestimable advantage to them in their relations with other people. The shop assistant, who had already taken down from the shelf the video requested, entered in the log book the title of the film and the day's date, then indicated to the customer the place where he should sign. Written after a moment's hesitation, the signature revealed only the last two names, Máximo Afonso, without the Tertuliano, but like someone determined to clarify in advance something that might become a cause of controversy, the customer murmured as he signed his name, It's quicker like that. This precautionary explanation proved of little use, for the assistant, as he transferred the information from the customer's ID onto an index card, pronounced the unfortunate, antiquated name out loud, in a tone that even an innocent child would have recognized as deliberate. No one, we believe, however free of obstacles his or her life may have been, would dare to claim that they had never suffered some similar humiliation. Although, sooner or later, we will all, inevitably, be confronted by one of those hearty types to whom human frailty, especially in its most refined and delicate forms, is the cause of mocking laughter, the truth is that the inarticulate sounds which, quite against our wishes, occasionally emerge from our own mouth, are merely the irrepressible moans from some ancient pain or sorrow, like a scar suddenly making its forgotten presence felt again. As he puts the video away in his battered, teacher's briefcase, Tertuliano Máximo Afonso, with admirable brio, struggles not to reveal the displeasure provoked by the shop assistant's gratuitous sneer, but he cannot help thinking, all the while scolding himself for the vile injustice of the thought, that the fault lay with his colleague and with the mania certain people have for handing out unasked-for advice. Such is our need to shower blame on some distant entity when it is we who lack the courage to face up to what is there before us. Tertuliano Máximo Afonso does not know, cannot imagine or even guess that the assistant already regrets his gross impertinence, indeed, another ear, more finely tuned than his and capable of dissecting the subtle vocal gradations in the assistant's At your service, sir, offered in response to the brusque Good afternoon thrown back at him, would have told him that a great desire for peace had installed itself behind the counter. After all, it is a benevolent commercial principle, laid down in antiquity and tried and tested over the centuries, that the customer is always right, even in the unlikely, but quite possible, eventuality that the customer's name should be Tertuliano.

Sitting now on the bus that will drop him near the building where he has lived for the last six or so years, that is, ever since his divorce, Máximo Afonso, and we use the shortened version of his name here, having been, in our view, authorized to do so by its sole lord and master, but mainly because the word Tertuliano, having appeared so recently, only six lines previously, could do a grave disservice to the fluency of the narrative, anyway, as we were saying, Máximo Afonso found himself wondering, suddenly intrigued, suddenly perplexed, what strange motives, what particular reasons had led his colleague from the Mathematics Department, we forgot to mention that his colleague teaches mathematics, to urge him so insistently to see the film he has just rented, when, up until then, the so-called seventh art had never been a topic of conversation between them. One could understand such a recommendation had it been an indisputably fine film, in which case the pleasure, satisfaction, and enthusiasm of discovering a work of high aesthetic quality might have obliged his colleague, over lunch in the canteen or during a break between classes, to tug anxiously at his sleeve and say, I don't believe we've ever talked about cinema before, but I have to tell you, my friend, that you absolutely must see *The Race Is to the Swift*, which is the title of the video Tertuliano Máximo Afonso has in his briefcase, something we also neglected to mention. Then the history teacher would ask, Where's it being shown, to which the mathematics teacher would respond, explaining, Oh, it's not being shown anywhere at the moment, it was on four or five years ago, I can't understand how I missed it when it first came out, and then, without a pause, concerned as to the possible futility of the advice he was so fervently offering, But maybe you've already seen it, No, I haven't, I hardly ever go to the cinema, I just make do with what they show on TV, and I don't see very much of that, Well, you should make a point of seeing it then, you'll find it in any video store, you can always rent it if you don't want to buy it. That is how the dialogue might have gone if the film had been worthy of praise, but things happened rather more prosaically, I don't want to stick my nose in where it isn't wanted, the mathematics teacher had said as he peeled an orange, but for a while now you've struck me as being rather down, and Tertuliano Máximo Afonso agreed, You're right, I have been feeling a bit low, Health problems, No, I'm not ill as far as I know, it's just that everything tires me and bores me, the wretched routine, the repetitiveness, the sense of marking time, Go out and have some fun, man, a bit of fun is always the best remedy, If you'll forgive me saying so, having fun is a remedy only for those who don't need one, A good answer, no doubt about it, but meanwhile, you've got to do something to shake off this feeling of apathy, Depression, Depression, apathy, it doesn't really matter, what we call the factors is arbitrary, But the intensity isn't, What do you do when you're not at school, Oh, I read, listen to music, occasionally visit a museum, And what about the cinema, No, I don't go to the cinema much, I make do with what they show on TV, You could buy a few videos, start a collection, a video library if you like, You're right, I could, except that I haven't even got enough space for my books, Well, rent some videos then, that's the best solution, Well, I do own a few videos, science documentaries, nature programs, archaeology, anthropology, the arts in general, and I'm interested in astronomy too, that sort of thing, That's all very well, but you need to distract yourself with stories that don't take up too much space in your head, I mean, given, for example, that you're interested in astronomy, you might well enjoy science fiction, adventures in outer space, star wars, special effects, As I see it, those so-called special effects are the real enemy of the imagination, that mysterious, enigmatic skill it took us human beings so much hard work to invent, Now you're exaggerating, No, I'm not, the people who are exaggerating are the ones who want me to believe that in less than a second, with a click of the fingers, a spaceship can travel a hundred thousand million kilometers, You have to agree, though, that to create the effects you so despise also takes imagination, Yes, but it's their imagination, not mine, You can always use theirs as a jumping-off point, Oh, I see, two hundred thousand million kilometers instead of one hundred thousand million, Don't forget that what we call reality today was mere imagination yesterday, just look at Jules Verne, Yes, but the reality is that a trip to Mars, for example, and Mars, in astronomical terms, is just around the corner, would take at least nine months, then you'd have to hang around there for another six months until the planet was in the right position to make the return journey, before traveling for another nine months back to Earth, that's two whole years of utter tedium, a film about a trip to Mars that respected the facts would be the dullest thing ever seen, Yes, I can see why you're bored, Why, Because you're not content with anything, I'd be content with very little if I had it, You must have something to hang on to, your career, your work, it doesn't seem to me that you have much reason for complaint, But it's my career and my work that are hanging on to me, not the other way around, Well, that's a malaise, always assuming it is a malaise, that I suffer from too, I mean, I myself would much rather be known as a mathematical genius than as the long-suffering, mediocre secondary school teacher I have no option but to continue to be, Maybe it's just that I don't really like myself, Now if you came to me with an equation containing two unknown factors, I could give you the benefit of my professional advice, but when it comes to an incompatibility of that sort, all my knowledge would only complicate things still further, that's why I suggested you pass the time watching a few films, as if you were taking a couple of tranquilizers, rather than devoting yourself to mathematics, which would really do your head in, Any suggestions, About what, About what would be an interesting, worthwhile film, There's no shortage of those, just go into a shop, have a look around, and choose one, Yes, but you could at least make a suggestion. The mathematics teacher thought and thought, then said, *The Race Is to the Swift*, What's that, A film, that's what you asked me for, It sounds more like a proverb, Well, it is a proverb, The whole thing or just the title, Wait and see, What sort is it, What, the proverb, No, the film, A comedy, You're sure it's not one of those old-fashioned, crime-of-passion melodramas, or one of those modern ones, all gunshots and explosions, It's a light, very amusing comedy, All right, I'll make a note of it, what did you say it was called, *The Race Is to the Swift*, Right, I've got it, It's not exactly a masterpiece of cinema, but it might keep you amused for an hour and a half.

Tertuliano Máximo Afonso is at home, he has a hesitant look on his face, not that this means very much, it isn't the first time it's happened, as he watches his will swing between spending time preparing something to eat, which generally means nothing more strenuous than opening a can and heating up the contents, or, alternatively, going out to eat in a nearby restaurant where he is known for his lack of interest in the menu, not because he is a proud, dissatisfied customer, he is merely indifferent, inattentive, reluctant to take the trouble to choose a dish from among those set out in the brief and all-too-familiar list. He is confirmed in his belief that it would be easier to eat in by the fact that he has homework to mark, his students' latest efforts, which he must read carefully and correct whenever they offend too extravagantly against the truths they have been taught or are overly free in their interpretations. The History that it is Tertuliano Máximo Afonso's mission to teach is like a bonsai tree the roots of which have to be trimmed now and then to stop it growing, a childish miniature of the gigantic tree of places and time and of all that happens there, we look, we notice the disparity in size and go no further, ignoring other equally obvious differences, the fact, for example, that no bird, no winged creature, not even the tiny hummingbird, could make its nest in the branches of a bonsai, and that if a lizard could find shelter in the tiny shadow the bonsai casts, always supposing its leaves were sufficiently luxuriant, there is every likelihood that the tip of the creature's tail would continue to protrude. The History that Tertuliano Máximo Afonso teaches, as he himself recognizes and will happily admit if asked, has a vast number of tails protruding, some still twitching, others nothing but wrinkled skin with a little row of loose vertebrae inside. Remembering the conversation with his colleague, he thought, Mathematics comes from another cerebral planet, in mathematics, those lizard tails would be mere abstractions. He took the homework out of his briefcase and placed it on the desk, he also took out the video of *The Race Is to the Swift*, these were the two tasks to which he could devote the evening, marking homework or watching a film, although he suspected that there wouldn't be time for both, especially since he neither liked nor was in the habit of working late into the night. Marking his students' homework was hardly a matter of life and death, and watching the film even less so. It would be best to settle down with the book he was reading, he thought. After a visit to the bathroom, he went into the bedroom to change his clothes, he donned different shoes and trousers, pulled a sweater on over his shirt, but left his tie, because he didn't like to leave his throat exposed, then went into the kitchen. He took three different cans out of the cupboard and, not knowing how else to choose, decided to leave the matter to chance, and resorted to a nonsensical, almost forgotten rhyme from childhood, which, in those days, had usually got him the result he least wanted, and it went like this, Eenie, meenie, minie, mo, catch a tiger by his toe, if he hollers let him go, eenie, meenie, minie, mo. The winner was a meat stew, which wasn't what he most fancied, but he felt it best not to go against fate. He ate in the kitchen, washing the food down with a glass of red wine, and when he finished, he repeated the rhyme, almost without thinking, with three crumbs of bread, the one on the left was the book, the one in the middle was the homework, the one on the right was the film. *The Race Is to the Swift* won, obviously what will be will be, don't quibble with fate over pears, it will eat all the ripe ones and give you the green ones. That's what people usually say, and because it is what people usually say, we accept it without further discussion when our duty as free people is to argue energetically with a despotic fate that has determined, with who knows what malicious intentions, that the green pear should be the film and not the homework or the book. As a teacher, and a teacher of history, this Tertuliano Máximo Afonso, for one has only to consider the scene we have just witnessed in the kitchen, entrusting his immediate future and possibly what will follow to three crumbs of bread and some senseless childhood drivel, this teacher, we were saying, is setting a bad example for the adolescents whom fate, whether the same or an entirely different one, has placed in his hands. Unfortunately, we do not have room in this story to anticipate the doubtless pernicious effects of the influence of such a teacher on the young souls of his pupils, so we will leave them here, hoping only that one day they may encounter on life's road a contrary influence that will free them, possibly in extremis, from the irrationalist perdition that currently hangs over them like a threat.

Tertuliano Máximo Afonso carefully washed up the supper dishes, for leaving everything clean and in its place after eating has always constituted for him an inviolable duty, which just goes to show, returning one last time to the young souls mentioned above, to whom such behavior might, indeed in all probability would, seem laughable and such a duty a mere dead letter, that it is still possible to learn something even from someone with so little to recommend him on all subjects, matters, and topics relating to free will. Tertuliano Máximo Afonso took this and other excellent lessons from the sensible customs of the family in which he was brought up, especially from his mother, who we are glad to say is alive and well, and whom he is sure to visit one of these days in the small provincial town where the future teacher first opened his eyes to the world, the cradle of the Máximos on his mother's side and the Afonsos on his father's side, and where he was the first Tertuliano to be born, almost forty years ago. He can only visit his father in the cemetery, that's what this bitch-of-a-life is like, it always runs out on us. The vulgar expression came into his mind unbidden, because, as he was leaving the kitchen, he happened to think about his father and to miss him, Tertuliano Máximo Afonso has never been one for using coarse language, so much so that on the rare occasions when he does, he himself is surprised by an awkwardness, by a lack of conviction in his phonatory organs, his vocal cords, palate, tongue, teeth, and lips, as if they were, against their will, articulating a word from a language hitherto unknown to them. In the small room that serves as both study and living room is a two-seater sofa and a coffee table, a rather welcoming armchair, with the television directly in front of it, at the vanishing point, and, placed at an angle to catch the light from the window, the desk where the history homework and the video are waiting to find out who will win. Two of the walls are lined with books, most of them dog-eared from use and wizened with age. On the floor, a carpet bearing a geometric design in subdued or possibly faded colors helps to create the no more than averagely cozy atmosphere, quite without affectation and making no pretense at appearing to be more than what it is, the home of a secondary school teacher who doesn't earn very much, a fact that may be capricious pigheadedness on the part of the teaching profession or the result of a historical penalty as yet still unpaid. The middle bread crumb, that is, the book that Tertuliano Máximo Afonso has been reading, a weighty tome on ancient Mesopotamian civilizations, lies where it was left the previous night, on the coffee table, waiting, like the other two bread crumbs, waiting, as all things always are, it's something they can't avoid, it is their ruling destiny, part, it seems, of their invincible nature as things. Given what we have so far seen of the character of Tertuliano Máximo Afonso, who, in the short time we have known him, has already shown signs of being something of a daydreamer, even somewhat noncommittal, it would come as no surprise now if he were to indulge in a display of certain conscious acts of self-deceit, leafing with feigned enthusiasm through his students' homework, opening the book at the page where he stopped reading, coolly studying both sides of the videocassette box, as if he had not yet decided what he wanted to do. But appearances, while not always as deceptive as people say, not infrequently belie themselves, revealing new modes of being that open the door to the possibility of real changes in a pattern of behavior, which, generally speaking, had been assumed to be defined already. This laborious explanation could have been avoided if, instead, we had got right to the point and said that Tertuliano Máximo Afonso headed straight for the desk, picked up the video, read the information on the front and back of the box, studied, on the former, the smiling, amiable faces of the actors, noted that only one of the names was known to him, the main one, that of a pretty, young actress, a sure sign that the film, when it came to drawing up contracts, had not been taken very seriously by the producers, and then, with the bold action of a will that seemed never to have wavered for a moment, slotted the cassette into the VCR, sat down in the armchair, pressed the PLAY button on the remote control, and settled back to enjoy the evening as best he could, although, given the unpromising material, any real enjoyment seemed unlikely. And so it proved. Tertuliano Máximo Afonso laughed twice and smiled three or four times, for the comedy was not just light, to use the mathematics teacher's conciliatory expression, it was, above all, absurd, ridiculous, a cinematic monster in which logic and common sense had been left protesting on the other side of the door, having been refused entry into the place where the madness was being perpetrated. The title, *The Race Is to the Swift*, was deployed merely as a very obvious metaphor, like one of those really easy riddles, what's white and is laid by hens, though there was no mention of races, runners, or speed, it was just a story of rampant personal ambition, which the pretty, young actress embodied as well as she had been trained to do, the plot being full of misunderstandings, hoaxes, mix-ups, and confusions, in the midst of which, alas, Tertuliano Máximo Afonso's depression found not the least relief. When the film ended, Tertuliano was more irritated with himself than with his colleague. The latter had the excuse of being well intentioned, but he himself was far too old to go chasing after sky rockets, and, as always happens with the ingenuous, what pained him most was his own ingenuousness. Out loud he said, I'll return this crap tomorrow, there was no surprise this time, he felt he had earned the right to vent his feelings using crude language, and one must bear in mind, too, that this was only the second vulgarity to escape him in recent weeks, what's more he had only thought the first one, and mere thoughts don't count. He glanced at his watch and saw that it wasn't yet eleven o'clock. It's early, he murmured, and by this he meant, as became apparent immediately, that he still had time to punish himself for his frivolity in having exchanged obligation for devotion, the authentic for the false, the enduring for the transient. He sat down at his desk, carefully drew the history homework toward him, as if seeking its forgiveness for his neglect, and worked into the night, like the scrupulous teacher he had always prided himself on being, full of pedagogical love for his pupils, but rigorous with dates and implacable when it came to epithets. It was late by the time he reached the end of the task he had set himself, but, still repentant for his lapse, still contrite for his sin, and like someone who has decided to swap one painful hairshirt for another no less punitive one, he took to bed with him the book on ancient Mesopotamian civilizations and began the chapter about the Amorites and, in particular, about their King Hammurabi and his code of law. After only four pages he fell peacefully asleep, a sign that he had been forgiven.

He awoke an hour later. He had not been dreaming, no horrible nightmare had disordered his brain, he had not been flailing around, trying to defend himself against a gelatinous monster that was stuck to his face, he merely opened his eyes and thought, There's someone in the apartment. Slowly, unhurriedly, he sat up in bed and listened. His bedroom has no windows, even during the day any outside noises are inaudible, and at this time of night, What time is it, the silence is usually complete. And it was complete. Whoever the intruder was, he was staying put. Tertuliano Máximo Afonso reached out to the bedside table and turned on the light. The clock said a quarter past four. Like most ordinary people, Tertuliano Máximo Afonso is a mixture of courage and cowardice, he isn't one of those invincible cinema heroes, but neither is he a wimp, the kind who pees his pants when, at midnight, he hears the door of the castle dungeon creak open. True, he felt all the hairs on his body prickle, but that even happens to wolves when faced by danger, and no one in their right mind would describe wolves as pathetic cowards. Tertuliano Máximo Afonso is about to prove that he certainly isn't either. He slid quietly out of bed, picked up a shoe for lack of any sturdier weapon, and, very cautiously, peered out into the corridor. He looked right and left. The sense of another presence that had woken him up grew slightly stronger. Turning on lights as he went, aware of his heart pounding in his chest like a galloping horse, Tertuliano Máximo Afonso went first into the bathroom and then into the kitchen. No one. And oddly enough, the presence seemed less intense there. He went back into the corridor and, as he approached the living room, he felt the invisible presence growing denser with each step, as if the atmosphere had been set vibrating by reverberations from some hidden incandescence, as if Tertuliano, in his nervousness, were walking over radioactive ground carrying in his hand a Geiger counter that, instead of sending out warning signals, was pumping out ectoplasm. There was no one in the room. Tertuliano Máximo Afonso looked around him, there they were, solid and impassive, the two tall, crowded bookshelves, the framed engravings on the walls, to which no reference has been made until now, but which are nonetheless there, and there, and there, and there, the desk with the typewriter on it, the chair, the coffee table in the middle with a small sculpture placed in its exact geometric center, and the two-seater sofa and the television set. Tertuliano Máximo Afonso muttered fearfully to himself, So that's what it was, and then, just as he uttered that last word, the presence, like a soap bubble bursting, silently disappeared. Yes, that's what it was, the television set, the VCR, the comedy called *The Race Is to the Swift*, an image from inside that had now returned to its place after going to rouse Tertuliano Máximo Afonso from his bed. He couldn't imagine what it could be, but he was sure he would recognize it as soon as it appeared. He went into the bedroom, put a dressing gown on over his pajamas, so as not to catch cold, and came back. He sat down in the armchair, pressed the PLAY button on the remote control, and leaning forward, all eyes, his elbows on his knees, no laughter or smiles this time, he replayed the story of that pretty, young woman who wanted to be a success in life. After twenty minutes, he saw her go into a hotel and walk over to the reception desk, he heard her say her name, My name's Inês de Castro, he had noticed this interesting historical coincidence earlier, then he heard her go on, I have a room reserved, the clerk looked straight at her, at the camera, not at her, or, rather, at her standing where the camera stood, but this time, Tertuliano Máximo Afonso barely understood what the clerk said, the thumb of the hand holding the remote control immediately pressed the PAUSE button, but the image had gone, obviously they weren't going to waste film on an actor who was little more than an extra, who only appeared twenty minutes into the plot, the tape rewound, past the receptionist's face, the pretty, young woman went into the hotel again, said again that her name was Inês de Castro and that she had reserved a room, and now, there it was, the frozen image of the clerk at the reception desk looking straight at the person looking at him. Tertuliano Máximo Afonso got up from the chair, knelt down in front of the television, his face as close to the screen as he could get it and still be able to see, It's me, he said, and once more he felt the hairs on his body stand on end, what he was seeing wasn't true, it couldn't be, any sensible person who happened to be there would say reassuringly, Come off it, Tertuliano, I mean, he's got a mustache, and you're clean shaven. Sensible people are like that, they tend to simplify everything, and then, but always too late, we witness their astonishment at the great diversity of life, they remember that mustaches and beards don't have minds of their own, they grow and prosper only when allowed to do so, or, occasionally, out of sheer indolence on the part of the wearer, but, from one moment to the next, because the fashion changes or because their hirsute monotony becomes an irritating sight in the mirror, they can also vanish without trace. Since, of course, anything can happen in the world of actors and the dramatic arts, there was also a strong probability that the clerk's fine, well-groomed mustache was, quite simply, false. It has been known. Tertuliano Máximo Afonso himself could have come up with these considerations, which, precisely because they were so obvious, would be bound to occur to anyone, had he not been so intent on finding other scenes involving this same extra or, to be more accurate, this supporting actor with a small speaking part. The man with the mustache appeared another five times in the film and on each occasion had very little to do, although in the last scene he was given a couple of supposedly saucy remarks to exchange with the mighty Inês de Castro and then, as she walked off, swaying her hips, he had to gaze after her with a grotesque leer on his face, which the director must have thought the audience would find irresistibly funny. Needless to say, if Tertuliano Máximo Afonso had failed to find this funny the first time, he found it still less so the second. He had gone back to the first image, the one in which the clerk at the reception desk, in close-up, is looking directly at Inês de Castro, and he was minutely analyzing the image, line by line, feature by feature, Apart from a few slight differences, he thought, especially the mustache, the different hairstyle, the thinner face, he's just like me. He felt calmer now, the resemblance was, to say the least, astonishing, but that was all it was, and there's no shortage of resemblances in the world, twins for example, the really amazing thing would be that out of the six thousand million people on the planet there weren't two people exactly alike. Obviously, they couldn't be exactly alike, the same in every detail, he said, as if he were talking to his almost—alter ego staring out at him from inside the television set. Seated once more in the armchair, thus occupying the position of the actress playing the part of Inês de Castro, he too pretended to be a customer at the hotel, My name's Tertuliano Máximo Afonso, he announced, then with a smile, What's yours, it was the rational thing to ask, if two identical people meet, it's only natural that they should want to know everything about each other, and the name is always the first thing we ask, because we imagine that this is the door through which one enters. Tertuliano Máximo Afonso fast-forwarded the tape to the end, there was the list of the supporting cast, he wondered if the roles they played would be mentioned too, but the names, and there were a lot of them, were simply listed alphabetically. He absentmindedly picked up the box, glanced again at what was on it, the smiling faces of the leading actors, a brief plot summary, and underneath, in small print, among the technical details, the date of the film. It's five years old, he muttered, and remembered that his colleague, the mathematics teacher, had told him this as well. Five years, he said again, and suddenly, the world gave another almighty shudder, it was not the effect of another impalpable, mysterious presence such as the one that had woken him, but of something concrete, not just concrete, but something that could be documented. With trembling hands, he opened and closed drawers, pulled out envelopes full of negatives and photographs, scattered them over his desk, and, at last, found what he was looking for, a photo of himself, five years ago. He had a mustache, a different hairstyle, and his face was thinner.

Nᴏᴛ ᴇᴠᴇɴ Tᴇʀᴛᴜʟɪᴀɴᴏ Mᴀ́xɪᴍᴏ Aғᴏɴsᴏ ʜɪᴍsᴇʟғ ᴄᴏᴜʟᴅ have said whether sleep once more opened her merciful arms to him after what, to him, had been the terrifying revelation of the existence, possibly in that same city, of a man who, to judge by his face and by his general appearance, was his very image. After a careful comparison of the photograph from five years ago with the close-up of the clerk in the film, and after finding no difference, however tiny, between the two, not even the smallest line present in one and absent in the other, Tertuliano Máximo Afonso fell onto the sofa, not into the armchair, which was not large enough to contain the physical and moral collapse of his body, and there, head in hands, nerves exhausted, stomach churning, he struggled to put his thoughts in order, untangling them from the chaos of emotions that had accumulated since the moment when memory, watching without his knowledge from behind the closed curtain of his eyelids, had woken him with a start from his initial and only sleep. What troubles me most, he finally managed to think, isn't so much the fact that the guy resembles me, is a copy, you might say, a duplicate of me, that's not so very unusual, there are twins, for example, there are look-alikes, species do repeat themselves, the human being repeats itself, head, trunk, arms, legs, and it could happen, although I can't be sure, it's just a hypothesis, that some unforeseen change in a particular genetic group could result in the creation of a being similar to one generated by another entirely unrelated genetic group, that doesn't trouble me as much as knowing that five years ago I was the same as he was then, I mean, both of us even had mustaches, and more than that, the possibility, or, rather, the probability that five years on, that is, now, right now, at this precise hour in the morning, that sameness continues, as if a change in me would occasion the same change in him, or worse still, that one of us changes not because the other one changes, but because any change is simultaneous, that's enough to send you stark staring mad, yes, all right, I mustn't make this into a tragedy, we know that everything that can happen will happen, but, first, there was the chance event that made us the same, then there was the chance event of my seeing a film I'd never even heard of, I could have lived out the rest of my life never imagining that a phenomenon like this would choose to manifest itself in an ordinary teacher of history, a man who only a few hours earlier was correcting his students' mistakes and who now doesn't know what to do with the mistake into which he himself, from one moment to the next, has seen himself transformed. Am I really a mistake, he wondered, and supposing I am, what significance, what consequences does it have for a human being to know that he's a mistake. A shiver of fear ran down his spine and he thought that some things were better left just as they are, to be what they are, because otherwise there is the danger that other people will notice and, even worse, that we too will begin to see through their eyes the hidden blunder that corrupted us at birth and which waits, impatiently chewing its nails, for the day when it can show itself and say, Here I am. The excessive weight of such deep thought, centered as it was on the possibility of the existence of absolute doubles, albeit intuited in brief flashes rather than put into words, made his head slowly droop and, eventually, sleep, a sleep that, in its own way, would continue the mental labors carried out up until then by wakefulness, overwhelmed his weary body and helped it make itself comfortable on the sofa cushions. Not that it was a rest that merited and justified that sweet name, for after a few moments, Tertuliano Máximo Afonso suddenly opened his eyes, like a talking doll whose mechanism has gone wrong, and repeated, in different words this time, the question he had just asked, What does it mean, being a mistake. He shrugged, as if the question had abruptly ceased to interest him. Whether this indifference was the understandable effect of extreme tiredness or, on the contrary, the beneficent consequence of that brief sleep, it is, nonetheless, both disconcerting and unacceptable because, as we well know, and he better than anyone, the problem was not resolved, it's still there untouched, waiting inside the VCR, having put into words that no one heard but which were there beneath the surface of the scripted dialogue, One of us is a mistake, that was what the clerk at the reception desk actually said to Tertuliano Máximo Afonso when, addressing the actress playing Inês de Castro, he informed her that the room reserved for her was number twelve-eighteen. How many unknown factors are there in this equation, the history teacher asked the mathematics teacher as he was once more crossing the threshold of sleep. His numerate colleague did not answer his question, he merely looked at him pityingly and said, We'll talk about it later, rest now, try to get some sleep, you need it. Sleep was indeed what Tertuliano Máximo Afonso most wanted at

21

that moment, but the attempt failed. Soon afterward, he was awake again, full of the brilliant idea that had suddenly occurred to him, which was to ask his colleague in mathematics to tell him why he had suggested watching *The Race Is to the Swift*, when it was a film of little merit, weighed down by five years of what had doubtless been a troubled existence, which in the case of any run-of-the-mill, low-budget movie is a surefire reason for being retired early on the grounds of disability or for meeting an inglorious end briefly postponed by the curiosity of a handful of eccentric viewers who, having heard talk of cult movies, erroneously thought that this was one. In this tangled equation, the first unknown factor he would have to resolve was whether his colleague had noticed the resemblance when he first saw the film and, if so, why he had not warned him when he suggested renting the video, even by jokily threatening him with, Prepare yourself, you're in for a shock. Although he does not really believe in Fate, distinguished from any lesser destiny by that respectful initial capital letter, Tertuliano Máximo Afonso cannot shake off the idea that so many chance events and coincidences coming all together could very well correspond to a plan, as yet unrevealed, but whose development and denouement are doubtless already to be found on the tablets on which that same Destiny, always assuming it does exist and does govern our lives, set down, at the very beginning of time, the date on which the first hair would fall from our head and the last smile die on our lips. Tertuliano Máximo Afonso has ceased lying on the sofa like an empty, crumpled suit, he has just stood up as steadily as he can manage after a night that, for violent emotions, has had no equal in his entire life, and, feeling that his head was not quite in its right place, he went over to the window to look out at the sky. The night was still clinging to the city's rooftops, the streetlamps were still lit, but the first, subtle wash of early-morning light was beginning to lend a certain transparency to the upper atmosphere. This was how he knew that the world would not end today, for it would be an unforgivable waste to make the sun rise in vain, merely to have the very entity that first gave life to everything witness the beginning of the void, and so, although the link between one thing and the other was not at all clear and certainly far from obvious, Tertuliano Máximo Afonso's common sense finally turned up to give the advice that had been noticeable by its absence ever since the clerk at the reception desk first appeared on the television screen, and this advice was as follows, If you feel you must ask your colleague for an explanation, then do so at once, that would be infinitely better than walking around with all kinds of questions and queries stuck in your throat, but I would recommend that you don't open your mouth too much, that you watch what you say, you're holding a very hot potato, so put it down before you get burned, take the video back to the shop today, that way you can draw a line under the whole business and put an end to the mystery before it begins to bring out things you would rather not know or see or do, besides, if there is another person who is a copy of you, or of whom you are the copy, as apparently there is, you're under no obligation to go looking for him, he exists and you knew nothing about him, you exist and he knows nothing about you, you've never seen each other, you've never passed in the street, the best thing you can do is, But what if one day I do meet him, what if I do pass him in the street, Tertuliano Máximo Afonso broke in, You just look the other way, as if to say, I haven't seen you and I don't know you, And what if he speaks to me, If he has even a grain of good sense, he'll do exactly the same, You can't expect everyone to be sensible, That's why the world's in the state it is, You didn't answer my question, Which one, What do I do if he speaks to me, You say, well, what an extraordinary, fantastic, strange coincidence, whatever seems appropriate, but emphasizing that it is just a coincidence, then you walk away, Just like that, Just like that, That would be rude, ill-mannered, Sometimes that's all you can do if you want to avoid the worst, if you don't, you know what will happen, one word will lead to another, after that first meeting there'll be a second and a third, and in no time at all, you'll be telling your life story to a complete stranger, and you've been around long enough to have learned that you can't be too careful with strangers when it comes to personal matters, and frankly, I can't imagine anything more personal, or more intimate, than the mess you seem about to step into, It's hard to think of someone identical to me as a stranger, Just let him continue to be what he has been up until now, someone you don't know, Yes, but he'll never be a stranger, We're all strangers, even us, Who do you mean, You and me, your common sense and you, we hardly ever meet to talk, only very occasionally, and, to be perfectly honest, it's hardly ever been worthwhile, That's my fault I suppose, No, it's my fault too, we are obliged by our nature and our condition to follow parallel roads, but the distance that separates or divides us is so great that mostly we don't hear each other, Yes, but I can hear you now, It was an emergency and emergencies bring people together, What will be, will be, Oh, I know that philosophy, it's what people call predestination, fatalism, fate, but what it really means is that, as usual, you'll do whatever you choose to do, It means that I'll do what I have to do, neither more nor less, For some people what they did is the same as what they thought they would have to do, Contrary to what you, common sense, may think, the things of the will are never simple, indecision, uncertainty, irresolution are simple, Who would have thought it, Don't be so surprised, there are always new things to learn, Well, my mission is at an end, you're obviously going to do exactly what you like, Precisely, Good-bye, then, see you next time, take care, See you at the next emergency, If I manage to get there in time. The streetlamps had been switched off, the traffic was growing thicker by the minute, the blue was gaining color in the sky. We all know that each day that dawns is the first for some and will be the last for others, and that for most people it will be just another day. For the history teacher Tertuliano Máximo Afonso, this day in which we find ourselves, in which we continue to exist, since there is no reason to believe it will be our last, will not be just another day. One might say that it appeared in the world with the possibility of being another first day, another beginning, and indicating, therefore, another destiny. Everything depends on what steps Tertuliano Máximo Afonso takes today. However, the procession, as people used to say in times gone by, is just about to leave the church. Let's follow it.

What a face, murmured Tertuliano Máximo Afonso, when he looked at himself in the mirror, and he was quite right. He had slept for only an hour, having spent the rest of the night struggling with the shock and horror described above, possibly in excessive detail, an excess entirely forgivable perhaps, given that never before in the history of humanity, the same history that Tertuliano Máximo Afonso tries so hard to teach his students, have two identical people existed in the same place and at the same time. There have been instances in far-distant times of a perfect physical resemblance between two people, sometimes men, sometimes women, but they were always separated by tens and hundreds and thousands of years and by tens and hundreds and thousands of kilometers. The most remarkable case we know was that of a particular town, long since disappeared, in which in the same street and in the same house, but not in the same family, and separated by an interval of two hundred and fifty years, two identical women were born. This marvelous event was not recorded in any chronicle, nor was it preserved in the oral tradition, which is perfectly understandable, really, given that when the first was born, no one knew there would be a second, and when the second came into the world, all memory had been lost of the first. Naturally. Notwithstanding the complete absence of any documentary proof or of eyewitness accounts, we are able to confirm, and even swear on our word of honor if necessary, that everything we have described or will describe or might describe as having happened in that now disappeared town did actually happen. The fact that history does not record a fact doesn't mean the fact did not exist. When he had reached the end of his morning shaving ritual, Tertuliano Máximo Afonso dispassionately examined the face before him and thought that, all in all, he looked better. Indeed, any impartial observer, whether male or female, would not shrink from describing his features, taken as a whole, as harmonious, and would definitely not neglect to give due importance to certain slight asymmetries and certain subtle volumetric variations that, if we may put it like this, constituted the salt that enlivened what would otherwise be an entirely savorless delicacy, so often the curse of faces endowed with an overly regular physiognomy. Not that we're saying Tertuliano Máximo Afonso is the perfect figure of a man, he would never be so immodest and we would never be so subjective, but, with just a pinch of talent he could doubtless have had a successful career as a leading man in the theater. And, of course, if he could act in a theater, he could act in movies too. An unavoidable parenthesis. There are moments in a narrative, and this, as you will see, has been one of them, when any parallel manifestation of ideas and feelings on the part of the narrator with respect to what the characters themselves might be feeling or thinking at that point should be expressly forbidden by the laws of good writing. The violation, either out of imprudence or a lack of respect, of such restrictive clauses, which, if they existed, would probably be of a nonobligatory nature, can mean that a character, instead of following, as is his inalienable right, an autonomous line of thought and feeling in keeping with the status conferred upon him, finds himself assailed quite arbitrarily by thoughts or feelings that, given their provenance, cannot be entirely alien to him, but which can, nonetheless, prove, at the very least, inopportune and, in some cases, disastrous. This was precisely what happened to Tertuliano Máximo Afonso. He was looking at himself in the mirror the way someone looks at himself simply in order to gauge the damage done by a bad night's sleep, he was thinking about this and nothing else, when, suddenly, the narrator's unfortunate thoughts about his physical features and the problematic possibility that, should he reveal the necessary talent, they might, at some future date, be placed at the service of the dramatic or cinematic arts, unleashed in him a reaction that it would be no exaggeration to describe as one of horror. If the man who played the part of the clerk at the reception desk were here, he thought melodramatically, if he were standing here in front of this mirror, the face he would see would be this face. We cannot blame Tertuliano Máximo Afonso for forgetting that the other man was wearing a mustache in the film, he did forget, it's true, but perhaps only because he was absolutely certain that the other man wouldn't

27

have a mustache now, which is why he has no need to resort to that mysterious source of knowledge, the presentiment, because he finds the best of all reasons in his own clean-shaven, utterly hairless face. Any feeling person will happily agree that the word horror, apparently ill suited to the domestic world of a person living alone, would describe with some accuracy what went through the mind of the man who has just come running back from his desk where he went to fetch a black felt-tipped pen and who now, standing once more before the mirror, traces on his own image, just above his own upper lip, a mustache identical to that worn by the clerk at the reception desk, the fine, pencil mustache of a leading man. At that moment, Tertuliano Máximo Afonso became the actor about whose name and life we know nothing, the teacher of history in a secondary school is no longer here, this apartment is not his, the face in the mirror has another owner. Had the situation lasted a minute longer, or not even that, anything could have happened in this bathroom, a nervous breakdown, a sudden fit of madness, a destructive rage. Fortunately, despite certain behavior which may have led one to believe the contrary, and which has doubtless not made its last appearance, Tertuliano Máximo Afonso is made of sterner stuff, and having, for a few moments, lost control of the situation, he has now regained it. However great an effort it may take, we know that all it requires to escape from a nightmare is to open our eyes, but the cure in this case was to close the eyes, not his own, but those reflected in the mirror. As effectively as any wall, a squirt of shaving foam separated these Siamese twins who have not yet met, and Tertuliano Máximo Afonso's right hand, splayed over the mirror, undid the faces of both men, so much so that neither would now be able to find or recognize himself in the surface smeared with white foam and with

gradually thinning trickles of black. Tertuliano Máximo
Afonso could no longer see the face in the mirror, now he was
alone in the apartment. He got into the shower, and although
he has always, since birth, been deeply skeptical about the
Spartan virtues of cold water, his father used to say that there
is no better way to prime the body or sharpen the brain, and
so it occurred to him this morning that a good blast of cold
water, without the addition of any decadent but delicious
warmer water, might prove beneficial to his feeble head and
might rouse once and for all the part inside him that is trying, all the time, surreptitiously, to slide into sleep. Washed
and dried, hair combed without the aid of the mirror, he
went into his bedroom, made the bed, got dressed, and then
went straight to the kitchen to prepare a breakfast composed,
as usual, of orange juice, toast, coffee, and yogurt, for teachers need to be well fed before they set off to school to face
that most difficult of tasks, planting trees or even bushes of
wisdom in ground that, in most cases, tends to be barren
rather than fertile. It is still very early, his class will not start
until eleven o'clock, but, in the circumstances, it is understandable that he would rather not be at home today. He returned to the bathroom to clean his teeth, and, while he was
doing so, it occurred to him that today was the day his upstairs neighbor usually came to clean the apartment, she was
an elderly woman, a widow with no children, who, as soon as
she realized that her new neighbor also lived alone, had appeared at his door six years ago to offer her services as a
cleaner. No, it's not her day today, he will leave the mirror as
it is, the foam is already starting to dry, it comes off with the
slightest touch of the fingers, but, for the moment, it's still
sticking to the surface and he can see no one peeping out from
underneath. Tertuliano Máximo Afonso is ready to leave, he

has already decided that he will go in the car in order to reflect calmly on the recent troubling events, without having to put up with the push and shove of public transport, which, for obvious economic reasons, it has been his habit to use. He put the homework books into his briefcase, paused for a few seconds to look at the empty video box, it would be a good time to follow the advice given by his common sense and take the video out of the VCR, put it back in its box, and go straight to the shop, Here you are, he would say to the assistant, I thought it would be interesting, but it wasn't, it was a waste of time, Do you want another one, the assistant would ask, struggling to recall the name of this customer who had only been in the day before, we've got a very wide selection, good films of every kind, old and new, ah, yes, Tertuliano, the last three words would only be thought, of course, and the accompanying ironic smile only imagined. Too late, the history teacher Tertuliano Máximo Afonso is already on his way down the stairs, this is not the first battle that common sense will have to resign itself to losing.

He drove slowly through the city, like someone who has decided to make the most of being out and about early, and while he did so, despite the help of a few red and amber lights slow to change, he vainly racked his brains to find some way out of a situation that, as would be clear to any reasonably informed person, was entirely in his hands. He knew where the difficulty lay and admitted it to himself out loud as he reached the street where the school stands, If only I could put all this nonsense behind me, forget about this insane business, just dismiss the whole absurd situation, here he paused to consider that the first part of this sentence would have been quite sufficient on its own, and then concluded, But I can't, which shows all too clearly how obsessed this disoriented man has become. As mentioned before, the history class doesn't start until eleven, which is two hours away. Sooner or later, his colleague the mathematics teacher will appear in the staff room where Tertuliano Máximo Afonso, who is waiting for him, is pretending, with apparent naturalness, to check through the homework in his briefcase. An attentive observer would not perhaps take long to notice this pretense, but for that he would have to be aware that no run-of-the-mill teacher would start reading for a second time what he had corrected a first time, not so much because there was a chance he would find new mistakes and therefore have to make new emendations, but as a matter of prestige, authority, and experience, or merely because what has been corrected stays corrected, and it is neither necessary nor possible to go back. That was all Tertuliano Máximo Afonso needed, to be correcting his own mistakes, always assuming that on one of the sheets of paper, which he is now reading without seeing, he had corrected what was right and put a lie in the place of an unexpected truth. As can never be stated too often, the best inventions are made by those who did not know what they were doing. At this point, the mathematics teacher entered the room. He saw his colleague the history teacher and went straight over to him. Good morning, he said, Good morning, Sorry, he said, I'm interrupting you, No, no, not at all, I was just having another quick glance through these, but I've corrected most of them already, How are they, Who, Your students, Oh, the usual, so-so, not too bad, Exactly like us when we were their age, said the mathematics teacher, smiling. Tertuliano Máximo Afonso was waiting for his colleague to ask him if he had, in the end, got around to renting the video, if he had seen it and liked it, but the mathematics teacher seemed to have forgotten entirely, his mind far from their interesting conversation of the previous day. He went and poured himself a coffee, came back, sat down, and calmly spread the newspaper out on the table, ready to learn about the general state of the world and the country. Having perused the headlines on the front page and wrinkled his nose at each of them, he said, Sometimes I wonder if the disastrous state the planet's in isn't all our own fault, Ours, whose, mine, yours, asked Tertuliano Máximo Afonso, pretending to be interested but hoping that this conversation, even though it was starting off with a subject so very far from his own concerns, would, eventually, lead them to the nub of the matter, Imagine a basket of oranges, said his colleague, imagine that one of them, at the bottom, starts to rot, and then imagine how each orange, one after the other, starts to rot too, who would then be able to say where the rot began, The oranges you're referring to, are they countries or people, asked Tertuliano Máximo Afonso, Within a country, they're the people, within the world, they're countries, and since there are no countries without people, it's obvious that the rot begins with the people, And why should it be us, you, me, who are the guilty parties, It must have been someone, Ah, but you're not taking society into account, Society, my dear friend, like humanity, is an abstraction, Like mathematics, Far more than mathematics, mathematics, in comparison, is as real as the wood this table's made of, What about social studies then, So-called social studies are often not studies about people at all, Let's just hope no sociologists are listening, they would condemn you to a civic death, at the very least, Contenting yourself with the music of the orchestra you play in and with the part you play in it is a common mistake, especially among nonmusicians, Some people are more responsible than others, you and I, for example, are relatively innocent, of the worst evils that is, Ah, the usual argument of the easy conscience, Just because it comes from an easy conscience doesn't mean it isn't true, The best way to achieve a universal exoneration is to conclude that since everyone is to blame, no one is guilty, Perhaps there's nothing we can do about it, perhaps they're just the world's problems, said Tertuliano Máximo Afonso, as if bringing the conversation to a close, but the mathematics teacher retorted, The only problems the world has are problems caused by people, and with that he stuck his nose in his paper. The minutes passed, it was nearly time for the history class, and Tertuliano Máximo Afonso could see no way of bringing up the subject that interested him. He could, of course, simply ask his colleague directly, put the question to him point-blank, By the way, except that he hadn't been coming that way at all, but these language fillers exist precisely for such situations, an urgent need to change the subject without appearing to insist, a kind of socially acceptable pretend-that-I-just-remembered-something, By the way, he would say, did you notice that the clerk in the film, the one at the reception desk, is the spitting image of me, but this would be tantamount to showing your strongest card in a game, making a third person party to a secret that wasn't even known as yet to two parties, with all the subsequent, future awkwardness of avoiding inquisitive questions, for example, So, have you met your double yet. Just then the mathematics teacher glanced up from the newspaper, So, he said, did you rent that video, Yes, I did, replied Tertuliano Máximo Afonso excitedly, almost happy, And what did you think of it, Quite amusing really, It helped with your depression, your apathy, I mean, Apathy or depression, it makes no odds, the name isn't the problem, It helped you though, Possibly, it made me laugh a couple of times. The mathematics teacher got up, he too had students waiting for him, what better opportunity for Tertuliano Máximo Afonso to say, By the way, when was the last time you saw *The Race Is to the Swift*, not that it really matters, of course, I was just curious, The last time was the first and the first time the last, When did you see it though, About a month ago, a friend lent it to me, Oh, I thought it was yours, part of your collection, No, if it had been, I would have lent it to you, not made you go spending good money on renting it. They were in the corridor now, on their way to the classrooms, Tertuliano Máximo Afonso felt easy and relaxed in his mind, as if his depression had suddenly evaporated, disappeared into infinite space, perhaps never to return. At the next corner, they would part and go their separate ways, and it was only when they had reached the corner and had both said, See you later, then, that the mathematics teacher, when he was about four paces away, turned and said, By the way, did you notice that one of the bit-part actors in the film looked incredibly like you, all you need is a mustache, and you'd be as alike as two peas in a pod. Like a devastating bolt of lightning, his depression fell from on high and reduced Tertuliano Máximo Afonso's buoyant mood to ashes. Despite this, he put on a brave face and managed to reply in a voice that seemed to break with every syllable, Yes, I did, it's an amazing coincidence, absolutely extraordinary, then added with a colorless smile, The only difference is that I haven't got a mustache and he's not a history teacher, otherwise we're identical. His colleague looked at him oddly, as if he had just met him again after a long absence, Now that I think of it, you had a mustache a few years ago too, he said, and Tertuliano Máximo Afonso, throwing caution to the wind, just like the lost man who will listen to no advice, replied, Perhaps, at the time, he was the teacher. The mathematics teacher came over to him, placed a paternal hand on his shoulder, You really are seriously depressed, I mean, something like that, a silly, unimportant coincidence, shouldn't upset you in this way, It didn't upset me, I just didn't sleep very much, I had a bad night, You probably had a bad night because you were upset. The mathematics teacher felt Tertuliano Máximo Afonso's shoulder tense beneath his hand, as if his whole body, from head to toe, had suddenly grown hard, and the shock was so great, the impression so strong, that it forced him to withdraw his hand. He did so as slowly as he could, trying not to show that he knew he had been rejected, but the unusual hardness in Tertuliano Máximo Afonso's eyes left no room for doubt, the pacific, docile, submissive history teacher whom he usually treated with friendly but superior benevolence is a different person right now. Perplexed, as if he had been set down in front of a game whose rules he did not know, he said, Right, I'll see you later, then, I won't be having lunch at school today. Tertuliano Máximo Afonso's only reply was to bow his head and go off to his class.

Contrary to the erroneous statement made a few lines back, which, however, we neglected to correct at the time, since this story is at least one step above a mere school exercise, the man had not changed, he was the same man. The sudden shift in mood observed in Tertuliano Máximo Afonso and which had so shaken the mathematics teacher was nothing but a simple somatic manifestation of a psychopathological state known as the wrath of the meek. Making a brief diversion from the central theme, we might be able to explain ourselves better if we were to refer to the old classification system, albeit somewhat discredited by modern advances in science, that divided the human temperament into four main types, namely, the melancholic, produced by black bile, the phlegmatic, produced, obviously, by phlegm, the sanguine, related no less obviously to the blood, and finally, the choleric, which was the consequence of white bile. As you can see, in this quaternary and primarily symmetrical division of the humors, there was no place for the community of the meek. Nevertheless, History, which is not always wrong, assures us that they already existed in those far-off times, indeed existed in great numbers, just as the Now, a chapter of History always waiting to be written, tells us that they still exist, that they exist in even greater numbers. The explanation of this anomaly, which, if we accept it, would serve as a way of understanding the dark shadows of Antiquity as well as the festive illuminations of the Now, may be found in the fact that when the clinical picture described above was defined and established, another humor had been forgotten. We are referring to the tear. It is surprising, not to say philosophically scandalous, that something so visible, so commonplace and abundant as tears have always been should have gone unnoticed by the venerable sages of Antiquity and received so little consideration from the no less wise, although far less venerable, sages of the Now. You will ask what this long digression has to do with the wrath of the meek, especially bearing in mind that Tertuliano Máximo Afonso, who gave such flagrant expression to it, has not yet been observed to cry. The statement we have just made regarding the absence of the tear from the humoral theory of medicine does not mean that the meek, who are naturally more sensitive and therefore more prone to that liquid manifestation of the emotions, spend all day, handkerchief in hand, blowing their nose or dabbing constantly at tear-reddened eyes. It does mean that, inside, a person, be they male or female, could well be tearing themselves to pieces as a result of loneliness, neglect, shyness, what the dictionaries define as an affective state triggered by social situations and which has volitive, postural, and neurovegetative effects, and yet, sometimes, all it takes is a simple word, a mere nothing, a well-intentioned but overprotective gesture, like the gesture made, quite unwittingly, by the mathematics teacher, for the pacific, docile, submissive person suddenly to vanish and be replaced, to the dismay and incomprehension of those who thought they knew all there was to know about the human soul, by the blind, devastating wrath of the meek. It doesn't usually last very long, but while it does, it inspires real fear. That is why the fervent bedtime prayer of many people is not the ubiquitous Lord's Prayer or the perennial Ave Maria, but Deliver us, O Lord, from evil and, in particular, from the wrath of the meek. The prayer seems to have worked well for Tertuliano Máximo Afonso's students, assuming they have habitual recourse to it, which, bearing in mind their extreme youth, is highly unlikely. Their time will come. It is true that Tertuliano Máximo Afonso entered the room frowning, which caused one student who thought himself more perspicacious than the others to whisper to the colleague beside him, He looks really pissed off, but this wasn't true, what could be seen on the teacher's face were merely the final effects of the storm, the last, scattered gusts of wind, a delayed flurry of rain, with the less flexible trees struggling to raise their heads. The proof of this was that, having called the register in a firm, serene voice, he said, I had intended saving the revision of our last written exercise for next week, but I had yesterday evening free and decided to get ahead of myself. He opened his briefcase, took out the papers, which he placed on the table, saying, I've corrected them all and given marks based on the number of errors made, but I'm not going to do as I usually do, simply hand the work back to you, instead, we're going to spend this class analyzing the mistakes, that is, I want each of you to explain the reasons for your mistakes, and the reasons you give me might even lead me to change your mark. There was a pause, and he added, For the better. The students' laughter blew the last clouds away.

After lunch, Tertuliano Máximo Afonso, along with most of his colleagues, took part in a meeting called by the headmaster to analyze the ministry's latest proposals for modernizing teaching practices, one of the many thousands of such proposals that make the lives of unfortunate teachers an arduous journey to Mars through an endless rain of threatening asteroids, some of which, all too often, hit their target. When it was his turn to speak, in a tone of voice that the other teachers found oddly indolent and monotonous, he merely repeated an idea that had long ceased to be a novelty and which always provoked a few benevolent smiles around the table as well as the ill-disguised annoyance of the headmaster, In my view, he said, the only important choice to make, the only serious decision to be taken as regards the teaching of history, is whether we should teach it from back to front or, as I believe, from front to back, everything else, while by no means insignificant, depends on that choice, and everyone knows this to be true, however much they may continue to pretend it is not. The effect of this speech was, as always, to elicit a resigned sigh from the headmaster and an exchange of glances and murmurs from the rest of the staff. The mathematics teacher smiled too, but his smile was one of friendly complicity, as if he were saying, You're quite right, none of this deserves to be taken seriously. The slight nod that Tertuliano Máximo Afonso sent back to him across the table meant that he was grateful for the message, but there was something else accompanying the gesture, something that, for lack of a better term, we will call a subgesture, telling him that the episode in the corridor had not yet been entirely forgotten. In other words, while the main gesture appeared to be openly conciliatory, saying, What's done is done, the subgesture hung back, adding, Yes, but not altogether. Meanwhile, it was the next teacher's turn to speak, and while he, unlike Tertuliano Máximo Afonso, discourses eloquently, pertinently, and proficiently, we will take the opportunity to discuss briefly, all too briefly given the complexity of the subject, the question of subgestures, which is, as far as we know, being raised here for the first time. People say, for example, that Tom, Dick, or Harry, in a particular situation, made this, that, or the other gesture, that's what we say, quite simply, as if the this, that, or the other, a gesture expressing doubt, solidarity, or warning, were all of a piece, doubt always prudent, support always unconditional, warning always disinterested, when the whole truth, if we're really interested, if we're not to content ourselves with only the banner headlines of communication, demands that we pay attention to the multiple scintillations of the subgestures that follow behind a gesture like the cosmic dust in the tail of a comet, because, to use a comparison that can be grasped by all ages and intelligences, these subgestures are like the small print in a contract, difficult to decipher, but nonetheless there. Putting aside the modesty that convention and good taste demand, we would not be the least bit surprised if, in the very near future, the study, identification, and classification of subgestures did not become, individually and as a whole, one of the most fertile branches of the science of semiotics in general. Stranger things have happened. The teacher who was speaking has just finished, the headmaster is about to move on to the next person, when Tertuliano Máximo Afonso shoots his right arm up in the air to indicate that he wishes to speak. The headmaster asked if he wished to comment on the points of view just expressed, adding that, if he did, according to the current rules of the meeting, as he doubtless knew, he must wait until everyone had had their say, but Tertuliano Máximo Afonso replied that, no, it wasn't a comment, nor was it to do with his colleague's very pertinent remarks, and that, yes, he knew and had always respected the rules, both those in current use and those fallen into disuse, all he wanted was to ask permission to be excused from the meeting because he had urgent matters to deal with outside of school. This time there was no subgesture, but there was a subtone, a harmonic, shall we say, which reinforced the incipient theory set out above as to the importance we should give to the many variations in communication, both gestural and oral, not just the second variation or the third, but also the fourth and the fifth. In the present case, for example, everyone at the meeting noticed that the subtone emitted by the headmaster expressed a feeling of deep relief underlying his actual words, Yes, of course, feel free. Tertuliano Máximo Afonso said good-bye with a generous wave of the hand, a gesture for the meeting as a whole, a subgesture for the headmaster, and left. His car was parked near the school, he was soon inside it, looking steadily at the road ahead, in the direction that would, for the moment, be the only appropriate destination given the events that had taken place since the previous afternoon, the shop where he had rented the video *The Race Is to the Swift.* He had sketched out a plan in the canteen, where he had lunched alone, had polished it under the protective shield of his colleagues' soporific speeches, and was now face-to-face with the assistant at the video shop, the one who had found this customer's name, Tertuliano, so very amusing and who, after the commercial transaction that will soon take place, will have more than enough reason to reflect upon the coincidence between the strangeness of the name and the extremely peculiar behavior of the person bearing that name. At first, there was no indication that this would happen, Tertuliano Máximo Afonso entered the shop like anyone else, he said good afternoon like anyone else, and, like anyone else, he started slowly perusing the shelves, stopping here and there, putting his head on one side to read the spines of the boxes containing the cassettes, until, finally, he went over to the counter and said, I'd like to buy the video I rented yesterday, I don't know if you remember, Yes, I remember perfectly, it was *The Race Is to the Swift*, Exactly, well, I'd like to buy it, With pleasure, but, if you don't mind my saying, and I only say this in your own interest, it would be best if you returned the video you rented and bought a new one, because, with use, you see, there's always some deterioration in both image and sound, minimal, it's true, but it does become more obvious over time, No, it's not worth it, said Tertuliano Máximo Afonso, the one I rented is fine for my purposes. The assistant heard with some perplexity the intriguing words for my purposes, it isn't a phrase generally considered necessary to apply to a video, you want a video to watch, that was what it was born for, the reason it was made, and that's all there is to it. The customer's eccentricities would not end there. In the hope of encouraging future transactions, the assistant had decided to treat Tertuliano Máximo Afonso with the most lavish display of appreciation and commercial consideration since the days of the Phoenicians, I'll deduct the rental price, he said, and as he was performing this subtraction, he heard the customer ask, Have you, by any chance, got any films by the same production company, Do you mean by the same director, asked the assistant cautiously, No, no, I mean the same production company, it's the production company I'm interested in, not the director, Forgive me, but in all my years in the business, no customer has ever asked me that, they ask for films by title, often by the name of a particular actor, and only very rarely does any one ask me about a director, but production companies, never, Let's just say I belong to a very select group of customers, So it would seem, Senhor Máximo Afonso, muttered the assistant, after a rapid glance at the customer's card. He felt stunned, confused, but pleased too by the sudden, happy inspiration that had prompted him to address the client by his surnames, which, since these could also be used as given names, might, from then on, manage to drive into the shadows of his memory the authentic name, the real name that had once, alas, made him feel like laughing. He had forgotten that he had neglected to reply to the customer as to whether he had in his shop other films by the same production company, Tertuliano Máximo Afonso had to repeat the question, adding an explanation that he hoped would correct the reputation for eccentricity he had clearly acquired in that establishment, The reason I'm interested in seeing other films by the same production company is that I'm currently working on a fairly advanced draft of a study of the tendencies, inclinations, intentions, and messages, explicit, implicit, and subliminal, in short, the ideological signals disseminated among its consumers, step by step, yard by yard, frame by frame, by a particular film-production company, always discounting, of course, the actual degree of awareness with which the company does so. As Tertuliano Máximo Afonso had developed his discourse, the assistant had opened his eyes wider and wider in pure astonishment and pure amazement, utterly won over by a customer who not only knew what he wanted but could give credible reasons for wanting it, something very rare indeed in commerce and, more particularly, in video-rental shops. It must be said, however, that the pure astonishment and pure amazement evident on the assistant's rapt face was tainted by the unpleasant stain of base commercial interest, the simultaneous thought that, since the production company in question was one of the most active and one of the oldest in the business, this customer, whom I must remember always to address as Senhor Máximo

Afonso, will end up by depositing a fair bit of money in the cash register when he finishes that work, study, essay, or whatever it is. Of course, one had to bear in mind that not all the films were available on video, but, even so, it was a promising deal, worth pursuing, Might I suggest, said the assistant, recovered now from his initial surprise, that we ask the production company for a list of all their films, Yes, possibly, said Tertuliano Máximo Afonso, but that isn't the most urgent thing at the moment, besides, I probably won't need to see every film they've produced, so we'll begin with what you have here, and then, depending on the results and conclusions reached, I'll decide what to do next. The assistant's hopes suddenly shriveled, the balloon was still on the ground and it already seemed to be losing gas. This, though, is precisely the kind of problem that besets small businesses, but just because the donkey kicked doesn't mean he'll break his leg, and if you haven't managed to get rich in twenty-four months, perhaps you'll make it if you work for twenty-four years. With his moral armor more or less restored thanks to the curative properties of these little nuggets of patience and resignation, the assistant announced as he came out from behind the counter and walked toward the shelves, Well, I'll just go and see what we've got, to which Tertuliano Máximo Afonso replied, If you do have any, then five or six will be enough to start with, just so that I can get down to work tonight, Six videos is equivalent to about nine hours' worth of viewing, the assistant remarked, it will be a long evening. This time Tertuliano Máximo Afonso did not reply, he was looking at a poster advertising what must have been a very recent film by the same production company, called *The Goddess of the Stage.* The names of the principal actors were written in different-sized fonts and were arranged on the poster in accordance with the greater or lesser importance of their place in the national cinematic firmament. The name of the actor who played the role of the hotel receptionist in *The Race Is to the Swift* would clearly not be there. The assistant returned from his explorations, bringing a pile of six videos, which he placed on the counter, We've got more, but you did say you only wanted five or six, That's fine, I'll come by tomorrow or the day after to pick up any others you find, Should I order those we don't already have, asked the assistant, in an attempt to rekindle dying hopes, Let's start with what we have here and then see. There was no point insisting, the customer really did know what he wanted. In his head, the assistant multiplied by six the individual prices of the videos, he belonged to the old school, to the age before pocket calculators, when these did not even exist in people's dreams, and said a number. Tertuliano Máximo Afonso corrected him, That's the sale price of the videos not the rental price, Oh, since you bought the other one, I assumed you'd want to buy these too, said the assistant by way of explanation, Yes, I might buy some or even all of them eventually, but first I have to see them, to view them, I think that's the right word, to find out if they have what I'm looking for. Overwhelmed by the customer's irrefutable logic, the assistant made a rapid recalculation and slipped the videos into a plastic bag. Tertuliano Máximo Afonso paid, said good afternoon, see you tomorrow, and left. Whoever named you Tertuliano knew what he was doing, muttered the frustrated vendor.

Given that preference is likely to be given to a device blessed with the seal of academic approval, the easiest thing for the relater or narrator, having reached this point, would be to say that nothing happened during the history teacher's homeward journey across the city. Like a time machine, especially when professional scruples will not permit the invention of a public fracas or a traffic accident just to fill in any gaps in the plot, those words, Nothing Happened, are used when there is an urgent need to move on to the next incident or when, for example, one does not know quite what to do with the character's own thoughts, especially if these bear no relation to the existential milieu in which the character is supposed to live and work. The teacher and fledgling lover of videos, Tertuliano Máximo Afonso, is in precisely this situation as he is driving his car. He was in fact thinking, a lot and very intensely, but his thoughts bore so little relevance to the last twenty-four hours he had just lived through that if we were to take them into account and include them in this novel, the story we had decided to tell would inevitably have to be replaced by another. True, it might be worthwhile, or rather, since we know everything about Tertuliano Máximo Afonso's thoughts, we know that it would be worthwhile, but this would mean declaring all our hard work, these forty or so dense, difficult pages, null and void, and going back to the beginning, to the ironic, insolent first page, throwing away all that honest toil to take a chance on an adventure, not just new and different, but also highly dangerous, for, of this we are sure, that is precisely where Tertuliano Máximo Afonso's thoughts would lead us. Let us remain therefore with this bird in the hand, rather than suffer the disappointment of seeing two fly away. Besides, we haven't got time for anything else. Tertuliano Máximo Afonso has just parked his car and is walking the short distance to his apartment, in one hand he has his teacher's briefcase, in the other the plastic bag, what will he be thinking about now apart from calculating how many videos he will manage to view, to use the more formal term, before going to bed, that's what comes of taking an interest in bit-part players, if he were a star, he'd be there in the very first scenes. Tertuliano Máximo Afonso has already opened the front door, gone in, and closed the door behind him, he puts the briefcase down on the desk and, beside it, the bag containing the videos. The air is free of any presences, or perhaps they are simply not apparent, as if what came into the apartment last night had meanwhile become an inseparable part of it. Tertuliano Máximo Afonso went to his room to change his clothes, opened the fridge in the kitchen to see if there was anything in it he fancied eating, closed it again, and went back into the living room with a can of beer and a glass. He took the videos out of the bag and arranged them in order of date of production, from the oldest, *The Accursed Code*, made two years before *The Race Is to the Swift*, which he has already seen, to the most recent, *The Goddess of the Stage*, from last year. The other four, in the same order, are *Passenger without a Ticket, Death Strikes at Dawn, The Alarm Rang Twice*, and *Phone Me Another Day*. An involuntary reflex movement, doubtless provoked by the last of these titles, made him turn and look at his own phone. The light on the machine was blinking, informing him that there were messages for him. He hesitated for a few seconds but ended up pressing the button to hear them. The first was a female voice that did not announce its identity, knowing presumably that it would be instantly recognized, it said only, It's me, then went on, I don't know what's wrong, but you haven't phoned me for a week now, if you want to end the relationship, then it would be better to tell me so to my face, surely this silence isn't to do with the fact that we quarreled the other day, well, only you know that, anyway, just to say that I still care about you, lots of love, bye. The second message was the same voice, Please phone me. There was a third message, but this was from the mathematics teacher, Listen, my friend, I got the impression that I did something today to annoy you, but, to be perfectly honest, I can't imagine what it was I did or said, I think we should talk and clear up any possible misunderstanding between us, if I owe you an apology, then please take this call as at least the beginning of one, all the best, and I'm sure I don't need to tell you that you have a friend in me. Tertuliano Máximo Afonso frowned, he vaguely remembered that something irritating or unpleasant had happened at school involving the mathematics teacher, but he couldn't remember what it was. He rewound the tape and listened again to the first two messages, this time with a half smile and a look on his face that is usually described as dreamy. He got up to remove the tape of *The Race Is to the Swift* from the VCR and to replace it with *The Accursed Code*, but at the last moment, his finger already on the PLAY button, he realized that, if he went on, he would be committing a grave infraction, omitting one of the sequential points in the plan of action he had drawn up, that is, copying down from the end of *The Race Is to the Swift* the names of the lowest-ranking bit-part actors, the ones who, even though they occupy time and space in the story, even though they say a few words and serve as satellites, tiny ones, of course, at the service of the interconnections and crossed orbits of the stars, do not even have the right to one of those temporary names, as necessary in life as in fiction, although we should not perhaps say so. He could, of course, do it afterward, at another time, but order, as people also say of the dog, is man's best friend, although, like the dog, it does occasionally bite. Everything in its place and a place for everything has always been the golden rule in prosperous families, just as, time and again, do what you have to do in good order has been shown to be the most solid insurance policy against the phantoms of chaos. Tertuliano Máximo Afonso quickly wound on the now familiar tape of *The Race Is to the Swift*, paused it at the relevant place, copied onto a sheet of paper the names of the men, only the men, because this time, most unusually, the object of the search is not a woman. We assume this provides an adequate explanation of the plan Tertuliano Máximo Afonso drew up during his long deliberations, that is, to try and identify the hotel receptionist, the one who was the spitting image of himself in the days when he had a mustache, and who doubtless continues to be so today without the mustache, and, who knows, tomorrow too, when the receding hairline of one begins to move in the direction of the baldness of the other. Tertuliano Máximo Afonso's plan was, like Columbus's discovery of the Indies, obvious once one had thought of it, to note down all the names of the supporting actors, both in the films in which the receptionist appeared and those in which he did not. For example, if his human copy does not appear in the film, *The Accursed Code*, that he has just slotted in the VCR, he can strike from the first list all those actors who also appeared in *The Race Is to the Swift*. As we know, a Neanderthal's brain would be no use at all in a situation like this, but for a history teacher accustomed to grappling with people from the most various places and times, why, only yesterday he was reading a chapter on the Amorites in that erudite tome about ancient Mesopotamian civilizations, this poor man's version of a treasure hunt is pure child's play and probably did not merit, on our part, such a detailed and comprehensive explanation. In the end, contrary to all our expectations, the hotel receptionist did appear in *The Accursed Code*, this time in the guise of a bank clerk being threatened by a gunman and, doubt-less to appear more convincing in the dissatisfied eyes of the director, exaggerating his fearful tremblings as he was forced to transfer the contents of the safe into a bag that the attacker hurled across the counter at him, at the same time snarling out of the corner of his mouth, a gesture so characteristic of the gangster genre, Either fill this up or I'll fill you full of lead. He had a certain taste for alliteration, this bandit. The bank clerk reappeared on two other occasions, the first time to answer police questions, the second when the bank man-ager decided to take him off counter duty because, trauma-tized by the incident, he had started to view all customers as potential thieves. Needless to say, the bank clerk sported the same fine, lustrous mustache as the hotel receptionist. This time, Tertuliano Máximo Afonso did not feel cold rivulets of sweat running down his back, this time his hands did not shake, he paused the image for a few seconds, studied it with cold curiosity, then moved on. Since this was a film in which the identical man, the look-alike, the unattached Siamese twin, the prisoner of Zenda, or some other thing still await-ing classification, had taken part, the method to be followed in the search for his real identity would clearly have to be dif-ferent, marking any names that had appeared on the first list and were repeated on the second. Tertuliano Máximo Afonso marked two, only two, with a cross. It was still some time until supper, his appetite showed no signs of impatience, he could therefore see the film that was next in chronological order, *Passenger without a Ticket* was the title, but it might just as well have been called A Complete Waste of Time, for the man in the iron mask had not been hired to appear in it. A Complete Waste of Time, we say, but not so complete, because thanks to the film a few more names could be crossed out on the first list and the second, By a process of elimination I'll get there in the end, Tertuliano Máximo Afonso said out loud, as if he had suddenly felt a need for company. The telephone rang. The least probable of all the possibilities was that it was his colleague the mathematics teacher, the most possible of all the probabilities that it was the same woman who had phoned twice before. It could also be his mother calling from far away, inquiring after the health of her beloved son. After a few rings, the telephone fell silent, a sign that the recording mechanism was about to start, from then on the recorded words will have to wait for the time when someone wants to listen to them, the mother asking, How have you been, my dear, the friend insisting, I don't think I said or did anything wrong, the lover despairing, I don't deserve to be treated like this by you. Whatever is now inside the machine, Tertuliano Máximo Afonso does not feel like listening to it. To distract himself, rather than because his stomach was demanding food, he went into the kitchen to make himself a sandwich and open another can of beer. He sat down on a stool, munched without pleasure on this frugal meal while his thoughts, set free, abandoned themselves to daydreaming. Realizing that conscious vigilance had faded away into a kind of swoon, common sense, which, after its first energetic intervention, had simply wandered off somewhere, insinuated itself in between two inconclusive fragments of that vague meditation and asked Tertuliano Máximo Afonso if he was happy with the situation he had created. Brought abruptly back to the bitter taste of a beer that had soon lost its coldness and to the soft, clammy consistency of a piece of low-quality ham squeezed between two slices of phony bread, the history teacher replied that happiness had nothing to do with what was going on here, and, as for the situation, he would just like to say that he had not created it. I agree you didn't create it, replied common sense, but most situations in which we find ourselves would never have got where they are if we hadn't helped them along, and you're not going to deny that you helped this one along, It was just curiosity, that's all, We've already discussed this, Have you got anything against curiosity, All I'm saying is that life hasn't yet taught you to understand that our finest gift, and by ours I mean common sense's, has always been curiosity, In my view, common sense and curiosity are incompatible, How wrong you are, sighed common sense, Prove it to me then, Who do you think invented the wheel, Nobody knows, Oh yes we do, the wheel was invented by common sense, only an enormous amount of common sense would have been capable of inventing it, And what about the atomic bomb, did common sense invent that too, asked Tertuliano Máximo Afonso in the triumphant tone of one who has just caught his opponent off guard, Oh, no, the atomic bomb was obviously invented by a sense, but there was nothing common about it, Forgive me saying so, but common sense is naturally conservative, I would go further and say reactionary, Ah, those accusing letters, sooner or later everyone writes them and everyone receives them, If all those people were sufficiently of one mind to write them, even those who had no alternative but to receive them, apart, that is, from writing them themselves, then it must be true, You know perfectly well that being of one mind doesn't always mean being in the right, what tends to happen is that people gather together under an opinion as if it were an umbrella. Tertuliano Máximo Afonso opened his mouth to speak, if the expression "opened his mouth" is allowable in a description of an entirely silent dialogue, taking place entirely in the mind as this one was, but common sense was no longer there, it had noiselessly withdrawn, not defeated exactly, but annoyed with itself for having allowed the conversation to be diverted from the matter that had provoked its reappearance. Always assuming, of course, that it hadn't been entirely common sense's fault that this had happened. Indeed, common sense has often been mistaken about consequences, badly so when it invented the wheel, disastrously so when it invented the atomic bomb. Tertuliano Máximo Afonso looked at his watch, calculated how long it would take to watch another film, for he was starting to feel the effects of that sleepless night, his eyelids, with the help of the beer he had drunk, were heavy as lead, and this was probably what lay behind the abstracted state into which he had fallen earlier. If I go to bed now, he said, I'll probably just wake up again in two or three hours' time, and then I'll feel even worse. He decided to see a bit of *Death Strikes at Dawn*, the guy might not even be in it, which would simplify everything, he could fast-forward to the end, make a note of the names, and then go to bed. He was quite wrong. There he was, playing the part of a hospital auxiliary, without a mustache this time. Tertuliano Máximo Afonso's hair stood on end again, this time only on his arms, the sweat left his back alone, and a normal sweat, not a cold one, contented itself with slightly dampening his forehead. He watched the whole film, put a cross next to another name that had appeared on other lists, and went to bed. He even read a couple of pages from the chapter on the Amorites before turning out the light. His last conscious thought was about his colleague the mathematics teacher. He really didn't know how to explain his sudden coldness toward him in the corridor at school. Was it because he put his hand on my shoulder, he asked, and immediately replied, I'll look like a complete fool if I tell him that and he turns his back on me, which is what I would do in his place. He used the final second before sleep to murmur, perhaps addressing himself, perhaps his colleague, There are some things you just can't explain in words.

WELL, THAT'S NOT QUITE TRUE. THERE WAS A TIME WHEN there were so few words that we did not even have enough to express something as simple as, This is my mouth, or, That is your mouth, still less ask, Why are our mouths touching. It doesn't occur to people nowadays what a lot of work was involved in creating those words, it was necessary, in the first place, to realize that there was a need for them, which may, who knows, have been the most difficult thing of all, then to reach a consensus on the significance of their immediate effects, and finally, a task that will never fully be completed, to imagine the consequences that might ensue, in the medium and long term, from these effects and from these words. Compared with this, and contrary to common sense's peremptory statement of last night, the invention of the wheel was no more than a lucky chance, as would be the discovery of the universal law of gravity, all because an apple happened to fall on Newton's head. The wheel was invented and stayed invented forever and ever, whereas words, those and all the others, came into the world with a vague, diffuse destiny, as highly provisional phonetic and morphological clusters, however much, thanks perhaps to the inherited glow of their glorious creation, they may insist on passing themselves off, not so much in their own right, but on behalf of the thing they variably mean and represent, as immortal, undying, or eternal, depending on the taste of the person doing the classifying. This congenital tendency, which they proved unable to resist, became, over time, a grave and possibly insoluble problem of communication, either in the collective or in the personal sense, getting their apples and their onions mixed up, their legacies with their legalese, the words usurping the place of the thing that, before, for better or worse, they had done their best to express, and out of which came, in the end, don't let the mask fool you, the thunderous clatter of empty cans, the carnivalesque cortege of canisters with labels on the outside but nothing inside, or merely, fading fast, the evocative smell of the food for mind and body that they once contained and conserved. This rambling reflection on the origins and destinies of words has led us so far from our real subject that we have no option but to start again at the beginning. Contrary to appearances, it was not mere chance that made us write the phrase, This is my mouth or the phrase, That is your mouth, still less, Why are our mouths touching. Had Tertuliano Máximo Afonso spent some of his time years ago, always assuming he had done so at the right moment, pondering the consequences and effects, short-term and long-term, of similar phrases and others that tend and incline to the same end, it is highly probable that he would not now be looking at the phone, scratching his head, a perplexed look on his face, wondering what the devil he will say to the woman who twice, possibly three times, left her voice and her lamentations on his answering machine. The smug half smile and dreamy expression we noticed last night when he listened to the messages were, after all, just a reprehensible sign of pride, and pride, especially among the male half of the world, is like one of those supposed friends who, at the first hint of trouble in our life, make themselves scarce or look the other way, whistling loudly. Maria da Paz, for that is the sweet, promising name of the woman who phoned, will soon be leaving for work, and if Tertuliano Máximo Afonso does not speak to her right now, the poor woman will have to spend another day worrying, which, whatever may have been her errors or her sins, if, indeed, she has committed any, really would be most unfair. Or undeserved, which was the term she preferred to use. It must be said, however, in respect and obedience to the rigor of the facts, that the difficulty Tertuliano Máximo Afonso is wrestling with at the moment has nothing to do with estimable questions of morality or scruples about justice or injustice, but the knowledge that if he doesn't phone her, she will phone him, and that the new call will bring down on him more recriminations, possibly tearful, possibly not. The wine has been poured and, in its time, savored, now he has to drink the bitter dregs in the bottom of the glass. As we will have ample opportunity to discover in the future, and in situations that will teach him some hard lessons, Tertuliano Máximo Afonso is not what one would call a bad person, we could even find him honorably included in a list of good people, if the list was drawn up according to some fairly undemanding criteria, but apart from being, as we have seen, extremely sensitive, which is a clear indication of a lack of self-confidence, his main weakness lies in his emotions, which have never been strong or enduring. His divorce, for example, was not one of those classic melodramas, all jealousies and betrayals, desertions and violence, it was merely the climax of a long process of continuous decay that had afflicted his own loving feelings and which he, whether out of distraction or indifference, would merely have sat back and watched to see what arid deserts would result, but which the woman to whom he was married, more honest and decent than him, finally found unbearable and unacceptable. I married you because I loved you, she said one famous day, but the only reason I would continue in this marriage now would be out of cowardice, And you're no coward, he said. No, she said, I'm not. The likelihood of this, in many ways, attractive person playing a part in the story we are telling is, alas, minimal, not to say nonexistent, it would depend on an action, gesture, or word from this her ex-husband, a word, gesture, or action that would doubtless be determined by some need or interest of his but about which, at this stage, we have no way of knowing. That is why we do not feel it necessary to give her a name. As for Maria da Paz, whether or not she continues to be a presence in these pages, for how long and to what end, is up to Tertuliano Máximo Afonso, he knows what he will say to her if and when he finally decides to pick up the phone and dial a number he knows by heart. He doesn't know by heart the mathematics teacher's number, which is why he is looking it up in his address book, it would seem, after all, that he is not going to phone Maria da Paz, he thought it more important, more urgent, to clear up an insignificant misunderstanding than to soothe a suffering female soul or deliver the coup de grâce. When Tertuliano Máximo Afonso's ex-wife said she was not a coward, she was at pains not to offend him with the assertion or even suggestion that he was, but in this case, as so often in life, a word to the wise is enough, and returning to the present emotional scene, the long-suffering, patient Maria da Paz is not even being granted half a word, although she has already grasped almost everything there is to understand, namely, that her boyfriend, lover, sexual partner, or whatever people call these things nowadays, is preparing to say good-bye. It was the mathematics teacher's wife who answered the phone and asked, Who is it, in a voice that barely disguised the irritation caused by a phone call at that hour in the morning, she didn't communicate this with half words but with a shrill, vibrant subtone, we are clearly in the presence here of a subject crying out for the attention of scholars from various disciplines, in particular that of sound theory, with appropriate help from those who have known most about the subject for centuries now, we are referring, of course, to people in the music world, to composers, in the first place, but also to the interpreters, to musicians, who are the ones who have to know how to make the sounds. Tertuliano Máximo Afonso began by apologizing, then gave his name and asked if he could speak to, Just a minute, I'll call him, the woman cut in, and shortly afterward there was his colleague saying, Good morning, and him responding, Good morning, he apologized again, said that he had only just heard his friend's message, I could have waited to talk to you at school but felt I should clear the air as quickly as possible so as not to leave room for any further misunderstandings, these things can so easily get out of hand, As far as I'm concerned, there is no misunderstanding, said the mathematics teacher, my conscience is as clear as a baby's, Yes, I know, I know, said Tertuliano Máximo Afonso, it's all my fault, the fault of this apathy, this depression that puts my nerves on edge, I get oversensitive, mistrustful, I imagine things, What things, asked his colleague, Oh, I don't know, just things, for example, that I'm not being treated with the consideration I think I deserve, sometimes I even have the feeling I don't really know what I am, that is, I know who I am, but not what I am, does that make sense, More or less, but it still doesn't explain the reason for your, what should I call it, reaction, yes, your reaction, To be perfectly honest, I don't understand it either, it was just a fleeting impression, as if you had treated me, how can I put it, in a paternalistic way, And when did I treat you in this paternalistic way, to use your terms, When we were standing in the corridor, about to go off to our respective classes, you placed your hand on my shoulder, it was obviously a friendly gesture, but I just took it the wrong way, it was as if you had hit me, Yes, I remember now, How could you not remember, if I'd had an electricity generator in my stomach you would have been struck down there and then, You mean your rejection of my gesture was that strong, Rejection may not be the right word, the snail doesn't reject the finger that touches it, it simply withdraws, That's the snail's way of rejecting it, Yes, But you haven't got much of the snail about you, Sometimes I think we're very similar, Who, you and me, No, me and the snail, Look, just shake off that depression and it will put a whole new complexion on things, That's odd, What is, That you should use those words, What words, About putting a whole new complexion on things, The meaning's fairly obvious, isn't it, Oh, yes, I understood what you meant, but what you've just said chimes in exactly with certain recent anxieties of mine, If I'm to continue following you, you're going to have to be more explicit, It's too soon for that now, but perhaps one day, Good, I'll look forward to it. Tertuliano Máximo Afonso thought, You can look forward to it all you like, and then, Coming back to what really matters, my friend, I just wanted to ask you to forgive me, You're forgiven, man, you're forgiven, although it's really not that important, you'd just created inside your head what people usually call a tempest in a teacup, fortunately, these shipwrecks nearly always happen within sight of the beach and no one drowns, Thanks for taking it all so well, That's all right, I'm glad to, If my common sense weren't so distracted with fantasies and phantoms and unwanted advice, I would have seen at once that the way I responded to your generous impulse wasn't just over the top, it was positively mad, Don't be deceived, common sense is much too common to really be sense, it's just a chapter from a statistics book, the one everyone always trots out, How interesting, I'd never thought of old, much-applauded common sense as being like a chapter from a statistics book, but when I think about it, that's exactly what it is, exactly, It could equally well be a chapter from a history book, in fact, now that we're on the subject, there's a book that should have been written, but which doesn't, as far as I know, exist, What book's that, A history of common sense, You're amazing, don't tell me you always produce ideas of this caliber first thing in the morning, said Tertuliano Máximo Afonso somewhat archly, If I get the right kind of stimulus, yes, but only after breakfast, replied the mathematics teacher, laughing, Well, I'll have to start phoning you every morning, then, Careful, remember what happened with the goose that laid the golden eggs, See you later, Yes, see you later, and I promise I won't go all paternalistic on you again, Even though you are almost old enough to be my father, All the more reason. Tertuliano Máximo Afonso replaced the receiver, he felt pleased, relieved, besides, the conversation had been both interesting and intelligent, it's not every day that someone turns up and tells us that common sense is nothing but a chapter from a statistics book and that what every library in the world lacks is a history of common sense from the time Adam and Eve were driven out of Paradise. A glance at the clock told him that Maria da Paz would have already left for her job at the bank and that the matter could be more or less sorted out, however temporarily, with a nice message left on her answering machine, Then I'll see. Out of prudence, just in case fate was conspiring against him, he decided to wait half an hour. Maria da Paz lives with her mother and they always leave the house together in the morning, one to go to work, the other to go to Mass and do the day's shopping. Maria da Paz's mother has been a great churchgoer ever since she was widowed. Deprived of the majesty of matrimony, in whose shadow, which she had always seen as a refuge, she had been shriveling up for years and years, she had gone in search of another gentleman to serve, a gentleman for life and for death too, a gentleman, moreover, whose one inestimable advantage was that he would never leave her a widow again. Once the half hour of waiting was over, Tertuliano Máximo Afonso was still unclear about the terms in which he should respond to the message, he had begun by thinking that a simple reply would be best, affectionate and natural, but, as we all know, the subtle shades of meaning between affectionate and cool and between natural and artificial are little less than infinite, normally, we come out with the right tone of voice for each circumstance spontaneously, but when there's an element of mistrust, as there is in this case, everything that strikes one at first as perfectly adequate and fitting will, the next moment, seem either abrupt or excessive. The eloquent silence, long favored by a particularly lazy kind of literature, does not exist, eloquent silences are just words that have got stuck in the throat, choked words that have been unable to escape the embrace of the glottis. After much racking of his brain, Tertuliano Máximo Afonso decided that, to be absolutely safe, the most prudent course of action would be to write the message down and then read it over the phone. This is what he came up with after several torn-up sheets of paper, Hi, Maria da Paz, I got your messages, and I'd just like to say that I think we should act with great caution and only make decisions that are right for both of us, bearing in mind that the only thing that lasts a whole lifetime is life itself, everything else is inevitably precarious, unstable, transient, time has taught me that one great truth, but I do know that we're friends and that we'll go on being friends, what we need is to have a good, long conversation and sort things out between us, I'll be in touch again soon. He hesitated for a second, what he was about to say was not on the piece of paper, then he ended the call with, Lots of love. When he had put the phone down, he reread what he had written and noticed the importunate presence of a few subtle shades of meaning to which he had not paid sufficient attention, some were less subtle than others, for example, that awful old chestnut, we're friends now and we'll always be friends, that's the worst thing anyone can say if they're trying to end a romantic relationship, it's as if we had closed the door only to find that we were still stuck fast in it, and then, quite apart from that pathetic Lots of love he had added at the end, there was the crass error of saying that they needed to have a long conversation, he should know by now, from personal experience and from the continual lessons learned from A History of Private Lives through the Ages, that long conversations, in situations such as this, are terribly danger-ous, how often has someone begun such a conversation feel-ing positively murderous toward the other person only to end up in their arms. What else could I do, he groaned, I obvi-ously couldn't tell her that everything between us would con-tinue as before, eternal love and all that, but neither could I, over the phone and when she's not there to pick it up, deliver the final blow, just like that, sorry, sweetheart, it's all over, that would be utter cowardice and I very much hope I never sink quite that low. With this conciliatory thought, along the lines of you win some, you lose some, Tertuliano Máximo Afonso decided to rest on his laurels, knowing, however, poor man, that the most difficult part was yet to come. At least I did my best, he concluded.

Up until now we have not needed to know on which day of the week these intriguing events are taking place, but Tertuliano Máximo Afonso's next actions, if they are to be understood, demand the information that today is a Friday, from which one will easily draw the conclusion that yesterday was Thursday and the day before that was Wednesday. Many readers will judge the complementary information we have given them about yesterday and the day before yesterday to be unnecessary, obvious, useless, absurd, even downright stupid, but, in anticipation of such a remark, we would counter by saying that any criticism along these lines reveals only bad faith and ignorance, given that, as is widely known, there are languages in the world that call Wednesday, for example, *mercredi, miércoles, mercoledì,* or *quarta-feira,* that call Thursday *jeudi, jueves, giovedì,* or *quinta-feira,* and as for Friday, if we had not taken the overt precaution of protecting its name, there would even be people out there who would start calling it *Freitag.* It may yet happen, all in good time, its moment will come. Having clarified this point, having agreed that today is Friday, having mentioned that the history teacher will have classes today only in the afternoon, and having noted that tomorrow, Saturday, *samedi, sábado, sabato,* there will be no classes, that we are therefore on the eve of the weekend, but, above all, because one should never put off till tomorrow what one can do today, it is clear that Tertuliano Máximo Afonso is quite right to go to the video-rental shop this morning so that he can rent the remaining films that interest him. He will return *Passenger without a Ticket* to its source, as being of no use in his researches, and will purchase copies of *Death Strikes at Dawn* and *The Accursed Code*. He still has three videos left from yesterday, which represent at least four and a half hours' viewing, and, along with whatever else he brings back from the shop, it promises to be an unforgettable weekend, a cinematic blowout if ever there was one, a real button-buster as country people used to say. He got dressed, ate breakfast, put the videos back in their respective boxes, locked them in one of the desk drawers, and left, first going upstairs to tell his neighbor that she could come down anytime to clean and tidy his apartment, Pop down whenever you like, I won't be back until later this afternoon, and then, far less agitated than he was the previous day but still afflicted by the nervousness of someone on his way to a meeting with a person who, although this is not the first of such meetings, will, for that very reason, brook no mistakes, he got into the car and set off for the video-rental shop. The moment has come to inform those readers who, given the, so far, rather scant urban descriptions, have created in their mind the idea that this is all taking place in a medium-sized city, one, that is, of fewer than a million inhabitants, but the moment has come, as we were saying, to inform them that, on the contrary, this teacher, Tertuliano Máximo Afonso, is one of the just over five million human beings who, with major differences in standards of living and other differences that defy all comparison, inhabit the vast metropolis that extends over what were, long ago, hills, valleys, and plains, and which is now a continuous labyrinthine duplication both horizontally and vertically, initially made more complicated by components we will term diagonals, but which, meanwhile, with the passing of time, have brought some measure of equilibrium to the chaotic urban mesh, for they established frontier lines that, paradoxically, instead of driving things apart, brought them closer together. The survival instinct, for that is what one is dealing with in big cities, applies both to the animal and to the inanimal, an admittedly abstruse term that does not appear in any dictionary and that we have had to invent so that, aptly and appositely, we can render transparent, at a glance, whether via the ordinary sense of the first word, animal, or via the unusual spelling of the second, inanimal, the differences and similarities between things and non-things, between the inanimate and the animate. From now on, whenever we use the word "inanimal," we will do so with the intention of being as clear and precise as when, in the other kingdom, where the novelty of being and all its designations has entirely worn off, we used to refer to both man and dog as animals. Tertuliano Máximo Afonso, despite being a teacher of history, has never understood that everything that is animal is destined to become inanimal and that, however great the names and deeds inscribed by human beings on History's pages, it is from the inanimal that we come and toward the inanimal that we are going. Meanwhile, though, between the lashes, as the above-mentioned country people used to say, meaning that in the briefest of brief intervals between one lash and the next the back had time to rest, Tertuliano Máximo Afonso is driving to the video-rental shop, one of the many intermediate destinations that await him in life. The assistant who had attended him on his two previous visits was busy with another customer. He gave a nod of recognition, however, and showed his teeth in a smile, which, though lacking any apparent special meaning, might have concealed some murky intention. A female assistant who stepped forward to ask the newly arrived customer what he wanted was stopped in her tracks by a few curt but imperious words, I'll deal with this, and she had to withdraw with a small, faint smile, which was at once understanding and apologetic. Being new to the profession and to that establishment, and therefore inexperienced in the sophisticated art of selling, she was not yet authorized to deal with first-class customers. Let us not forget that Tertuliano Máximo Afonso, who is, as we know, a respected teacher of history and a renowned scholar of serious audiovisual matters, is also a large-scale renter of videos, as was shown yesterday and as will be shown again today. Having dealt with his other customer, the assistant, bright-eyed and zealous, came over to him, Good morning, sir, lovely to see you again, he said. While not wishing to cast doubt on the sincerity or cordiality of this greeting, it is, nevertheless, impossible to allow to pass without comment the evident and apparently unbridgeable contradiction between it and the final words muttered yesterday by this same assistant when this same customer left the shop, Whoever named you Tertuliano knew what he was doing. The explanation, let us hasten to add, lies in the pile of videos on the counter, about thirty at least. Expert in the aforesaid art of selling, the assistant, having given vehement but sotto voce expression to his feelings, decided that it would be a mistake to let himself be blinded by disappointment and that, although he had been unable to make the big sale he had initially hoped for, there was still the possibility that this Tertuliano fellow could be encouraged to rent all the videos available from the same production company, thus, and not without some basis, preserving the hope of being able to sell him a large number of the videos he had rented. Business life is full of trapdoors and pitfalls, a real lucky dip, although not always so lucky, you have to play your cards close to your chest, you have to be sly and calculating but without the client noticing your subtle maneuverings, you have to wear away at any preconceived ideas he may have brought with him to protect himself, to lay siege to any show of resistance, and to probe his innermost desires, in short, the new assistant will have to eat a lot of bread and a lot of salt if she is ever to reach such heights. What the assistant does not know is that Tertuliano Máximo Afonso has gone there with the precise aim of stocking up with videos for the weekend, determined now to get through as many as he can lay his hands on, rather than, as he did yesterday, content himself with a mere half dozen. In this way, vice once more paid homage to virtue, in this way vice raised virtue up, rather than trampling it underfoot as it had hoped. Tertuliano Máximo Afonso put *Passenger without a Ticket* on the counter and said, I'm not interested in this one, And what about the others you rented, have you decided what to do with them, asked the assistant, Yes, I'll keep *Death Strikes at Dawn* and *The Accursed Code*, but the other three I haven't yet seen, Now correct me if I'm wrong, but those three are *The Goddess of the Stage, The Alarm Rang Twice*, and *Phone Me Another Day*, recited the assistant, after consulting the relevant index card, Exactly, So that means you're renting *Passenger* and buying *Death* and the *Code*, Exactly, Right, so what can we do for you today, here we have, but Tertuliano Máximo Afonso did not give him time to finish his sentence, Those videos over there were, I assume, set aside for me, Exactly, echoed the assistant, caught, in his mind, between contentment at having won without a struggle and disappointment at not having had to struggle in order to win, How many are there, Thirty-six, How many hours is that, If we continue to calculate on the basis of an average hour and a half per film, let me see now, said the assistant, reaching for his calculator, Don't worry, I can tell you the answer, it's fifty-four, How did you manage to do that so quickly, asked the assistant, ever since these machines became available, and even though I haven't lost the ability to do sums in my head, I always use them for more complicated calculations, It's really easy, said Tertuliano Máximo Afonso, thirty-six half hours equals eighteen, so if you add the thirty-six whole hours we already had to the eighteen from the half hours, you get fifty-four, Are you a mathematics teacher, No, history, not mathematics, in fact, I've never been much good at figures, Well, you'd never know it, knowledge really is a wonderful thing, It depends what you know, It depends too, I think, who knows it, If you were capable of reaching that conclusion on your own, said Tertuliano Máximo Afonso, then you don't need calculators at all. The assistant was not sure he had entirely grasped the meaning of the customer's words, but they struck him as pleasant, friendly, even flattering, and as soon as he got home, assuming he hadn't forgotten them en route, he would repeat them to his wife. He decided to do the multiplication with pencil and paper, so many videos at so much, because he had resolved that, at least in front of this customer, he would never again use a calculator. It came to quite a tidy sum, not as much as it would have if, instead of renting, he had been buying, but this selfish thought went as quickly as it came, the peace had definitely been signed. Tertuliano Máximo Afonso paid, then asked, Would you very much mind making up two packages of eighteen cassettes each while I go and fetch my car, it's parked too far away for me to be able to carry them all there. A quarter of an hour later, it was the assistant himself who came and put the packages in the trunk, closed the car door after Tertuliano Máximo Afonso had got in, said good-bye with a smile and a wave that were the very embodiment of fond affection, and who murmured as he returned to the counter, People may say that it's first impressions that count, but here's a person whom I didn't take to at all to start with, and yet. Tertuliano Máximo Afonso's thoughts were following a very different route, Two days equals forty-eight hours, mathematically, of course, that's not enough time for me to watch all the films even if I don't sleep for those two days, but if I start tonight, with the whole of Saturday and Sunday ahead of me, and make it a serious rule not to watch a film all the way through if the fellow hasn't appeared by the halfway point, I'm sure I'll have finished the task by Monday. The plan of action was complete in its objective and perfect in its form, there was no need for addenda, appendices, or footnotes, but Tertuliano Máximo Afonso insisted, If he doesn't appear by the halfway point, he won't appear afterward. Yes, afterward. That is the word that has been hanging around ever since the actor who played the part of the hotel receptionist appeared for the first time in that interesting and amusing film *The Race Is to the Swift*. And afterward, asked the history teacher, like a child who does not know that there is no point asking about something that has not yet happened, what will I do afterward, what will I do after finding out that this man has appeared in fifteen or twenty films, that, so far as I have been able to ascertain, as well as playing a hotel receptionist, he has also been a bank clerk and a medical auxiliary, what will I do then. He had the answer on the tip of his tongue, but he only gave that answer a minute later, Find him and meet him.

BY CHANCE OR FOR SOME OTHER UNKNOWN REASON, SOME-one must have gone to tell the headmaster that Tertuliano Máximo Afonso was in the staff room, apparently filling in time until lunch, since all he had done since going in there had been to read the newspapers. He wasn't marking home-work, he wasn't putting the final touches to a lesson plan, he wasn't making notes, he was just reading the newspapers. He had begun by taking from his briefcase the receipt for the rental of the thirty-six videos, which he unfolded and placed on the table, then he looked for the entertainment page in the first newspaper, the cinema section. He would do the same with another two newspapers. Although, as we know, his ad-diction to the seventh art is very recent and his ignorance about anything to do with the image industry unchanged, he knew, assumed, imagined, or guessed that any new releases would not be launched immediately onto the video market. In order to reach this conclusion he did not need to be en-dowed with a prodigious deductive intelligence or with some extraordinary access to a knowledge beyond reason, it was a simple and obvious matter of applying very ordinary com-mon sense and looking under the section devoted to videos to buy and rent. He looked for cinemas that showed older films, and, one by one, ballpoint in hand, he compared the titles of the films shown there with those on the receipt, marking the titles on the latter with a small cross whenever they coincided. If anyone were to ask Tertuliano Máximo Afonso why he was doing this, if he intended going to those cinemas to see films he already had on video, he would probably look at us surprised, astonished, perhaps offended that we judged him capable of such an absurd act, not that he would give us an acceptable explanation either, apart from the one that erects walls to keep out other people's curiosity and which in two words says, Just because. Meanwhile, we, who have been privy to the history teacher's intimate thoughts and have insinuated ourselves into his secrets, can tell you that the sole point of this absurd undertaking is to keep his attention fixed on the one objective that has obsessed him for the last three days, or to prevent his attention from becoming distracted, for example, by reading the news in the newspapers, as the other teachers present in the room probably imagine he is doing now. Life, however, is made in such a way that even doors we considered firmly locked and bolted against the world find themselves at the mercy of the modest, solicitous errand boy who has just come into the room to announce to the history teacher that the headmaster would very much like to see him in his office. Tertuliano Máximo Afonso got to his feet, folded up the newspapers, put the receipt back in his briefcase, and went out into the corridor where some of the classrooms were. The headmaster's office was on the floor above, and the stairs that led up to it had, in the roof, a skylight so opaque inside and so grimy outside that, winter and summer, it allowed in only a miserly amount of natural light. He went down another passageway and stopped at the sec-

72

ond door. The green light was lit, and so he rapped on the door and opened it when he heard a voice inside say, Come in, then he said his good mornings, shook the headmaster's hand, and, at a sign from him, sat down. Whenever he went into this room, he had the feeling that he had seen this same office somewhere else, it was like one of those dreams we know we have dreamed but which we cannot manage to recall when we wake up. The floor was carpeted, there were thick curtains at the window, the desk was large and old-fashioned, the black leather armchair modern. Tertuliano Máximo Afonso knew this furniture, these curtains, this carpet, or thought he did, one possibility is that he had one day read in a novel or a story the brief description of another office belonging to another headmaster of another school, in which case, if this could be proved with book in hand, he would be forced to replace, with a banal occurrence that could happen to anyone endowed with a reasonable memory, something that he had always thought, up until now, was an intersection between his routine life and the majestic circular flow of the eternal return. Fantasies. Absorbed in these visions, the history teacher had not heard the headmaster's first words, but we, who will always be around lest anything be missed, can safely say that he did not miss much, merely the reciprocation of his good morning, the question, How have you been, the preamble I asked you to come and see me, but from then on, Tertuliano Máximo Afonso was there in body and in spirit, with the light of his eyes and understanding awake. I asked you to come and see me, said the headmaster again because he noticed what appeared to be an air of distraction on the other man's face, to talk to you about what you said at yesterday's meeting about the teaching of history, What did I say at yesterday's meeting, asked Tertuliano Máximo Afonso, Don't you remember, Well, I have a vague idea, but my head's not very clear, I didn't sleep much last night, Are you ill, No, not ill, just slightly anxious, that's all, That's bad enough, Really, sir, it's of no importance, there's no need to worry, What you said, word for word, I've got it written down on this piece of paper, was that the only serious decision to be taken as regards the teaching of history is whether we should teach it from back to front or from front to back, It's not the first time I've said that, Precisely, you've said it so often that your colleagues no longer take it seriously, they start to smile as soon as you say the first words, My colleagues are lucky, they're easily amused, and you, And I what, Do you take me seriously, I wonder, or do you too smile as soon as I say the first words, or perhaps the second, You know me well enough to realize that I'm not easily amused, still less in a situation like that, as for taking you seriously, there's no question, you're one of our best teachers, the students admire and respect you, which, these days, is nothing short of miraculous, So why did you ask to see me, Just to ask you not to repeat, That business about the only serious decision to be taken, Yes, In that case, I won't open my mouth in meetings anymore, if someone thinks they have something important to say and the others don't want to hear it, then it's best to keep quiet, Personally, I've always found your idea very interesting, Thank you, sir, but don't tell me that, tell my colleagues, tell the ministry, besides, it's not even my idea, I didn't invent it, people far more competent than me have proposed and defended it, Without noticeable success, That's understandable, sir, talking about the past is the easiest thing there is, it's all written down, it's just a question of repeating, of parroting, of checking in books what students write in their essays or say in the oral exams, whereas talking about a present that is exploding in our face at every minute, talking about it every day of the year and at the same time navigating the river of History back to the source, or thereabouts, always struggling to get a better understanding of the chain of events that has brought us where we are now, that's quite another story, it's a lot of work, requires great perseverance in its application, you have to keep the rope pulled tight all the time, What you've just said is admirable, indeed, I think even the minister would be persuaded by your eloquence, Hm, I doubt it, sir, ministers are put there in order to persuade us, Look, I withdraw what I said before, from now on, I'll support you all the way, Thank you, but it's best not to foster illusions, the system has to render accounts to the person in charge and that's a kind of arithmetic they don't like at all, We'll insist, Someone once said that all the great truths are basically trivial and so we have to find new ways, preferably paradoxical ways, of expressing them, in order to keep them from falling into oblivion, Who said that, A German, a man called Schlegel, but others probably said it before him, It makes you think, though, Yes, but what I like most about it is the fascinating assertion that the great truths are just so much trivia, the rest, the supposed need for a new, paradoxical way of expressing them and thus prolonging their existence and giving them substance doesn't really concern me, after all, I'm just a history teacher in a secondary school, We should talk more, my friend, There isn't time to do everything, sir, besides, there are my other colleagues who doubtless have more important things to tell you, for example, how to find easy amusement in difficult words, and the students, we mustn't forget the students, poor things, who, if they didn't have someone to talk to, might one day end up with nothing to say, imagine what school life would be like with everyone talking to each other, we'd never get anything done, and work calls. The headmaster looked at his watch and said, So does lunch, let's go and eat. He got up, walked around his desk, and, in a spontaneous expression of real regard, placed his hand on the shoulder of the history teacher, who had also stood up. There was, inevitably, something paternalistic about this gesture, but coming as it did from the headmaster, this was only natural, only right even, human relations being what we know them to be. Tertuliano Máximo Afonso's hypersensitive electricity generator did not react to this touch, a sign that there had been no troublesome hyperbole in the headmaster's show of appreciation, or, who knows, perhaps it was just that this morning's illuminating conversation with the mathematics teacher had simply unplugged the generator. One can never repeat too often that other trivial truth, that small causes can produce great results. When the headmaster went back to his desk to fetch his glasses, Tertuliano Máximo Afonso looked around the room, saw the curtains, the black leather armchair, the carpet, and again thought, I've been here before. Then, perhaps because someone had suggested that he might merely have read somewhere a description of an office similar to this, he added another thought, Reading is probably another way of being in a place. The headmaster's glasses were now safely in his top jacket pocket and he was saying, smiling, Off we go then, and Tertuliano Máximo Afonso will be unable to explain now or ever why the air seems to have thickened, as if impregnated with an invisible presence, as intense and powerful as the one that roused him brusquely from his bed after watching that first video. He thought, If I had been here before I became a schoolteacher, what I'm feeling now could be nothing more than a memory of myself reactivated by my current nervous state. The remainder of that thought, if there was a remainder, was never developed, the headmaster was taking his arm and saying something about great lies, wondering if they were also trivial, and if paradoxes could stop them from falling into oblivion too. Tertuliano Máximo Afonso just managed to pick up the thread at the very last moment, Great truths, great lies, I suppose in time everything becomes trivial, the usual dishes with the same old sauce, he replied, Now I hope that isn't a criticism of our kitchens, joked the headmaster, Certainly not, I'm a regular customer, responded Tertuliano Máximo Afonso in the same vein. They went downstairs to the canteen and, on the way, were joined by the mathematics teacher and a teacher of English, which meant that the headmaster's table was full for that lunchtime. So, said the mathematics teacher in a low voice, while the headmaster and the English teacher went on ahead of them, how are you feeling, Good, very good actually, Did you have a little chat, Yes, he called me to his office to ask me not to bring up that business of teaching topsy-turvy history again, Topsy-turvy, It's just a figure of speech, And what did you say, Oh, I explained my point of view for the hundredth time and I think I finally managed to persuade him that my crazy idea was not quite as dotty as he had always thought, A victory, Which won't get us anywhere, True enough, though, of course, one can never be quite sure where exactly victories get us anyway, sighed the mathematics teacher, Whereas everyone knows where defeats get us, especially the people who poured everything they were and everything they had into the battle, but no one pays any attention to that particular lesson from history, Anyone would think you were fed up with your job, Perhaps I am, it's just that we seem to be putting the same old sauce on the usual dishes, nothing changes, Are you thinking of leaving teaching, I don't know exactly, or even vaguely, what I think or want, but I imagine it would be a good idea, To abandon teaching, To abandon anything. They went into the canteen, sat down at a table for four, and the headmaster, as he unfurled his napkin, said to Tertuliano Máximo Afonso, I'd like you to tell our colleagues here what you told me just now, About what, About your very original concept for the teaching of history. The English teacher began to smile, but the look that the history teacher gave her, deadpan, absent, and, at the same time, cold, froze the smile just beginning to appear on her lips. Always assuming concept is the right word, sir, it's not in the least original, that particular laurel wreath was not meant for my head, said Tertuliano Máximo Afonso after a pause, Ah, yes, but the speech that convinced me was yours, retorted the headmaster. In an instant, the history teacher's gaze left the canteen, went down the corridor, up to the next floor, through the locked door of the headmaster's office, saw what it was expecting to see, then returned by the same route, and became present again, but this time, there was in his gaze a look of troubled perplexity, a tremor of disquiet that bordered on fear. It was him, it was him, it was him, Tertuliano Máximo Afonso repeated over and over to himself, while, with his eyes fixed on his colleague the mathematics teacher, he restated, using more or less the same words, the various stages of his metaphorical navigation up the river of Time. He didn't say the river of History now, he felt that river of Time would have more impact. The English teacher was looking at him, grave faced. She is about sixty years old, a mother and a grandmother, and contrary to first impressions, she is not one of those people who go through life dispensing mocking smiles right, left, and center. What happened was only what has happened to so many of us, we go astray not because we intended to but because we saw in that going astray a connecting link, a comfortable complicity, a knowing wink from someone who thought they understood what was going on, purely on the say-so of others. When Tertuliano Máximo Afonso ended his brief speech, he saw that he had convinced someone else. The English teacher murmured shyly, You could do the same thing with languages, I mean, teach them in the same way, and navigate back up to the source of the river, perhaps that way we might get a clearer understanding of what it means to speak, There's no shortage of specialists on that subject, commented the headmaster, But I'm not one of them, I'm expected to teach English in a complete void, as if nothing had existed before. The mathematics teacher said, smiling, I don't think these methods would work with arithmetic, the number ten is stubbornly invariable, it didn't even have to be a nine first nor is it consumed with ambition to be an eleven. The food had been brought to the table and the conversation turned to other things. Tertuliano Máximo Afonso was no longer so sure that the person responsible for the invisible plasma dissolving in the atmosphere of the headmaster's office was the bank clerk. Or the hotel receptionist. Especially not with that ridiculous little mustache, he thought, and then, smiling sadly to himself, I must be losing my mind. In the class he gave after lunch, he spent the whole lesson, completely inappropriately and apropos of nothing, since the subject was not part of the syllabus, discoursing on the Amorites, on Hammurabi's code of law, the Babylonian legal system, the god Marduk, the Accadian language, with the result that he changed the view of the student who, the day before, had whispered to his neighbor that the teacher looked really pissed off. The much more radical diagnosis now was that he either had a screw loose or else a screw with a badly worn thread. Fortunately, the next class, for younger students, went smoothly enough. A single passing reference to historical films was greeted with passionate interest by the class, but that was as far as the divertimento went, there was no mention of Cleopatra or Spartacus, nor of the Hunchback of Notre Dame, nor even of the ever-reliable Emperor Napoléon Bonaparte. A fairly forgettable day, thought Tertuliano Máximo Afonso when he got into his car to go home. He was being unjust to the day and to himself, after all, he had won over the headmaster and the English teacher to his reforming ideas, there would be one less person smiling at the next staff meeting, and, anyway, he has nothing to fear from the former, who, as we found out a few hours ago, is not easily amused.

The house was clean and tidy, the bed as neat as a marriage bed, the kitchen bright as a new pin, the bathroom exuding detergent odors, a sort of lemon smell, which one had only to breathe in for one's body to be purified and one's soul to be exalted. On the days when the upstairs neighbor comes to bring order to this single man's apartment, the occupier eats supper out, he feels it would show a lack of respect to soil plates, light matches, peel potatoes, open cans, and then put a frying pan on the stove, that would be unthinkable, the oil would spurt everywhere. The restaurant is close by, last time he was there he ate meat, this evening he will eat fish, it's good to make changes, if we're not careful, life can quickly become predictable, monotonous, a drag. Tertuliano Máximo Afonso has always been a very careful man. The thirty-six videos he brought from the shop are piled up on the small coffee table in the living room, the three remaining from the previous visit, and which have not yet been seen, are in a drawer in the desk, the magnitude of the task ahead is quite simply overwhelming, Tertuliano Máximo Afonso would not wish it on his worst enemy, not that he knows who that might be, perhaps because he is still young, perhaps because he has always been so careful with life. To pass the time until supper, he started putting the videos in order according to the dates when the original film was issued, and since they would not fit on the table or on the desk, he decided to line them up on the floor, at the bottom of one of the bookshelves, the oldest, on the left, is called *A Man Like Any Other*, the most recent, on the right, *The Goddess of the Stage*. If Tertuliano Máximo Afonso had been consistent with the ideas he has been defending about the teaching of history to the point of applying them, insofar as this was possible, to his everyday activities, he would watch this row of videos from front to back, that is, he would begin with *The Goddess of the Stage* and end with *A Man Like Any Other*. We all know, however, that the enormous weight of tradition, habit, and custom that occupies the greater part of our brain bears down pitilessly on the more brilliant and innovative ideas of which the remaining part is capable, and although it is true that, in some cases, this weight can balance the excesses and extravagances of the imagination that would lead us God knows where were they given free rein, it is equally true that it often has a way of subtly submitting what we believed to be our free will to unconscious tropisms, like a plant that does not know why it will always have to lean toward the side from which the light comes. The history teacher will therefore faithfully follow the teaching program placed in his hands and will therefore watch the videos from back to front, from the oldest to the most recent, from the days of effects that we did not need to call natural to these days of effects we call special and which, because we don't know how they are created, fabricated, or produced, should really be given a much more neutral name. Tertuliano

Máximo Afonso has returned from supper, he did not, after all, have fish, the dish on offer was monkfish, and he does not like monkfish, that benthonic marine creature that lives on the sandy or muddy sea bottom, from inshore areas to depths greater than a thousand meters, that can measure up to two meters in length and weigh more than forty kilos, with a vast, flat head equipped with very strong teeth, which, in short, is a most disagreeable animal to look at and one that Tertuliano Máximo Afonso's palate, nose, and stomach have never been able to tolerate. He is gleaning all this information now from an encyclopedia, finally prompted by curiosity to find out something about this creature that he has detested since the first day he saw it. This curiosity dates from times past, from years back, but today, inexplicably, he is giving it due satisfaction. Inexplicably, we said, and yet we should know that this is not so, we should know that there is no logical, objective explanation for the fact that Tertuliano Máximo Afonso has spent years and years knowing nothing about the monkfish apart from its appearance and the taste and consistency of the pieces put on his plate, and then suddenly, at a certain moment on a certain day, as if he had nothing more urgent to do, he opens the encyclopedia and finds out more. We have an odd relationship with words. We learn a few when we are small, throughout our lives we collect others through education, conversation, our contact with books, and yet, in comparison, there are only a tiny number about whose meaning, sense, and denotation we would have absolutely no doubts if, one day, we were to ask ourselves seriously what they meant. Thus we affirm and deny, thus we convince and are convinced, thus we argue, deduce, and conclude, wandering fearlessly over the surface of concepts about which we have only the vaguest of ideas, and, despite the false air of confidence that we generally affect as we feel our way along the road in the verbal darkness, we manage, more or less, to understand each other and even, sometimes, to find each other. If we had time and if impatient curiosity were to prick us, we would always end up finding out exactly what a monkfish was. The next time the waiter at the restaurant suggests this inelegant member of the *Lophiidae* family, the history teacher will know what to say, What, that hideous benthonic creature that lives in the sand or on the muddy sea bottom, and will add firmly, Certainly not. Responsibility for this tedious piscine and linguistic digression lies entirely with Tertuliano Máximo Afonso for having taken such a long time to put *A Man Like Any Other* in the VCR, as if he were hesitating at the foot of a mountain, pondering the effort required to reach the summit. Like nature, they say, a narrative abhors a vacuum, which is why, since Tertuliano Máximo Afonso has, in this interval, done nothing worth telling, we had no option but to improvise some padding to more or less fill up the time required by the situation. Now that he has decided to take the video out of its box and put it in the VCR, we can relax.

After an hour, the actor still had not appeared, and it seemed likely that he was not in the film. Tertuliano Máximo Afonso fast-forwarded the tape to the end, carefully read the credits, and removed from his list of participants any names that were repeated. If we had asked him to explain in his own words what he had just watched, he would probably have shot us the angry glance one reserves for the impertinent and replied with another question, Do I look like someone who would be interested in such vulgarities. We would have to agree with him here, because the films he has so far seen clearly belong to the so-called B-movie category, films made quickly for quick consumption and which aspire only to help pass the time without troubling the spirit, as the mathematics teacher had so neatly put it, albeit in other words. Another video has been put in the VCR, this one is called *A Merry Life*, and Tertuliano Máximo Afonso's twin will appear in the role of doorman at a cabaret or nightclub, it will be impossible to gauge with any clarity which of the two definitions best suits this place of worldly delights that is the scene of jollities shamelessly copied from various versions of *The Merry Widow*. Tertuliano Máximo Afonso thought at first that it wasn't worth watching the whole film, he already knew what he needed to know, that is, whether his other self appeared in the story, but the plot was so gratuitously convoluted that he let himself be carried along until the end, surprised to notice stirrings inside him of compassion for the poor devil who, apart from opening and closing the doors of cars, did nothing but raise and lower his peaked cap to greet the elegant clientele as they came and went, with a grave though not always subtle blend of respect and complicity. At least I'm a teacher of history, he murmured. A statement like that, made with the overt intention of pointing up and emphasizing his superiority, not only professionally, but also morally and socially, compared with the insignificance of the character's role, was crying out for a response that would restore courtesy to its proper place, and this was supplied by his common sense with an unusual touch of irony, Beware of pride, Tertuliano, think of what you've missed by not being an actor, they could have made your character a headmaster, a teacher of mathematics, but since you obviously couldn't be an English teacher of the female sex, you'll just have to be a plain old male teacher. Pleased with the warning note it had sounded, common sense, deciding to strike while the iron was hot, again brought the hammer down hard, Obviously, you'd have to have some slight talent for acting, but apart from that, my friend, as sure as my name is Common Sense, they would be bound to make you change your name, no self-respecting actor would dare to appear in public with that ridiculous Tertuliano, you'd have no option but to adopt an attractive pseudonym, although, on second thoughts, that might not be necessary, Máximo Afonso wouldn't be bad, think about it. *A Merry Life* returned to its box, the next film appeared with an intriguing title, very promising in the circumstances, *Tell Me Who You Are* it was called, but it contributed nothing to Tertuliano Máximo Afonso's knowledge of himself and nothing to the research he is embroiled in. To amuse himself, he fast-forwarded it to the end, added a few crosses to his list, and, with a glance at the clock, decided to go to bed. His eyes were red, his temples throbbed, and he could feel a weight on his forehead. I'm not going to kill myself over this, he thought, the world won't end if I don't manage to watch all the videos this weekend, and if it did end, this wouldn't be the only mystery left unresolved. He was in bed, waiting for sleep to answer the call of the tablet he had taken, when something that might have been common sense again, but which did not announce itself as such, said that, quite frankly, in his opinion, the easiest route would be to telephone or to go in person to the production company and ask straight out for the name of the actor in this, this, and this film who played the parts of receptionist, bank clerk, medical auxiliary, and nightclub doorman, they must be used to it, they might find it odd that such a question should be about an insignificant, bit-part actor, little more than an extra, but at least it would make a change from having to talk about stars and superstars all the time. Vaguely, as the first tangled mesh of sleep was wrapping around him, Tertuliano Máximo Afonso replied that it was a stupid idea, far too simple, too humdrum, I didn't study history just to come up with ideas like that, he added. These last words had nothing to do with anything, they were just another display of pride, but we must forgive him, it's the sleeping tablet talking, not the person who took it. From Tertuliano Máximo Afonso, on the very threshold of sleep, came the final remark, as strangely lucid as the flame of a candle about to burn out, I want to find him without anyone knowing and without him suspecting. These were definitive words that brooked no argument. Sleep closed the door. And Tertuliano Máximo Afonso is now slumbering.

B Y ELEVEN O'CLOCK IN THE MORNING, TERTULIANO MÁXIMO Afonso had already watched three films, although none of them from beginning to end. He had risen very early, breakfasted on a couple of biscuits and a warmed-up cup of coffee, and, without wasting time on shaving, and omitting all but the most necessary ablutions, still in his pajamas and dressing gown, like someone who is expecting no visitors, he launched into the day's task. The first two films passed in vain, but the third, entitled *The Parallel of Terror,* brought to the scene of the crime a jolly, gum-chewing police photographer who kept saying, in Tertuliano Máximo Afonso's voice, that in life and death it's all a question of angle. At the end, the list was again brought up-to-date, a name struck through, new crosses added. There were five actors marked five times, as many as the number of films in which the history teacher's double had appeared, and their names, in impartial alphabetical order, were Pedro Félix, Adriano Maia, Carlos Martinho, Daniel Santa-Clara, and Luís Augusto Ventura. Up until then, Tertuliano Máximo Afonso had been lost on the great sea of the more than five million inhabitants of the city, but from now on, he will only have to deal with fewer than half a dozen, possibly even fewer than that if one or more of those names is struck off for not answering the roll call, Quite an achievement, he muttered, but it immediately leaped to his notice that this new labor of Hercules had not, after all, been so very arduous, given that at least two million, five hundred thousand people belonged to the female sex and were, therefore, excluded from the field of his research. Tertuliano Máximo Afonso's oversight should not surprise us, since, in calculations involving such large numbers, as in the present case, the tendency not to take women into account is irresistible. Despite this blow to his statistics, Tertuliano Máximo Afonso went into the kitchen to celebrate the promising results with another cup of coffee. The doorbell rang just as he was taking his second sip, the cup remained suspended in midair, halfway on its journey to the tabletop, Who can that be, he asked, at the same time putting the cup lightly down. It could be his helpful upstairs neighbor, wanting to know if he had found everything to his liking, it could be one of those young people selling encyclopedias that explain the habits of the monkfish, it could be his colleague the mathematics teacher, no, it wouldn't be him, they had never visited each other's homes, Who can it be, he said again. He quickly finished his coffee and went to see. Crossing the room, he cast a worried glance at the video boxes scattered about, at the impassive line of videos on the floor at the foot of the bookshelf, waiting their turns, his upstairs neighbor, always assuming it was her, wouldn't be at all pleased to see the deplorable mess he had made of the place she had taken such pains to tidy up yesterday. It doesn't matter, she doesn't have to come in, he thought, and opened the door. It wasn't his upstairs neighbor standing there before him, it wasn't a young saleswoman bearing encyclopedias and telling him that, at last, he had within his grasp the enormous privilege of knowing everything there was to know about the habits of the monkfish, it was a woman who has not yet appeared in person but whose name we already know, Maria da Paz, bank employee. Oh, it's you, exclaimed Tertuliano Máximo Afonso, and then, trying to hide his perturbation, his confusion, Hello, this is a surprise. He should have asked her in, Come in, come in, I was just having a cup of coffee, or, How nice of you to drop by, just make yourself comfortable while I shave and have a shower, but it was only with an effort that he stood to one side and let her pass, ah, if only he could say to her, Just wait right here while I hide some videos I don't want you to see, ah, if only he could say, Sorry, but you've come at a bad time, I can't really talk to you right now, come back tomorrow, ah, if only he could say something, but it's too late now, he should have thought of this before, it's all his fault, the prudent man should always be on his guard, alert, he should foresee all eventualities, he should, above all, never forget that the best way to proceed is always the simplest, for example, not ingenuously to open the door just because the bell rings, haste always brings complications in its wake, no doubt about it. Maria da Paz entered the apartment with the ease of someone who knows every corner, and asked, How have you been, and then, I got your message and I agree, we need to talk, I hope I haven't come at a bad moment, No, of course not, said Tertuliano Máximo Afonso, you must forgive me for receiving you like this, hair uncombed, face unshaven, and looking as if I'd just got out of bed, When I've seen you like this on other occasions, you've never felt the need to apologize, Today is different, In what way, You know what I mean, I've never opened the door to you dressed like this, in pajamas and a dressing gown, It has a certain novelty, and there's not much of that between you and me anymore. She was only three steps from the living room, her astonishment would soon become apparent, What the hell's all this, what are you doing with all these videos, but Maria da Paz pauses to ask, Aren't you going to kiss me, Of course, was Tertuliano Máximo Afonso's unfortunate and embarrassed response, as he made to kiss her on the cheek. This masculine modesty, if that's what it was, proved vain, Maria da Paz's mouth had come to meet his and was now sucking, pressing, devouring it, while her body glued itself to his from head to toe, as if there were no clothes separating them. Maria da Paz was the first to draw back and murmur, panting, a sentence she never managed to finish, Even if I regret what I've just done, even if I'm ashamed of having done it, Don't be silly, said Tertuliano Máximo Afonso, improvising furiously to gain time, what nonsense, regret, shame, why on earth should anyone regret and feel ashamed of expressing their feelings, You know perfectly well what I mean, so don't pretend you don't, You came in, we kissed, what could be more normal, more natural, We didn't kiss, I kissed you, Yes, but I kissed you back, Only because you had no option, You're exaggerating as usual, dramatizing, You're right, I do exaggerate and I do dramatize, I exaggerated in coming to your apartment, I dramatized by embracing a man who no longer loves me, I should leave this very instant, regretful and ashamed, despite all those charitable phrases about how it really doesn't matter. The possibility that she might leave, although obviously a remote one, sent a ray of hopeful light into the tortuous crannies of Tertuliano Máximo Afonso's mind, but the words that emerged from his mouth, some might say escaped against his will, expressed a very different sentiment, Honestly, I don't know where you've got this peculiar idea that I don't care about you, You expressed yourself pretty clearly on the subject the last time we met, But I never said I didn't care about you, I never said that, In matters of the heart, about which you know so little, even the most obtuse of intelligences can understand what wasn't said. To imagine that those words of Tertuliano Máximo Afonso's, currently under analysis, escaped against his will would be to forget that the skein of the human spirit has many and various ends, and that the function of some of its threads, while seeming to lead the interlocutor to a knowledge of what lies inside, is to give false directions, to suggest detours that will end up in culs-de-sac, to distract from the fundamental subject, or, as in the case that concerns us now, to lessen, in anticipation, the shock of what is to come. In affirming that he had never said he didn't care about Maria da Paz, thus letting it be understood that he really did care about her, Tertuliano Máximo Afonso's intention was, if you'll forgive the banality of the images, to wrap her in cotton wool, to surround her with muffling pillows, to bind her to him with loving feelings when it was no longer possible to detain her further outside the living-room door. Which is what is happening now. Maria da Paz has just taken the necessary three steps, she goes in, she doesn't want to think about the sweet nightingale song that lightly brushed her ears, but she can think of nothing else, she would even be prepared to recognize, contritely, that her ironic allusion to obtuse intelligences had been not merely impertinent but unjust too, and with a smile on her lips she turns to Tertuliano Máximo Afonso, ready to fall into his arms and determined to forget all about grievances and complaints. Chance, however, chose, although it would be more exact to say that it was inevitable, since alluring concepts like fate, fortune, and destiny really have no place in this narrative, that the arc described by Maria da Paz's eyes would pass, first, the television set, turned on, then the videos that had not yet resumed their appointed positions, and, finally, the row of videos itself, an unheard-of, inexplicable presence to anyone, like her, who had an intimate knowledge of this place and of the occupier's tastes and habits. What's all this, what are all these videos doing here, she asked, It's material for some work I'm engaged in at the moment, replied Tertuliano Máximo Afonso, looking away, Unless I'm very much mistaken, your work, for as long as I've known you, has involved teaching history, said Maria da Paz, and this thing, she was studying the video with curious eyes, called *The Parallel of Terror*, doesn't look to me as if it has very much to do with your speciality, There's no law that says I can only study history for the rest of my life, No, of course not, but it's only natural that I should find it odd to see you surrounded by videos, as if you had suddenly developed a passion for the cinema, when, before, you weren't really interested at all, As I said, I'm engaged in a piece of work, a sociological study, if you like, Look, I may be an ordinary clerk, a bank employee, but even my rather dim intelligence can sense you're not telling the truth, Not telling the truth, exclaimed Tertuliano Máximo Afonso indignantly, not telling the truth, that really is the limit, There's no point getting angry, I'm just saying how it seems to me, Now I know I'm not perfect, but dishonesty is not one of my faults, you should know me better than that, Forgive me, That's all right, you're forgiven, we won't mention the matter again. That is what he said, but he would in fact have preferred to continue talking about it, if only to avoid talking about the other subject he was much more afraid to broach. Maria da Paz sat down in the armchair in front of the television set and said, I came to talk to you, I'm not interested in your videos. The nightingale's song had got lost in the stratospheric regions of the ceiling, it was already, as they used to say in days gone by, but a sweet memory, and Tertuliano Máximo Afonso, who cut a deplorable figure in his dressing gown and slippers, his face unshaven, all of which put him in a position of clear inferiority, was aware that an acerbic conversation, even though the angry words he might use would suit what we know to be his final aim, that is, to end his relationship with Maria da Paz, would be difficult to conduct and doubtless even harder to bring to a close. So he sat down on the sofa, covered his legs with his dressing gown, and began in a conciliatory tone of voice, My idea, What are you talking about, broke in Maria da Paz, us or your videos, We'll talk about us afterward, for the moment I just want to explain to you the kind of work I'm involved in, If you must, replied Maria da Paz, reining in her impatience. Tertuliano Máximo Afonso prolonged the ensuing silence for as long as possible, he racked his brain for the words he had used to put the assistant in the video shop off the track, and he experienced a strange and contradictory feeling. Although he knows he is going to lie, he thinks, nevertheless, that this lie will be a kind of warped version of the truth, that is, although the explanation may be completely false, the mere fact of repeating it will, in a way, make it plausible, and all the more plausible if Tertuliano Máximo Afonso does not stop at this first attempt. At last, feeling himself master of his material, he began, My interest in looking at a number of films by this production company, chosen at random, for, as you will see, they are all made by the same company, was born out of an idea I had some time ago, that of making a study of the tendencies, inclinations, intentions, and messages, explicit, implicit, and subliminal, in short, the ideological signals disseminated among its consumers, image by image, by a particular film company, And how did it come about this sudden interest, or as you call it, this idea, what has it got to do with your work as a history teacher, asked Maria da Paz, completely unaware that she had just handed to Tertuliano Máximo Afonso on a plate the very answer which, in his hour of dialectical need, he might not have been capable of finding for himself, It's very simple, he replied with a look of relief on his face that could easily have been mistaken for the virtuous satisfaction experienced by any good teacher taking delight in the act of transmitting his knowledge to the class, It's very simple, he said again, just as the history that we write, study, or teach penetrates every line, every word, and even every date, what I termed ideological signals, inherent not just in the interpretation of facts, but also in the language we use to express those facts, not forgetting the various types and degrees of intentionality in our use of that language, so it is that the cinema, a storytelling mode that, given its particular efficacy, acts upon the actual contents of history, at once contaminating and falsifying them, so it is, I repeat, that the cinema, with far greater speed and no less intentionality, participates in the general propagation of a whole network of those ideological signals, usually in a way that promotes its own interests. He paused and, with the indulgent half smile of someone apologizing for the aridity of an explanation that failed to take into consideration his audience's inadequate ability to understand, added, I hope to clarify my ideas when I write them down. Despite her more than justified reservations, Maria da Paz couldn't help looking at him with a certain admiration, after all, he is a skilled history teacher, a trained professional of proven competence, one presumes he knows what he's talking about even when he ventures into matters outside his speciality, while she is a mere middle-ranking bank employee, without the necessary preparation to take full cognizance of any ideological signals unless they first explained who they were and what they wanted. However, throughout Tertuliano Máximo Afonso's speech, she had noticed a kind of embarrassed catch in his voice, a disharmony that occasionally distorted his delivery, like the characteristic vibrato produced by a cracked water jar when struck with the knuckles, quick, someone, go to Maria da Paz's aid and tell her that it is with precisely this sound that our words leave our mouth when the truth we appear to be saying is the lie we are concealing. Apparently, yes, apparently someone did warn her or else intimated as much with the usual hints and suggestions, what other explanation can there be for the fact that the admiring light in her eyes was suddenly extinguished and replaced by a wounded expression, an air of compassionate pity, whether for herself or for the man sitting opposite we do not know. Tertuliano Máximo Afonso realized that his discourse had been not only offensive but useless too, that there are many ways of showing one's disrespect for other people's intelligence and sensitivity and that this had been one of the grosser examples. Maria da Paz did not come to see him in order to be given explanations about procedures that are neither here nor there, or anywhere else for that matter, she came to find out how much she would have to pay to have restored to her, if such a thing were still possible, the small happiness she had believed to be hers during the last six months. It is also true that Tertuliano Máximo Afonso is not going to say, as if it were the most natural thing in the world, You won't believe this, but I've discovered a man who is my exact double and who appears as an actor in some of these films, there was no way he would say that to her, if, indeed, such words could legitimately follow the words that immediately preceded them, for this could be interpreted by Maria da Paz as yet another diversionary tactic, when all she had come to find out was how much she would have to pay to have restored to her the small happiness she had believed to be hers during the last six months, and please forgive the repetition, which we make in the name of the right we all have to say over and over where the pain is. There was an awkward silence. Maria da Paz should really speak now and say defiantly, Right, if you've finished your stupid spiel about nonexistent ideological signals, let's talk about us, but dread has formed a lump in her throat, the fear that the simplest word could shatter the glass of her fragile hope, which is why she says nothing, which is why she waits for Tertuliano Máximo Afonso to begin, but Tertuliano Máximo Afonso is sitting, eyes downcast, apparently absorbed in contemplation of his slippers and the pale fringe of skin that appears where his pajama bottoms end, the truth, however, is very different, Tertuliano Máximo Afonso does not dare to look up in case his eyes drift over to the papers on the desk, the list of films and actors' names, with its little crosses, deletions, and question marks, all so far removed from his unfortunate discourse on ideological signals, which seems to him now the work of another person. Contrary to popular belief, the helpful words that open the way to great, dramatic dialogues are, in general, modest, ordinary, banal, no one would think that Would you like a cup of coffee could serve as an introduction to a bitter debate about feelings that have died or to the sweetness of a reconciliation that neither person knows how to bring about. Maria da Paz should have responded with due coolness, I didn't come here to drink coffee, but, looking inside herself, she saw that this wasn't true, she saw that she really had come there to drink coffee, that her own happiness, imagine, depended on that coffee. In a voice that was intended to reveal only weary resignation but which shook with nerves, she said, Yes, I would, and added, I'll make it. She got up from her chair, and it wasn't that she stopped as she walked past Tertuliano Máximo Afonso, how can we explain what happened, we pile up words, words, and more words, the very words we talked about elsewhere, a personal pronoun, an adverb, a verb, an adjective, and, however we try, however hard we struggle, we always find ourselves outside the feelings we so ingenuously hoped to describe, as if a feeling were like a landscape with mountains in the distance and trees in the foreground, but the truth is that Maria da Paz's spirit subtly froze the rectilinear movement of her body, hoping, who knows what, perhaps that Tertuliano Máximo Afonso would stand up and embrace her, or softly take the hand hanging loose by her side, which is indeed what happened, first his hand taking hold of hers, then the embrace that did not dare to go beyond a discreet proximity, she did not offer him her lips and he did not seek them, there are times when it is a thousand times better to do less than to do more, to hand the matter over to sensibility, which will know better than rational intelligence how best to proceed toward the full perfection of the following moments, if, that is, they were born to reach such heights. They slowly separated, she smiled a little, he smiled a little, but we know that Tertuliano Máximo Afonso has another idea in his head, which is to remove from Maria da Paz's eyes, as quickly as possible, the telltale papers, which is why we need not be surprised by the way he almost propels her toward the kitchen, Go on, then, you make the coffee while I try to bring some order to this chaos, and then the unexpected happened, for, as if giving no particular importance to the words emerging from her mouth or as if she did not entirely understand them, she murmured,

Chaos is merely order waiting to be deciphered, What, what did you say, asked Tertuliano Máximo Afonso, who had already removed the list of names, Chaos is merely order waiting to be deciphered, Where did you read that, or did you hear someone say it, No, it just occurred to me now, I don't think I read it anywhere and I certainly never heard anyone say it, But how could you just come out with something like that, Is there something special about it, There certainly is, Oh, I don't know, perhaps it's because my work at the bank is all to do with numbers, and numbers, when they're all mixed together, muddled up, can seem like chaotic elements to people who don't know them, and yet there exists in them a latent order, in fact I don't think numbers have any sense at all outside some sort of order you impose on them, the problem lies in finding that order, There aren't any numbers here, But there is a chaos, you yourself said so, A few videos out of place, that's all, And the images inside them, attached to each other so as to tell a story, i.e., an order, as well as the successive chaoses they would form if we jumbled them up before putting them together to make different stories, and the successive orders that would come out of that, always leaving behind an ordered chaos, always advancing into a chaos waiting to be put into an order, Ideological signals, said Tertuliano Máximo Afonso, not entirely sure that the reference was pertinent, Yes, ideological signals if you want, It sounds to me like you don't believe me, It doesn't matter whether I believe you or not, you presumably know what you're after, What I find hard to understand is how you stumbled upon that discovery, the idea of order being contained within a chaos and which can be deciphered from within, Do you mean to say that in all these months, ever since our relationship first began, you have never considered me intelligent enough to have ideas, Oh, come on, that's got nothing to do with it, you're a very intelligent person, but, Oh, I know, but not as intelligent as you, and, needless to say, I haven't got the necessary training, I am, after all, just a poor little bank employee, There's no need to be ironic, I've never once thought you were less intelligent than me, I just meant that your idea is really original, And you didn't expect such originality from me, No, in a way, I didn't, You're the historian, but I would say that it was only after our ancestors had had the ideas that made them intelligent that they actually began to be intelligent enough to have ideas, Now you've gone all paradoxical on me, I can't keep up with all these surprises, said Tertuliano Máximo Afonso, Well, before you turn into a pillar of salt, I'll go and make the coffee, said Maria da Paz with a smile, and as she headed off down the corridor that led to the kitchen, she said, Tidy up that chaos, Máximo, tidy up that chaos. The list of names was swiftly locked away in a drawer, the loose videos were returned to their respective boxes, and *The Parallel of Terror*, which was still in the video player, followed the same route, it hadn't been so easy to impose order on chaos since the world began. Experience has taught us, however, that there are always a few ends left untied, always some milk spilled along the way, always a line that comes out of alignment, which, when applied to the situation under scrutiny, means that Tertuliano Máximo Afonso is aware that his war is lost even before it's begun. The way things stand now, thanks to the sovereign stupidity of his speech on ideological signals, and after her masterstroke, that comment about the existence of order in chaos, of a decipherable order, it is impossible to tell the woman who is now in the kitchen making coffee, Our relationship has come to an end, we can still be friends if you like, but that's all, or else, I hate to have to tell you this, but I've been weighing up my feelings for you and I just don't feel that first flush of enthusiasm anymore, or even, It's been very nice, my dear, but it's over, from now on, you go your way and I'll go mine. Tertuliano Máximo Afonso goes over the conversation, trying to find out where his tactic failed, always assuming he had a tactic and wasn't just led by Maria da Paz's changes of mood, as if they were sudden minor fires he had to put out as they arose, unaware that flames were meanwhile licking around his feet. She always was more confident than me, he thought, and at that moment he saw the reasons for his defeat quite differently, who was this grotesque figure, disheveled and unshaven, in down-at-the-heels slippers, the stripes on his pajama bottoms like faded fringes peeping out from beneath his dressing gown, which has been tied clumsily so that one edge is higher than the other, there are some decisions in life that must be taken only when dressed to the nines, with one's tie knotted and one's shoes polished, so that one can exclaim in noble, wounded tones, If my presence bothers you, madam, say not another word, then sweep out of the door, without looking back, looking back brings with it terrible risks, a person can be turned into a pillar of salt at the mercy of the first shower of rain. But Tertuliano Máximo Afonso now has another problem to solve, one that requires great tact, great diplomacy, a talent for maneuvering which has so far eluded him, especially since, as we have seen, the initiative always lay in Maria da Paz's hands, even right at the start, when she arrived and threw herself into her lover's arms like a woman about to drown. This was precisely what Tertuliano Máximo Afonso thought, caught between admiration, annoyance, and a kind of dangerous tenderness, She looked as if she were about to drown, but she actually had her feet firmly on the ground. Returning to the problem, what Tertuliano Máximo Afonso cannot allow is for Maria da Paz to be left alone in the living room. What if she appears with the coffee, and, by the way, why is she taking so long, coffee takes only a few minutes to make, gone are the days when you had to strain it, what if, after drinking their coffee in sweet harmony, she says to him, either with or without ulterior motives, You go and get dressed while I have a look at one of these videos of yours, to see if I can spot any of your famous ideological signals, what if cruel fate were to make Tertuliano Máximo Afonso's double appear in the role of nightclub doorman or bank clerk, imagine Maria da Paz's scream, Máximo, Máximo, come here, quick, come and see this actor playing a medical auxiliary and who looks just like you, really, you can call him anything you like, good Samaritan, divine Providence, brother of charity, but he's certainly no ideological signal. None of this, however, will happen, Maria da Paz will bring in the coffee, you can hear her coming down the corridor now, the tray with two cups and a sugar bowl on it, a few biscuits to placate the stomach, and everything will pass off as Tertuliano Máximo Afonso would never have dared to dream, they drank their coffee in silence, but it was a companionable silence, not hostile, the perfect domestic bliss that, as far as Tertuliano Máximo Afonso was concerned, turned into utter heaven when he heard her say, While you're getting dressed, I'll sort out the chaos in the kitchen, then I'll leave you in peace to get on with your work, Oh, don't let's talk any more about that, said Tertuliano Máximo Afonso in order to remove this importunate stone from the middle of the road, but aware that he had just put another stone there in its place, more difficult to remove, as he will soon find out. In any case, Tertuliano Máximo Afonso did not want to leave anything to chance, he shaved in a trice, washed in a twinkling, got dressed in a flash, did all this, in short, so rapidly that when he went into the kitchen, he was still in plenty of time to dry the dishes. The most touchingly familiar of all scenes then took place in this apartment, the man drying the plates and the woman putting them away, it could have been the other way around, but destiny or fate, call it what you will, decided that it should be thus so that what had to happen happened as Maria da Paz was reaching up to place a serving dish on a shelf, thus, either wittingly or unwittingly, offering up her slender waist to the hands of a man incapable of resisting the temptation. Tertuliano Máximo Afonso put down the tea towel, and while the cup, slipping from his grasp, shattered on the floor, he embraced Maria da Paz, clasped her furiously to him, and the most objective and impartial of spectators would readily have admitted that his so-called first flush of enthusiasm could never have been greater than this. The question, the painful and eternal question, is how long will this last, will this really mean a rekindling of an affection that will have occasionally been confused with love, with passion even, or do we merely find ourselves once more before the familiar phenomenon of the candle that, as it goes out, burns with a higher and unbearably brighter flame, unbearable only because it is the last, not because it is rejected by our eyes, which would happily remain absorbed in looking. It is said and has been said before that between the lashes the back takes its pleasure, but it is not the back, in fact, that is taking its pleasure, indeed we would go so far as to say, if we can allow ourselves to be so crude, that it is, rather, the lash that is taking its pleasure, however, the truth is, although this is not the moment for high-flown lyricism, that the joy, pleasure, and delight of these two people stretched out on the bed, one on top of the other, arms and legs literally entwined, should prompt us respectfully to doff our hat and hope that it will be always thus for them, or for each of them, whoever their future partners might be, if, that is, the candle that is burning now does not last beyond this brief, final spasm, the very spasm that, even as it melts us, also hardens and drives us apart. Bodies, thoughts. Tertuliano Máximo Afonso is thinking about life's contradictions, about the fact that in order to win a battle it might sometimes be necessary to lose it, the present situation is a case in point, to win would have been to guide the conversation in the direction of the desired total and definitive split, and that battle, at least for the time being, had to be given up as lost, but to win would also be to distract Maria da Paz's attention from the videos and the imaginary study on ideological signals, and that battle has, for the moment, been won. According to popular wisdom, you can't have everything, and there's a good deal of truth in that, the balance of human lives is constantly swinging back and forth between what is gained and what is lost, the problem lies in the equally human impossibility of coming to an agreement on the relative merits of what should be lost and what should be gained, which is why the world is in the state it's in. Maria da Paz is also thinking, but, being a woman, and therefore closer to things fundamental and essential, she is remembering her anxiety of mind when she entered the apartment, her certainty that she would leave here vanquished and humiliated, and yet, after all, the one thing that she had never for a moment imagined would happen has happened, going to bed with the man she loves, which just goes to show how much this woman still has to learn if she does not know that it is in bed that so many dramatic arguments between couples end up and are resolved, not because having sex is a panacea for all physical and moral ills, although there are plenty of people who think it is, but because, when bodies are exhausted, minds take the opportunity to raise a timid finger and ask permission to enter, ask if their reasons can be heard now and if they, the bodies, are prepared to listen. That is when the man says to the woman, or the woman to the man, We must be mad, what fools we've been, and one of them, out of compassion, does not respond as in fairness they could, Well, you might have been, but I've been here all the time. Impossible though it may seem, it is this silence full of unspoken words that saves what had been judged to be lost, like a raft that looms out of the fog looking for its sailors, with its oars and its compass, with its candle and its cache of bread. Tertuliano Máximo Afonso said, We could have lunch together, if you're free that is, Of course I am, I always have been, No, what I meant was that there's your mother to be considered, Oh, I told her I fancied going for a walk alone and that I might not be home for lunch, An excuse to come here, Not exactly, it was only after I'd left the house that I decided to come and speak to you, And now we've spoken, Meaning, asked Maria da Paz, that everything between us will continue as before, Of course. One might have expected a little more eloquence from Tertuliano Máximo Afonso, but he will always be able to say, I didn't have time, she flung her arms around my neck and kissed me and I did the same, and, God help us, there we were once more entwined, And did God help, asked the unknown voice that we haven't heard for a while now, Well, I don't know if it was God exactly, but it was certainly good, So what next, We're going to have lunch, And you're not going to talk about it, About what, About you and her, We've talked, No, you haven't, Yes, we have, So the clouds have all blown away, They have, Does that mean you're no longer considering ending the relationship, then, That's another matter, let's leave for tomorrow what belongs to the morrow, A good philosophy, The best, As long as you know what does belong to the morrow, We can't know that until we get there, You've got an answer for everything, You would too if you had had to lie as much as I have in the last few days, So, you're going out to lunch, Yes, we are, Well, *bon appétit*, and what will you do afterward, Afterward, I'll take her home and come back here, To watch the videos, Yes, to watch the videos, Well, have a good time, said the unknown voice. Maria da Paz had already got up, one can hear the sound of the water in the shower, they always used to take a shower together after making love, but this time she didn't think of it and he didn't remember, or they both remembered but preferred to say nothing, there are times when it is best to be content with what one has, so as not to lose everything.

It was past five o'clock in the afternoon when Tertuliano Máximo Afonso got home. All that time wasted, he thought, as he opened the drawer where he had put the list and while he hesitated between *Arm-in-arm with Fate* and *Angels Dance Too*. He will never put either in the VCR, which is why he will never know that his double, the actor who looks just like him, as Maria da Paz might have said, plays a croupier in the first film and a dance teacher in the second. He suddenly rebelled against the self-imposed obligation to keep to the chronological order in which the films had been produced, from oldest all the way up to the most recent, he thought it wouldn't be a bad idea to vary things a bit, to break with routine, I'm going to watch *The Goddess of the Stage*, he said. Within ten minutes his double appeared, playing the part of a theater impresario. Tertuliano Máximo Afonso felt a jolt in the pit of his stomach, a lot of things must have changed in this actor's life for him to be playing a character who was gaining in importance all the time, after years of playing, fleetingly, a hotel receptionist, a bank clerk, a medical auxiliary, a nightclub doorman, and a police photographer. After half an hour, he couldn't stand it anymore, so he fast-forwarded the tape to the end, but, contrary to expectation, he failed to find in the credits any of the names on his list. He rewound back to the beginning, to the opening credits, which, out of force of habit, he had ignored, and there it was. The actor playing the part of the theater impresario in the film *The Goddess of the Stage* is called Daniel Santa-Clara.

Discoveries made over the weekend are no less valid or valuable than those that first find being or expression on other, so-called working days. In both cases, the person who has made the discovery will inform his assistants, if they happen to be working overtime, or his family, if they happen to be near, and, if there's no champagne on hand, they will toast the success with the bottle of sparkling wine that has been waiting in the fridge for just such an occasion, congratulations will be given and received, details for the patent noted down, and life, imperturbable, will move on, having shown yet again that inspiration, talent, or chance are not particular about either time or place when it comes to revealing themselves. There can have been few cases when the discoverer, because he lived alone or had no assistants, did not have at least one person with whom he could share the joy of having bestowed on the world the light of a new piece of knowledge. More extraordinary and rarer still, not to say unique, is the situation in which Tertuliano Máximo Afonso finds himself at this precise moment, for not only has he no one to whom he can communicate his discovery of the name of the actor who is the very image of himself, he must also take great care to keep this discovery secret. Indeed, it is impossible to imagine Tertuliano Máximo Afonso rushing off to phone his mother, or Maria da Paz, or his colleague the mathematics teacher, and saying, the words tumbling over themselves in his excitement, I've found him, I've found him, the guy's name is Daniel Santa-Clara. If there is one secret in life he wants to keep under wraps so that no one even suspects its existence, it is this. For fear of the consequences, Tertuliano Máximo Afonso is obliged, possibly forever, to maintain absolute silence on the results of his investigations, both the results of this first phase, which ended today, and of any further investigations he may carry out in the future. He is also condemned, at least until Monday, to total inactivity. He knows the man is called Daniel Santa-Clara, but knowing this is about as useful as being able to say that a particular star is called Aldebaran, but knowing nothing else about it. The production company will be closed today and tomorrow, so there is no point in trying to phone them, at best a security guard would answer and he would only say, Phone back on Monday, no one's here today, Oh, Tertuliano Máximo Afonso would declare in an attempt to drag the conversation out, I thought there were no Sundays or holidays for a production company, that they filmed every day the Good Lord sent, especially in spring and summer, so as not to waste all those daylight hours, That's not my business, it's not my responsibility, I'm just a security guard, A well-informed security guard should know everything, They don't pay me to know everything, That's a shame, Anything else, the man would ask impatiently, Can you at least tell me who I should contact there to find out about actors, Look, I don't know, I don't know anything, I've already told you I'm just a security guard, phone back on Monday, the man will say again in exasperation, if he doesn't unleash a few choice words that the caller's impertinence more than justifies. Sitting in the armchair, in front of the television, surrounded by videos, Tertuliano Máximo Afonso comes to the conclusion, There's nothing I can do about it, I'm just going to have to wait until Monday to phone the production company. He said this and immediately felt his stomach contract as if with sudden fear. It was very quick, but the subsequent tremor lasted a few seconds longer, like the troubling vibration of a double-bass string. In order not to think about what had seemed to him some kind of threat, he asked himself what he could do with the rest of the weekend, what remains of today and all of tomorrow, how to occupy all those empty hours, one possibility would be to watch the remaining films, but that wouldn't provide him with any further information, he would merely see his face in other roles, perhaps as a dance teacher, perhaps as a fireman, perhaps as a croupier, a pickpocket, an architect, a primary school teacher, an actor looking for work, his face, his body, his words, his gestures, repeated ad nauseam. He could phone Maria da Paz, ask her to come and see him, to-morrow if not today, but that would mean tying his own hands, no self-respecting man asks for help from a woman, even if the woman doesn't know he's asking for help, to just send her away again afterward. It was at this point that a thought which had occasionally raised its head behind other more fortunate thoughts, without Tertuliano Máximo Afonso paying it the slightest attention, suddenly managed to push its way to the front, If you went and looked in the phone directory, it said, you could find out where he lives, you wouldn't have to bother the production company then, you could even, always assuming you felt up to it, go and see the street where he lives, and the house, although obviously you'd have to take the elementary precaution of disguising yourself, don't ask me as what, that's your problem. Tertuliano Máximo Afonso's stomach gave another lurch, this man refuses to understand that emotions are wise things, they worry about us, tomorrow they'll say, We warned you, but by then, in all probability, it will be too late. Tertuliano Máximo Afonso has the phone directory in his hands, which tremble as they search for the letter S, they leaf backward and forward, here it is. There are three Santa-Claras, but none of them is a Daniel.

It wasn't such a big disappointment. Such an arduous search couldn't just end like that, it would be too ridiculously easy. It's true that telephone directories have always been one of the prime investigatory tools of any private detective or local policeman endowed with a little basic intelligence, a kind of paper microscope capable of bringing the suspect bacterium to the investigator's visual curve of perception, but it is also true that this method of identification has had its difficulties and failures, all those people with the same name, heartless answering machines, wary silences, that frequent, discouraging reply, Sorry, that person doesn't live here anymore. Tertuliano Máximo Afonso's first and, logically speaking, correct thought was that Daniel Santa-Clara had not wanted his name to appear in the directory. Some influential people, with a high social profile, adopt this procedure, it's called defending their sacred right to privacy, businessmen and financiers do it, for example, as do corrupt politicians of the first order, the stars, planets, comets, and meteorites of the cinema, brooding writers of genius, soccer wizards, Formula One racing drivers, models from the worlds of high and medium fashion, and from low fashion too, and, for rather more understandable reasons, criminals with various crime specialities have also preferred the reserve, discretion, and modesty of an anonymity that, up to a point, protects them from unhealthy curiosity. In these cases, even if their exploits make them famous, we can be sure that we will never find their names in the phone book. Now, since Daniel Santa-Clara, at least from what we know of him so far, is not a criminal, and since he is not, and of this we have not the slightest doubt, a film star, despite belonging to the same profession, the reason for his absence from the small group of people bearing the surname Santa-Clara is bound to cause real perplexity, from which only profound thought will free us. This was precisely what Tertuliano Máximo Afonso was engaged in while we, with reprehensible frivolity, have been discussing the sociological type of those people who, deep down, would like to be included in a private, confidential, secret telephone directory, a kind of *Almanach de Gotha* that would record the new forms of ennoblement that exist in modern societies. The conclusion reached by Tertuliano Máximo Afonso, even though it belongs to the category of the blindingly obvious, is no less deserving of applause, for it demonstrates that the mental confusion which has tormented the history teacher's past few days has not proved an impediment to free and impartial thought. It is true that Daniel Santa-Clara's name does not appear in the telephone directory, but this doesn't mean that there isn't some, shall we say, family connection between one of the three people who do appear and Santa-Clara the film actor. Equally admissible is the probability that they all belong to the same family or even, if we are going down that road, that Daniel Santa-Clara does, in fact, live in one of those houses and that the telephone he uses is still, for example, registered in the name of his late grandfather. If, as children used to be told, in order to illustrate the relationship between small causes and great effects, for want of a shoe the horse was lost, for want of a horse the battle was lost, the trajectory followed by the deductions and inductions that brought Tertuliano Máximo Afonso to the conclusion set out above seems to us no less dubious and problematic than that edifying episode from the history of wars whose first agent and ultimate culprit must have been, when all's said and done and with no room for objections, the professional incompetence of the vanquished army's farrier. What will Tertuliano Máximo Afonso do next, that is the burning question. Perhaps he will be satisfied with having whittled away at the problem with a view to a subsequent study of the necessary conditions for drawing up an oblique approach strategy, of the prudent kind that proceeds by small advances and constant vigilance. To look at him, sitting in the chair where there began what is now, by any measure, a new phase of his life, back bent, elbows resting on his knees, and head in his hands, you would not imagine the hard work going on inside that brain, weighing up alternatives, pondering options, considering other variants, anticipating moves, like a chess master. Half an hour has gone by, and he hasn't moved. And another half an hour will have to pass before we suddenly see him get up and go over to the desk with the telephone directory open at the page containing the enigma. He has clearly taken a bold decision, let us admire the courage of this man who has finally put prudence behind him and decided to attack head on. He dialed the number of the first Santa-Clara and waited. No one picked up the phone and no answering machine came on. He dialed the second number and a woman's voice said, Hello, Good afternoon, madam, I'm sorry to bother you, but I'd like to speak to Senhor Daniel Santa-Clara, I understand he lives at this address, No, you're wrong, he doesn't live here and

never has, But the surname, The surname is just a coincidence, like many others, Oh, I thought you might perhaps be
related and be able to help me find him, Look, I don't even
know you, Forgive me, I should have told you my name, No,
don't, I don't want to know, It would seem I was badly informed, It would indeed, Many thanks for your time, That's
all right, Good-bye, then, sorry to have troubled you, Good-
bye. It would have been natural, after this inexplicably tense
exchange of words, for Tertuliano Máximo Afonso to pause
in order to regain his composure and his normal pulse rate,
but this was not the case. There are times in our lives when we
think that we might as well be hanged for a sheep as a lamb,
and when all we want is to find out as quickly as possible the
true dimensions of the disaster, and then, if possible, never
to think about the matter again. Therefore, the third number
was dialed without hesitation, a man's voice asked abruptly,
Who is it. Tertuliano Máximo Afonso felt as if he had been
caught out and so mumbled some name or other, What do
you want, the voice asked in the same harsh tone, although
curiously there was no hostility in it, some people are like
that, their voice comes out in a way that makes it sound as if
they were angry with everyone, and, in the end, you discover
that they have a heart of gold. On this occasion, given the
brevity of the conversation, we will never find out if the heart
of this person really is made of that most noble of metals.
Tertuliano Máximo Afonso expressed a desire to speak to
Senhor Daniel Santa-Clara, and the man with the angry voice
replied that no one of that name lived there, and the conversation seemed unlikely to progress any further, there was no
point in revisiting the curious coincidence of surnames or the
chance possibility of a family relationship that might lead the

questioner to his destination, in such cases the questions and answers are always the same, Is so-and-so there, No, so-and-so doesn't live here, but this time something new happened, the man with the dissonant vocal cords mentioned that more or less a week before someone else had phoned with exactly the same question, It wasn't you, was it, no, the voice is different, I have a very good ear for voices, No, it wasn't me, said Tertuliano Máximo Afonso, feeling troubled, and was this person a man or a woman, A man, of course. Yes, of course, a man, stupid fool, it stands out a mile that however many differences there may exist between the voices of two men, there are far more between a female voice and a male voice, Although, the man added, now that I think about it, there was a moment when I thought he was trying to disguise his voice. Having duly thanked the man for all his help, Tertuliano Máximo Afonso replaced the receiver and sat looking at the three names in the directory. If the man who phoned had been asking for Daniel Santa-Clara, simple logic dictated that, as he himself had just done, he too must have phoned all three numbers. Obviously Tertuliano Máximo Afonso could not know if anyone would have answered at the first number, and everything indicated that the ill-disposed woman with whom he had spoken, and who really was rude despite her neutral tone of voice, had either forgotten or deemed it unnecessary to mention the fact, or, and this was a far likelier reason, she had not taken the previous call. Perhaps because I live alone, Tertuliano Máximo Afonso said to himself, I tend to assume that other people do as well. The deep disquiet caused by the news that an unknown man was also looking for Daniel Santa-Clara left him with a troubling sense of bewilderment as if he had been handed a quadratic equation to solve when he had already forgotten how to do simple ones.

It was probably a creditor, he thought, yes, that's probably who it was, a creditor, artists and literary people tend to lead fairly disorganized lives, he probably owes money in one of those places where people gamble and now they want it back. Tertuliano Máximo Afonso had read some time ago that gambling debts are the most sacred of all debts, some people even call them debts of honor, and although he did not quite see why these debts should be any more honorable than others, he had accepted both code and prescription as something that had nothing to do with him, Ah, well, it's up to them, he had thought. Now, however, he would have preferred those debts to be less sacred, to be ordinary ones, of the kind that are forgiven and forgotten, as was not only prayed for but promised too in the old Lord's Prayer. To calm his mind, he went into the kitchen to make some coffee, and, while he drank it, he took stock of the situation, I've still got to make that call, now, two things could happen when I do, they will either tell me that they know neither the name nor the person, and that will be that, or they'll say, yes, he lives here, and then I'll hang up, at the moment, all I need to know is where he lives.

With his spirit fortified by the impeccable logic he had just produced and by his no less impeccable conclusion, he went back into the living room. The phone directory lay open on the desk, the three Santa-Claras had not moved. He dialed the first number and waited. He waited and continued to wait long after he was sure no one would answer. It's Saturday today, he thought, they're probably out. He hung up, he had done everything he could, no one could accuse him of irresolution or timidity. He looked at his watch, it was about time to go out to supper, but the gloomy memory of the tablecloths, white as shrouds, the miserable little vases of plastic flowers on the tables, and, above all, the permanent threat of monkfish, made him change his mind. In a city of five million inhabitants, there is, naturally, a proportionate number of restaurants, a few thousand at least, and even excluding, at the one extreme, the luxurious, and at the other, the frankly repellent, he would still be left with a large range to choose from, for example, the charming place where he had had lunch with Maria da Paz today, and which they had simply happened upon, but Tertuliano Máximo Afonso disliked the idea of dining there alone when, at lunchtime, he had been in company. He therefore decided not to go out, he would, as the time-honored expression has it, just have a bite to eat at home and go to bed early. He wouldn't even need to draw back the sheets, the bed was exactly as they had left it, the sheets rumpled, the pillows unplumped, the smell of cold love. He thought that he really should phone Maria da Paz and say something nice, send her a smile that she would doubtless feel at the other end of the line, it's true that their relationship is bound to come to an end one of these days, but there are tacit obligations that cannot and should not be ignored, it would show gross insensitivity, not to mention an unforgivable moral coarseness, to behave as if, that morning, in that apartment, they had not enjoyed some of the pleasurable, beneficial, agreeable activities that, sleeping aside, tend to take place in bed. Being a man should never be an impediment to behaving like a gentleman. And we have no doubt that Tertuliano Máximo Afonso would have acted like one if, however odd this may at first seem, the thought of Maria da Paz had not returned him to his obsessive preoccupation of the last few days, that is, how to find Daniel Santa-Clara. His zero success in his attempts at phoning had left him no alternative but to write a letter to the production company, since it would be out of the question to go there himself, in the flesh, running the risk that the person of whom he was asking the information might say to him, How are you, Senhor Santa-Clara. Resorting to a disguise, the classic false beard, mustache, and wig, apart from being totally ridiculous, would be utterly stupid too, it would make him feel like a bad actor in an eighteenth-century melodrama, like an aristocratic father or the rake who turns up in the fourth act, and since he had always feared that life might choose him to be the victim of one of the frequent and tasteless practical jokes on which it preens itself, he was convinced that the mustache and beard would fall off just as he was inquiring about Daniel Santa-Clara and that the person he asked would burst out laughing and summon his or her colleagues to join in the fun, Oh, very good, very good, come over here everyone, it's Senhor Santa-Clara inquiring about himself. A letter was, therefore, the only way, and probably the safest, of achieving his conspiratorial ends, with the one condition, sine qua non, that he did not sign his own name or mention his address. As we can testify, he had lately been pondering this tangle of tactics, although in such a diffuse and confused manner that such mental labors should not properly be called thought, it was more like a drift or a meander of vacillating fragments of ideas that had only now managed to come together and organize themselves in a sufficiently focused way, which is also why we have only now recorded them here. The decision that Tertuliano Máximo Afonso has just taken is one of truly startling simplicity, of brilliant, transparent clarity. Common sense does not share this view and has just bustled in through the door asking indignantly, How could such an idea even enter your head, It's the only one and it's the best one too, said Tertuliano Máximo Afonso coldly, It might well be the only one and it might well be the best, but if you'd care to know my opinion, I think it would be shameful of you to write that letter in Maria da Paz's name and giving her address, Why shameful, Well, if you need it explained, more fool you, She won't mind, How do you know if you haven't even talked to her about it, I have my reasons, We know about your reasons, my friend, they're known as the presumptuousness of the male, the vanity of the seducer, and the arrogance of the conqueror, Well, I am male, that's my sex, but I've never seen the seducer you describe reflected in the mirror, and as for me being a conqueror of women, please, if my life is a book, then that's one chapter that's missing, Really, Believe me, I'm never the conqueror, always the conquered, And how are you going to explain your reasons for writing a letter asking for information about an actor, But I won't tell her I'm interested in finding out about an actor, What will you say, then, That the letter is to do with the work I mentioned to her, What work, Oh, don't make me go through it all again, All right, but you obviously think that all you have to do is snap your fingers and Maria da Paz will come running to satisfy your every whim, All I'm doing is asking her a favor, The current state of your relationship means that you've lost any right to ask her favors, It might prove awkward signing my own name, Why, You never know what consequences it might have in the future, So why not use a false name, The name would be false, but the address would be real, Frankly, I still think you should forget all about this business of doubles, twins, and duplicates, Maybe I should, but I can't, it's something that's stronger than me now, My feeling is that you've set in motion a great crushing machine that is slowly advancing toward you, warned common sense, but since his companion did not reply, he withdrew, shaking his head, saddened by the outcome of the conversation. Tertuliano Máximo Afonso dialed Maria da Paz's number, her mother would probably answer, and their brief dialogue would be another small comedy of pretenses, grotesque and with just a touch of the pathetic, May I speak to Maria da Paz, he would ask, Who's calling, A friend, What's your name, Just tell her it's a friend, she'll know who it is, My daughter does have other gentleman friends, you know, Not that many, Many or few, the ones she has have names, All right, tell her it's Máximo. During the six months that he has been seeing Maria da Paz, Tertuliano Máximo Afonso has not often had to phone her at home and still less often has her mother answered first, but the tone of words and voice has always been, on her part, one of suspicion, and, on his part, one of ill-disguised impatience, she perhaps because she doesn't know as much about the affair as she would like, he doubtless annoyed that she should know so much. The previous dialogues had not differed very much from the example given above, which is merely a rather pricklier version of how it might have been but, in the end, was not, since Maria da Paz was the one to answer the phone, however, all of these dialogues, this one and the others, would, without exception, have been found in the index of any Manual of Human Relations under Mutual Incomprehension. I was beginning to think you weren't going to phone me, said Maria da Paz, As you see, you were wrong, here I am, Your silence would have meant that today didn't mean the same thing to you as it did to me, Whatever it meant, it was the same for us both, But perhaps not in the same way or for the same reasons, We don't have the instruments to measure such differences, if there were any, You still care about me, Yes, I still care about you, You don't sound very enthusiastic, all you did was repeat what I said, Tell me why those words shouldn't serve me as well as they served you, Because in being repeated they lose some of the conviction they would have carried if they had been spoken first, Of course, a round of applause for the ingenuity and subtlety of the analyst, You'd know that too if you read more fiction, How am I supposed to read fiction, novels, and stories, or whatever, if I don't even have time for history, which is my job, right now I'm struggling through a major work on Mesopotamian civilizations, Yes, I noticed it on the bedside table, You see, But I'm still not convinced you're that pressed for time, If you knew what my life was like, you wouldn't say that, But I would know what your life was like if you'd let me, We're not talking about that, we're talking about my professional life, Well, I'd say that your professional life was far more likely to be suffering because of that famous study you're immersed in, with all those films to watch, than because of any novel you might be reading in your spare time. Tertuliano Máximo Afonso had realized that the direction the conversation had taken was not to his advantage, that he was moving further and further away from his main objective, which was to mention, as naturally as possible, the matter of the letter, and now, for the second time that day, as if it were some automatic game of actions and reactions, Maria da Paz herself had just given him the opportunity, almost in the palm of her hand. He would still have to be cautious, though, and not let her think that his phone call was motivated entirely by self-interest, that he hadn't in fact called in order to talk about feelings, or even the good time they had had in bed, given that his tongue refused to pronounce the word love. I am interested in the subject, he said in a conciliatory manner, but rather less than you think, No one would have thought as much seeing you as I did, hair all over the place, in your dressing gown and slippers, still unshaven, with videos all over the place, you certainly didn't look like the sensible, levelheaded man I thought I knew, That's perfectly understandable, I was relaxing alone at home, but now that you mention it, I did have an idea that could facilitate and speed up the work, Well, I hope you're not going to make me watch your films, surely I didn't do anything to deserve such a punishment, Don't worry, my cruel instincts don't go that far, my idea was simply to write to the production company asking them for various specific facts related, in particular, to their distribution network, the location of cinemas and the number of viewers per film, it could be very useful to me I think, and would help me draw a few conclusions, Hm, I don't really see what that has got to do with the ideological signals you were looking for, It may not have as much to do with them as I imagine, but I'd still like to try, Fine, then, it's up to you, Yes, but there's one small problem, What's that, Well, I don't want to be the one to write the letter, Why don't you go and see them personally, then, some things are best done face to face, and they would probably be flattered, a history teacher taking an interest in the films they produce, That's precisely what I don't want, mixing up my scientific and professional qualifications with a study that's outside my speciality, Why, Well, I'm not sure I can explain really, but perhaps it's a matter of scruples, Then I don't really know how you're going to resolve a difficulty that you yourself are creating, You could write the letter, What an absurd idea, just how am I going to write a letter about a subject that is as mysterious to me as Chinese, When I say that you could write the letter, I mean that I would write it in your name and giving your address, and that way I would be safe from any indiscretion, Oh, that's all right then, I suppose that way your honor wouldn't be placed in jeopardy or your dignity in doubt,

Don't be ironic, as I said, it's merely a matter of scruples, Yes, so you said, And you don't believe me, Oh, don't worry, I believe you, Maria da Paz, Yes, speaking, You know I love you, don't you, Well, I think I do when you say you do, then I wonder if it's true, It is true, And did you phone because you couldn't wait to tell me so, or simply to ask me to write that letter, The idea of the letter came up in the course of the conversation, Yes, but you're not expecting me to believe that you had the idea while we were talking, No, I had thought about it vaguely before, Vaguely, Yes, vaguely, Listen, Máximo, Yes, my love, Go ahead and write the letter, Thanks so much for saying yes, I didn't honestly think you would mind, it's such a simple thing, Life, my dear Máximo, has taught me that nothing is simple, it just seems simple sometimes, and it's always when it looks simplest that we should most doubt it, You're being very skeptical, As far as I know, no one is born skeptical, Anyway, if you're in agreement, I'll write the letter in your name, Presumably I'll have to sign it, That won't be necessary, I'll invent a signature myself, At least make it look a bit like mine, Well, I never was much good at copying other people's handwriting, but I'll do my best, Be careful, watch yourself, once a person starts falsifying things there's no telling where it will end, Falsify isn't quite the right word, you probably mean forge, Thank you for the correction, my dear Máximo, but what I was trying to do was find one word that meant both things, As far as I know, there is no one word that combines both forge and falsify, If the action exists, then the word should exist too, All the words we have are in the dictionaries, All the dictionaries put together don't contain half the terms we would need in order for us to understand each other, For example, For example, I don't know of a word that could describe the confused mixture of feelings I feel inside me at the moment, Feelings about what, Not about what, about whom, About me, Yes, about you, Well, I hope it's nothing very bad, There's a little bit of everything, a pot-pourri if you like, but don't worry, I wouldn't be able to explain it to you even if I tried, We can return to the subject another day, Does that mean our conversation has come to an end, That's not what I said or what I meant, It really wasn't, well, forgive me then, Although, on second thought, it would perhaps be best if we just leave it for now, there's obviously too much tension between us, sparks fly off every remark that leaves our mouths, That isn't how I wanted it to be, Nor did I, But that's how it is, Yes, that's how it is, That's why we're going to say good-bye like the well-brought-up children we are and wish each other a good night's sleep and sweet dreams, see you soon, Call me whenever you want, Yes, I will, and Maria da Paz, Yes, I'm still here, Just to say that I do care about you, So you said.

Having replaced the receiver on the rest, Tertuliano Máximo Afonso wiped the sweat from his forehead with the back of his hand. He had got what he wanted and had more than enough reason to be pleased with himself, but the fact was that their long, difficult conversation had always been dictated by her even when it appeared not to be, subjecting him to a kind of continual humiliation that never found explicit expression in the words spoken by either of them, and yet those words, one by one, left an increasingly bitter taste in his mouth, which is precisely how people often describe the taste of defeat. He knew he had won, but he was aware too that his victory was in part illusory, as if each advance he had made had been only the mechanical consequence of a tactical withdrawal by the enemy, golden bridges skilfully placed to draw him on, with flags flying and drums and bugles sounding, until there came a point perhaps when he would find himself hopelessly encircled. In order to gain his objectives, he had thrown around Maria da Paz a net of sly, calculating speeches, but the knots with which he thought he was binding her had merely ended up limiting his own freedom of movement. During the six months they had known each other, he had deliberately kept Maria da Paz on the margins of his private life, so as not to let himself become too involved, and now that he had decided to end the relationship, and was only waiting for the right moment to do so, he found himself obliged not only to ask for her help, but to make her an accomplice in actions of whose origins and causes, as well as whose final end, she knew nothing. Common sense would call him an unscrupulous exploiter, but he would reply that the situation he was living through was unique in the world, that there were no antecedents by which to establish the guidelines for socially acceptable behavior, that no law had foreseen the extraordinary circumstance of a person being duplicated, and so, he, Tertuliano Máximo Afonso, had to invent, at every turn, the procedures, correct or incorrect, that would lead him to his objective. The letter was just one of those procedures, and if, to write it, he had been obliged to abuse the trust of a woman who said she loved him, it wasn't such a very grave crime, other people had done far worse things and no one was marking them out for public condemnation.

Tertuliano Máximo Afonso put a sheet of paper in the typewriter and paused to think. The letter would have to look as if it came from an admirer, it would have to be enthusiastic, but not too enthusiastic, after all, the actor Daniel Santa-Clara was not exactly a star capable of provoking hysterical outbursts of feeling, the letter should go through the ritual of asking for a signed photograph, even though what Tertuliano

Máximo Afonso really wants to know is where the actor lives, as well as his real name, if, as everything seems to indicate, Daniel Santa-Clara is the pseudonym of a man who may, who knows, also be called Tertuliano. Once the letter has been sent, there are two possible hypotheses as to what will happen next, the production company will either respond directly, giving the information requested, or say that it is not authorized to do so, in which case they will probably send the letter on to the person to whom it is really addressed. Is that what will happen, wondered Tertuliano Máximo Afonso. A moment's brief reflection made him see that the last hypothesis was the least likely because it would show a complete lack of professionalism and even less consideration on the part of the company in burdening its actors with the task and with the expense of replying to letters and sending out photographs. Let's hope so, he muttered, the whole thing will fall apart if he sends Maria da Paz a personal reply. For a moment, he seemed to see before him the thunderous collapse of the house of cards that, for a week now, he has been so painstakingly building, but administrative logic and an awareness that there was no other possible route helped him, gradually, to restore his shaken spirits. Writing the letter did not prove easy, which explains why his upstairs neighbor heard the hammering of the typewriter for over an hour. At one point, the phone rang, rang insistently, but Tertuliano Máximo Afonso did not pick it up. It was probably Maria da Paz.

HE WOKE LATE. HE HAD SPENT A TROUBLED NIGHT, SHOT through with fleeting, disquieting dreams, a staff meeting at which none of the teachers were present, an endless corridor, a videocassette that refused to fit into the VCR, a cinema with a black screen on which a black film was being shown, a telephone directory with the same name repeated on every line and which he could not read, a parcel with a fish inside, a man carrying a stone on his back and saying, I'm an Amorite, an algebraic equation with people's faces where there should have been letters. The only dream he could remember with any clarity was the one about the parcel, although he had been unable to identify the fish, and now, still barely awake, he consoled himself with the thought that at least it couldn't have been a monkfish, because a monkfish wouldn't have fit inside the box. He got up with some difficulty, as if his joints had stiffened after some excessive and unaccustomed physical effort, and went into the kitchen to get a drink of water, a full glass gulped down with all the urgency of someone who had eaten something salty for supper. He was hungry but didn't feel like preparing breakfast. He went back into the bedroom to fetch his dressing gown, then returned to the living room. The letter to the production company was there on the desk, the final and definitive version of the many versions with which the wastepaper basket was filled almost to overflowing. He reread it and it seemed to him to serve his present purposes, he had not only requested a signed photograph of the actor, he had also, as if in passing, asked for his address. A final comment, which Tertuliano Máximo Afonso was immodest enough to consider an imaginative and strategic masterstroke, suggested that there was an urgent need for a study of the importance of supporting actors, who were, according to the writer of the letter, as essential to the development of filmic action as small tributaries are to the formation of great rivers. Tertuliano Máximo Afonso was convinced that such a metaphorical, sibylline conclusion would remove any possibility of the company forwarding the letter to an actor, who, even though his name had appeared in the opening credits of the most recent films he had acted in, was, nevertheless, one of the legion of actors considered to be inferior, subaltern, and incidental, a kind of necessary evil, an indispensable nuisance, who, in the opinion of the producer, always takes up too much space in the budget. If Daniel Santa-Clara were to receive a letter written in these terms, his thoughts would naturally turn to financial and social rewards in keeping with his role as a tributary of the Nile and the Amazon of the major stars. And if that first individual action, begun in order to defend the simple, selfish well-being of one claimant, were to multiply, to spread, to expand into a vast collective action of solidarity, then the pyramid structure of the film industry would collapse like another house of cards, and we would be granted the extraordinary fate or, better still, the historic privilege of witnessing the birth of a new and revolutionary concept of the cinema and of life. There is no danger, however, that such a cataclysm will occur. The letter, signed with the name of a woman called Maria da Paz, will be sent to the appropriate department, where a clerk will call the boss's attention to the ominous suggestion contained in the final paragraph, the boss will at once pass on the dangerous item for consideration by his immediate superior, and, that same day, before the virus slips, by mistake, out into the streets, the few people who know about the letter will be instantly sworn to absolute secrecy, rewarded in advance with appropriate promotions and substantial increases in salary. A decision will then have to be taken as to what to do with the letter, whether to grant the requests for a signed photograph and for information about where the actor lives, the first purely routine, the second rather unusual, or to behave simply as if it had never been written or had got lost in the confusion of the postal service. The discussion held by the board of directors will take up the whole of the following day, not because it proved difficult to reach initial unanimity, but because every foreseeable consequence became the object of prolonged consideration, and not only those consequences, but others that seemed to be the products of sick imaginations. The final decision will be both radical and clever. Radical because the letter will be burned at the end of the meeting, with the whole board of directors present to witness it and breathe a sigh of relief, clever because it will satisfy the two requests in a way that will guarantee the double gratitude of the writer, the first, purely routine as we said, no problem at all, the second, With reference to your letter, which we read with great interest, those were the terms in which it was put, underlining the exceptional nature of the information being given. This did not exclude the possibility that the writer of the letter, Maria da Paz, would one day meet Daniel

Santa-Clara, now that she has his address, and would mention to him her theory about tributaries as applied to the distribution of roles in the dramatic arts, but, as experience in communications has abundantly shown, the mobilizing power of the spoken word, which is in no way inferior to that of the written word and may even, in the short term, prove more effective in marshaling minds and multitudes, has a more limited historical range, given that, when a speech is repeated, it soon runs out of breath and strays from its original aims and intentions. Why else are the laws that rule us written down. It is more likely, though, that, if such a meeting were to take place and if such a matter were to be brought up, Daniel Santa-Clara would pay only scant attention to Maria da Paz's tributarial theories and suggest diverting the conversation to less arid subjects, if we can be forgiven such a flagrant contradiction, given that it was of water that we were speaking and the rivers that carry it away.

Having placed before him one of the letters that Maria da Paz had written to him some time before, and after a few trial runs to loosen up and prepare his hand, Tertuliano Máximo Afonso transcribed as best he could the sober but elegant signature that concluded the letter. He did this out of respect for the childish and somewhat melancholy desire she had expressed, and not because he thought that the more perfect the forgery the more credible the document would appear, a document that, as mentioned above, will, within a matter of a few days, have vanished from this earth, burned to ashes. It makes one feel like saying, All that work for nothing. The letter is already in the envelope, the stamp is in its place, all he needs to do now is to go down to the street and put it in the postbox on the corner. Since today is a Sunday, the postal van won't be picking up the correspondence, but Tertuliano

Máximo Afonso is anxious to be free of the letter as soon as possible. As long as it is here, time will remain as still as a deserted stage, or this, at least, is his vivid impression. The row of videos on the floor provokes in him the same nervous impatience. He wants to clear the stage, to leave no traces, the first act is over, it is time to remove the props. No more of Daniel Santa-Clara's films and no more anxiety, Will he be in this one, Perhaps he won't appear, Will he have a mustache, Will he wear his hair parted in the middle, no more putting little crosses by names, the puzzle has been solved. It was at this moment that he remembered the call he had made to the first of the Santa-Claras in the phone book, that house where no one had responded. Shall I try again, he wondered. If he did, if someone answered, if they said, yes, Daniel Santa-Clara did live there, the letter that had cost him so much mental labor would become unnecessary, dispensable, he could tear it up and throw it in the wastepaper basket, as useless as the failed drafts that had prepared the way for the final version. He realized that he needed a pause, a respite, even just a week or two, the time it would take for the production company to reply, a period in which he could pretend that he had never seen *The Race Is to the Swift* or the hotel receptionist, knowing that this false calm, this appearance of tranquility, would have a limit, an imminent expiration date, and that when it was time, the curtain would rise inexorably on the second act. But he realized too that if he didn't try to phone again, he would remain tethered thereafter to the obsessive idea that he had behaved in a cowardly fashion in a fight to which no one had challenged him and into which he had entered of his own free will, having himself provoked it. Searching for a man called Daniel Santa-Clara who did not even know he was the object of a search, this was the absurd situation Tertuliano Máximo

Afonso had created, more suited to the plot of a detective novel with no known criminal, and quite unjustifiable in the hitherto uneventful life of a history teacher. Caught thus with his back to the wall, he made an agreement with himself, I'll phone once more, if someone answers and says that Daniel Santa-Clara lives there, I'll throw the letter away and deal with whatever the consequences might be, I'll decide then whether to speak or not, but, if they don't answer, then the letter will be sent off and I'll never phone the number again, come what may. The feeling of hunger he had felt up until then had been replaced by a kind of nervous palpitation in the pit of his stomach, but the decision had been made, he would not go back on it. The number was dialed, the phone rang somewhere in the distance, the sweat started trickling slowly down his face, the phone rang and rang, it was clear there was no one at home, but Tertuliano Máximo Afonso defied fate, he gave his adversary one last chance to pick up the phone, until the ringing became a strident victory cry and the telephone fell silent of its own accord. Right, he said out loud, let no one say of me that I failed in my duty. He felt suddenly calmer than he had in a long time. His period of rest had begun, he could go into the bathroom with a clear head, shave, shower unhurriedly, and get dressed carefully, Sundays tend to be dull, gloomy days, but there are some when one feels glad to have been born. It was too late to have breakfast and too early for lunch, he would have to fill the time somehow, he could go out and buy a newspaper and come back, he could look over the lesson he has to teach tomorrow, he could sit down and read a few more pages of *A History of Mesopotamian Civilizations*, he could, he could, then a light came on in one small corner of his memory, the recollection of one of his dreams of the previous night, the one in which a man was carrying a stone on his back and saying, I'm an Amorite, it would be nice if that stone had been King Hammurabi's famous Code and not just any old stone picked up from the ground, it's only logical really that historians, having studied so hard, should dream historical dreams. It is hardly surprising that *A History of Mesopotamian Civilizations* should lead him to King Hammurabi's laws, it was a transition as natural as opening the door into the next room, but the fact that the boulder carried on the back of the Amorite should have reminded him that he hadn't phoned his mother for nearly a week, even the most skilled interpreter of dreams would have been incapable of explaining to us, having excluded outright as insulting and ill intentioned, the easy interpretation that, deep down, and never daring to confess as much to himself, Tertuliano Máximo Afonso thinks of his progenitor as a heavy burden. Poor woman, far away, bereft of news, so discreet and respectful of her son's life, I mean, he's a secondary school teacher, and only in an emergency would she dare to phone, for fear of interrupting a labor that, to some extent, she finds beyond her comprehension, not that she lacks education, not that she didn't study history herself as a child, but what she has always found bewildering is that history can be taught at all. When she used to sit on the benches at school and hear the teacher talking about the events of the past, it seemed to her that all these things were pure imaginings and that if the teacher had those imaginings, she could have them too, just as she occasionally found herself imagining her own life. Finding these events set down in the history book did not change her mind in the least, all the textbook did was collect together the free-flowing fantasies of the person who had written it, and there was clearly little difference between those fantasies and the ones you could find in a novel. Tertuliano Máximo Afonso's mother, whose name, Carolina, surname Máximo, finally appears here, is a fervent and assiduous reader of novels. As such, she knows all about telephones that ring unexpectedly and of others that ring when you are desperately hoping they will. This was not the case now, Tertuliano Máximo Afonso's mother has just been thinking, I wonder when my son will phone, and there, suddenly, is his voice in her ear, Hello, Mama, how have you been, Oh, fine, fine, pretty much as usual, what about you, Oh, I'm fine too, as always, Have you had a lot of work at school, No more than normal, homework, tests, the occasional staff meeting, And when do your classes end this year, In about two weeks' time, then I'll have a week of exams, Does that mean that you'll be here with me within a month, Of course I'll come and see you, but I won't be able to stay for more than a few days, Why's that, Because I've got some things to sort out here, a few loose ends to tie up, What sort of things, what loose ends, the school closes for the holidays, and holidays, as I understand it, were made for people to rest, Don't worry, I'll rest, but there are some matters I need to sort out first, And are they serious matters, Yes, I believe so, What do you mean, if they're serious, they're serious, it's not a question of belief, It was just a manner of speaking, Has it anything to do with your girlfriend, with Maria da Paz, In a way, You're like a character in a book I've been reading, a woman who always answers questions with another question, You're the one who has been asking the questions, my only question was to ask how you've been, That's because you don't speak to me clearly and directly, I believe so, you say, in a way, you say, I'm not used to you being so mysterious with me, Don't get angry, I'm not getting angry, it's just that I find it odd that, once the holidays start, you won't be coming straight here, it's never happened before as I recall, Look, I'll tell you all about it later, Are you going on a trip somewhere, Another question, Are you or aren't you, If I was, I would tell you, What I don't understand is why you said that Maria da Paz had something to do with these things that oblige you to stay, It isn't quite like that, perhaps I was exaggerating, Are you thinking of getting married again, Oh, Mama, please, Well, perhaps you should, People don't tend to get married so much these days, you must have gleaned that from your novels, Now I'm not stupid and I know perfectly well the kind of world I'm living in, it's just that I don't think you should keep the girl dangling, But I've never promised her marriage or even suggested we live together, As far as she's concerned, a relationship that's lasted six months is like a promise, you don't know women, No, I don't know the women of your day, And you don't know much about the women of yours either, Possibly, I don't really have that much experience of women, I've been married once, divorced once, and the rest doesn't really count for much, There's Maria da Paz, She doesn't really count for much either, Don't you realize how cruel you're being, Cruel, that's a very solemn word, Yes, I know it sounds like something out of a cheap romance, but cruelty can take many forms, sometimes it even comes disguised as indifference or indolence, shall I give you an example, delaying a decision can become a conscious weapon of mental aggression against other people, Well, I knew you had a talent for psychology, but I had no idea you knew so much, Oh, I don't know a thing about psychology, I've never read a single word about it, but I know a thing or two about people, All right, I'll let you know when the time comes, Don't keep me waiting too long, from now on I won't have a moment's peace, Please don't worry, one way or another everything in this world finds a solution, Sometimes in the worst possible way, Not in this case, Well, I certainly hope not, Take care, Mama, You too, son, take care, Yes, I will. His mother's anxiety dissipated the sense of well-being that had lent a new vivacity to Tertuliano Máximo Afonso's spirit after phoning the Santa-Clara who was not at home. Mentioning the serious matters he would have to deal with when school was over had been an unforgivable mistake. True, the conversation had got diverted afterward onto his relationship with Maria da Paz and, at a certain point, seemed set to stay there, but when, to soothe her, he had said that everything in this world finds a solution, his mother's words, Sometimes in the worst possible way, sounded to him now like an augury of disaster, a warning of future misfortunes, as if, in the place of the elderly lady called Carolina Máximo, who also happened to be his mother, a sibyl or a Cassandra had spoken to him from the other end of the line, telling him in so many words, There's still time to stop. For a moment, he considered jumping in his car and making the five-hour journey that would bring him to the small town where his mother lived, telling her everything, then, his soul washed clean of unhealthy miasmas, coming back to his job as a history teacher with no taste for cinema, determined to turn this confusing page of his life and even, who knows, prepared seriously to consider the possibility of marrying Maria da Paz. *Les jeux sont faits, rien ne va plus,* said Tertuliano Máximo Afonso out loud, this man who had never been inside a casino in his life, but who has among his assets as a reader a few famous novels from the belle epoque. He put the letter addressed to the production company in one of his jacket pockets and went out. He will forget to post it, have lunch in a restaurant somewhere, and come back home to drain to the bitter dregs this Sunday afternoon and evening.

Tertuliano Máximo Afonso's first task the following day was to make two parcels out of the cassettes that he
would return to the shop. Then he gathered the others together, fastened them with string, and put them away in a
cupboard in his bedroom, under lock and key. He methodically tore up the sheets of paper on which he had written the
names of the actors, did the same with the various drafts of
the letter that he still had in his jacket pocket and which will
have to wait a few more minutes before taking its first step
along the road that will lead it to the addressee, and, finally,
as if he had a pressing reason to erase his fingerprints, he ran
a damp cloth over all the furniture in the living room that
he had touched during the past few days. He also erased any
prints left behind by Maria da Paz, but he did not think of
that. The traces he wanted to expunge were not his or hers,
they were those left behind by the presence that had wrenched
him from sleep that first night. There was no point in telling
him that such a presence had existed only in his head, doubtless the fabrication of an anxiety generated in his mind by a
dream he had since forgotten, there was no point in suggesting to him that it might have been no more than the super-

natural consequence of an ill-digested beef stew, there was no point, in short, in demonstrating to him, with all the reasons due to reason, that, even if we were prepared to accept the hypothesis that the products of the mind have a certain capacity to take on material form in the external world, what we absolutely cannot accept is that the impalpable and invisible presence of the cinematic image of the hotel receptionist could have left vestiges of its sweaty fingertips scattered about the apartment. As far as is known, ectoplasm does not perspire. Once this work was completed, Tertuliano Máximo Afonso got dressed, picked up his teacher's briefcase and the two packages, and left. On the stairs, he met his upstairs neighbor, who asked if he needed any help, he thanked her very much, but said that, no, he didn't, and, in turn, inquired after her weekend, so-so, she said, as usual, but that she had heard him working away on his typewriter, and he said that one of these days he would have to buy a computer because they, at least, were quiet, but she said that the noise of the typewriter didn't bother her in the least, on the contrary, it kept her company. Since today was a cleaning day, she asked if he would be coming home before lunch, and he said that he would not, that he would be having lunch at school and wouldn't be back until the afternoon. They said good-bye, and Tertuliano Máximo Afonso, aware that his neighbor was watching him pityingly, went down the stairs, struggled to keep a grip on both parcels and briefcase, taking great care where he placed his feet so that he wouldn't fall flat on his face and die of embarrassment. His car was parked opposite the postbox. He put the parcels in the trunk, then turned around, at the same time taking the letter out of his pocket. A boy came running past and accidentally bumped into him, causing the letter to slip from Tertuliano Máximo Afonso's fingers and fall onto the pavement. The lad stopped a few steps farther on and apologized but, perhaps afraid he would be told off or punished, did not come back, as he should have done, to pick the letter up and return it. Tertuliano Máximo Afonso made an indulgent gesture, the gesture of one who has decided to accept the apology and forgive the rest, then bent down himself to retrieve the letter. It occurred to him that he could make a wager with himself, leave it where it was and surrender his fate and that of the letter to the hands of chance. The next passerby might find the letter, see that it had a stamp on it, and, like a good citizen, place it carefully in the postbox, he might open it to see what was inside and then discard it once he had read it, he might not even notice it at all and trample it indifferently underfoot, and through-out the day many more people might do the same, so that it grew steadily dirtier and more crumpled, until someone de-cided to kick it with the tip of their shoe into the gutter where the street sweeper would find it. The wager did not take place, the letter was picked up and taken to the postbox, and the wheel of fortune was finally set in motion. Now Ter-tuliano Máximo Afonso will visit the video-rental shop and, with the assistant, go through the videos in the two parcels, and, taking into account those he intends to purchase and those he has left at home, he will then pay what he owes and possibly tell himself that he will never enter that shop again. In the end, much to his relief, the unctuous assistant was not there, and he was attended instead by the new, inexperienced young woman, which is why the process took a little longer than expected, although the customer's facility for mental arith-metic again came in handy when it was time to draw up the final bill. The assistant asked if he wanted to rent or buy any more videos and he replied in the negative, saying that he had finished the study he was engaged in, forgetting that the young woman was not in the shop when he made his famous speech about the ideological signals present in any cinematic narrative, in cinematic masterpieces too, of course, but, above all, in the more ordinary productions, second- or even third-rate movies, those generally ignored by everyone but which are all the more effective because they catch the viewer unawares. It seemed to him that the shop was smaller than when he had entered it for the first time, not even a week ago, it really was incredible how, in such a short space of time, his life had been transformed, at that moment, he felt as if he were floating in a kind of limbo, in a corridor joining heaven and hell, which made him wonder, with some amazement, where he had come from and where he would go to next, because, judging by current ideas on the subject, it cannot be the same thing for a soul to be transported from hell to heaven as to be pushed out of heaven into hell. He was driving toward the school when these eschatological reflections were replaced by an analogy of another type, this time taken from natural history, the entomological section, which made him view himself as a chrysalis in a state of profound withdrawal and undergoing a secret process of transformation. Despite the somber mood that had been with him ever since he got out of bed, he smiled at the comparison, thinking that, were this the case, then, having entered the cocoon as a caterpillar, he would emerge from it a butterfly. Me, a butterfly, he murmured, now I've seen everything. He parked the car not far from the school and consulted his watch, he would still have time for a cup of coffee and to have a quick look through the newspapers, if they hadn't all been taken. He knew he had neglected his lesson preparation but his years of experience would remedy that fault, he had improvised on other occasions and no one had noticed the difference. What he would never do was to go into the classroom and announce to those innocent children point-blank, Right, today we've got a test. That would be an act of disloyalty, the despotism of someone who, having the knife in his hand, does whatever he likes with it and varies the thickness of the cheese slices depending on the whim of the occasion and on established preferences. When he went into the staff room, he saw that there were still a few newspapers left on the display stand, but in order to get there, he would have to walk past a table at which, surrounded by coffee cups and glasses of water, three colleagues were talking. He could hardly walk straight past, especially when one of them was his friend, the mathematics teacher, to whom he owed so much in terms of understanding and patience. The others were an older woman who taught literature and a young man who taught natural sciences and with whom he had never felt any close bond of friendship. He said good morning, asked if he could join them, and, without waiting for a reply, drew up a chair and sat down. To anyone unfamiliar with the customs of the place, such behavior could appear to verge on bad manners, but the staff-room protocol governing such things had come into being, shall we say, naturally, it had not been written down, but was built on the solid foundations of consensus, and since it had never entered anyone's head to respond negatively to the question, it was best not to bother with a chorus of agreement, some of it sincere, some less so, but accept it as a fait accompli. The only delicate point still capable of creating tension between those who were already there and any new arrivals lay in the possibility that the matter under discussion was of a confidential nature, but this too had been resolved by tacit recourse to the question, to that piece of redundancy par excellence, Am

I interrupting, to which there was only one socially acceptable reply, Of course not, come and join us. Saying to the newcomer, for example, however politely, Yes, you are interrupting actually, go and sit somewhere else, would cause such a commotion that the intra-relational network of the group would be seriously shaken and placed in jeopardy. Tertuliano Máximo Afonso returned with the cup of coffee he had gone to fetch, sat down, and asked, Any news, Are you referring to news from outside or from inside, asked the mathematics teacher, It's still too early to know about the news from inside, I meant news from outside, since I haven't yet had time to read the newspapers, The wars that were being fought yesterday are still being fought today, said the literature teacher, And there is, needless to say, a high probability or even certainty that another war is just about to start, said the natural sciences teacher, as if they had rehearsed their answers together, How about you, how was your weekend, asked the mathematics teacher, Oh, quiet, peaceful, I spent most of it reading a book I think I've mentioned to you before, about Mesopotamian civilizations, the chapter on the Amorites is fascinating, Well, I went to the cinema with my wife, Ah, said Tertuliano Máximo Afonso, glancing away, Our colleague here is not a great lover of the cinema, explained the mathematics teacher to the others, Look, I've never said outright that I don't like it, all I said and say again now is that cinema is not one of my cultural interests, I prefer books, My dear friend, there's no need to get aerated about it, it's of no importance, as you know, it was with the very best of intentions that I suggested you watch that film, What does getting aerated mean exactly, asked the literature teacher, as much out of curiosity as to pour oil on troubled waters, To get aerated, said the mathematics teacher, means to get angry, to bridle, or, more precisely, to take the hump, And why, in your opinion, is to take the hump more precise than getting angry or bridling, asked the natural sciences teacher, It's just a personal interpretation really that has its roots in childhood memories, whenever my mother told me off or punished me for some mischief I'd committed, I would scowl and refuse to talk, I would maintain total silence for hours on end, and then she used to say I had taken the hump, Or were aerated, Exactly, In my house, when I was about that age, said the literature teacher, the metaphorical language for childish sulks was different, In what way, Well, it tended to the asinine, What do you mean, We used to call it tethering the donkey, and don't go looking it up in any dictionary, because you won't find it, so I assume it was exclusive to our family. Everyone laughed, apart from Tertuliano Máximo Afonso, who gave a slightly irritated smile and said, Well, I don't know about it being exclusive to your family, because they used the expression in my house too. More laughter, and peace reigned once more. The literature teacher and the natural sciences teacher got up and said good-bye, see you later, their classrooms are probably farther off, possibly on the upper floor, so those who remained have a few more minutes in which to say, In a person who claims to have spent the last two days serenely reading a history book, remarked the mathematics teacher, I would expect anything but that tormented expression, That's just your imagination, there isn't anything tormenting me, although I might have the face of someone who hasn't slept very much, You can say what you like, but you haven't been the same since you saw that film, What do you mean, I haven't been the same, asked Tertuliano Máximo Afonso in an unexpectedly alarmed tone of voice, Just what I said, you're different, But I'm the same person, Of course you are, It's true I am a bit worried at the moment about a matter of a sentimental nature which has lately got rather complicated, the kind of thing that could happen to anyone, but that doesn't mean I've turned into another person, And I didn't say you had, nor have I the slightest doubt that you are still called Tertuliano Máximo Afonso and that you work as a teacher of history here in this school, Then I don't know why you keep insisting that I'm not the same person, Only since you saw the film, Don't let's talk about the film, you know my views, All right, But I am the same person, Of course you are, Need I remind you that I've been suffering from depression lately, Or apathy, that was the other name you gave it, Exactly, and that deserves a bit of consideration I think, It has my wholehearted consideration, as well you know, but that isn't what we were talking about, Well, I am the same person, Now you're the one who's insisting, True enough, but it was only a few days ago that I told you I was going through a period of great psychological stress, and it's only natural that this should be apparent in my face and in the way I behave, Of course, But that doesn't mean I've changed so much morally or physically that I resemble someone else, All I said was that you don't seem the same, not that you resembled someone else, There isn't a great deal of difference, Our colleague in literature would say that, on the contrary, the difference is enormous, and she knows about these things, when it comes to subtleties and nuances, literature is almost like mathematics, Alas, I belong in the field of history, where nuances and subtleties don't exist, They would exist if, how can I put it, history could be a portrait of life, You surprise me, it's not like you to resort to such banal rhetoric, You're quite right, in that case history wouldn't be life, but only one of the many possible portraits of life, similar, but never the same. Tertuliano Máximo Afonso glanced away again, then, with an effort of will, turned and looked at his colleague, just to see what might lie hidden behind the apparent serenity of his face. The mathematics teacher held his gaze without apparently giving it any particular importance, then, with a smile as full of sympathetic irony as it was of frank benevolence, said, One day, I might take another look at that film, maybe I'll manage to find out what it was that so upset you, always supposing the film is the origin of your ills. A shudder ran through Tertuliano Máximo Afonso from head to foot, but in the midst of his confusion, in the midst of his panic, he managed to come up with a plausible response, I wouldn't bother if I were you, what's upset me, to use your word, is a relationship I don't know how to extricate myself from, if you've ever found yourself in a similar situation, you'll know how it feels, but I've got to get to my class now, I'm late, If you don't mind, I'll go with you to the corner of the corridor, even though in the history of that place there has already been at least one dangerous incident, said the mathematics teacher, and I therefore solemnly promise not to repeat the imprudent gesture of placing my hand on your shoulder, Well, you know, today I might not mind at all, Oh, I'm not going to run any risks, you look to me as if you've got your batteries fully charged. They both laughed, the mathematics teacher unreservedly, Tertuliano Máximo Afonso somewhat more stiffly, for the words that had filled him with panic, the worst threat anyone could have made just then, still rang in his ears. They parted at the corner of the corridor and went off to their different destinations. The arrival of the history teacher put to rest the students' fond hope, to which the delay had already given rise, that today there would be no class. Even before he sat down, Tertuliano Máximo Afonso had announced that in three days' time, next

Thursday, there would be a final piece of written work, This will be a decisive piece of work when it comes to calculating your final mark, he said, as I have decided not to hold oral exams in the remaining last two weeks of term, moreover, this class and the next two classes will be devoted exclusively to revising what we've learned so far, so that you can bring some fresh ideas to your work. This preamble was well received by the most impartial section of the class, for it was clear, thank God, that Tertuliano did not intend spilling any more blood than he could possibly help. From then on, all the students' attention will be focused on the emphasis given by the teacher to each subject covered in the course, for, if the logic of weights and measures is essentially a human thing and good luck one of its variable factors, such changes in communicative intensity might foreshadow, without the teacher noticing the unconscious revelation, the choice of questions for the test. Although it is a well-known fact that no human being, including those who have reached what we term senescence, can live solely on hope, that strange psychic disorder indispensable to normal life, what can we say about these boys and girls who, having lost the hope that there would be no class today, are now engaged in feeding another far more problematic hope, that Thursday's test will be for each of them, and therefore for all of them, the golden bridge over which they will triumphantly cross into the next year. The class was just finishing when a clerk knocked on the door and came in to tell Tertuliano Máximo Afonso that the headmaster had asked if he would be so kind as to go to his office as soon as the lesson ended. The exposition being developed about some treaty or other was dispatched in less than two minutes, so cursorily, in fact, that Tertuliano Máximo Afonso felt bound to say, Don't worry too much about that, it won't be on the test. The students exchanged knowing looks, from which one gleaned that their ideas about evaluating emphases had finally been confirmed in a case in which the meaning of the words meant less than the dismissive tone in which they had been spoken. Rarely has a class finished in such an atmosphere of concord.

Tertuliano Máximo Afonso put his papers back in his briefcase and left. The corridors were rapidly filling up with students who came bursting out of every door, discussing subjects that had nothing whatsoever to do with what had been taught to them one minute before, here and there, teachers were trying to pass unnoticed amid the choppy sea of heads that surrounded them on every side, dodging as best they could the reefs that rose up before them as they slunk toward their natural harbor, the staff room. Tertuliano Máximo Afonso took a shortcut up to the part of the building where the headmaster had his office, he stopped to speak to the literature teacher whose path crossed his, What we need is a good dictionary of colloquial expressions, she said, tugging at the sleeve of his jacket, Surely most general dictionaries already include most of them, he replied, Yes, but not in any systematic or analytical way, not with the aim of being really exhaustive, for example, recording that expression about tethering the donkey and explaining what it means wouldn't be enough, it would need to range much more widely, to identify in each expression's component parts the analogies, direct and indirect, with the state of mind they are intended to represent, You're quite right, said the history teacher, more in order to seem pleasant than because the subject really interested him, but now, if you'll excuse me, I have to go, the headmaster asked to see me, Oh, you'd better go then, keeping God waiting is the very worst of sins. Three minutes later,

Tertuliano Máximo Afonso was knocking on the office door, he entered when the green light came on, said good morning, received a good morning in return, and, at a gesture from the headmaster, sat down and waited. He felt no intrusive presence there, either astral or otherwise. The headmaster set aside the papers on his desk and said, smiling, I've been giving a lot of thought to our last conversation, the one about the teaching of history, and I've come to a conclusion, What's that, sir, To ask you to do some work during the school holidays, Work, sir, You could say to me that holidays were made for resting and that it's simply not acceptable to ask a teacher, once the classes are over, to continue to concern himself with school matters, You know perfectly well, sir, that I would never put it in those words, You might say it in other words that meant exactly the same thing, Yes, but I have yet to pronounce any words at all, either the former or the latter, so please tell me what your idea is, Well, I thought we might try to persuade the ministry not to turn the teaching program upside down exactly, that would be expecting too much, and the minister has never been one for revolutions, but to study, organize, and put into practice a little experiment, a pilot study, limited, to begin with, to one school and to a small number of students, preferably volunteers, in which the historical material was studied from the present to the past, rather than from the past to the present, in short, the very thesis that you have for so long defended and of whose excellence you have, I'm pleased to say, finally persuaded me, And this work you want me to do, what form would it take exactly, asked Tertuliano Máximo Afonso, To draw up a solid, well-thought-out proposal to send to the ministry, Me, sir, Now I'm not saying this to flatter you, but the truth is that I can't think of anyone else in the school better qualified for the job, you've already shown that you've given the matter a great deal of thought, you obviously have very clear ideas about it, and, I say this in all sincerity, it would give me real pleasure if you would take on the task, and the work would, of course, be remunerated, I'm sure we can find room in our budget for such a commission, But I very much doubt that my ideas, as regards either quality or quantity, because, as you know, quantity also counts, would be enough to persuade the ministry, you know them better than I do, Alas, all too well, So, So allow me to insist, because I genuinely think that this would be a good moment to make clear to them that we are a school capable of producing innovative ideas, Even if they tell us to get lost, They might well do that, they might simply relegate the proposal to their files, but there it will be, and someone, someday, will remember it, And we'll just have to wait around until they do, No, meanwhile, we could ask other schools to participate in the project, organize debates, conferences, get the media involved, Until the director-general writes a letter telling us to be quiet, It seems my suggestion doesn't enthuse you, There are few things in this world that do, sir, but that isn't the problem, it's just that I don't know what the coming holidays might hold for me, Sorry, I don't understand, Well, I'm going to have to deal with a number of important problems that have come up recently in my life, and I'm afraid I won't have either the time or the necessary peace of mind to devote myself to a task that would demand all my concentration, In that case, let's just forget about it, Let me think about it a little longer, sir, give me a few days, I promise I'll give you an answer by the end of the week, And am I to hope that it will be a positive one, Possibly, sir, but I can't say for sure, You're obviously very preoccupied about something, I do hope you find a solution to your problems, So do I, How was the class, Oh, it went really well, the class is working hard, Excellent, We're having a written test on Thursday, And on Friday you'll give me your answer, Yes, Give the matter some thought, Yes, I will, There's no need to tell you whom I have in mind to lead the pilot study, Thank you, sir. Tertuliano Máximo Afonso went down to the staff room, intending to read the newspapers until it was time for lunch. However, as the hour approached, he began to realize that he couldn't bear to be with other people, that he couldn't stand another conversation like the one this morning, even if it didn't involve him directly, even if, from beginning to end, it was all about such innocent colloquial expressions as to tether the donkey, to have a face as long as Monday, or has the cat got your tongue. Before the bell went, he left and had lunch in a restaurant. He returned to school for his second class, spoke to no one, and was back home before evening. He lay down on the sofa, closed his eyes, tried to empty his mind of thoughts, to sleep if he could, to be like a stone that simply lies where it's left, but not even the enormous mental effort he made afterward to concentrate on the headmaster's request could erase the shadow under which he would have to live until he received an answer to the letter he had written in Maria da Paz's name.

He waited for nearly two weeks. In the meantime, he taught, telephoned his mother twice, prepared the written test for Thursday and sketched out another that he would give to the students of his other class, on Friday he told the headmaster that he would accept his kind offer, on the weekend he did not leave his apartment, he spoke on the phone to Maria da Paz to find out how she was and if she had had a reply, he answered a call from his colleague the mathematics teacher who wanted to know if there was anything wrong, he finished reading the chapter on the Amorites and moved on to the Assyrians, he watched a documentary on the Ice Age in Europe and another about man's remote ancestors, he thought that this period of his life could be made into a novel, then thought it would be a complete waste of time because no one would believe such a story, he phoned Maria da Paz again, but in such a lackluster voice that she became worried and asked if she could help at all, he told her to come and she came, they went to bed and then went out to supper, and the following day it was her turn to phone him to say that the letter from the production company had arrived, I'm phoning from the bank if you want to drop in, otherwise I can bring it over on my way home. Trembling inside, shaken by excitement, Tertuliano Máximo Afonso only just managed to suppress the question that he should not, on any account, have asked, Did you open it, and this led him to delay for a couple of seconds the categorical answer that would do away with any doubts that might exist over whether he was prepared to share with her the contents of the letter, I'll come to the bank. If Maria da Paz had imagined a tender domestic scene in which she saw herself listening to him read the letter out loud while she sipped the tea she had prepared in the kitchen of the man she loved, she could forget it. We can see her now, sitting at her small desk in the bank, her hand still resting on the receiver she has just replaced, the oblong-shaped envelope before her and in it the letter that honesty will not allow her to read because it is not hers, even though it is addressed to her. Less than an hour had passed when Tertuliano Máximo Afonso hurried into the bank and asked to speak to Maria da Paz. No one knew him there, no one would suspect that affairs of the heart and dark secrets existed between him and the young woman walking over to the counter. She had seen him from the back of the large room where she has her post as a worker with numbers, which is why she has the letter already in her hand, Here you are, she says, they did not greet each other, they did not wish each other good afternoon, they did not say, Hi, how are you, nothing of the sort, there was the letter to hand over and it has been handed over, he says, See you later, I'll give you a ring, and she, having fulfilled the role that had fallen to her in the urban postal distribution service, returns to her seat, oblivious of the suspicious glances of an older male colleague who, some time before, had come sniffing around her without success and who, from then on, out of pique, has always kept a beady eye on her. Outside in the street, Tertuliano Máximo Afonso is walking quickly, almost running, he left the car in an underground garage three blocks away, he is carrying the letter not in his briefcase but in an inside pocket in his jacket, for fear it might be snatched from him by some small urchin, as boys brought up in the freedom of the streets were once called, then angels with dirty faces, then rebels without a cause, now delinquents who are denied the benefits of either euphemism or metaphor. He is telling himself that he will not open the letter until he gets home, that he is too old to be behaving like an anxious adolescent, but, at the same time, he knows that these adult notions will evaporate once he is inside the car, in the gloom of the garage, with the door closed to defend himself from the morbid curiosity of the world. It took him a while to find where he had left the car, which only aggravated his state of nervous anxiety, the poor man resembled, if you'll forgive the comparison, a dog abandoned in the middle of the desert, looking forlornly this way and that, with not one familiar smell to guide him home, It was on this level, I'm sure of it, but the fact is he wasn't sure. He did in the end find the car, he had been only a few steps from it on three occasions but had failed to see it. He got in quickly, as if he were being pursued, closed the door, locked it, and turned on the interior light. He has the envelope in his hands, the moment has finally come to know what lies inside, just as the commander of a ship, having reached the point where the coordinates cross, opens the sealed instructions that will tell him where he is to go next. Out of the envelope come a photograph and a sheet of paper. The photograph is of Tertuliano Máximo Afonso but bears the signature of Daniel Santa-Clara beneath the words, Yours truly. As for the sheet of paper, it not only informs him that Daniel Santa-Clara is the stage name of António Claro but, additionally and exceptionally, gives him his private address, Given the special consideration we felt your letter merited, it says. Tertuliano Máximo Afonso remembers the terms in which he wrote the letter and congratulates himself on the brilliant idea of suggesting to the production company that a study should be made of the importance of supporting actors, I threw the mud at the wall and it stuck, he murmured, and at the same time, he realized, without surprise, that his mind has recovered its former calm, that his body is relaxed, no sign of nervousness, no sign of anxiety, the tributary simply flowed into the river and the volume of the river increased, Tertuliano Máximo Afonso knows now which direction to take. He removed a map of the city from the pocket in the driver's door and looked for the street where Daniel Santa-Clara lives. It is in a part of the city he does not know, at least he has no memory of ever having been there, moreover it is far from the center, as he has just discovered from the map, which he has unfolded and which is now resting against the steering wheel. It doesn't matter, he has time, he has all the time in the world. He got out to pay the parking fee, went back to the car, turned out the interior light, and started the engine. His destination, as one can easily guess, is the street where the actor lives. He wants to see the building, to gaze up at the actor's apartment, at the windows, to see what the neighbors are like, what the atmosphere is like, what clothes people wear, how they behave. The traffic is very heavy, the cars move with exasperating slowness, but Tertuliano Máximo Afonso does not get impatient, there is no danger that the road he is driving toward will move, it is the prisoner of the city road network that surrounds it on all sides, as the map only confirms. It was while Tertuliano Máximo Afonso was waiting at a red light, drumming his fingers on the steering wheel in time to a wordless song, that common sense got into the car. Good afternoon, it said, Who invited you, was the driver's response, Frankly, I can't remember a single occasion when you've invited me anywhere, Well, I might if I didn't know beforehand what you would say, Like today, Yes, you're going to tell me to think carefully, not to get involved, that it's imprudent in the extreme, that there's no guarantee the devil isn't lurking behind the door, the usual spiel, Well, this time you're wrong, what you're about to do isn't just imprudent, it's stupid, Stupid, Yes, sir, stupid, utterly stupid, Well, I don't see why, Of course you don't, one of the secondary forms of mental blindness is stupidity, Explain yourself, Well, I don't need you to tell me that you're driving to the street where your Daniel Santa-Clara lives, it's odd, the cat's tail was dangling out of the bag and you didn't even notice, What cat, what tail, stop talking in riddles and get to the point, It's very simple, out of his surname Claro he created the pseudonym Santa-Clara, It's not a pseudonym, it's his stage name, Oh, yes, there was that other fellow who disliked the plebeian vulgarity of pseudonyms so much that he called them heteronyms, And what use would it have been if I had spotted the cat's tail, Not much I agree, you would still have had to find him, but by looking under the name of Claro in the telephone directory, you would have found him in the end, Look, I've got what I need, And now you're going to the street where he lives, you're going to see the building, to gaze up at the apartment where he lives, at the windows, to see what the neighbors are like, what the atmosphere is like, what clothes people wear, how they behave, those, if I'm not mistaken, were your words, They were, Just imagine if, while you're gazing up at the windows, the actor's old lady, or, to put it more respectfully, António Claro's wife, appears at one of them and asks why you don't come up, or, worse still, asks you to go to the pharmacy to buy some aspirin or some cough syrup, Nonsense, If you think that's nonsense, imagine someone walking past and greeting you, not as the Tertuliano Máximo Afonso that you are, but as the António Claro you will never be, More nonsense, All right, if that hypothesis is nonsense, imagine that when you're strolling around, gazing up at the windows or studying the way the locals dress, Daniel Santa-Clara appears before you in the flesh, and the two of you stand there staring at each other just like two china dogs, each one a reflection of the other, except that this reflection, unlike the one in the mirror, will show the left side where the left side is and the right side where the right is, how would you react if that happened. Tertuliano Máximo Afonso did not respond at once, he remained silent for two or three minutes, then he said, The solution would be to stay in the car, Oh, I wouldn't be so sure even then, objected common sense, you might have to stop at a red light, there might be a traffic jam, a truck unloading, an ambulance loading up, and there you would be, on show, like a fish in an aquarium, at the mercy of the inquisitive, adolescent movie buff who lives on the first floor of your building and asks you what your next film will be, So what should I do, That I don't know, that's not part of my job, the role of common sense in the history of your species has never gone beyond advising caution and chicken soup, especially in those cases where stupidity has already taken the floor and looks set to take the reins too, Then I'll just have to disguise myself, As what, Well, I don't know, I'll have to think, It seems to me that, being who you are, your only option is to look like someone else, Yes, I really need to have a think, About time too, And I suppose I might as well go home, If it isn't too much bother, could you just drop me at the door, then I can make my own way after that, Don't you want to come up, You've never asked me up before, Well, I'm asking you now, Thank you, but I shouldn't really accept, Why not, Because it's not healthy for the mind to live cheek by jowl with common sense, eating at the same table, sleeping in the same bed, taking it along to work, and asking its approval or permission before making a move, you've got to take a few risks of your own, Who do you mean, All of you, the human race, But I took a risk getting this letter, and, at the time, you told me off, The way you got that letter is certainly nothing to be proud of, using another person's honesty the way you did is a form of blackmail at its most repellent, Are you referring to Maria da Paz, Yes, I'm referring to Maria da Paz, in her place, I would have opened the letter, read it, and then rubbed it in your face until you begged forgiveness on your knees, That's how common sense behaves, is it, That's how it should behave, Right, then, see you again sometime, I have to consider my disguise now, The more you disguise yourself, the more you'll look like you. Tertuliano Máximo Afonso found a parking space almost immediately outside the door of the building where he lived, he parked the car, picked up the street map, and got out. On the pavement on the other side of the street, a man was standing, face lifted, gazing at the upper stories of the building opposite. The man did not resemble him facially or physically, his presence there was pure coincidence, but Tertuliano Máximo Afonso felt a shiver run down his spine as the thought went through his mind, he couldn't help it, his unhealthy imagination was stronger than he was, that Daniel Santa-Clara might be looking for him, me looking for you, you looking for me. He shrugged off the discomfiting fantasy, I'm seeing ghosts, the guy doesn't even know I exist, yet his legs were still trembling when he went into his apartment and fell exhausted onto the sofa. For a few moments he lay plunged in a kind of torpor, absent from himself, like a marathon runner whose strength has suddenly drained away as he crossed the finishing line. Of the calm energy that had filled him as he left the garage and, afterward, when he was driving to a destination he did not, in the end, reach, all that remained was a very vague memory, like the memory of something not really experienced, or that had been experienced only by a part of him that was now absent. He got up with some difficulty, his legs felt odd, as if they belonged to someone else, and he went into the kitchen to make some coffee. He drank it in slow sips, conscious of the comforting warmth that went down his throat into his stomach, then he washed the cup and saucer and went back into the living room. All his gestures had become slow and deliberate, as if he were busy handling dangerous substances in a chemical laboratory, and yet all he had to do was open the telephone directory at *C* and confirm the information given in the letter. And then what will I do, he wondered, leafing through the pages until he found it. There were a lot of Claros, but only half a dozen Antónios. Here it was, at last, the thing that had cost him so much effort, so easy that anyone could have done it, a name, an address, a telephone number. He copied the details onto a piece of paper and repeated the question, Now what shall I do. In a reflex reaction, his right hand reached for the phone, he let it rest there while he read and reread what he had written down, then he withdrew his hand, got up, and paced about the apartment, arguing with himself over whether it wouldn't be more sensible to leave the next stage until after the exams were over, at least in that way he would have one less thing to worry about, unfortunately, he had told the headmaster he would write a proposal for that project on the teaching of history, and that was one obliga-tion he couldn't get out of, Sooner or later I'll have to sit down and write a proposal that no one is going to take any notice of, it was madness to take on the project in the first place, but there was no point trying to deceive himself, pre-tending that he could ever accept the idea of putting off until after his schoolwork the first step on the road that will lead him to António Claro, since Daniel Santa-Clara does not, strictly speaking, exist, he's a shadow, a puppet, a shifting shape that moves and talks inside a videocassette and returns to silence and immobility once the role he has been taught ends, while the other man, António Claro, is real, concrete, as solid as Tertuliano Máximo Afonso, the history teacher who lives in this apartment and whose name can be found under *A* in the telephone book, regardless of the fact that some say Afonso isn't a surname at all but a first name. He is sitting at his desk again, he is holding the piece of paper with the notes he wrote on it, his right hand is again resting on the re-ceiver, he looks as if he is finally about to make the phone call, but how very long this man takes to make up his mind, how vacillating, how irresolute he has turned out to be, no one would think he was the same person who only a few hours ago almost snatched the letter from Maria da Paz's hands. Then, abruptly, without thinking, as the only way of overcoming this paralyzing cowardice, he dials the number. Tertuliano Máximo Afonso listens to the phone ringing, once, twice, three times, many times, and just as he is about to hang up, thinking, half relieved, half disappointed, that no one is there, a woman, out of breath, as if she had had to run from the other end of the apartment, said simply, Hello. A sudden muscular contraction tightened Tertuliano Máximo Afonso's throat, he did not reply, giving time for the woman to say again, impatiently, Hello, who is it, at last the history teacher managed to say three words, Good afternoon, madam, but instead of responding in the reserved tone of someone addressing a stranger whose face she cannot even see, the woman said with a smile that shone through every word, If you're trying to fool me, don't bother, Excuse me, stammered Tertuliano Máximo Afonso, I just needed some information, What can a person who knows everything about the apartment he is phoning possibly need to know, All I wanted to know is whether the actor Daniel Santa-Clara lives there, My dear sir, I will be sure to tell the actor Daniel Santa-Clara, when he gets in, that António Claro phoned to ask if they both lived here, Sorry, I don't understand, Tertuliano Máximo Afonso began to say, just to gain time, but the woman broke in, This isn't like you, you don't usually play tricks like this, just tell me what you want, has filming been delayed, is that it, Forgive me, madam, there's been some mistake, my name isn't António Claro, You're not my husband, she asked, No, I'm just someone wanting to know if the actor Daniel Santa-Clara lives at this address, Given my answer, you now know that he does, Yes, but the way you gave the answer left me confused, puzzled, That wasn't my intention, I just thought it was my husband having a joke, You can be quite sure that I am not your husband, Well, I find that very hard to believe, That I'm not your husband, It's your voice, I mean, your voice is exactly like his, It must just be a coincidence, Coincidences like that don't happen, two voices, like two people, might be similar, but not absolutely identical, Perhaps it's your imagination, Every word you say sounds to me as if it were coming out of his mouth, Well, I find that very hard to believe, Would you like to give me your name so that I can tell him you called, No, it's all right, besides, your husband doesn't know me, You're a fan, are you, Not exactly, Nevertheless, he'll want to know, No, I'll phone another day, Listen. The connection was cut, Tertuliano Máximo Afonso had slowly replaced the phone on the rest.

THE DAYS PASSED AND TERTULIANO MÁXIMO AFONSO DID NOT
phone. He was pleased by the way the conversation with António Claro's wife had gone, and he felt, therefore, confident
enough to try again, but on further consideration, he had
decided to opt for silence. For two reasons. The first was his
realization that he enjoyed the idea of prolonging and in-
creasing the atmosphere of mystery that his phone call must
have created, he even amused himself by imagining the dialogue between husband and wife, his doubts about the supposed absolute identity of the two voices, her insistence that
she would never have confused them if they hadn't been identical, Well, I just hope you're home next time he calls, then
you'll be able to judge for yourself, she would say, and he
would say, If he does call again, after all, he's already found
out from you what he wanted to know, that I live here, He
asked for Daniel Santa-Clara, remember, not António Claro,
Yes, that is odd. The second and more pressing reason was
that he now accepted as entirely justified his original idea as
to the advantages of clearing the decks before taking the next
step, in other words, waiting until the classes and the exams
were over before, with a cool head, drawing up new strategies

for approach and siege. It is true that awaiting him is the dull task the headmaster had asked him to undertake, but during the nearly three months of holiday that lie ahead, he is bound to be able to find both the time and the necessary disposition of mind for such arid studies. In fulfillment of the promise he had made, it is even likely that he will go and spend a few days, though only a few, with his mother, on condition, however, that he can find some sure way of confirming his near certainty that the actor and his wife will not be taking their holidays early, we need only remember the question asked by her when she thought she was speaking to her husband, Has filming been delayed, to conclude, putting two and two together, that Daniel Santa-Clara is making a new film and that, if his career is on the rise, as *The Goddess of the Stage* demonstrated, he must, of necessity, spend much more time working than he did in his early days when he was little more than an extra. Tertuliano Máximo Afonso's reasons for delaying the call are, therefore, as we have seen, convincing and substantive. They do not, however, oblige him or condemn him to inactivity. His idea of going to see the street where Daniel Santa-Clara lives, despite the brutal bucket of cold water thrown on the idea by common sense, had not been entirely discarded. He even considered this, shall we say, prospective act of surveillance to be indispensable to the success of subsequent operations, since it constituted a way of gauging the situation, rather like, as used to happen in time of war, sending out a reconnaissance party in order to evaluate the enemy's strength. Fortunately, for his own safety, common sense's providentially sarcastic remarks about the more-than-likely effects of his appearing there barefaced have not been wiped from his memory. He could, it is true, grow a beard or a mustache, place on his nose a pair of dark glasses, wear a hat on his head, but, apart from the hat and the glasses, which can be put on and taken off, he was certain that these hairier ornaments, beard and mustache, whether by some capricious decision on the part of the production company or by some last-minute change to the script, would already be starting to grow on Daniel Santa-Clara's face. Consequently, the inevitable disguise would have to resort to the fakery of all ancient and modern masquerades, this unanswerable necessity overriding the fears he had felt the other day, when he had started imagining the catastrophes that might have ensued if, thus disguised, he had gone to the production company in person to request information about the actor Santa-Clara. Like everyone else, he knew of the existence of establishments that specialized in the sale and hire of costumes, props, and all the other paraphernalia indispensable both to the art of theatrical trickery and to the protean transformations of the spy. The possibility that he might be mistaken for Daniel Santa-Clara when he made his purchases could be taken seriously only if it were the actors themselves who went to buy false beards, mustaches, and eyebrows, wigs and hairpieces, eye patches for perfectly healthy eyes, warts and moles, stuffing to plump out cheeks, various kinds of padding for either sex, not to mention cosmetics capable of producing chromatic variations at the whim of the client. Certainly not. Any production company worth its salt will have everything it might need in its warehouses and will buy anything else that isn't, and, should there be budget constraints, or if something simply isn't worth buying, then they will rent it, it won't blacken their family's reputation. Honest housewives used to put blankets and overcoats in hock as soon as the warm spring days arrived, and their lives were considered no less deserving of the respect of society, which must, surely, know all about need. There is some doubt as to whether what we have just written, from the word "Honest" to the word "need," was actually generated by Tertuliano Máximo Afonso's own thought processes, but since these words, and what lies between them, represent the holiest and purest of truths, it seemed a shame to pass up the opportunity to set them down. What should finally reassure us, now that it is clear what steps he should take, is the certainty that Tertuliano Máximo Afonso will, without fear, be able to visit the shop selling disguises and props, to choose and purchase the kind of beard that best suits his face, on the absolute condition, however, that a pathetic little beard of the kind generally known as a flea trap, even were it to transform him into an arbiter of elegance, would have to be firmly rejected, without haggling and without succumbing to the temptations of a discount, since the ear-to-ear design and the relative shortness of the hair, not to mention the bare upper lip, would leave revealed to the broad light of day the very features he is trying to conceal. For quite the opposite reason, that is, because it would attract the attention of the curious, any kind of very long beard should also be resisted, even if it isn't of the apostolic variety. The best choice would therefore be a full, fairly thick beard, tending more to the short than to the long. Tertuliano Máximo Afonso will spend hours trying it out in front of the bathroom mirror, sticking on and pulling off the thin film in which the hairs have been implanted, carefully adjusting it to his own sideburns and to the shape of his jaw, eyes, and lips, particularly the latter, since he will have to move them in order to speak and even, who knows, to eat, or even, for one never really does know, to kiss. When he first saw his new physiognomy, he felt a terrible tremor inside him, the intimate, insistent, nervous palpitation in his solar plexus that he knows so well, however, this shock was caused not merely by seeing himself looking entirely different but, and this is much more interesting when we bear in mind the peculiar situation in which he has recently found himself, by his having a whole new sense of himself, as if, finally, he had come face-to-face with his own authentic identity. It was as if, by looking different, he had become more himself. So intense was the sense of shock, so extreme the feeling of energy rushing through him, so exalted and incomprehensible the joy filling him, that an urgent need to preserve the image made him go out, taking every care not to be seen, and head for a photographic studio far from where he lived in order to have his picture taken. He did not want to subject himself to the erratic lighting and blind mechanisms of a photo booth, he wanted a proper portrait, which it would please him to keep and to contemplate, an image before which he could say to himself, This is me. He paid a surcharge for having the photograph developed on the spot and sat down to wait. To the comment from the assistant who said, It will take a while yet, and suggested he go for a walk to kill time, he replied that he would prefer to wait right there, adding unnecessarily, It's for a present, you see. Now and then, he would raise his hands to his beard, as if to smooth it, and check with his fingers that everything was in place, then go back to the pile of photography magazines set out on a table. When he left, he took with him, as well as the respective enlargement, half a dozen medium-sized portraits, which he had already decided to destroy so as not to have to see himself multiplied. He dropped in at a nearby shopping center, went into a public toilet, and there, safe from prying eyes, removed the beard. If anyone had noticed a bearded man going into the toilets, he would have been hard pushed to swear that it was this same clean-shaven man who has just emerged five minutes later. Generally speaking, one does not notice what a bearded man is carrying, but the telltale envelope he had been clutching in his hand is now hidden between shirt and jacket. Tertuliano Máximo Afonso, up until now a placid teacher of history at a secondary school, clearly has talent enough for the exercise of either of these two professional activities, that of the disguised criminal or that of the policeman on his trail. Time will tell which of these two vocations will prevail. When he got home, he burned the six small copies of the enlarged photo in the sink, turned on the tap to wash the ashes down the plughole, and, after smugly studying his new, clandestine image, restored it to the envelope, which he then hid on one of his bookshelves, behind a history of the Industrial Revolution that he himself had never read.

A few more days passed, the school term ended with the last exam and the pinning up of the list of marks, his colleague the mathematics teacher said good-bye to him, I'm off on holiday now, but afterward, if you need anything, phone me, and be careful, be very careful, Don't forget what we agreed, the headmaster told him, and I'll phone you when I get back from holiday to find out how the work's going, but if you do decide to go away, because you do, after all, have a right to some rest, leave me a contact number on your answering machine. Some days later, Tertuliano Máximo Afonso invited Maria da Paz out to supper, his appalling treatment of her had finally begun to weigh on his conscience, not even so much as a formal thank-you for her help, not even some explanation of what the letter had said, even if he had to invent one. They met in the restaurant, she arrived a little late, sat down immediately, and blamed her lateness on her mother, to look at them no one would think they were lovers, or you might perhaps think that they had been lovers until recently and were still not yet used to their new state of mutual indifference, or having to pretend to be indifferent. They exchanged a few polite words, How are you, How have you been, Are you very busy, Me too, and while Tertuliano Máximo Afonso was once again hesitating as to which way the conversation should go, she anticipated him and jumped in with both feet, Did the letter tell you what you wanted to know, she asked, did it give you all the information you needed, Yes, he said, all too aware that his response was at once true and false, That wasn't my impression, Why's that, Well, I was expecting a bulkier envelope, Sorry, I don't understand, If I remember rightly, the facts you needed were so many and so detailed that they couldn't possibly have fit on one sheet of paper, and that was all the envelope contained, How do you know, did you open it, asked Tertuliano Máximo Afonso sharply and knowing, even as he said it, what response this gratuitous provocation would receive. Maria da Paz looked him straight in the eye and said serenely, No, I didn't, as you well know, Forgive me, I spoke without thinking, he said, Oh, I'll forgive you if you insist, but I can go no further than that, Further than what, For example, I can't forget that you considered me capable of opening a letter intended for you, Deep down, you know that isn't what I really think, Deep down, I know that you don't know me at all, If I didn't trust you, I would never have asked you if it was all right for the letter to be sent to you, My name was just a mask, a mask for your name, a mask for you, But I explained at the time why I thought that was the best way to proceed, Yes, you explained, And you agreed, Yes, I agreed, So, So, from now on I will be expecting you to show me this information you say you received, not because I'm interested, but simply because I think it's your duty to do so, Now you're the one who distrusts me, Yes, but I'll stop distrusting you if you can tell me how all the facts you asked for could possibly have fit on one sheet of paper, They didn't give me all the facts, Ah, they didn't give you all the facts, That's what I said, Then you'll have to show me what you've got. The food was growing cold on their plates, the sauce on the meat was congealing, the wine was sleeping forgotten in their glasses, and there were tears in Maria da Paz's eyes. For a moment, Tertuliano Máximo Afonso thought what an infinite relief it would be to tell her the whole story from the beginning, about this extraordinary, singular, astonishing, and never-before-seen case of the duplicate man, the unimaginable become reality, the absurd reconciled with reason, the final proof that for God nothing is impossible, and that the science of this century is, as someone said, a fool. If he did so, if he was open with her, then all his previous troubling actions would be explained, including those that had been, as far as Maria da Paz was concerned, aggressive, rude, or disloyal, or that had, in short, offended against the most elementary common sense, that is to say almost all his actions. Then harmony would be restored, all errors and mistakes would be unconditionally and unreservedly forgiven, Maria da Paz would beg him, Don't go on with this madness, it might turn out badly, and he would reply, You sound like my mother, and she would ask, Have you told her, and he would say, No, I just said that I had a few problems at the moment, and she would conclude, Now that you've talked to me about it, let's sort it out together. Not many tables are occupied, they have been given a corner table, and no one is paying them any particular attention, situations like this, couples who come to air their sentimental or domestic grievances between the fish and the meat courses or, worse, because the conflicts have taken longer to resolve, between the aperitif and paying the bill, form an integral part of the catering trade, whether in restaurants or in cafeterias. Tertuliano Máximo Afonso's well-intentioned thought vanished as quickly as it came, the waiter asked if they had finished and took away the plates, Maria da Paz's eyes are almost dry, it's been said thousands of times before that there's no point crying over spilled milk, the problem in this case is what has happened to the jug, which lay shattered on the floor. The waiter brought the coffee and the bill that Tertuliano Máximo Afonso had asked for, and a few minutes later, they were in his car. I'll take you home, he had said, Yes, if you wouldn't mind, she had said. They did not speak until they reached the street where Maria da Paz lived. Before they reached the place where he normally dropped her, Tertuliano Máximo Afonso parked the car by the sidewalk and turned off the engine. Surprised by this unusual gesture, she shot him a glance, but still said nothing. Without turning his head, without looking at her, in a tense, determined voice, he said, Every word that has come out of my mouth during these last few weeks, including the conversation we've just had in the restaurant, has been a lie, but don't ask me what the truth is because I can't tell you, So it wasn't statistical data you wanted from the production company, Exactly, And I suppose there's no point expecting you to tell me what the real reason for your interest was, No, Presumably it's something to do with the videos you've got in your apartment, Just be satisfied with what I've told you and stop asking questions and making suppositions, Oh, I can promise you I won't ask you any questions, but I'm free to make all the suppositions I want, however absurd you may think them, You seem oddly unsurprised, Why should I be surprised, You know what I mean, don't make me repeat it, Sooner or later you would have had to tell me, I just didn't expect it to be today, And why would I have had to tell you, Because you're more honest than you think, Although not honest enough to tell you the truth, The reason for that isn't a lack of honesty, something else is keeping your lips sealed, What, A doubt, an anxiety, a fear, What makes you think that, Because I've read it in your face and heard it in your words, But the words were lying, They were, yes, but not the way they sounded, The moment has come to use the phrase politicians always use, I can neither confirm nor deny it, That's just one of those low rhetorical tricks that deceive no one, Why, Because anyone can see that the phrase inclines more toward confirmation than toward denial, Well, I've never noticed that, Neither have I, it only occurred to me now, thanks to you, But I didn't confirm the fear, the anxiety, or the doubt, You didn't deny them either, Now is not the time for word games, Well, it's better than sitting at a restaurant table with tears in your eyes, Forgive me, This time there's nothing to forgive, now I know half of what there is to know, so I can't complain, But all I said was that everything I told you was a lie, That's the half I know, from now on I hope to be able to sleep better, You might not be able to sleep at all if you knew the other half, Don't frighten me, please, There's no reason to be frightened, don't worry, there are no corpses involved, Don't frighten me, It's all right, as my mother usually says, in the end everything finds a solution, Promise me you'll take care, Yes, I promise, Great care, Yes, And if, among all the secrets I'm incapable of imagining, you find one you can tell me about, you will tell me, won't you, however insignificant it may seem to you, It's a promise, but, in this case, it's either all or nothing, Even so, I'll wait. Maria da Paz bent toward him, kissed him lightly on the cheek, and made to get out of the car. He placed one hand on her arm and stopped her, Stay, come back home with me. She gently pulled away, No, not tonight, you couldn't give me more than you already have, Unless I told you everything, No, not even then. She opened the door, turned once more to say good-bye with a smile, and got out. Tertuliano Máximo Afonso started the engine, waited until she had gone into the building, and then, with a weary gesture, set the car in motion and drove home, where, patient and confident of its power, loneliness was waiting for him.

The following day, about midmorning, he set off for his first reconnoitering of the unknown territory where Daniel Santa-Clara lived with his wife. He was wearing the false beard meticulously fixed to his face and a peaked cap to throw a protective shadow over his eyes, which he decided at the last moment not to conceal behind a pair of dark glasses because, in conjunction with the rest of the disguise, they gave him an outlaw air likely to awaken the suspicions of the whole neighborhood and to be the cause of a full-scale police hunt, with the all-too-foreseeable consequences of capture, identification, and public opprobrium. He was not making this expedition in the expectation of collecting any particularly significant facts, at most he would learn something of the exterior of things, gain a topographical knowledge of places, the street, the building, but little more. It would be the most extraordinary fluke to see Daniel Santa-Clara going into the building, with remnants of makeup still on his face, and wearing the irresolute, perplexed expression of someone who is taking rather too long to emerge from the skin of the character he had been playing an hour before. Real life has always seemed to us more frugal in coincidences than the novel or other forms of fiction, unless we were to allow that the principle of coincidence is the one true ruler of the world, in which case, we should give as much value to the coincidence one actually experiences as to that which is written about, and vice versa. During the half hour that Tertuliano Máximo Afonso spent there, stopping to look in shopwindows and to buy a newspaper, then sitting reading the paper outside a café right next to the building, Daniel Santa-Clara was seen neither entering nor leaving. Perhaps he's resting in the peace of his home with his wife and his children, if he has any, perhaps, as he was the other day, he is busy at a film shoot, perhaps there is no one in the apartment, the children because they have gone to spend the holidays with their grandparents, the mother because, like so many others, she has a job to go to, either to safeguard a position of real or imagined personal independence or because the household finances cannot survive without her material contribution, for the fact is that, however quickly a supporting actor scurries from small role to small role, however often he is selected by the production company that uses him now on a more or less tacitly exclusive basis, the money he can earn will always be subordinated to the rigors of the law of supply and demand, which is never based on the objective needs of the subject but purely on the latter's real or imagined talents and abilities, those that it favors him with recognizing or those that, with unknown and usually negative intent, are attributed to him, forgetting that he might have other, less visible talents and abilities that might be worth putting to the test. This means that Daniel Santa-Clara could become a big star if fortune were to decide to have him noticed by a clever producer who didn't mind taking a risk, the sort who, while he might occasionally take it into his head to destroy a really first-rate star, has also been known, with great generosity, to polish up the shine on second-rate or even third-rate stars. Letting time do its work has always been the best option ever since the world began, Daniel

Santa-Clara is still young, he has a pleasant face, a good physique, and undeniable gifts as an actor, it wouldn't be right for him to have to spend the rest of his life playing hotel receptionists or other such occupations. It is not long since we saw him playing a theater impresario in *The Goddess of the Stage*, at last duly acknowledged in the opening credits, and this could be a sign that he has begun to be noticed. The future, wherever it is, and although it is hardly a novelty to say so, awaits. Tertuliano Máximo Afonso, on the other hand, had better not wait around very much longer, for fear that the troubling blackness of his general appearance should become etched on the photographic memory of the waiters in the café, we neglected, by the way, to mention that he is wearing a dark suit and that, as protection against the glare of the sun, he has now had to resort to dark glasses. He left the money on the table, so as not to have to summon the waiter, and walked quickly over to the telephone booth on the other side of the road. From his top jacket pocket he removed a piece of paper bearing Daniel Santa-Clara's telephone number, which he dialed. He didn't want to speak to anyone, just to know if anyone would answer, and who. This time no woman came running from the other end of the apartment, nor did a child tell him Mummy's not home, nor did he hear a voice identical to Tertuliano Máximo Afonso's say, Hello. She must be at work, he thought, and he's probably filming, playing a traffic cop or a public-works contractor. He emerged from the telephone booth and looked at his watch. It was nearly lunchtime, neither of them will be coming home, he said, but at that moment, a woman passed, he didn't manage to see her face, she was crossing the street in the direction of the café, she looked as if she was going to sit down at a table outside, but she didn't, she went on, took a few more steps, and entered the building where Daniel Santa-Clara lives. Tertuliano Máximo Afonso made a gesture of barely contained frustration, It must have been her, he muttered, for this man's worst defect, at least since we have known him, has been an excess of imagination, no one would think he was a history teacher, someone who should be interested only in facts, here we have him inventing identities after catching only a brief rear view of the woman who passed him, someone he does not know and has never seen before, either from behind or from in front. To be fair to Tertuliano Máximo Afonso though, despite this tendency to imaginative flights of fancy, he can still manage, at decisive moments, to impose upon himself a calculating coolness that would make the most hardened of stock-exchange speculators turn pale with professional envy. There is, in fact, a simple, not to say elementary, way, although, as with all things, it is necessary first to have had the idea, of finding out if the woman who went into the building was going up to Daniel Santa-Clara's apartment, he would just have to wait a few minutes, to allow time for the lift to reach the fifth floor where António Claro lives, to wait for her to open the front door and go in, two more minutes for her to put her bag down on the sofa and make herself comfortable, it wouldn't be right to make her run as he had the other day, as you could tell from her breathing. The phone rang and rang, rang and rang again, but no one answered. So it wasn't her, said Tertuliano Máximo Afonso as he hung up. He has nothing more to do here, this latest preliminary act of investigation is over, many of the previous ones had been absolutely vital to the success of the operation, others had not really been worth wasting time on, but they had, at least, served to deceive his doubts, anxieties, and fears, to allow him to pretend that marking time was the same as going forward and that retreat was merely an opportunity to think things through. He had left his car on a nearby street and was setting off to find it, his work as a spy had ended, or so we thought, but Tertuliano Máximo Afonso, and heaven knows what they'll think, cannot help shooting glances of burning intensity at every woman he passes, well, not every woman, some are excluded as being too old or too young to be married to a thirty-eight-year-old man, Which is my age and, therefore, presumably his age, now it should be said at this point that Tertuliano Máximo Afonso's thoughts set off along two different paths, some to question the discriminatory idea underlying his allusion to age differences in marriage and other similar unions, thus upholding the prejudices of social consensus where the fluctuating but deep-rooted concepts of what is proper and improper are generated, and others, the thoughts we mentioned, to dispute the possibility subsequently aired, which is that the history teacher and the actor, based on the fact that each is the spitting image of the other, as established earlier by videographic evidence, are exactly the same age. As regards the first branch of reflections, Tertuliano Máximo Afonso had no option but to recognize that every human being, insuperable and private moral impediments apart, has the right to be bound to whomever they like, where and how they like, as long as the other interested party wants this too. As for the second line of thought, this suddenly revived in Tertuliano Máximo Afonso's mind, and for more pressing reasons now, the troubling question of who is the duplicate of whom, rejecting as improbable the hypothesis that both were born, not only on the same day, but also at the same hour, at the same minute, and same fraction of a second, for this would imply that, as well as seeing the light at the very same moment, they would, at that very same moment, both have experienced crying for the first time too. Coincidences are fine as long as they respect the minimum degree of probability demanded by common sense. Tertuliano Máximo Afonso is troubled now by the possibility that he might be the younger of the two, that the other man might be the original and he nothing but a mere and, of course, devalued repetition. Obviously, his nonexistent powers of divination do not allow him to peer into the fog of the yet-to-be and see if this will have any influence on a future that we have every reason to describe as impenetrable, but the fact that he was the discoverer of the supernatural miracle we know so well had given rise in his mind, without him noticing, to a kind of sense of primogeniture that, at this moment, is rebelling against the threat, as if an ambitious bastard brother had come to turn him off his throne. Absorbed in these ponderous thoughts, harried by these insidious anxieties, Tertuliano Máximo Afonso, still wearing his beard, turned into the street where he lives and where everyone knows him, running the risk that someone might suddenly start shouting that the teacher's car is being stolen and for a determined neighbor to block the way with his own car. Solidarity, however, has lost many of its former virtues, in this case it would be quite appropriate to say fortunately so, and Tertuliano Máximo Afonso proceeded on his way without impediment, and, without anyone giving any sign that they had recognized him or the car he was driving, he left the area and its environs and, now that necessity has made of him a frequent visitor to shopping centers, went into the first one he found. Ten minutes later, he emerged, cleanshaven, apart from the tiny amount of his own beard that had grown since the morning. When he got home there was a message from Maria da Paz on the answering machine, nothing important, just to ask how he was. I'm fine, he murmured, absolutely fine. He promised himself that he would phone her that night, but he probably won't if he decides to take the next step, which cannot be delayed for even a page longer, that of phoning Daniel Santa-Clara.

M AY I SPEAK TO SENHOR DANIEL SANTA-CLARA, ASKED
Tertuliano Máximo Afonso when the man's wife answered,
You're the same person, I presume, who phoned the other day,
I recognize your voice, she said, Yes, I am, May I ask who's
calling, That hardly seems necessary, your husband doesn't
know me, You don't know him either, but you know his
name, That's only natural, he's an actor, and therefore a public figure, So are we all, we are all more or less public figures,
it's only the number of spectators that varies, My name is
Máximo Afonso, Just a moment. The receiver was placed on
the table, then picked up again, the voices of both men will
repeat themselves as a mirror repeats itself when placed in
front of another mirror, António Claro speaking, how may I
help you, My name's Tertuliano Máximo Afonso and I'm a
history teacher in a secondary school, My wife said your
name was Máximo Afonso, That was just for brevity's sake,
my full name is Tertuliano Máximo Afonso, Fine, how may I
help you, You have doubtless already noticed that our voices
are identical, Yes, Totally identical, So it seems, You see I have
already had several occasions now to confirm this, How, By
watching some of the films you've appeared in in recent years,

the first was a fairly old comedy entitled *The Race Is to the Swift*, and the last was *The Goddess of the Stage*, I've probably seen eight or maybe ten in all, Really, I must say I feel rather flattered, I had no idea that the kind of film that I was, for some years, obliged to appear in could be of such interest to a history teacher, although, needless to say, the roles I'm playing now are quite different, Well, I have a good reason for watching them, which is why I would like to talk to you in person, Why in person, It isn't only our voices that are identical, What do you mean, Anyone seeing us together would swear on their own life that we were twins, Twins, More than twins, identical, In what way identical, Identical, quite simply identical, My dear sir, I don't know you and I can't even be sure that your name is what you say it is or that you really are a historian, I'm not a historian, I'm just a history teacher, as for my name I've never had any other, we don't use pseudonyms in teaching, for better or worse, we teach with our faces uncovered, That hardly seems relevant, look, let's just stop the conversation right here, I have things to do, So you don't believe me, No, I don't believe in impossibilities, Do you have two moles on your right forearm, one above the other in a line, Yes, I do, So do I, That doesn't prove anything, Do you have a scar under your left kneecap, Yes, So do I, And how do you know all this if we have never met, For me it was easy, I saw you in a beach scene, I can't remember which film it was now, but there was a close-up, And how am I to know that you have the same moles as I do, the same scar, That depends on you, The impossibilities of a coincidence are infinite, The possibilities are too, it's true that our moles could have been there at birth or developed later, over time, but a scar is always the consequence of an accident that affected a particular part of the body, we both had that accident and, in all probability, on the same occasion, Even admitting that such an absolute likeness could exist, and notice I'm only admitting it as a hypothesis, I can see no reason for us to meet and I don't understand why you've phoned, Out of curiosity, nothing but curiosity, it isn't every day that you find two identical people, Look, I've lived my whole life without knowing it, and I haven't missed knowing it at all, But now you do know, Then I'll pretend I don't, The same thing will happen to you as to me, every time you look at yourself in the mirror you will never be sure whether you are seeing your own virtual image or my real image, Frankly, I'm starting to think I've been talking to a madman, Remember that scar, if I'm mad, then we probably both are, I'll call the police, Oh, I doubt very much if the police would be interested, all I've done is make two phone calls asking to speak to the actor Daniel Santa-Clara, whom I did not threaten or insult or harm in any way, what crime have I committed exactly, You've upset my wife and myself, anyway, that's enough, I'm going to hang up now, You're quite sure you don't want to meet me, you don't feel the slightest twinge of curiosity, No, I don't feel any curiosity and I don't want to meet you, That's your last word, The first and the last, In that case, I must apologize, I had no evil intentions, Promise me you won't phone again, I promise, We have a right to our peace of mind, to our privacy, Of course, Good, I'm glad you agree, There's just one thing I'm not quite clear about, if you'll allow me, What's that, If we're identical, then will we also die at the same moment, People who are not identical and don't live in the same city die at the same moment every day, That's just coincidence, simple, banal coincidence, This conversation has come to an end, we have nothing more to say, I just hope now you have the decency to keep your word, Look, I promised I wouldn't phone you again at home and I won't, Excellent, Once more, please accept my apology, Apology accepted, Good-bye, Good-bye. There is something strange about Tertuliano Máximo Afonso's calm demeanor, when the natural, logical, human reaction would be, in this order, to slam down the phone, thump the desk in justifiable irritation, and exclaim bitterly, All that work for nothing. Week after week spent drawing up strategies, developing tactics, weighing every new step, pondering the effects of the previous step, maneuvering the sails to take advantage of favorable winds, wherever they came from, and all this to arrive at the end and humbly beg forgiveness, promising, like a child caught red-handed in the pantry, that he will never do it again. Contrary to all reasonable expectations, however, Tertuliano Máximo Afonso is pleased. Firstly, because he feels that during the conversation he coped with the situation well, he was never intimidated, he argued, and here the expression is appropriate, as equal to equal, and even, occasionally, leaped nimbly onto the offensive. Secondly, because he considers it simply unthinkable that things will stop here, doubtless a highly subjective view, but one backed up by countless actions which, despite the force of curiosity that should set them immediately in motion, are often delayed, to the point, in some cases, where they appear to have been forgotten for good. Even if the immediate effect of the revelation is not as momentous as it was for Tertuliano Máximo Afonso, it is impossible that António Claro will not, one of these days, take steps, either openly or covertly, to compare one face with the other and one scar with the other. I don't know what to do, António Claro said to his wife after adding to his part of the conversation that of the other man, which she had not been able to hear, he speaks with such confidence it makes me feel like finding out if his story is actually true, If I were you, I would just wipe the matter from my mind, I would repeat to myself a hundred times a day that there cannot possibly be two identical people in the world, until I had convinced myself and could forget all about it, And you wouldn't make any attempt to get in touch with him, No, I don't think so, Why not, I'm not sure really, out of fear I suppose, It's obviously not a very common situation, but I don't see why you should be afraid, The other day, I felt almost dizzy when I realized it wasn't you on the phone, Well, I can understand that, because listening to him is just like listening to me, What I thought, no, it wasn't a thought, it was more of a feeling, like a wave of panic closing over me, making my skin creep, and I felt that if the voice was the same, then everything else would be too, Not necessarily, we might not be completely identical, He says you are, We would have to prove it, And how would we do that, invite him over here so that you could undress and he could undress, and I, nominated judge by you both, could pronounce sentence, or not pronounce sentence at all, because it turned out that you actually were identical, and if I was to leave the room and come back in afterward, I wouldn't know who was one and who was the other, and if either of you was to go out, to leave this apartment, which one of you would I be left with afterward, tell me that, with you or with him, You'd be able to tell us apart by our clothes, Unless you had swapped, Look, don't worry, we're only talking, nothing like that will happen, Imagine it, though, having to make a decision based on what's outside rather than what's inside, Calm down, And I wonder now what he meant when he talked about how if you were identical, then you would both have to die at the same moment, He didn't state it as a fact, he was merely expressing a thought, a supposition, as if he were asking himself the question, Yes, but why mention it then, out of the blue, He probably did it to shock me, Who is this man, what does he want with us, You know as much as I do about who he is and what he wants, which is nothing, He said he was a history teacher, That must be true, he wouldn't invent that, and he did strike me as an educated man, as for him telephoning us, I would probably have done the same if, instead of him, I had been the one to discover the resemblance, And how are we going to feel now, with that ghostlike presence in the house, every time I look at you, it will be as if I were seeing him, We're still suffering the effects of the shock, the surprise, tomorrow it will all seem much simpler, one more oddity among many, after all, it's not like a cat with two heads or a calf with five legs, we're just a couple of Siamese twins who happen to have been born apart, A little while ago, I spoke of fear, panic, but I realize now that it's something else I'm feeling, What, Well, I'm not sure, a presentiment perhaps, Good or bad, It's just a presentiment, like a closed door behind another closed door, You're trembling, Yes, I am. Helena, for that is her name, although we did not know it until now, responded abstractedly to her husband's embrace, then sat huddled in one corner of the sofa and closed her eyes. António Claro tried to distract her, to cheer her up with a joke, If I ever get top billing, this Tertuliano fellow can be my double, I'll have him do all the dangerous scenes or the boring bits, and I can stay at home, and no one will notice the difference. She opened her eyes, smiled wanly, and said, A history teacher playing someone's double would certainly be a sight to see, the only thing is that cinema doubles come when they're called, and this one has invaded our house, Look, try not to think about it, read a book, watch television, do something, No, I don't feel like reading, still less like watching TV,

I'm going to lie down. When António Claro went to bed an hour later, Helena appeared to be sleeping. He pretended to believe her and turned out the light, knowing beforehand that it would take him a while to get to sleep too. He remembered the disquieting dialogue he had had with the intruder, sifting his phrases and even his words for hidden meanings, until the words, which were as tired as he was, began to grow neutral, to lose their significance, as if they no longer had anything to do with the mental world of the man who was silently, desperately continuing to pronounce them, The infinite possibilities of a coincidence, Those who are identical die together, he had said, and, The virtual image of the person looking at himself in the mirror, The real image of the person looking out at him from the mirror, then the conversation with his wife, her presentiment, her fear, he made a purely private decision, for it was getting late, that the matter would have to be resolved for good or ill, whatever happened, and quickly too, I'll go and talk to him. The decision deceived his mind, tricked the tensions in his body, and sleep, finding the way clear, crept in and lay down. Worn out by an immobility against which every nerve in her body protested, Helena had also finally fallen asleep, and for two hours she managed to rest beside her husband, António Claro, as if no other man had come between them, and she would probably have remained so until dawn if her dream had not startled her awake. She opened her eyes to find the room immersed in a gloom that was almost darkness, she heard her husband's slow, regular breathing, and was suddenly aware that there was another breathing in the house, someone had come in, someone was moving around, perhaps in the living room, perhaps in the kitchen, behind the door that leads into the corridor, anyway, right here. Shaking with fear, Helena reached out her arm to wake her husband, but, at the last moment, reason stopped her. There's no one here, she thought, there can't possibly be anyone out there, it's just my imagination, sometimes dreams do step out of the brain that dreamed them, then we call them visions, phantasmagoria, premonitions, omens, warnings from beyond, the person who was breathing and walking about the house, the person who just sat down on my sofa, the person hidden behind the curtains, isn't that man, but a fantasy I have inside my head, this figure heading straight toward me, touching me with hands identical to those of this other man asleep by my side, looking at me with the same eyes, who would kiss me with the same lips, who in the same voice would say the everyday words and the other, tender, intimate words, those of the spirit and those of the flesh, is a fantasy, nothing but a mad fantasy, a nightmare borne out of fear and anxiety, tomorrow everything will return to its place, I won't need the cockerel to crow to drive away bad dreams, the alarm clock will be enough, everyone knows that no man can be exactly the same as another man in a world in which they make machines to wake us up. A ridiculous conclusion that offended both good sense and a simple respect for logic, but to this woman, who had spent all night wandering among the vaguenesses of obscure thoughts composed of shifting scraps of fog constantly changing form and direction, the conclusion seemed unanswerable and irrefutable. We must even be grateful to absurd reasoning if, in the midst of the bitter night, it restores to us a little serenity, however illusory, and gives us the key with which we can finally, hesitantly, open the door to sleep. Helena opened her eyes before the alarm was due to go off, she silenced it so that her husband would not wake up, and, lying on her back, staring up at the ceiling, she allowed her confused ideas to gradually come to order and to follow the route that would at last draw them all together into rational, coherent thought, free of inexplicable phantasms and all-too-easily explained fantasies. She could hardly believe that given all the real and mythological chimera, the sort that spit fire and have the head of a lion, the tail of a dragon, and the body of a goat, for the flaccid monsters of her insomnia could have appeared to her in this form too, she could hardly believe that she could have been tormented, like some lewd, not to say indecent, temptation, by the image of another man whom she would not even need to undress in order to know what he was like physically, from head to toe, every inch of him, because an identical man lies beside her now. She was not ashamed of herself because these ideas did not really belong to her, they were the ambiguous fruit of an imagination that, shaken by unusual, violent emotions, had jumped the rails, what matters is that she is lucid and alert now, the mistress of her thoughts and her desires, the hallucinations of the night, be they of the flesh or of the spirit, always dissolve into air with the first light of morning, the light that reorders the world and restores it to its usual orbit, once more rewriting the books of the law. It is time to get up, the travel agency she works for is on the other side of the city, every morning on her way there she thinks how wonderful it would be if she could get them to transfer her to one of the offices in the center, the wretched traffic, at this time of day, more than deserves the term "infernal" coined by someone in some happy moment of inspiration, who knows when, who knows where. Her husband will remain in bed for another hour or two, he has no filming to do today, and the current project, it seems, is coming to an end. Helena slipped out of bed with a lightness that, though natural to her, has been perfected during her ten years as attentive, devoted spouse, then she moved noiselessly about the room while she took clothes off hangers and got dressed, before going out into the corridor. This is where the night visitor had walked, she heard his breathing next to this gap in the door before he came in and hid behind the curtain, no, don't worry, this is not another evil assault made by Helena's imagination, she herself is making fun of her own temptations, so trivial, now that she can compare them with the rosy glow coming in through that window, the one in the living room where, last night, she had felt as frightened as a little girl left alone in a wood in a fairy tale. There is the sofa on which the visitor sat, and it was not by chance that he did so, of all the places where he could have rested, if that was what he wanted, he chose that one, Helena's sofa, as if to share it with her or to appropriate it for himself. There are plenty of reasons to think that the more we try to drive our imaginations away, the more they will amuse themselves by seeking out and attacking those points in our armor that, consciously or unconsciously, we left unprotected. One day, this woman Helena, who is in a hurry and has a professional timetable to keep to, will tell us why she too went and sat down on the sofa, why, during one long minute, she cozily lingered there, and why, having been so resolute when she woke up, she is behaving now as if the dream had taken her in its arms again and was gently rocking her. And why too, dressed and ready to leave, she opened the telephone directory and copied Tertuliano Máximo Afonso's address onto a piece of paper. She pushed open the bedroom door, her husband is still apparently asleep, but his sleep is nothing more than the final, diffuse threshold of wakefulness, she can therefore approach the bed, kiss him on the forehead, and say, I'm off now, and then receive on her mouth his kiss and the other man's lips, good heavens, this woman must be mad, the things she does, the things she thinks of. Are you late, asked António Claro, rubbing his eyes, No, I've still got a couple of minutes, she replied and sat down on the edge of the bed, What shall we do about this man, What do you want to do, Last night, while I was trying to get to sleep, I thought I should go and talk to him, but now I'm not so sure that would be a good idea, We either open the door to him, or we close it, to be honest, I don't see any other solution, one way or another our life has changed and will never be the same again, The decision is in our hands, But it's not in our hands, or anyone else's, to make what happened unhappen, the arrival of this man is a fact that we can neither erase nor remove, even if we don't let him in, even if we close the door on him, he'll be there waiting on the other side until we can't stand it anymore, You're taking a very grim view of things, perhaps, after all, we can resolve matters with a simple meeting, he proves that he's identical to me, I tell him, yes, sir, you're quite right, and once that's done, it's good-bye and good riddance, please don't bother us again, He'll still be waiting on the other side of the door, Well, we won't open it, He's already come in, he's inside your head and inside mine, We'll forget him eventually, Possibly, but we can't be sure. Helena got up, looked at her watch, and said, I've got to go, I'm going to be late, she took two steps toward the door but still had time to ask, Are you going to phone him, are you going to arrange to meet, Not today, replied her husband, raising himself up on one elbow, or tomorrow, I'll wait a few days, it might not be a bad idea to let indifference and silence do their work, to allow time for the matter to die a natural death, Oh, well, it's up to you, see you later. The apartment door opened and closed, and we will never know if Tertuliano Máximo Afonso was sitting on the stairs outside waiting.

António Claro stretched out in bed again, if life really hadn't changed, as his wife claimed it had, he would turn over and sleep for another hour, it seems to be true what the envious say, that actors need a lot of sleep, it must be a consequence of the irregular life they lead, even when they go out at night as rarely as Daniel Santa-Clara. However, five minutes later, António Claro was up, unaccustomed to the early hour, although, to be fair, when his professional duties demand it, this actor, who gives every appearance of being somewhat lazy, is as capable of getting up as the most early-rising of larks. He peered at the sky out of the bedroom window, it was not hard to predict that it was going to be another hot day, then he went into the kitchen to make some breakfast. He thought about what his wife had said, He's inside our heads, but she was like that, peremptory, no, not peremptory exactly, what she has is the gift of concision, of coming out with short, condensed, pithy phrases, using four words to say what others wouldn't be able to say in forty. He wasn't sure if his was the best solution, waiting a while before going on the offensive, either in the form of a secret meeting, face-to-face, without any witnesses who might blab afterward, or in the form of a terse telephone conversation, of the kind that leaves the other party dumbstruck, breathless, nonplussed. However, he doubted the efficacy of his dialectical skills to put a stop, once and for all, to any plans, present or future, that this wretch, Tertuliano Máximo Afonso, might have to introduce into their lives the kind of pernicious psychological and conjugal disquiet of which he had implicitly boasted and to which he had explicitly given rise, for example, Helena, last night, having the boldness to declare, Every time I look at you, it will be as if I were seeing him. Only a woman whose moral foundations had been severely shaken would have thrown such words in the face of her own husband unaware of the adulterous element they contained, diaphanous, it is true, but highly revealing. Meanwhile, going around and around in António Claro's head, although he would doubtless angrily deny this if we so much as mentioned it, is the outline of an idea that, out of pure caution, we will not go so far as to classify as being on a par with a Machiavelli, at least not until its eventual effects, doubtless negative, have been revealed. This idea, which, at the moment, is nothing but a mental sketch, consists, neither more nor less, and however shocking it may seem to us, in working out whether, with skill and cunning, it would be possible to obtain from the resemblance, similarity, or absolute identity, should this be confirmed, some advantage of a personal nature, that is, whether António Claro or Daniel Santa-Clara could find a way of profiting from a business that, at the moment, appears not at all favorable to their interests. Since we cannot, at the moment, expect the person responsible for the idea to illumine the doubtless tortuous routes via which he vaguely imagines that he will reach his objectives, do not count on us, mere transcribers of other people's thoughts and faithful copyists of their actions, to anticipate the next steps of a procession that has still got no farther than the vestibule. What can, however, be excluded from this embryonic plan is the suggestion that Tertuliano Máximo Afonso might serve as the actor Daniel Santa-Clara's double, we must all concur that it would show a grave lack of intellectual respect to ask a history teacher to take part in the hirsute frivolities of the seventh art. António Claro was just taking his last sip of coffee when another idea crossed his synapses, and this was to get in his car and go and have a look at the street and the building where Tertuliano Máximo Afonso lives. Despite no longer being driven by irresistible hereditary instincts, the actions of human beings are repeated with such startling regularity that we believe it would be permissible, without stretching a point, to hypothesize the slow but steady formation of a new kind of instinct, perhaps "sociocultural" would be the right word, which, based on variants of repeated tropisms and in response, of course, to identical stimuli, would mean that any idea that had occurred to one person would, necessarily, occur to someone else. First it was Tertuliano Máximo Afonso coming to this street dramatically disguised, all in black on a brilliant summer's morning, now it is António Claro who is preparing to go to Tertuliano Máximo Afonso's street without even considering the complications that might ensue if he appears there barefaced, then, while he is shaving, showering, and getting dressed, the finger of inspiration touches his forehead, reminding him that in a drawer somewhere, stored away in an empty cigar box, as a touching professional souvenir, is the mustache Daniel Santa-Clara wore five years ago when playing the role of receptionist in the comedy *The Race Is to the Swift*. As the wise old proverb almost says, Keep a thing five years and you'll always find a use for it. It will not take long for António Claro to discover where the history teacher lives thanks to the estimable telephone directory, now sitting slightly askew on the bookshelf where they usually keep it, as if it had been replaced by a nervous hand after having been nervously consulted. He has noted down the address in his pocket diary, as well as the telephone number, for, although making use of the latter is not in his plans for the day, if he ever does phone Tertuliano Máximo Afonso's apartment, he wants to be able to do so from wherever he happens to be, without having to depend on a telephone directory that he may have neglected to put back in its place and which he might then be unable to find when he most needs it. He is ready to leave now, his mustache in position, although not particularly securely since it has lost some of its adhesive qualities over the years, but it is unlikely to fall off at the critical moment, since walking by the teacher's building and having a quick look at it will take him only a matter of seconds. When he was putting the mustache on, using his reflection in the mirror to guide him, he remembered that, five years before, he had had to shave off the natural mustache that at the time adorned the space between his nose and upper lip, merely because the director had thought both its shape and design to be inappropriate for what he had in mind. At this point, let us prepare ourselves for the attentive reader, a direct descendant of those ingenuous but extremely bright young lads who, in the early days of cinema, used to call out to the boy on the screen that the map of the mine was hidden in the hatband of the evil, cynical enemy fallen at his feet, let us prepare ourselves for them to call us to order and denounce as an unforgivable lapse the difference in behavior between the character Tertuliano Máximo Afonso and the character António Claro, since, in identical situations, the former had to go into a shopping center in order to put on and take off his false beard and mustache, while the latter is blithely preparing to leave the house in the equally blithe light of day wearing on his face a mustache that, while it may belong to him, is not in fact his. That attentive reader is forgetting what has already been pointed out during this narrative, that just as Tertuliano Máximo Afonso is, in every respect, the double of the actor Daniel Santa-Clara, so the actor Daniel Santa-Clara, although for different reasons, is the double of António Claro. No one living in the building or in the street will find it strange that the man who entered the building yesterday without a mustache should be leaving it today with one, at most, if they notice at all, they would say, He's obviously already made up for filming. Sitting in his car, with the window open, António Claro consults the route map and the *A–Z* and learns from them what we know already, that the street where Tertuliano Máximo Afonso lives is on the other side of the city, and, having bade a friendly good morning to a neighbor, he sets off. It will take nearly an hour to reach his destination, he will try tempting fate by driving past the building three times at ten-minute intervals, as if he were looking for a place to park, who knows, some happy coincidence might draw Tertuliano Máximo Afonso down into the street, although, those of us who are fully informed of the duties the history teacher has to fulfill know that, at this precise moment, he is sitting quietly at his desk, working hard on the proposal the headmaster commissioned him to write, as if his future depended on the result of this effort, when the truth is, and this we can tell you now, Tertuliano Máximo Afonso will never again enter a classroom, either in the school to which we have occasionally accompanied him or in any other. The reason will be revealed later. António Claro saw what there was to see, a nondescript street, a building like many others, no one would imagine that in that second-floor apartment, behind those innocent curtains, lives a phenomenon of nature no less extraordinary than the seven heads of the Lernaean Hydra and other such marvels. Whether Tertuliano Máximo Afonso truly merits a description that would exclude him from human normality is something that remains to be seen, for we still do not know which of these two men was the first to be born. If the first-born was Tertuliano Máximo Afonso, then it is António Claro who deserves the designation phenomenon of nature, since, having come into being second, he appeared in this world on false pretenses to occupy a place not his own, just like the Lernaean Hydra, which is why Hercules killed it. The sovereign equilibrium of the universe would not have been disturbed one iota if António Claro had been born and become an actor in some other solar system, but here, in the same city, and, therefore, as far as an observer watching us from the moon is concerned, right next door, all kinds of disorders and confusions are possible, especially the worst, especially the most terrible. And just in case you think that, because we have known him longer, we harbor some special preference for Tertuliano Máximo Afonso, we would point out that, mathematically speaking, as many inexorable probabilities of his having been the second-born hang over his head as over António Claro's. Nevertheless, however strange to sensitive eyes and ears the following syntactical construction might appear, it is legitimate to say that what will be has been, and all that's lacking now is for it to be written down. António Claro did not drive along the street again, four blocks farther on, he removed Daniel Santa-Clara's mustache, furtively, in case some good citizen should catch him in the act and call the police, then, having nothing else to do, he set off for home, where the script for his next film awaited him for study and annotation. He left the house again only to go for lunch in a nearby restaurant, then took a short nap and resumed work until his wife came home. He was not yet one of the main characters in the film, but his name would appear on the posters that would be placed strategically about the city when the time came, and he was pretty sure that he would garner some critical praise, however brief, for his performance as a lawyer, which is the role he had been given this time. His only difficulty was the enormous number of lawyers in all shapes and sizes who had appeared in films and on television, public and private prosecutors with various styles of legal patter, from the caressing to the aggressive, defense lawyers blessed with varying degrees of eloquence and for whom being convinced of the innocence of their client did not always appear to be of great importance. He would like to create a new kind of lawyer, a person who would be capable of astonishing the judge with his every word and every gesture and of dazzling the public with the sharpness of his ripostes, with his implacable powers of reasoning, with his superhuman intelligence. It was true that none of this was in the script, but the director might allow himself to be persuaded to steer the screenwriter in that direction if the producer put in a good word for him. He would have to think about it. Having muttered to himself that he would have to think about it immediately transported his thoughts to other parts, to the history teacher, to his street, to the building, to the curtained windows, and from there, in retrospect, to last night's phone call, to his conversations with Helena, to the decisions that he would sooner or later have to take, he wasn't so sure now that he could profit from the situation, but, as he has just said, he would have to think about it. His wife arrived slightly later than usual, no, she hadn't been shopping, it was the usual problem, the traffic, you could never predict what might happen, as António Claro knew, for it had taken him an hour to reach Tertuliano Máximo Afonso's street, but I'd better not mention that today, I'm sure she wouldn't understand why I did it. Helena will likewise say nothing either, she is equally sure that her husband would not understand what she had done.

THREE DAYS LATER, ABOUT MIDMORNING, TERTULIANO MÁXimo Afonso's phone rang. It wasn't his mother phoning because she missed him, it wasn't Maria da Paz phoning out of love, it wasn't the mathematics teacher phoning out of friendship, nor was it the headmaster from school wanting to know how the work was going. Hello, this is António Claro, the voice said, Oh, hello, Perhaps I'm phoning too early, No, don't worry, I'm up and working, If I'm interrupting, I can always call later, What I was doing can easily wait for an hour, there's no danger of my losing the thread, Coming straight to the point, then, I've been having a serious think these last few days and I've reached the conclusion that we should meet, That's my view too, it doesn't make sense for two people in our situation not to, My wife had a few doubts about it, but I've managed to persuade her that things couldn't simply stay as they were, Good, The problem is that we can't possibly appear in public together, we would gain nothing by becoming a news item on TV and in the press, especially me, it would be prejudicial to my career if people knew I had a look-alike who even had the same voice as me, More than a look-alike, A twin, More than a twin, That's precisely what I want to confirm, although I confess I find it hard to believe that we are as identical as you say, It's in your power to find out, We'll have to meet, then, Yes, but where, Any ideas, One possibility would be to come to my apartment, but there's the problem of the neighbors, the lady who lives upstairs, for example, knows I haven't gone out, imagine how she would feel if she saw me walking into the building I'm already in, What if I disguise myself, How, With a mustache, No, a mustache wouldn't be enough, she would just ask you, that is, ask me, because she would assume she was talking to me, if I was now a fugitive from the police, She knows you that well, She does my cleaning for me, Ah, I see, no, it clearly wouldn't be very sensible, and then there are the other neighbors too, Exactly, In that case, I think we'll have to meet outside the city, in some deserted place in the country, where no one will see us and where we can talk freely, That sounds like a good idea, Actually, I know just the place, about thirty kilometers out of the city, In which direction, Explaining it over the phone would be impossible, look, I'll send you a sketch map today, giving all the directions, we can meet in, say, four days' time so that we can be sure the letter has arrived, Four days' time brings us to Sunday, As good a day as any, But why thirty kilometers away, You know how it is with cities, just getting out of them takes a while, where the streets end, the factories begin, and where the factories end, the shantytowns begin, not to mention the villages that have already become part of the city without even knowing it, You put it well, Thank you, anyway I'll phone you on Saturday to confirm the meeting, All right, There is one other thing I'd like you to know, What's that, Well, I'll be armed, Why, Because I don't know you and I don't know what other intentions you might have, If you're afraid I'll kidnap you, for example, or eliminate you so that I can be alone in the world with this face that we both have, I can tell you now that I won't have any weapons on me, not even a penknife, No, no, I don't suspect you of that, You'll still be armed though, Just a precaution, All I want to do is prove to you that I'm right, and as for what you say about not knowing me, allow me to object that we're in exactly the same position, it's true you've never seen me, but, up until now, I've only seen you pretending to be someone else, playing a part, so that makes us equal, Let's not argue, we should go to our meeting calmly, without any previous declarations of war, But I'm not the one who'll be armed, The gun won't be loaded, What's the point of taking it then, if it won't be loaded, Pretend that I'm playing another one of my roles, that of a person drawn into an ambush from which he knows he will emerge alive because someone has given him the script to read, in short, the movies, It's just the opposite in history, you only find out afterward, What an interesting idea, I'd never thought of that before, Nor had I, it only occurred to me now, So we're in agreement, then, we'll meet on Sunday, Yes, I'll await your call, Don't worry, I won't forget, it's been a pleasure talking to you, Same here, Good-bye, Good-bye, and give my regards to your wife. Like Tertuliano Máximo Afonso, António Claro was alone at home. He had warned Helena that he was going to phone the history teacher, but had said he would prefer her not to be there and that he would tell her about the conversation afterward. She didn't try to stop him, she said she thought it a good idea, that she understood his desire to feel comfortable when embarking on a conversation that would clearly not be easy, but what he will never know is that Helena made two phone calls from the travel agency where she works, the first to her own number and the second to Tertuliano Máximo Afonso's, as fate would have it, she did so precisely when he and her husband were talking to each other, that way she could be sure that the matter was going ahead, but again she could not have said why she did this, it is becoming more and more evident that, after many more or less failed attempts, the only way to arrive at some proper explanation of our actions would be for us to say why we do the things about which we always say we don't know why we do them. A trusting and conciliatory spirit would presume that, had Tertuliano Máximo Afonso's number not been engaged, António Claro's wife would have hung up without waiting for a reply, she would certainly not announce herself with, Hello, I'm Helena, António Claro's wife, she wouldn't say, I was just phoning to see how you are, such words, in the current situation, would be in a way improper, if not downright indiscreet, given that these two people, even though they have spoken twice, are not on close enough terms for it to seem natural for either of them to inquire about the state of mind or health of the other, neither can we accept as an excuse for such an excess of familiarity the fact that these are perfectly normal, everyday expressions, the kind that, in principle, do not oblige or commit anyone to anything, unless, that is, we were to tune our auditory organ to the complex range of possible underlying subtones, as set out in the exhaustive explanation given elsewhere in this story for the enlightenment of those readers more interested in what lies hidden than in what is shown. As for Tertuliano Máximo Afonso, it was with evident relief that he leaned back in his chair and took a deep breath when the conversation with António Claro came to an end. If asked which of the two, in his opinion, at the point we have now reached, was in charge of the game, he would feel inclined to reply, I am, although he was equally sure that the other man would think he had reason enough to give exactly the same answer if asked the same question. It did not worry him that the place chosen for the meeting was so far from the city, it did not trouble him that António Claro was intending to go armed, even though he was convinced that, contrary to his assurances, the pistol, because it would in all probability be a pistol, would be loaded. In a way that he himself realized to be totally lacking in logic, rationality, and common sense, he believed that the false beard he would wear would protect him while he was wearing it, basing this absurd belief on the firm idea that he would not take it off when they first met, only later on, when the absolute identity of hands, eyes, eyebrows, forehead, ears, nose, hair, had been agreed to the satisfaction of both. He would take with him a mirror large enough so that, when he does finally remove his beard, their two faces, side by side, could be compared directly, so that their eyes could pass from the face to which they belonged to the face to which they could have belonged, a mirror that would state definitively, If what you can see is identical, then the rest must be too, I really don't think it's necessary for you to take all your clothes off in order to continue the comparison, this isn't a nudist beach or a weight-lifting contest. Calmly and confidently, as if this particular chess move had been foreseen from the start, Tertuliano Máximo Afonso resumed his work, thinking that, just as with his bold proposal for the study of history, people's lives could also be told from front to back, one could wait until they ended and then, gradually, follow the stream back to the source, identifying the tributaries on the way and sailing up them too, aware that each one, even the smallest and feeblest, was, in its time and in itself, a major river, and in this slow, deliberate way, alert to every scintillation on the surface of the water, every bubble risen from the bottom, every sudden downward flurry, every stagnant stillness, reach the end of the narrative and place after the first of all moments the final full stop, and to take the same amount of time that the lives thus told had actually lasted. Let's not hurry, we have so much to say when we fall silent, murmured Tertuliano Máximo Afonso and went back to his work. Halfway through the afternoon, he phoned Maria da Paz and asked if she would like to drop by when she finished work, she said she would but that she couldn't stay long because her mother wasn't well, and then he said not to bother, that family duties came first, and she said, No, I'd like to see you, and he agreed and said, Yes, it would be good to see each other, as if she were his beloved, and we know that she is not, or perhaps she is and he doesn't know it, or perhaps, he stopped at this word because he didn't know how to complete the sentence honestly, what lie or what pretend truth he would say to himself, it's true that his eyes had grown misty with emotion, she wanted to see him, yes, sometimes it's good to have someone who wants to see us and who tells us so, but the treacherous tear, already wiped away with the back of his hand, appeared only because he was alone and because solitude suddenly weighed on him more than in his darkest hours. Maria da Paz duly arrived, they kissed each other on both cheeks, then sat down to talk, he asked if her mother's illness was serious, she said no, fortunately not, just one of those problems that comes with old age, they come and go, go and come, and finally stay. He asked when her holidays began, she said in two weeks' time, but that they probably wouldn't be going away, it all depended on her mother's health. He asked how work was at the bank, and she said, oh, the usual, some days better than others. Then she asked if he didn't get terribly bored, now that the classes were over, and he said no, he didn't actually, the headmaster had set him a task, to draw up a proposal for the ministry on methods of teaching history. She said, How interesting, and then they fell silent, until she asked if he had anything to tell her, and he said no, it wasn't the right time yet, that she must be patient a little longer. She said she would wait as long as she had to, that the conversation they had had in the car after supper the other night, when he had admitted that he had lied, had been like a door opening only to close again at once, but that at least she had found out that the thing separating them was only a door and not a wall. He said nothing, merely nodded and thought to himself that worse than any wall is a door to which one has never had the key, a key he didn't know where to find, or even if it existed. Then, when he didn't speak, she said, It's getting late, I'd better go, and he said, Don't go yet, But I've got to, my mother's expecting me, Of course, forgive me. She got up, he did too, they looked at each other, they kissed each other on the cheek as they had when she arrived, Good-bye, then, she said, Good-bye, he said, phone me when you get home, Yes, they looked at each other again, then she took the hand he was about to place on her shoulder by way of farewell, and, very gently, as if he were a child, led him into the bedroom.

António Claro's letter arrived on the Friday. Accompanying the map was a handwritten note, unsigned and with no salutation, it said, Let's meet at six in the evening, I hope you don't have too much difficulty finding the place. The writing isn't exactly like mine, but there's very little difference, and it's mainly in the way he writes his capital letters, murmured Tertuliano Máximo Afonso. The map showed a road leading out from the city and, on either side of the road, two villages separated by eight kilometers, and between them, a road off to the right, heading into the countryside toward another village, smaller than the others to judge by the drawing. From there, another narrower road came to a halt about a kilometer farther on, at a house. This was indicated by the word "house," not by a rudimentary drawing, the simple outline that even the least skillful of hands can draw, a roof with a chimney, a facade with a door and a window on either side. Above the word, a red arrow left no room for doubt, Go no farther. Tertuliano Máximo Afonso opened a drawer, took out a map of the city and environs, found and identified the right exit, here's the first village, the road that turns off to the right before reaching the second, the little village up ahead, all that's missing is the final stretch of track. Tertuliano Máximo Afonso looked at the sketch map again, If it's a house, he thought, then I don't need to take a mirror, all houses have mirrors in them. He had imagined that the meeting would take place in open countryside, far from prying eyes, perhaps beneath the protection of some leafy tree, and instead it would take place under a roof, rather like a meeting of acquaintances, with a glass in one hand and some nuts to nibble on. He wondered if António Claro's wife would go too, if she would go there in order to confirm the size and shape of the scars on the left knee, to measure the distance between the two moles on the right forearm and the distance that separates one from the epicondyle and the other from the wrist bone, and then say, Don't leave my sight, so that I don't get you muddled up. He thought not, it wouldn't make sense for any man worthy of the name to go to a potentially difficult, not to say hazardous, meeting, one has only to remember António Claro's gentlemanly warning to Tertuliano Máximo Afonso that he would be armed, and to drag his wife along with him, as if ready to hide behind her skirts at the slightest sign of danger. No, he'll go alone, I won't take Maria da Paz either, Tertuliano Máximo Afonso pronounced these disconcerting words unaware of the profound difference that exists between a legitimate spouse, adorned with all the inherent rights and duties, and a temporary romantic relationship, however steadfast the aforementioned Maria da Paz's affections have always seemed to us, and given that it is reasonable, if not obligatory, to doubt those of the other party. Tertuliano Máximo Afonso put the city map and the sketch map away in the drawer, but not the handwritten note. He put it in front of him, picked up his pen, and wrote the whole sentence on a piece of paper, in a hand that tried to imitate as closely as possible the other hand, especially the capital letters, which is where the difference was most noticeable. He kept writing, repeating the sentence, until he had covered the whole sheet, and in the last attempt, not even the most experienced of graphologists would have been able to discover even the most insignificant suggestion of forgery, what Tertuliano Máximo Afonso achieved when he quickly copied Maria da Paz's signature is a mere shadow of the work of art he has just produced. From now on, all he will have to find out is how António Claro forms the capital letters from A to H, J to K, and M to Z, and then learn to imitate them. This does not mean, however, that Tertuliano Máximo Afonso is nurturing in his mind future projects that involve the person of the actor Daniel Santa-Clara, he is merely, in this particular case, satisfying the taste for study that led him, when still a young man, to the public exercise of the praiseworthy profession of schoolmastering. Just as it is always possible that it might prove useful to know how to stand an egg on its end, so one should not exclude the possibility that being able to produce an accurate imitation of António Claro's capital letters might also serve some purpose in Tertuliano Máximo Afonso's life. As the ancients taught, never say, Of this water I will not drink, especially, we would add, if you have no other water. Since these thoughts were not formulated by Tertuliano Máximo Afonso, it is not in our power to analyze the connection that might nevertheless exist between them and the decision he has just taken and to which he was obviously led by some thought of his own that we failed to catch. This decision reveals the, shall we say, inevitable nature of the obvious, for now that Tertuliano Máximo Afonso has the sketch map that will guide him to the location where the meeting will take place, what could be more natural than that it should occur to him to go and inspect the location first, to study its entrances and exits, to take its measure, if we can use that expression, with the added and not insignificant advantage that, by doing so, he will avoid the risk of getting lost on Sunday. The thought that this short journey would distract him for some hours from the painful duty of writing the proposal to the ministry not only brightened his thoughts, it also, in truly surprising fashion, lifted the gloom from his face. Tertuliano Máximo Afonso does not belong to that extraordinary group of people who can smile even when alone, his nature inclines him more to melancholy, to reverie, to an exaggerated awareness of the transience of life, to an incurable perplexity when faced by the genuine Cretan labyrinths of human relationships. He does not properly understand the mysterious workings of a beehive nor why the branch of a tree should spring out where and in the way it does, that is, neither higher up nor lower down, neither thicker nor thinner, but he attributes his difficulty in understanding this to the fact that he does not know the genetic and gestural communication codes used among the bees, still less the flow of information that more or less blindly circulates along the tangled network of vegetal motorways that link the roots deep down in the earth to the leaves that clothe the tree and which rest in the noonday stillness and stir when the wind moves them. What he absolutely does not understand, however much he cudgels his brain, is why it is that while communication technologies continue to develop in a genuinely geometric progression, from improvement to improvement, the other form of communication, proper, real communication, from me to you, from us to them, should still be this confusion crisscrossed with culs-de-sac, so deceiving with its illusory esplanades, and as devious in expression as in concealment. Tertuliano Máximo Afonso might not perhaps mind becoming a tree, but he will never be one, his life, like that of all humans who have lived and will live, will never know the supreme experience of the vegetal. Supreme, or so we imagine, since, up until now, no one has read the biography or the memoirs of an oak tree, written by the same. Let Tertuliano Máximo Afonso, therefore, concern himself with the things of the world to which he belongs, the world of men and women who shout and boast in every natural and artificial setting, and let him leave in peace the arboreal world, which has quite enough things to cope with, phytopathological diseases, the electric saw, and forest fires, to name but a few. He is preoccupied too with driving the car that is taking him out into the countryside, carrying him away from a city that is the very model of modern difficulties in communication, in the form of vehicles and pedestrians, especially on days like today, Friday afternoon, when everyone is leaving for the weekend. Tertuliano Máximo Afonso is leaving, but he will soon be back. The worst of the traffic is behind him now, the road he must take is not very busy, soon he will find himself outside the house where, the day after tomorrow, António Claro will be waiting for him. He has his beard on, carefully stuck to his face, just in case, as he is driving through the last village, someone addresses him as Daniel Santa-Clara and invites him to have a beer, always assuming that the house he has come to see belongs to António Claro or is rented by him, a house in the country, a second home, these supporting actors who work in films certainly live high on the hog if they already have access to luxuries that, not so very long ago, were the privilege of the few. Meanwhile, Tertuliano Máximo Afonso is concerned that the narrow road that leads to the house and which is now there before him may have no other use, that is, if it does not go beyond the house and there are no other houses nearby, then the woman who appeared at the window will be asking herself or her neighbor beside her, Where's that car going, there's no one staying at António Claro's house at the moment as far as I know, and I didn't like the look of that man's face, men with beards have usually got something to hide, it's just as well Tertuliano Máximo Afonso didn't hear her, he would have had yet another serious reason to feel worried. There is scarcely room on the tarmac road for two cars to pass, there obviously isn't much traffic here. To the left, the stony ground slopes gently down to a valley where a long, unbroken line of tall trees, which from here look to be ash trees and white poplars, marks the probable course of a river. Even at the prudent speed at which Tertuliano Máximo Afonso is driving, in case a car should suddenly appear coming toward him, a kilometer takes no time at all to cover, and this kilometer is covered already, and this must be the house. The road continues, snaking up two hills set one above the other, then disappearing around the other side, it probably serves other houses that cannot be seen from here, the distrustful woman seems, after all, to be concerned solely with what is near the village where she lives, what lies beyond her frontiers doesn't interest her. From the broad terrace in front of the house another, even narrower road and in even worse condition leads down toward the valley, That must be another way to get here, thought Tertuliano Máximo Afonso. He is aware that he should not go too near the house, lest some walker or goatherd, for it looks like the kind of area where goats might be kept, should sound the alarm, Stop thief, and in two ticks the police would be there, or, if not them, a detachment of locals armed, as in the old days, with sticks and scythes. He must behave like a traveler just passing through, who has paused for a moment to admire the view and who, now that he's there, casts an appreciative eye over a house whose owners, now absent, are fortunate enough to enjoy this magnificent vista. The house is a simple one-story building, a typical rural dwelling that looks as if it had undergone some careful restoration work, although there are signs of neglect too, as if the owners did not come here very often and only on brief visits. One usually expects a house in the country to have potted plants outside the door and on the window ledges, but this has hardly any, a few dry stalks, the occasional fading flower, and a single brave geranium that continues to do battle against absence. The house is separated from the road by a low wall, and, behind it, raising their branches up above the roof, are two chestnut trees that, judging by their height and their evident great age, must have been there long before the house was built. A solitary place, ideal for contemplative people, for those who love nature for what it is, making no distinction between sun and rain, heat and cold, wind and stillness, between the ease that some of these bring and that others withhold. Tertuliano Máximo Afonso walked around to the back of the house, through a garden that once merited the name but which is now no more than a barely-walled-in space invaded by thistles, a tangle of rampant weeds swamping an atrophied apple tree, a peach tree whose trunk is covered with lichen, and a few thorn apples, or *Datura stramonium,* to give them their Latin name. For António Claro, and perhaps for his wife too, the country house must have been a love of only brief duration, one of those short-lived bucolic passions that occasionally assail city dwellers and which, like loose straw, burn with the lightest touch of a match and are reduced immediately to black ash. Tertuliano Máximo Afonso can now return to his second-floor apartment with a view of the other side of the road and await the phone call that will bring him back here on Sunday. He got into the car, drove back the way he had come, and, to show the woman at the window that no crime committed against another person's property weighed heavy on his conscience, he drove slowly through the village as if he were nudging his way through a herd of goats as calmly accustomed to the streets as they were to the fields where they grazed among the broom and the thyme. Tertuliano Máximo Afonso wondered if, just to satisfy curiosity, it would be worth investigating the shortcut that seemed to lead from the house down to the river, but he soon changed his mind, the fewer people who saw him around these parts, the better. After Sunday, of course, he will never come here again, but it would still be best if people forgot the man with the beard. As he left the village, he accelerated, and in a few minutes he was back on the main road, and less than an hour afterward he was home. He had a bath, which restored him after the heat of the journey, changed his clothes, and, accompanied by a lemon drink that he took from the fridge, sat down at his desk. He is not going to continue work on the proposal for the ministry, he is, like a good son, going to telephone his mother. He will ask how she's been, she'll say fine, how are you, oh, much as usual, no complaints, I was beginning to wonder why you hadn't phoned, sorry, but I've had a lot to do, in human beings these words are presumably the equivalent of the rapid touches of recognition that ants give to each other with their antennae when they meet on a path, as if they were saying, You're one of us, now we can talk about serious matters. So how are your problems, his mother asked, On the way to being resolved, don't worry, The very idea, as if I had nothing better to do with my life than to worry about you, Well, I'm glad you're not taking it all too seriously, You can't see my face, Come on, now, Mama, calm down, Oh, I'll calm down, but only once you're here, It won't be long now, And what about your relationship with Maria da Paz, how does that stand at the moment, It's not easy to explain actually, You could at least try, Well, I do like her and need her, Other people have got married for lesser reasons, Yes, but I think that my need for her is just a thing of the moment, nothing more, and what if I stop feeling it tomorrow, what will I do then, And what about liking her, That's only to be expected in a man who lives alone and has been lucky enough to meet a nice woman, with a pretty face, a good figure, and who is, as people say, a very caring person, Oh, so not very much then, It's not that it's not much, just that it's not enough, You loved your wife, Did I, I can't remember now, that was six years ago, Six years isn't very long to forget so much, Well, I thought I loved her, and she must have thought the same about me, but it turns out we were both mistaken, that's what tends to happen, And you don't want to make the same mistake with Maria da Paz, No, I don't, For your sake or for hers, For both our sakes, More for your own sake than for hers though, Look, I know I'm not perfect, it will be enough that I save her from the evil I don't want to happen to me, but at least my selfishness, in this case, doesn't mean I don't care about protecting her as well, Perhaps Maria da Paz wouldn't mind taking the risk, Another divorce, my second, her first, no, Mama, absolutely not, It might turn out well, we don't know precisely what awaits us beyond each action we take, True enough, Why do you say it like that, Like what, As if we were sitting in the dark and you had suddenly turned a light on and off, It's just your imagination, Say it again, Say what again, What you said, Why, Repeat it, please, As you wish, true enough, Say just the two words, True enough, No, it wasn't the same, What do you mean it wasn't the same, It just wasn't the same, Come on, Mama, stop imagining things, please, too much imagination is not the best way to gain peace of mind, the words I said just signified agreement, conformity, Thanks, I could work that out for myself, I too used to consult dictionaries when I was young, you know, Now don't get angry, When are you coming, Like I said, soon, We need to have a talk, We can have all the talks you want, Yes, but I just want the one talk, Which one, Don't pretend you don't know, I want to know what's going on, and please don't come with any ready-prepared stories, fair play and cards on the table, that's what I expect from you, That doesn't sound like you talking, It's what your father often used to say, do you remember, All right, I'll put all my cards on the table, And you promise you'll play fair, no tricks, Yes, I'll play fair and there'll be no tricks, That's what I like to hear from my son, We'll see what you have to say when I lay down the first card in the pack, Oh, I think I've seen just about all there is to see in life, Cherish that illusion until we have that conversation, Is it so very serious, Time will tell when we get there, Well, don't take too long, please, It could be as soon as the middle of next week,

Well, I certainly hope so, Take care, Mama, Take care, son. Tertuliano Máximo Afonso put down the receiver, then he let his thoughts wander, as if he were still talking to his mother, Words can be the very devil, there we are thinking we allow out of our mouths only the words that suit us, and suddenly another word slips out, where it came from we don't know, we didn't ask for it to appear, and because of that word, which we often have difficulty remembering afterward, the whole conversation abruptly changes direction, and we find ourselves affirming what we denied before, or vice versa, what happened just now was a perfect example, I hadn't intended to speak to my mother so soon about this whole mad story, if I ever really intended to do so at all, and then, from one moment to the next, how I don't know, she has my formal promise that I'll tell her everything, she's probably already putting a cross on the calendar, for next Monday, just in case I should turn up unannounced, I know her, the day she chooses is the day I should arrive, and it won't be her fault if I don't. Tertuliano Máximo Afonso isn't annoyed, on the contrary, he feels an indescribable sense of relief, as if a weight had suddenly been lifted from his shoulders, he wonders what he has gained by remaining silent all these days and he cannot find a single decent answer, in a while he might be able to come up with a thousand explanations, each more plausible than the last, now all he can think of is getting it off his chest as soon as possible, he'll have the meeting with António Claro on Sunday, in two days' time, so there's nothing stopping him getting in the car on Monday morning and going to show his mother all the cards that make up this puzzle, all of them, because it would be one thing to have told her some time ago, There's a man who looks so like me that even you couldn't tell us apart, and quite a different thing to say, I've met him and now

I don't know who I am. At that moment, the tiny fragment of consolation that had been charitably caressing him vanished, and in its place, like a pain that suddenly reasserts itself, fear reappeared. We don't know precisely what awaits us beyond each action we take, his mother had said, and this banal truth, within the grasp of a mere provincial housewife, this trivial truth that forms part of the infinite list of those truths not worth saying because they won't cause anyone any sleepless nights, this truth that belongs to everyone and means the same thing to everyone, can, in certain situations, afflict and frighten more than the worst of threats. Every second that passes is like a door that opens to allow in what has not yet happened, what we call the future, but, to challenge the contradictory nature of what we have just said, perhaps it would be more accurate to say that the future is just an immense void, that the future is just the time on which the eternal present feeds. If the future is empty, thought Tertuliano Máximo Afonso, then nothing that one might call Sunday exists, its possible existence depends on my existence, if I were to die now, part of the future or part of possible futures would be canceled out forever. The conclusion Tertuliano Máximo Afonso was about to reach, For Sunday to exist I must continue to exist, was interrupted by the phone. It was António Claro asking, Did you get the map, Yes, I did, Any problems, None, Look, I know I said I'd ring tomorrow, but I thought the letter must have arrived by now and so I thought I'd just call to confirm the meeting, Fine, I'll be there at six, Don't worry about having to drive through the village, I'll be taking a shortcut that goes straight to the house, that way no one will find it odd seeing two people with the same face driving past, And what about the car, Which car, Mine, Oh, that doesn't matter, if anyone does mistake you for me, they'll just think I've got a new car, besides, I haven't been to the house much lately, All right then, See you the day after tomorrow, Yes, see you on Sunday. After hanging up, it occurred to Tertuliano Máximo Afonso that he should have mentioned he would be wearing a beard. Not that it matters, he will take it off as soon as he gets there. Sunday has just taken a great step forward.

IT WAS FIVE MINUTES PAST SIX WHEN TERTULIANO MÁXIMO
Afonso parked the car opposite the house on the other side
of the road. António Claro's car was already there, by the en-
trance, by the wall. Their cars are a whole mechanical generation apart, Daniel Santa-Clara would never have exchanged
his car for anything that looked like Tertuliano Máximo
Afonso's car. The garden gate stands open, so does the front
door, but the windows are closed. Inside stands a barely dis-
tinguishable figure, however the voice that emerges from
within is clear and precise, as the voice of a film actor should
be, Come in, make yourself at home. Tertuliano Máximo
Afonso went up the four steps and paused on the threshold.
Come in, come in, said the voice, don't stand on ceremony,
although, judging from what I see, you are not the person I
was expecting, I thought I was the actor, but I was wrong.
Without a word, very carefully, Tertuliano Máximo Afonso
removed his beard and went in. That's what I call a sense of
theater, it puts me in mind of those people who like to burst
into a room, shouting, I'm here, as if their presence actually
mattered, said António Claro, while he emerged from the
shadows and stood in the bright light coming in through the

open door. They stood stock-still, looking at each other. Slowly, as if painfully dragging itself up from the depths of the impossible, stupefaction wrote itself across António Claro's face, not across Tertuliano Máximo Afonso's face, for he knew what he was going to find. I'm the person who phoned you, he said, I'm here so that you can see with your own eyes that I was not just having fun at your expense when I said we were identical, So I see, stammered António Claro in a voice that no longer resembled that of Daniel Santa-Clara, I had imagined, because you were so insistent, that there was a strong resemblance, but I confess I wasn't prepared for what I have before me now, my own image, Well, now that you have the proof, I'll leave, said Tertuliano Máximo Afonso, No, no, I asked you to come in, now I'm asking you to sit down so that we can talk, the house is a bit of a mess but these sofas are serviceable enough and I've probably got something to drink too, but no ice, Oh, I wouldn't want to put you to any bother, It's no bother, although you'd get much better service if my wife was here, but it's not hard to imagine what she would be feeling right now, more confused and troubled than I am, that's for sure, Speaking for myself, I have no doubt about it, what I've had to live through these past few weeks I wouldn't wish on my worst enemy, Sit down, please, what would you like to drink, whiskey or brandy, Oh, I'm not a great drinker, but I think I'll have a brandy, just a drop, nothing more. António Claro brought bottles and glasses and poured the visitor a drink, then poured himself three fingers of whiskey without water and sat down on the other side of the small table separating them. I just can't get over it, he said, Oh, I've got past that stage, replied Tertuliano Máximo Afonso, now my only concern is what will happen next, How did you find out, As I told you when I phoned, I saw you in a film, Ah, yes, I remember now, the one where I played a hotel receptionist, Exactly, Then you saw me in other films, Exactly, And how did you track me down, since the name Daniel Santa-Clara isn't in the phone book, Before I could do that, I had to find a way of identifying you among all the other supporting actors who appear in the final credits with no mention of which character they played, Yes, of course, It took time, but I got there in the end, And why did you go to so much trouble, It seems to me that anyone in my position would have done the same, Yes, I suppose so, it's such an extraordinary situation, you couldn't really ignore it, Then I rang all the people listed in the phone book under the surname Santa-Clara, And they, of course, said they didn't know me, Yes, although one of them mentioned that this was the second time someone had rung him up asking for Daniel Santa-Clara, Someone else, before you, had asked for me, Yes, A female fan perhaps, No, it was a man, How strange, Stranger still, he said the man seemed to be trying to disguise his voice, How odd, why would he want to disguise his voice, No idea, The person you spoke to might have imagined it, Possibly, So how did you find me in the end, I wrote to the production company, Well, I'm surprised they gave you my address, They told me your real name too, Oh, I thought you only found that out when you spoke to my wife on that first occasion, No, the production company told me, As far as I know, at least as regards myself, that's the first time they've done anything like that, Well, I did stick in a paragraph about the importance of supporting actors, maybe that convinced them, That would be more likely to have the opposite effect, Anyway, I got your name, And here we are, Yes, here we are. António Claro drank some of his whiskey, Tertuliano Máximo Afonso took a sip of his brandy, then they looked at each other and immediately looked away. The light from the declining afternoon sun came in through the still-open door. Tertuliano Máximo Afonso pushed his glass to one side and spread his two hands out on the tabletop, his fingers splayed, Let's compare, he said. António Claro took another sip of his whiskey and placed his hands symmetrically opposite, pressing them down hard on the table to conceal the fact that they were shaking. Tertuliano Máximo Afonso seemed to be doing the same. Their hands were identical in every respect, every vein, every wrinkle, every hair, each and every finger, as if they had come out of a mold. The only difference was the gold wedding ring that António Claro was wearing on his ring finger. Let's have a look at the moles on our right forearms, said Tertuliano Máximo Afonso. He got up, took off his jacket, which he deposited on the sofa, and rolled up his shirtsleeve to his elbow. António Claro had got up too, but, first, he went and closed the front door and turned on the lights in the living room. When he draped his jacket over the back of a chair, there was a dull clunk. Is that your pistol, asked Tertuliano Máximo Afonso, Yes, Oh, I thought perhaps you'd decided not to bring it, It's not loaded, It's not loaded are just three words that say it's not loaded, Do you want me to show you, since you obviously don't believe me, Do what you like. António Claro put his hand into the inside pocket of the jacket and showed him the gun, Here it is. With deft, rapid movements, he removed the empty clip and pulled back the breech to reveal the equally empty chamber. Convinced, he asked, Convinced, And you don't suspect me of having another pistol in another pocket, That would be too many pistols, It would be the right number of pistols if I was planning to get rid of you, And why would the actor Daniel Santa-Clara want to get rid of the history teacher Tertuliano Máximo Afonso, You yourself put your finger on the problem when you wondered out loud what will happen next, Yes, but I was all set to leave right away, you were the one who asked me to stay, That's true, but your withdrawal wouldn't have solved anything, here or at home or teaching your classes or sleeping with your wife, Actually, I'm not married, You would still be my copy, my duplicate, a permanent image of me in a mirror in which I would not be looking at myself, and that would probably be unbearable, Two bullets would solve the problem before it even presented itself, They would, But the pistol isn't loaded, Exactly, And you haven't got another one in the other pocket, Precisely, Which brings us back to the beginning, to not knowing what will happen next. António Claro had now also rolled up his shirtsleeve, at the distance they were standing one from the other it was not easy to see the marks on their skin, but when they went over to a light, there they were, clear, precise, identical. This is like a science-fiction film written, directed, and acted by clones under orders from a mad philosopher, said António Claro, We still haven't looked at the scars on our knees, said Tertuliano Máximo Afonso, It hardly seems worth it, we don't need any further proof, hands, arms, faces, voices, everything about us is the same, we'll be taking all our clothes off next. He poured himself more whiskey, he looked at the liquid as if expecting some idea to emerge from it, then said, Why not, yes, why not, Because it would be grotesque, you yourself said that no further proof was needed, Why would it be grotesque, either from the waist up or from the waist up and down, we cinema actors, theater actors too, do little else but take our clothes off, But I'm not an actor, Don't take your clothes off if you don't want to, but I'm going to, it's no big deal, I'm used to it, and if our bodies are the same all over, you'll be seeing yourself even when you're looking at me, said António Claro. He removed his shirt in one movement, he took off his shoes and then his trousers, followed by his underwear and, finally, his socks. He was naked from head to toe, and from head to toe he was Tertuliano Máximo Afonso, history teacher. Not wanting to be left behind, and feeling he had to accept the challenge, Tertuliano Máximo Afonso got up from the sofa and started getting undressed as well, more inhibited in his gestures out of modesty and lack of habit, but when he had done, his body slightly hunched in shyness, he had turned into Daniel Santa-Clara, cinema actor, with the one visible exception of his feet, for he had kept his socks on. They looked at each other in silence, conscious of the utter futility of any word they might utter, gripped by a confused sense of humiliation and loss that drove out any quite natural sense of amazement, as if the shocking sameness of their bodies had stolen something from the identity of each. The first to get dressed was Tertuliano Máximo Afonso. He stood there like someone who thinks it is time to leave, but António Claro said, Would you mind sitting down, there's one last point I'd like to clarify with you, I won't take up much more of your time, What is it, asked Tertuliano Máximo Afonso as he reluctantly sat down again, I'm talking about the dates when we were born and the time, said António Claro, taking his wallet out of his jacket pocket and removing his identity card, then handing the card to Tertuliano Máximo Afonso across the table. The latter glanced at it quickly, then gave it back, saying, I was born on the same date, year, month and day, Would you be offended if I asked you to show me your identification, Not at all. Tertuliano Máximo Afonso's card passed into António Claro's hands, where it remained for ten seconds before being returned to its owner, who asked, Satisfied, Not yet, we still don't know what time each of us was born, my idea is that we should write down the time on a piece of paper, Why, So that the second person to speak, if we were to do it that way, wouldn't give in to the temptation to subtract fifteen minutes from the time the first one gave, And why wouldn't he add those fifteen minutes, Because any increase would be against the interests of the second of us to speak, But the piece of paper doesn't guarantee the seriousness of the procedure either, there's nothing to stop me from writing, and this is just an example, that I was born the very first minute of the day, even if that wasn't true, You would be lying, Yes, I would, but either of us, if he chooses, can lie even if we just say out loud the time we were born, You're right, it's a matter of integrity and good faith. Tertuliano Máximo Afonso was trembling inside, he had been sure from the very beginning that this moment would arrive, he had simply not imagined that he would be the one to invite the moment to reveal itself, to break the final seal, to reveal the one difference. He already knew what António Claro's answer would be, but he still asked, And what difference would it make telling each other what time we came into the world, Then we would know which of us, you or me, was the duplicate of the other, And what would happen to either of us if we knew that, I haven't the faintest idea, although my imagination, because we actors do have some imagination, tells me that, at the very least, it would be uncomfortable to live knowing that one was the duplicate of another person, And are you prepared, on your part, to run that risk, More than prepared, And no lying, That, I hope, won't be necessary, replied António Claro with a studied smile, an expressive composition of lips and teeth in which frankness and malice, innocence and impudence were united in identical but indiscernible doses. Then he added, Naturally, if you would prefer, we can draw lots to see who should speak first, That's not necessary, you yourself said it was a question of integrity and good faith, said Tertuliano Máximo Afonso, So what time were you born, At two o'clock in the afternoon. António Claro pulled a regretful face and said, I was born half an hour before or, to put it with absolute chronometrical exactitude, I stuck my head out at thirteen hundred hours twenty-nine minutes, sorry, old pal, but I was already here when you were born, so you are the duplicate. Tertuliano Máximo Afonso drank down the rest of his brandy, got up, and said, It was curiosity that brought me to this meeting, now that my curiosity is satisfied, I'll go, So soon, let's talk a little more, it's still early, in fact, if you haven't anything else to do, we could have supper together, there's a good restaurant near here, you could wear your beard, so there wouldn't be any danger, Thanks for the invitation, but I'll have to say no, we probably wouldn't have much to say to each other, since you are not, I would think, very interested in history, and I've been cured of cinema for the foreseeable future, You're upset because you weren't the first to be born, because I'm the original and you're the duplicate, Upset isn't quite the right word, don't ask me why, but I would simply have preferred that it hadn't happened like this, anyway, I didn't lose out entirely, I still have one small compensation, What compensation is that, The fact that you will gain nothing by going around boasting to all and sundry that, of the two of us, you're the original, if I, the duplicate, am not around for the necessary corroboration, Look, I have no intention of shouting this whole incredible story from the rooftops, after all, I'm a movie actor, not a circus freak, And I'm a history teacher, not a teratological phenomenon, There we agree, So there's no reason whatsoever for us to meet again, Not as far as I'm concerned, All that remains, then, is for me to wish you every happiness in carrying out a role from which you will gain absolutely no advantage, since there will be no audience to applaud you, and I promise you that this particular duplicate will keep well out of the way of scientific curiosity, however legitimate, and out of the way, too, of the media ghouls, whose interest is equally legitimate, since they live off such stuff, for I suppose you will have heard the phrase custom is nine-tenths of the law, if that were not the case, I can assure you that the Hammurabi Code would never have been written, We'll stay away from each other, That shouldn't be hard in a city as large as the one we live in, and our professional lives are so different that I would never even have known of your existence if it hadn't been for that wretched film, and as for the likelihood of a movie actor taking an interest in a history teacher, that's probably off the scale of mathematical probability, You never know, the probability of us existing as we do was zero, and yet here we are, Well, I will try to imagine that I never saw that film or any of the others, or else remember only that I endured a long, painful nightmare before realizing at last that it wasn't worth it, after all, two identical men, what does it matter, to be perfectly frank the only thing that really worries me at the moment is whether, since we were both born on the same day, we will both die on the same day, What's the point of worrying about that now, Death is always to the point, You seem to be suffering from some morbid obsession, when you phoned me, you said the same thing, and I couldn't see the point even then, At the time, I just said it without thinking, it was one of those expressions out of place and context that slip into a conversation without being called, That wasn't the case just now, Does it bother you, No, not at all, It might bother you if you heard the idea that had just popped into my head, What idea is that, That if we are as identical as we have seen we are today, the logic of the identity that seems to unite us would mean that you will die before me, precisely thirty-one minutes before me, and during those thirty-one minutes, the duplicate will take the place of the original and himself be the original, Well, I hope you enjoy those thirty-one minutes of personal, absolute, and exclusive identity, because that is all you will enjoy from now on, How kind, said Tertuliano Máximo Afonso. He carefully put on his false beard, patting it delicately into place with his fingertips, his hands no longer trembling, then he said good-bye and headed for the door. There he stopped, turned, and said, Ah, I forgot the most important thing, we've done all the tests except one, What's that, asked António Claro, A DNA test, an analysis of our genetic information, or, put in the simplest of terms, so that anyone can understand it, the decisive argument, the ultimate proof, No way, No, you're right, because that would mean us going to the genetic laboratory together, hand in hand, for them to pare off a bit of nail or extract a drop of blood, and then we would know if our identity was just a chance coincidence of colors and external forms, or if we really are the double proof, the original and the duplicate proof I should say, that the impossibility of this happening was our one remaining illusion, They would classify us as monsters, Or circus freaks, Which would be unbearable for us both, Absolutely, Well, I'm glad we agree on that, We'd have to agree on something, Good-bye, Good-bye.

The sun had sunk behind the mountains that obscured the horizon on the far side of the river, but the light from the cloudless sky was almost undiminished, except where the harsh intensity of the blue had been tempered by a pale, slowly spreading pink. Tertuliano Máximo Afonso started the car and turned the wheel to head off down the road that went through the village. Looking back at the house, he saw António Claro standing at the door, but he continued on. Neither of them waved good-bye. You're still wearing that ridiculous beard, said common sense, I'll take it off when we get to the main road, and this will be the last time you catch me wearing it, from now on, I'll go around barefaced, let other people disguise themselves if they want to, How do you know it's the last time, Oh, I couldn't honestly say, it's just an idea I have, a feeling, an intuition, Well, I have to confess I didn't expect you to cope so well, you behaved admirably, like a man, But I am a man, Yes, I'm not saying you're not, but in the past your weaknesses have always tended to get the better of your strengths, So a man is anyone who isn't subject to weaknesses, A man is also someone who isn't dominated by them, In that case, a woman capable of overcoming her female weaknesses is a man, or is like a man, In a figurative sense, yes, you could say that, Well, it seems to me that common sense has a very chauvinistic way of expressing itself, That's not my fault, it's just the way I was made, That's hardly a good excuse from someone who does nothing but offer advice and opinions, But I'm not always wrong, This sudden rush of modesty suits you, Look, I would be better than I am, more efficient, more useful, if you helped me, Who, All of you, men and women, after all, common sense is just a kind of arithmetic mean that rises and falls according to the tide, Predictable, you mean, Yes, I am the most predictable of all things, Which is why you were waiting for me in the car, It was time I came back, indeed, I could even be accused of having been away too long, You heard everything, From start to finish, Do you think I was wrong to come and talk to him, That depends on what you mean by wrong or right, besides, it doesn't matter, given the situation you were in, there wasn't really any alternative, This was the only way of drawing a line under the matter, What line, We've agreed between us that there will be no more meetings, Are you trying to tell me that after all the fuss you've made it's going to end just like that, that you'll go back to your work and he to his, you to your Maria da Paz, for as long as that lasts, and he to his Helena or whatever her name is, and everything will be discreetly brushed under the carpet, is that what you're trying to say, There's no reason why it should be any other way, There is every reason why it should be another way, believe you me, It's entirely up to us, If you turned off the engine, the car would continue to move, But we're going downhill, Even if we were on a flat surface, it would still continue to move, although admittedly for much less time, it's called inertia, as you should know, even though it's nothing to do with history, or perhaps it is, now that I think of it, I would say that it is precisely in history that one is most aware of inertia, Don't give opinions about things you know nothing about, a game of chess can be interrupted at any moment, But I was talking about history, And I'm talking about chess, All right, have it your way, one of the players can go on playing alone if he wants to, and, without resorting to tricks, he will inevitably end up winning, whether he plays white or black, because he's playing with all the pieces, Let's say I've got up from the table, left the room, am no longer there, There are still three players remaining, You're referring, I suppose, to António Claro, And to his wife and to Maria da Paz, What's Maria da Paz got to do with it, You have a very poor memory, my friend, you seem to have forgotten that you used her name in your investigations, sooner or later, either through you or someone else, Maria da Paz will find out all about the plot she is unwittingly involved in, and as for the actor's wife, always assuming she hasn't yet made a move, tomorrow she could be the victorious queen, You have rather too much imagination for common sense, Remember what I said to you a few weeks ago, that only a common sense with the imagination of a poet could have invented the wheel, That isn't quite what you said, It doesn't matter, that's what I'm saying now, You would be better company if you didn't always want to be right, But I've never claimed to be always right, whenever I make a mistake, I'm always the first to hold out my hand for the cane, Possibly, but always with the look on your face of someone who has been the victim of the most terrible miscarriage of justice, What about the horseshoe, What about the horseshoe, Well, I, common sense, also invented the horseshoe, With the imagination of a poet I suppose, Horses would be inclined to say so, All right, that's enough, we're in the realms of fantasy now, What do you think you'll do next, Make two phone calls, one to my mother to tell her that I'll be coming to see her the day after tomorrow and another to Maria da Paz to tell her that the day after tomorrow I'll be going to see my mother and will be away for a week, as you see, nothing could be simpler, more innocent, nothing could be more familiar and domestic. At that moment, a car overtook them at great speed, the driver waved with his right hand. Do you know that man, who is he, asked common sense, He's the man I was talking to, António Claro, Daniel Santa-Clara, the original of which I am the duplicate, I'd have thought you'd recognize him, How can I recognize someone I've never seen, Seeing me is the same as seeing him, But not behind a beard like that, With all this talking I'd forgotten to take it off, there you are, how do I look now, His car is more powerful than yours, Much more powerful, He was gone in an instant, He'll be racing back to tell his wife about our meeting, Possibly, but I wouldn't be so sure, You're a systematic doubting Thomas, No, I'm not, I'm just what you call common sense because you haven't yet found a better name for me, The inventor of the wheel and the horseshoe, In my poetic moments, only in my poetic moments, It's a shame there aren't more of them, When we arrive, just drop me at the end of the street, if you don't mind, Don't you want to come up and have a bit of a rest, No, I'd rather set my imagination to work, because we're certainly going to need it.

WHEN TERTULIANO MÁXIMO AFONSO WOKE UP THE NEXT day, he knew why he had told common sense, as soon as it got into the car, that that would be the last time it would see him wearing the false beard and that, from then on, he would go about barefaced, for everyone to see. Let other people disguise themselves if they want to, had been his categorical words. What at the time might have seemed to the unwary little more than an emotional statement of intent provoked by the justifiable impatience of someone who has been through a series of very tough trials, was, in fact, unbeknownst to us, the seed of an action pregnant with future consequences, like sending off a letter of challenge to the enemy, in the knowledge that things could not possibly stay as they were. Before we go on, however, it would be beneficial to the harmony of the story if we were to devote a few lines to the analysis of any inadvertent contradiction there might be between the action we will describe shortly and the resolutions announced by Tertuliano Máximo Afonso during his brief car journey with common sense. A rapid perusal of the final pages of the previous chapter will immediately reveal the existence of a basic contradiction made manifest in a variety of different expressions, such as those spoken by Tertuliano Máximo Afonso and received with prudent scepticism by common sense, firstly, that he had drawn a line under the matter of the two identical men, secondly, that he and António Claro had agreed they would never meet again, and, thirdly, employing the ingenuous rhetoric of a dramatic final scene, that he had got up from the table, had left the room, was no longer there. That is the contradiction. How can Tertuliano Máximo Afonso say he was no longer there, that he had left the room, had got up from the table when, no sooner has he finished breakfast than we see him rush out to the nearest stationer's and buy a cardboard box in which he will send to António Claro, through the post, the very beard we have just seen him use as a disguise. Should António Claro one day have a need to disguise himself, that's up to him, but this will have nothing to do with the Tertuliano Máximo Afonso who slammed out of the house, saying that he would never be back. When, in two or three days' time, António Claro opens the box at home and finds an immediately-recognizable false beard, he will inevitably say to his wife, What you're seeing here may look like a beard, but it's actually a letter of challenge, and his wife will ask, But how can that be, you don't have any enemies. António Claro will not waste his breath by replying that it's impossible not to have enemies, that enemies are born not out of our will to have them but out of their irresistible desire to have us. In the world of actors, for example, roles with ten lines arouse, with discouraging frequency, the envy of roles with only five lines, that is where it always begins, with envy, and if the roles with ten lines then go on to have twenty and those with five have to content themselves with seven, then the ground has been well manured to encourage the growth of a leafy, prosperous, and lasting enmity. But what role does the beard play in all this, Helena will ask, This beard, as I forgot to mention the other day, is the one that Tertuliano Máximo Afonso was wearing when he came to meet me, it's quite understandable really, in fact, I'm grateful to him, I mean, imagine the complications that could have arisen if someone had seen him driving through the village and mistaken him for me, So what are you going to do with it, Well, I could return it with a curt note putting the wretched meddler in his place, but that would mean getting involved in a tit for tat with unforeseeable consequences, you know how it starts but not how it will end, and I have a career to think about now that I'm getting roles with fifty lines, with the possibility of getting more if everything continues to go as well as the script over there promises it will, If I were you, I would tear it up and throw it away or burn it, after all, dead dogs don't bite, It's hardly a matter of life or death, Besides, I don't think the beard would suit you, This is no joke, It was just a manner of speaking, all I know is that it unsettles my mind, it even troubles my body to know that there is a man in this city who looks exactly like you, although I still can't believe the resemblance can be so exact, But I'm telling you the resemblance is total, absolute, even the fingerprints on our identity cards are identical, I looked, It makes me dizzy just to think about it, Don't let it get to you, take a tranquilizer, Oh, I already have, I've been taking them ever since that man first phoned, Well, I hadn't noticed, You never do notice much about me, That's not true, how could I know you were taking pills if you were doing it secretly, Sorry, my nerves are on edge, it doesn't matter, it will pass, The day will come when we won't even remember this wretched affair, Until that day comes, you'll have to decide what to do with that horrible hairy thing, I think I'll put it with the mustache I wore in that film, Why would you want to keep a beard that has been on someone else's face, That's precisely the point, it does belong to someone else, but the face is the same, It's not the same, It is, If you really want me to go mad, then just keep on saying that your face is his face, Please, calm down, Anyway, how do you square your intention of keeping the beard, as if it were some kind of relic, with calling it a letter of challenge sent by an enemy, which is what you said when you opened the box, I didn't say it came from an enemy, No, but you thought it, Possibly, though I'm not sure it's the right word, the man's never done me any actual harm, He exists, He exists for me just as I exist for him, Yes, but you weren't the one who went looking for him, In his place, I wouldn't have behaved any differently, You would have if you had asked my advice first, Look, I know it isn't exactly a pleasant situation for either of us, but I can't understand why you're getting so inflamed about it, What do you mean inflamed, Any moment now there'll be flames starting from your eyes. Unexpectedly, tears, not flames, started from Helena's eyes. She turned her back on her husband and ran into the bedroom, slamming the door loudly behind her. Anyone of a superstitious bent, and who had witnessed the deplorable conjugal scene we have just described, would probably lose no time in attributing the cause of the conflict to some malign influence emanating from the false beard that António Claro is determined to keep alongside the mustache with which he more or less began his career as an actor. That person would probably shake his head, put on a pitying air, and say in oracular fashion, If you invite your enemy into the house, don't come complaining to me about it afterward, you were warned and you took no notice.

More than four hundred kilometers from here, in his childhood bedroom, Tertuliano Máximo Afonso is preparing to go to sleep. Having left the city on Tuesday morning, he spent the whole journey arguing with himself about whether he should tell his mother at least part of what was going on or if, on the contrary, it would make more sense to keep his mouth firmly shut. After fifty kilometers, he decided that it would be best to make a clean breast of things, after a hundred twenty, he raged against himself for having even been capable of such an idea, after two hundred ten, it seemed to him that a superficial explanation given in an anecdotal tone might be sufficient to satisfy his mother's curiosity, after three hundred fourteen, he called himself a fool and said that surely he knew his mother better than that, at four hundred forty-seven, when he stopped outside the door of the family home, he had absolutely no idea what to do. And now, as he puts on his pajamas, he is thinking that the trip was a grave error, an out-and-out mistake, that he would have been better off not leaving his apartment, staying shut up in his protective shell, waiting. It's true that here he is out of the way, but, no offense to Dona Carolina, who does not deserve such comparisons either on physical or on moral grounds, Tertuliano Máximo Afonso feels as if he had fallen into the wolf's mouth like an unwary sparrow that has flown into the trap without realizing the consequences. His mother did not ask him any questions, she just looked at him expectantly now and then, then immediately looked away again, the look said, I don't mean to be indiscreet, but the message said, If you think you're going to leave here without telling me, you can think again. Lying on his bed, Tertuliano Máximo Afonso goes over and over the problem in his head but reaches no solution. His mother is made of sterner stuff than Maria da Paz, who is satisfied, or so she allows him to believe, with any explanation that he gives her and would wait her whole life, if necessary, for the moment of revelation. Tertuliano Máximo Afonso's mother, with every gesture, every movement, when she puts his plate down in front of him, when she helps him on with his jacket, when she hands him a newly laundered shirt, is saying to him, I'm not asking you to tell me everything, you have a right to your secrets, but with one absolute exception, the secrets on which your life, future, and happiness depend, those I want to know, it's my right, and that you cannot deny me. Tertuliano Máximo Afonso turned out the bedside lamp, he had brought some books with him, but tonight his spirit does not want reading matter, and as for the Mesopotamian civilizations, which doubtless would have gently carried him off to the diaphanous threshold of sleep, these were too heavy and so stayed at home on the bedside table, with the bookmark placed at the beginning of the illustrative chapter on King Tukulti-Ninurta I, who flourished, as they say of historical figures, between the thirteenth and twelfth centuries before Christ. The bedroom door, which was only pushed to, opened softly in the darkness. Tomarctus, the household dog, had come in. He came to find out if this master, who only turns up very infrequently, was still here. He is a medium-sized dog, and ink black, not like other dogs that, when seen from up close, are really gray. The strange name was given to him by Tertuliano Máximo Afonso, that's what happens when you have an erudite master, instead of christening the creature with a name that he could pick up easily through direct genetic routes, as must have been the case with Faithful, Pilot, Sultan, or Admiral, names inherited and then transmitted from generation to generation, he gave him the name of a canine said to have lived about fifteen million years ago and that, according to the paleontologists, is the fossil-Adam of these four-legged creatures who run, sniff, and scratch their fleas and who, as is only natural in a friend, occasionally bite. Tomarctus has not come to stay for very long, he will sleep for a few minutes curled at the foot of the bed, then he will get up and take a turn about the house to see if everything is in order, and then, for the rest of the night, will be the watchful companion of his constant mistress, apart from the odd sortie into the yard to bark and, while he's there, drink some water from his bowl and lift his leg against the bed of geraniums or the rosemary bush. He will return to Tertuliano Máximo Afonso's bedroom at first light to check that nothing has moved on this side of the earth either, for what dogs most want in life is for no one to go away. When Tertuliano Máximo Afonso wakes, the bedroom door will be closed, a sign that his mother is already up and about and that Tomarctus has gone out with her. Tertuliano Máximo Afonso looks at his watch, says to himself, It's still early, as long as this last, vague sleep endures his worries can wait.

He would have woken with a start if a mischievous goblin had come to whisper in his ear that something of extreme importance is happening at this same hour in the home of António Claro or, to be more precise, more accurate, in the tortuous innards of his brain. The tranquilizers have proved a boon to Helena, the proof of this is to see how she sleeps, her breathing regular, her face as placid and absent as a child's, but we cannot say the same of her husband, who has not spent the nights well, his thoughts returning again and again to the false beard, wondering what Tertuliano Máximo Afonso's intentions had been in sending it, dreaming about the meeting at the house in the country, waking up in a state of anxiety, sometimes bathed in sweat. Not today though. The night proved as inimical as the previous nights, but dawn

234

came like a savior as all dawns should. He opened his eyes and waited, surprised to find himself watching for something that should have been about to explode, and which did explode, a flash, a bolt of lightning that filled the whole room with light, remembering what Tertuliano Máximo Afonso had said at the beginning of their conversation, I wrote to the production company, that was his reply to the question he had asked, So how did you find me in the end. He smiled with pure pleasure as must all discoverers when they first catch sight of the unknown island, but the exultant thrill of discovery did not last long, these morning ideas generally come with a manufacturer's flaw, we think we have just invented the perpetual-motion machine, and as soon as we turn our backs, it stops. The one thing film companies never have a shortage of is letters asking for actors' photographs and autographs, the big stars, as long as they enjoy the public's favor, receive thousands of them a week, well, when we say "receive," they don't actually receive them in the normal sense of the word, they wouldn't even waste their time looking at them, that's what the staff at the production company are for, they go to the appropriate shelf to find the desired photograph, stick it in an envelope with the dedication already printed on it, the same for everyone, and then it's, hurry up now, it's getting late, next, please. Obviously, Daniel Santa-Clara is no star, indeed, if the company were ever to receive three letters in one day asking for his photograph, it would be an occasion to hang out the flags and declare a national holiday, and such letters are never kept, of course, they all pass through the paper shredder, all those longings and emotions reduced to the misery of a pile of indecipherable little strips. Assuming, however, that the filing clerks at the production company had instructions to record, order, and judiciously classify everything, so as not to lose a single scrap of that evidence of the public's admiration for their artistes, we must inevitably ask what possible use Tertuliano Máximo Afonso's letter could be to António Claro, or, more precisely, how that letter could contribute to his finding a way out, if such a thing exists, of that complicated, freakish, never-before-seen case of two identical men. It must be said that it was this unrealistic hope, immediately shattered by the logic of the facts, that brought such joy and cheer to António Claro's awakening, and if something of that mood remains, it is only because there is a remote possibility that the part of the letter in which Tertuliano Máximo Afonso mentioned the importance of supporting actors might have been deemed of sufficient interest to merit the honor of a place in the files and even, who knows, the attention of a marketing specialist to whom the human factor would not be entirely a matter of indifference. All this boils down to is a need for the minuscule satisfaction it would afford to Daniel Santa-Clara's ego, via the pen of the history teacher, to have some recognition of the importance of the cabin boys in the running of an aircraft carrier, even if all they've done on the voyage is keep the brasses nice and shiny. That this would be enough to make António Claro decide to visit the production company that morning in order to inquire about a letter written by one Tertuliano Máximo Afonso is, to be perfectly frank, questionable, given the unlikelihood of his finding what he so ingenuously imagined, but there are times in life when an urgent need to drag oneself out of the slough of indecision, to do something, anything, however useless, however superfluous, is the final sign that we are still capable of doing something of our own volition, like looking through the keyhole of a door we have been forbidden to enter. António Claro is already out of bed, he slipped out taking every precaution not to wake his wife, now he is sprawled on the big sofa in the sitting room, with the script of his next film open on his lap, that will be his excuse for going to visit the production company, he who has never needed excuses before nor been asked for them at home, but that's what happens when one's conscience is not entirely easy, There's a point I need to clear up, he will say when Helena finally appears, there seems to be a bit of dialogue missing, the way it reads now, it just doesn't make sense. He will, in fact, be asleep when his wife comes into the living room, but the effect will not be entirely lost, for she thought he had got up to study his role, some people are like that, people whose overly acute sense of responsibility keeps them in a state of permanent unrest, as if, at every moment, they were not doing their duty and were being accused of just that. He had woken up suddenly, he explained in somewhat garbled fashion, had slept badly, and she asked him why he didn't go back to bed, and then he told her how he had found a mistake in the script that could be rectified only by the production company, and she said that there was no need to go rushing over there, he could go after lunch, but that now he should sleep. He insisted and she desisted, saying only that, personally, she would love to be able to slip back in between the sheets again, The holidays begin in two weeks' time, you'll see then how much I sleep, especially with these tablets, it will be paradise, You're not going to spend your whole holiday in bed, are you, he said, My bed is my castle, she replied, I'm safe behind its walls, You should go to a doctor, you never used to be like this, That's understandable, up until now, I've never had two men on my mind at the same time, You're not serious, are you, Not the way you mean it, no, besides, you must admit it would be pretty ridiculous to feel jealous of a person I don't even know and who, if I have anything to do with it, I never will know. This would be the right moment for António Claro to confess that he isn't going to visit the production company because of any supposed deficiencies in the script, but to read, if he can, a letter written by the second of the men occupying his wife's thoughts, although it is reasonable to presume, given the way in which the human brain works, always ready to slide into some form of delirium, that, at least in these last few agitated days, the second man will have overtaken the first. We recognize, however, that such an explanation, as well as demanding too much effort from António Claro's confused mind, would only complicate the situation still further and would not, in all probability, be received by Helena with great sympathy. António Claro merely said that he wasn't jealous, that it would be stupid to be jealous, he was just worried about her health, We should make the most of your holidays and go somewhere far away from here, he said, To be honest, I'd rather stay at home, and, besides, you've got that film, Yes, but shooting isn't due to start just yet, Even so, We could go and stay at the house in the country, I'll ask someone in the village to tidy up the garden for us, The solitude there is suffocating, Well, let's go somewhere else then, Like I said, I'd rather stay at home, Isn't that just a different kind of solitude, Yes, but I like it here, If that's what you really want, Yes, that's what I really want. There was no more to be said. They ate breakfast in silence, and half an hour later, Helena had left for work. António Claro was not in quite such a hurry, but he nevertheless left soon afterward. He got into his car thinking that he was about to go on the attack. He just didn't know why.

Actors do not often visit the offices of the production company, and this must be the first time that one of them has come to make inquiries about a letter from an admirer, even though this letter differed from the others in that, unusually, it asked not only for a photograph or an autograph but also for an address, António Claro does not know what the letter says, he assumes it merely asks for his home address. António Claro's task would be a difficult one were it not for the fortunate circumstance that he knows one of the department heads, who was at school with him and who received him with open arms and the usual words, So, what brings you here, Well, I was told that someone wrote in asking for my address, and I was just curious to read the letter, he said, Well, I don't deal with such matters myself, but I'll get someone to help you. He spoke to someone over the intercom, explained briefly what was needed, and moments later, a young woman entered, smiling, with her words already prepared, Good morning, I really enjoyed seeing you in your last film, That's very kind of you, Now what would you like to know, It's about a letter written by someone called Tertuliano Máximo Afonso, If all he wanted was a photograph, the letter won't be here, we don't keep those ones, if we did, the files would be bursting at the seams, As far as I know, he asked for my address and made some other rather interesting comment, which is what brings me here today, What did you say his name was, Tertuliano Máximo Afonso, he's a history teacher, Do you know him, Yes and no, that is, I've heard of him, How long ago was the letter written, More than two weeks and less than three, I think, but I'm not sure, Well, I'll look in the letter register first, although, to be honest, the name doesn't ring a bell, Are you in charge of the register, No, a colleague of mine is but she's on holiday, although a name like that must have caused some comment, there can't be too many Tertulianos around nowadays, No, I suppose not, Would you mind coming with me, said the woman. António Claro said good-bye to his friend and followed her, which was certainly no hardship, she had a good figure and was wearing a nice perfume. They walked through a room where several people were working, two of them smiled shyly when they saw him pass, which just goes to show, despite opinions to the contrary, which tend to be governed by ancient class prejudices, that some people do notice supporting actors. They went into an office lined with shelves, almost all of which were filled with large record books. An identical book lay open on the only table. It's like stepping back in time, said António Claro, it's like the archive in a Central Registry Office, Well, it is an archive, but only a temporary one, as soon as the book on the table is full, the oldest of the others will be thrown out, it's not like a real Registry Office, where everything is kept, the living and the dead, Compared with the other room we walked through, though, this is another world, You probably get rooms like this in even the most modern of offices, like a rusty anchor chained to the past and with no purpose in life. António Claro looked at her intently and said, You know, you've come out with a number of interesting comments since we came into this room, Do you think so, Yes, I do, Perhaps it's a bit like a sparrow who suddenly starts singing like a canary, You see, another interesting idea. The woman did not respond, she turned a few pages in the book, going back three weeks, and began running through the list of names with her right index finger, one by one. The third week passed, the second too, we're on the first week, we've reached today's date, and the name of Tertuliano Máximo Afonso has still not appeared. You must have been misinformed, said the woman, no such name has been recorded, which would mean that the letter, if it was written, didn't come through here, it must have got lost en route, Oh dear, I'm putting you to an awful lot of trouble, wasting your time, but, António Claro added sweetly, perhaps we could just go back another week, Of course. The woman turned more pages and sighed. The fourth week had seen a superabundance of requests for photographs, it would take a good while to get to Saturday, but let us raise our hands to heaven and give thanks to God that the requests concerning more important actors are dealt with in a department equipped with computer systems, nothing like the near-incunabular archaism of this mountain of folios reserved for the masses. It took a while for António Claro to realize that the search being carried out by this amiable woman was one he could do equally well himself and that he really should have offered to take her place, especially since the elementary nature of the facts recorded, no more than a list of names and addresses, the sort of thing anyone could find in an ordinary telephone directory, did not demand any degree of confidentiality or discretion that would require them to be kept away from the inquisitive eyes of non–staff members. The woman smiled, thanked him for his offer of help, but did not accept, she couldn't stand idly by watching him work, she said. The minutes passed, the pages passed, it was Thursday already and still no sign of Tertuliano Máximo Afonso. António Claro was beginning to feel uneasy, to curse himself for having thought of coming here, to wonder what use the wretched letter would be to him if it did turn up, and he could find no answer to justify the awkwardness of the situation, and even the tiny satisfaction his ego had come looking for, like a greedy cat, was rapidly turning into embarrassment. The woman closed the book, I'm terribly sorry, but it isn't here, And I must apologize for giving you so much work and all for nothing, The fact that you were so keen to see the letter means that it can't have been nothing, said the woman generously, I was told there was a paragraph in the letter that might interest me, What paragraph, Oh, I'm not quite sure, but I think it was about the important contribution made by supporting actors to the success of films, or something like that. The woman started, as if, inside her, a memory had shaken her, and asked, Did you say it was about supporting actors, Yes, said António Claro, not wanting to believe that some remnant of hope could yet come from that quarter, But that letter was written by a woman, By a woman, repeated António Claro, feeling his head give a sudden lurch, Yes, by a woman, And what happened to her, to the letter I mean, The first person who read it thought it was pretty eccentric and immediately rushed off to show it to the former head of the department, who, in turn, sent it up to the admin department, And then, It was never sent back, it was either locked up in a safe or put through the shredder by the managing director's secretary, But why, why, Those are two very pertinent questions, probably because of that paragraph, probably because the management did not look kindly on the possibility of a petition going around, inside and outside the company, throughout the country, demanding equality and justice for supporting actors, there would be a revolution in the industry, and imagine what would happen if the demand was taken up by the lower orders, by the supporting players in society as a whole, You mentioned a former head of the department, why former, Because, thanks to his great foresight, he was immediately promoted, So the letter disappeared, vanished, murmured António Claro glumly, The original did, yes, but I kept a copy for my own use, a duplicate, You kept a copy, echoed António Claro, aware that the shudder that had just run through him had been caused not by the first word, copy, but by the sec-

242

ond, duplicate, It struck me as such an extraordinary idea that I decided to commit a minor infraction of staff regulations, And do you have that letter with you, No, I have it at home, Ah, at home, If you'd like a duplicate, I'd be more than happy to send you one, after all, the letter was intended for the actor Daniel Santa-Clara, whose legal representative you are, I really don't know how to thank you and let me just say again what a pleasure it's been to meet you and talk to you, Well, I have my moments, today you found me in a good mood, or perhaps it's because I felt as if I were a character in a book, What book, what character, Oh, it doesn't matter, let's get back to real life, and leave aside fantasies and fictions, tomorrow I'll make you a photocopy of the letter and post it to you at home, Look, I don't want to put you to any more trouble, I can always drop by, Absolutely not, imagine what people here would think if I was seen passing you a bit of paper, Would your reputation be at risk, asked António Claro, with just the hint of a mischievous smile, Worse than that, she said tartly, my job would be at risk, Forgive me, I must have seemed indiscreet, I didn't mean to hurt your feelings, No, I suppose not, you merely mistook the meaning of the words, which is a common-enough occurrence, that's the purpose of the filters that get woven into us over time and through continual listening, What filters are those, They act like voice-sieves, and any words, as they pass through, leave behind them a kind of sediment, and to find out what those words actually intended to communicate, you have to analyze the sediment carefully, It seems an awfully complicated process, On the contrary, the necessary procedures happen instantaneously, like on a computer, but they never get in each other's way, there's a strict order to be followed, from start to finish, it's all a matter of training, Or a natural gift, like perfect pitch,

You don't need quite that degree of accuracy, you just have to be capable of hearing the word, the acuteness lies elsewhere, but don't go thinking it's roses all the way, sometimes, and I'm speaking for myself here, I don't know how it is with other people, I get home and it feels as if my filters were all clogged up, it's just a shame that the showers we take for our outsides can't be used to clean up our insides too, You know I'm beginning to think that this sparrow isn't singing like a canary, but like a nightingale, Good heavens, there's an awful lot of sediment there, exclaimed the woman, Listen, I'd like to see you again, So I thought, my filter just told me so, Really, I'm serious, But not serious enough, Look, I don't even know your name, Why do you want to know, Don't get annoyed, it's normal for people to introduce themselves, When there's a reason, And isn't there, asked António Claro, To be perfectly honest, I can't see one, What if I come here again needing your help, That's simple enough, you just ask my boss to call the clerk who helped you this time, although you'll probably get my colleague, the one who's on holiday at the moment, So I won't be hearing from you again, No, but I'll keep my promise, you'll receive the letter from the person who asked for your address, And that's all, That's all, replied the woman. António Claro went to thank his former school friend, they chatted for a while, then he asked, What's the name of the clerk who helped me, Maria, why, Oh, no reason really, that doesn't tell me any more than I knew before, And what did you know before, Nothing.

THE ARITHMETIC WAS EASY ENOUGH TO DO. IF SOMEONE TELLS us that they wrote a letter and that letter subsequently turns up bearing the signature of another person, there are only two hypotheses to choose from, either the second person wrote the letter at the request of the first, or the first person, for reasons António Claro does not know, forged the name of the second person. And that's that. Whatever the truth may be, bearing in mind that the sender's address on the letter is not that of the first person but that of the second, to whom the reply from the production company had clearly been addressed, bearing in mind that all the steps taken as a result of knowing the letter's contents were taken by the first person and not a single step taken by the second, the conclusions to be drawn from this case are not just logical but transparent. Firstly, as is obvious, patent, and manifest, the two parties agreed between them to carry out this piece of epistolary mystification, secondly, for reasons that António Claro again does not know, the aim of the first person was to remain in the shadows until the last possible moment, as he had succeeded in doing. António Claro went over and over these very elementary deductions during the three days it took for the letter sent by the enigmatic Maria to reach him. The letter was accompanied by a card bearing the following handwritten words, but no signature, I hope this proves useful to you. This was precisely the question that António Claro was asking himself, And now what do I do. Nevertheless, it must be said that were we to apply the theory of filters and word-sieves to the current situation, we would notice the presence of lees, of a residue, a deposit or sediment, as Maria chose to describe it, the same Maria whom António Claro dared to call, although only he will know with what intentions, first, a canary and then a nightingale, anyway, now that we are trained in the analytical process, we would say that the above-mentioned sediment betrays the existence of a purpose, perhaps still undefined, diffuse, but which we would bet our boots would not have arisen if the letter received had been signed not by a woman but by a man. This means that if Tertuliano Máximo Afonso had, for example, a close male friend and had worked out this crafty trick with him, Daniel Santa-Clara would have simply torn up the letter because he would consider it an unimportant detail vis-à-vis the fundamental issue, that is, the complete identity that brought them together and, at this rate, will very probably drive them apart. Alas, the letter is signed by a woman, Maria da Paz is her name, and António Claro, who, in his professional life, has never been cast as the elegant seducer, or even as a lowlier class of cad, does his best to find some balancing compensations in real life, although not always with very auspicious results, as we have recently had occasion to verify in that episode with the assistant at the production company, we should perhaps point out that the reason we have made no previous reference to his amatory propensities is simply because they did not seem relevant to the events being recounted at the time. Since, however, human actions, generally speaking, are determined by a concurrence of impulses flowing from all the cardinal and collateral points of the instinctive being, we still are, along, of course, with a few rational factors that, against all the odds, we still manage to slip into the motivational web, and since, in these actions, the pure and the sordid are present in equal parts, and honesty counts as much as prevarication, we would not be using António Claro fairly if we refused to accept, however provisionally, the explanation he would doubtless offer us regarding the evident interest he is showing in the signatory of the letter, that is, his natural and very human curiosity to know what kind of relationship exists between Tertuliano Máximo Afonso, the letter's intellectual author, and, or so he thinks, its material author, this Maria da Paz. We have had many opportunities to observe that António Claro does not lack perspicacity or vision, but the truth is that not even the most subtle of investigators to have left their mark on the science of criminology would have ever imagined that, in this strange matter, and against all the evidence, especially the documentary evidence, the moral author and the material author were one and the same. Two obvious hypotheses cry out for consideration, in ascending order of gravity, either they are simply friends or they are simply lovers. António Claro inclines to the latter hypothesis, firstly, because it fits in with the sentimental plots to which he is a mere witness in the films he usually appears in, and secondly and consequently, because he finds himself then in familiar territory and with a prepared script. It is time we asked if Helena knows what is going on, if António Claro has bothered to tell her about his visit to the production company, about the search through the register and his conversation with the intelligent and aromatic Maria, if he showed her or is going to show her the letter signed by Maria da Paz, if, in short, given that she is his wife, he will share with her his dangerously fluctuating thoughts. The answer is no, three times no. The letter arrived yesterday morning, and António Claro's one concern was to find a place to put it where no one else would find it. There it is, pressed between the pages of a history of the cinema that has not caught Helena's interest since she very cursorily read it during the first few months of their marriage. Out of respect for the truth, we should say that, as yet, and despite the enormous amount of thought he has given to the matter, António Claro has still not produced a satisfactory plan of action deserving of the name. However, the privilege we enjoy of knowing everything that is going to happen up until the very last page of this story, apart from those things that might still need to be invented, allows us to say that tomorrow, the actor Daniel Santa-Clara will make a phone call to Maria da Paz's apartment, purely to find out if anyone is there, we are, don't forget, in high summer, the holiday period, but he will not say a word, not a single sound will issue from his lips, total silence, lest there should be any confusion, on the part of the person at the other end, between his voice and that of Tertuliano Máximo Afonso, for in that case, he would probably have no option but to pretend, to assume his identity, with, bearing in mind the current state of affairs, entirely unforeseeable consequences. However unexpected this may seem, in a few minutes' time, before Helena gets back from work, and, again, to find out if he is away, he will phone the history teacher's apartment, but this time he will not lack for words, António Claro has his speech already prepared, regardless of whether there is someone there to listen to him or whether he has to speak to the answering machine. This is what he will say, this is what he is saying, Hello, it's António Claro here, I don't suppose you were expecting a call from me, in fact, I'd be surprised if you were, I assume you're not at home, perhaps you're off enjoying a holiday in the country somewhere, it's only natural, it is, after all, the holiday season, anyway, whether you're there or not, I wanted to ask you a big favor, to phone me as soon as you get back, I genuinely think we have a lot more to say to each other, I believe we should meet, not at my house in the country, which is, frankly, too out-of-the-way, but somewhere else, somewhere discreet where we will be safe from prying eyes, which would do us no good at all, anyway, I hope you agree, the best time to call me is between ten in the morning and six o'clock in the evening, any day except Saturday and Sunday, but, please note, only until the end of next week. He did not add, Because from then on, Helena, that's my wife's name, I don't know if I've mentioned it before, will be at home on holiday, but even though I'm not shooting a film, we won't be going anywhere. That would be tantamount to admitting that she doesn't know what's going on, and where there is no trust, nonexistent in the present case, no sensible, well-balanced person would lay bare the secrets of his married life, especially in view of the gravity of the situation. António Claro, whose sharp wits have been shown to be in no way inferior to those of Tertuliano Máximo Afonso, realizes that the roles they have been playing up until now have been switched and that, from now on, he will be the one who has to disguise himself, and what had, at first sight, appeared to be a tardy and gratuitous provocation on the part of the history teacher, sending him, like a slap in the face, that false beard, did, it appears, have meaning and purpose, was born out of some presentiment. António Claro, not Tertuliano Máximo Afonso, will be the one who has to go in disguise to wherever their next meeting place will be. And just as Tertuliano

Máximo Afonso came to this street, wearing a false beard, in order to catch a glimpse of António Claro and his wife, so António Claro, complete with false beard, will go to the street where Maria da Paz lives to find out what kind of woman she is, and will follow her to the bank and occasionally even to within sight of where Tertuliano Máximo Afonso lives, thus he will be her shadow for however long is necessary and until the compelling force of what is written and what might be written disposes otherwise. After what has been said, it will come as no surprise that António Claro should go to the chest of drawers where he keeps the box containing the mustache that, in times past, adorned the face of Daniel Santa-Clara, a disguise clearly inadequate for the present situation, the same empty cigar box that for some days now has also been home to the false beard that António Claro is going to wear. Also in times past, there lived a king considered to be very wise and who, in a moment of easy philosophical inspiration, stated, one assumes with all the solemnity due to his position, that there was nothing new under the sun. We should never take these phrases too seriously, just in case we should still be saying them when everything around us has changed and the sun itself is not what it once was. The movements and gestures people make, on the other hand, have not changed very much, not just since the third king of Israel, but since that imme-morial day when a human face first saw itself in the smooth surface of a pond and thought, That's me. Now, here, where we are, where we have our existence, even after the passing of four or five million years, those primeval gestures continue to be monotonously repeated, oblivious to any changes in the sun and in the world illumined by that sun, if we need further proof that this is so we have only to watch as, before the smooth surface of his bathroom mirror, António Claro adjusts the beard that once belonged to Tertuliano Máximo Afonso with the same care, with the same concentration of mind, and perhaps with the same tremor of fear with which, not many weeks ago, Tertuliano Máximo Afonso, in another bathroom and before another mirror, had drawn António Claro's mustache on his own face. Less sure of themselves than their brutish common ancestor, they did not fall into the ingenuous temptation of saying, That's me, for fears have changed a lot since then and doubts have changed even more, now, here, instead of a confident affirmation, all that emerges from our mouth is the question, Who's that, and probably not even another four or five million years will be enough to provide an answer. António Claro took off the beard and put it back in the box, Helena will be home soon, tired from work, even more silent than usual, moving about the apartment as if it were not her home, as if the furniture were unfamiliar to her, as if the corners and edges of the furniture did not recognize her and, like zealous guard dogs, growled threateningly at her as she passed. A single word from her husband might perhaps change things, but we know that neither António Claro nor Daniel Santa-Clara will say it. Perhaps they don't want to, perhaps they can't, all fate's reasons are human, purely human, and anyone who, basing themselves on the lessons of the past, says otherwise, be it in prose or in verse, doesn't know what he or she is talking about, if you'll forgive such a bold opinion.

The following day, after Helena had gone out, António Claro phoned Maria da Paz's house. He did not feel particularly nervous or excited, silence would be his protective shield. The voice that answered was flat, with the hesitant fragility of someone recovering from some physical ailment, and yet although everything indicated that the voice belonged to a woman of a certain age, it did not sound as frail as that of an old woman, or, if you prefer euphemisms, an elderly lady. She did not say much, Hello, hello, who is it, say something, will you, hello, hello, honestly, how rude, a person can't even get any peace in her own home, and she hung up, but Daniel Santa-Clara, although he does not orbit the solar system of the really famous actors, has an excellent ear, for relationships in this case, and so it was easy for him to work out that the elderly woman, if she isn't the mother, is the grandmother, and if she isn't the grandmother, she's the aunt, excluding out of hand, because it bears no relation to actuality, that tired old literary cliché of the old-servant-who-never-got-married-out-of-love-for-her-master-and-mistress. Obviously, given his method of approach, he still doesn't know if there are any men at home, a father, a grandfather, an uncle, or a brother, but António Claro need not worry overmuch about such a possibility, since, in every respect, in sickness and in health, in life and in death, he will appear before Maria da Paz not as Daniel Santa-Clara, but as Tertuliano Máximo Afonso, who, while they may not fling wide the doors for him, either as friend or lover, must at least enjoy the advantages of a tacitly acknowledged relationship. Were we to ask António Claro what his preference would be, in accordance with the objectives he has in mind, as to the nature of the relationship between Tertuliano Máximo Afonso and Maria da Paz, whether they are lovers or friends, we have no doubt whatsoever as to his reply, that if the relationship were merely one of friendship, it would not hold half the attraction for him as it would if they were lovers. As we can see, the plan of action that António Claro has been working on has not only advanced greatly as regards the setting of objectives, it is also beginning to grow in strength as regards the motivation it previously lacked, although that strength, unless we have made a grave error of interpretation, seems to be based entirely on malevolent ideas of personal revenge that the situation, as we see it, neither promised nor in any way justified. True, Tertuliano Máximo Afonso did challenge Daniel Santa-Clara directly when, without a word, and that, perhaps, was the worst thing, he sent him the false beard, but with a little common sense, the matter could have ended there, António Claro could have shrugged and said to his wife, The man's a fool, if he thinks he can provoke me that easily, he's very much mistaken, throw it in the bin, will you, and if he's stupid enough to repeat this nonsense, then we'll call the police and put a stop to this whole story once and for all, whatever the consequences. Unfortunately, common sense does not always appear when it is needed, and its brief absences have often resulted in some major dramas and in some of the most terrifying of catastrophes. The proof that the universe was not as well-thought-out as it should have been lies in the fact that the Creator ordered the star that illumines us to be called the sun. Had the king of the stars borne the name Common Sense, imagine how enlightened the human spirit would be now, both by day and by night, because, as everyone knows, the light we call moonlight comes not from the moon but always and solely from the sun. It's worth considering that the reason so many theories about the origin of the universe have been created since the birth of speech and the word is that all of them, one by one, have failed miserably, with a regularity that augurs rather ill for the one that, with a few variations, is currently in vogue. Let us return, however, to António Claro. It is clear that he wishes, as soon as possible, to meet Maria da Paz, and that, for entirely wrongheaded reasons, he has become obsessed with revenge, and, as you will no doubt already have noticed, there is no power in heaven or on earth that will dissuade him from this. Obviously, he cannot go and stand outside the building where she lives and ask every woman who goes in or out, Are you Maria da Paz, nor could he entrust himself to the hands of chance and fortune and, for example, walk up and down her street once, twice, three times and, on the third occasion, address the first woman he saw, You look like Maria da Paz, you can't imagine what a pleasure it is finally to meet you, I'm a movie actor and my name's Daniel Santa-Clara, allow me to invite you to a coffee, it's just across the road, I'm sure we're going to have lots to talk about, ah, the beard, yes, I congratulate you on your perspicacity, on not being deceived, but I ask you, please, don't be alarmed, keep calm, when we can meet in some more private place, a place where I can remove the beard without danger, you will see before you a person you know well, intimately I believe, and whom I, without a flicker of envy, would congratulate were he here, our very own Tertuliano Máximo Afonso. The poor woman would be utterly overwhelmed by the prodigious transformation, which would, however, be quite inexplicable at this point in the narrative, for it is vital to keep in mind the fundamental, guiding idea that things should patiently await their moment and not push or reach over the shoulders of those who arrived first, shouting, I'm here, although we would not entirely reject the hypothesis that if, occasionally, we did let them through, certain potential evils might lose some of their virulence or vanish like smoke in the air, for the banal reason that they had missed their turn. This outpouring of thoughts and analyses, this benevolent scattering of reflections and their offshoots over which we have been lingering, should not make us lose sight of the prosaic reality that, deep down, what António Claro wants to know is if

Maria da Paz is worth it, if she is really worth all the trouble he is going to. If she was unattractive, as thin as a rail, or, on the contrary, suffering from an excess of fat, neither of which, we hasten to add, would constitute any great obstacle if love were playing a part, then, we would see Daniel Santa-Clara taking a rapid step backward, as must have happened so often in the past, during encounters based on friendships formed through correspondence, the ridiculous stratagems, the ingenuous means of identification, I'll be carrying a blue parasol in my right hand, I'll be wearing a white flower in my buttonhole, and, in the end, no parasol and no flower, perhaps one person waiting in vain at the arranged spot, perhaps neither, the flower thrown hastily into the gutter, the parasol hiding a face that preferred not to be seen. Daniel Santa-Clara, however, need not worry, Maria da Paz is young, pretty, elegant, with a nice figure and a good character, that last attribute, though, is irrelevant to the matter at hand, for, nowadays, the scales on which the fate of the parasol or the destiny of the flower were once decided are not particularly sensitive to considerations of this nature. Meanwhile, António Claro has an important problem to resolve if he does not want to spend hours and hours hanging about on the pavement outside Maria da Paz's building, waiting for her to appear, with fatal and dangerous consequences arising from the natural apprehensions of the neighbors, who would, in no time, be phoning the police to alert them to the suspicious presence of a bearded man who certainly wasn't there just to keep the building propped up. He must have recourse, therefore, to reason and to logic. It is likely that Maria da Paz works, that she has a regular job and leaves and returns at regular hours. Like Helena. But António Claro does not want to think about Helena, he tells himself that the two things have nothing to do with each other, that whatever happens with Maria da Paz will not put his marriage at risk, you could almost call it a whim, of the kind to which men are said to be so easily prone, if, in the present case, the right words were not vengeance, revenge, retaliation, retribution, redress, reprisal, rancor, vindictiveness, if not the very worst of them all, hatred. Good heavens, how ridiculous, where will it all end, cry those happy people who have never come face-to-face with a copy of themselves, who have never suffered the terrible affront of receiving in the post a false beard in a box without even a pleasant, good-humored note to soften the blow. What is, at this moment, going through António Claro's head will show to what extent, and contrary to the most elementary good sense, a mind dominated by base feelings can make its own conscience fall in with them, slyly forcing it to reconcile the worst actions with the best reasons and to use both to justify each other, in a kind of double game in which the same player will always win or lose. What António Claro has just thought, incredible though it may seem, is that taking Tertuliano Máximo Afonso's lover to bed under false pretenses would, as well as being a way of returning the slap in the face with a still more resounding one, be the most extreme way, now can you imagine anything more absurd, of avenging his wife Helena's wounded dignity. However hard we pleaded, António Claro would be unable to explain what extraordinary offenses these were that could, theoretically, be avenged only by a new and no less shocking offense. This has now become in him an idée fixe, and there is nothing to be done. It is something of an achievement that he is still capable of returning to his interrupted reasoning, when he recalled that Helena was similar to Maria da Paz in having work obligations, a regular job, and particular hours for leaving and returning. Instead of walking up and down the street in the hope of some highly unlikely chance encounter, what he should do is get there really early, stand somewhere inconspicuous, wait for Maria da Paz to come out, and then follow her to work. What could be easier, one might think, and yet how wrong one would be. The first problem is that he does not know if Maria da Paz, on leaving her building, will turn left or right, and therefore to what extent the position he chooses to keep watch from, as regards both the direction she chooses to take and the place where he will leave his car, will complicate or facilitate the task of following her, not forgetting, and here is the second and no less serious problem, the possibility that she may have her own car parked outside the door, which would not give him enough time to run back to his car and join the traffic without losing sight of her. What will probably happen is that he will fail completely on the first day, return on the second to fail in one respect but succeed in another, and then trust that the patron saint of detectives, impressed by his pertinacity, will take it upon himself to make the third day a perfect and definitive triumph in the art of following a trail. António Claro will still have one other problem to resolve, relatively insignificant, it is true, compared with the enormous difficulties already overcome, but which will have to be dealt with using a remarkable degree of tact and spontaneity. Apart from when he has to drag himself from between the sheets when obliged to do so by work, an early-morning shoot or one taking place outside the city, Daniel Santa-Clara, as you will have noticed, prefers to remain snug in his bed for one or two hours after Helena has left for the day. He will, therefore, have to come up with a good explanation for the unusual fact that he intends to get up at the crack of dawn, not on one day, but on two, possibly even three, when, as we know, he is currently resting professionally, waiting for the call for action on *The Trial of the Charming Thief*, in which he will play the part of a lawyer's assistant. Telling Helena that he has a meeting with the producers wouldn't be a bad idea if his investigations into Maria da Paz were concluded in one day, but, given the circumstances, the likelihood of this happening is remote to say the least. On the other hand, he does not necessarily need to carry out his inquiries on consecutive days, in fact, when he thinks about it, this could even prove inappropriate for the purpose he has in mind, since the appearance of a bearded man three days in a row on the street where Maria da Paz lives, quite apart from arousing the suspicion and alarm of the neighbors, as we said earlier, could provoke the anachronistic, and thus doubly traumatic, rebirth of childish nightmares just when we were convinced that the advent of television had once and for all erased from the imaginations of modern children the terrible threat that the bearded bogeyman represented to generation upon generation of innocent infants. Thinking along these lines, António Claro rapidly reached the conclusion that there was no sense in worrying about hypothetical second and third days before he even knew what the first might have to offer. He will therefore tell Helena that he has a meeting tomorrow with the producers, I have to be there by eight at the latest, That's awfully early, she will say, although without a great deal of interest, Yes, I know, but it has to be at eight because the director's leaving for the airport at noon, Fine, she said and went into the kitchen, closing the door behind her, to decide what to make for supper. She had more than enough time, but she wanted to be alone. She had said the other day that her bed was her castle, she could equally well have said that the kitchen was her fortress. Meanwhile, deft and silent as the charming thief, António Claro went and opened the drawer where he kept the box containing the false beard and mustache, removed the beard, and, silent and deft, hid it under one of the cushions on the big sofa in the living room, on the side where they hardly ever sit. So that it doesn't get too squashed, he thought.

It was a few minutes after eight o'clock the following morning when he parked the car almost opposite the door out of which he expected Maria da Paz to emerge, on the other side of the street. It seemed that the patron saint of detectives had been there all night, saving the place for him. Most of the shops are still closed, some of them, according to the notices fixed on the doors, for the purpose of staff holidays, there are not many people about, a queue of them, shorter rather than long, is waiting for the bus. António Claro soon realized that his laborious musings on how and where he should place himself in order to spy on Maria da Paz had been not only a waste of time, but also a useless waste of mental energy. Inside the car, reading the newspaper, is where he is least at risk of attracting attention, he'll just look like he's waiting for someone, which is true but can't be spoken out loud. A few people, mainly men, occasionally emerge from the building under surveillance, but none of the women correspond to the image that António Claro, without realizing it, had been forming in his mind with the help of a few female characters from films in which he has taken part. It was half past eight on the dot when the building door opened and a pretty, young woman, pleasing to look at from head to toe, came out, accompanied by an elderly lady. That's them, he thought. He put down his newspaper, turned on the engine, and waited, as restless as a horse in the starting gate before the pistol sounds. The two women continued slowly along on the right-hand side of the pavement, the younger giving her arm to the older, there is no doubt about it, they are mother and daughter and probably live alone. The old lady is the one who answered the phone yesterday, and by the way she's walking, she must have been ill, but the other one, I would bet anything you like that the other one is the famous Maria da Paz, and she's got a pretty good body, yes, sir, the history teacher has excellent taste. The two of them were moving off, and António Claro didn't know what to do. He could follow them and come back when they got into the car, but then he would risk losing them. What shall I do, shall I stay or go, where's she taking the old biddy, his rather nervous state is to blame for this somewhat discourteous expression, António Claro does not normally talk like that, it just came out. Ready for anything, he leaped out of the car and strode after the two women. When they were about thirty meters away, he slowed his pace and tried to match his speed to theirs. To avoid getting too close, he had to stop now and then and pretend he was looking in the shop windows. He was surprised to find that the slowness was beginning to irritate him, as if he saw in it an obstacle to future actions that, although not yet fully defined in his head, would, in any case, brook no impediment. The false beard was making him itch, the walk seemed endless, and he hadn't even gone very far, about three hundred meters in all, the next corner brought the end of the journey, Maria da Paz helps her mother up the steps of the church, kisses her good-bye, and is now walking back the way she came, with the nimble step of certain women who walk as if they were dancing. António Claro crossed over to the other side of the street and paused farther on outside a shop in whose window, shortly afterward, the slender figure of Maria da Paz would pass. Alertness is all now, a moment of indecision could ruin everything, if she gets into one of these cars and he doesn't manage to reach his quickly enough, then he can kiss all his carefully laid plans good-bye until the next time. What António Claro does not know is that Maria da Paz doesn't own a car, she is calmly going to wait for the bus that will drop her close to the bank where she works, so the detectives' handbook, completely up-to-date as regards the latest technology, had forgotten that, of the five million people in this city, some of them would have lagged behind in acquiring their own means of transport. The queue had not grown much, Maria da Paz joined it, and António Claro, so as not to stand too close, allowed three people to go ahead of him, the false beard covers his face but not his eyes, his nose, his eyebrows, head, hair, or ears. Someone educated in the esoteric doctrines would choose to add the soul to the list of things that a beard does not cover, but on this point we will remain silent, we would not want to add fuel to a debate that has been going on pretty much since time began and which will go on for a long time yet. The bus arrived, Maria da Paz managed to find a free seat, António Claro will stand in the aisle, at the back. It's worked out well, he thought, this way we can travel together.

WHAT TERTULIANO MÁXIMO AFONSO TOLD HIS MOTHER
was that he had met someone, a man, who was so like him
that anybody who did not know them intimately would be
bound to confuse them, that he had had a meeting with this
man and regretted having done so, because it was one thing
to see yourself repeated, with a few tiny differences, in one
or two genuine twin brothers, since it's all in the family, but
to come face to face with a stranger you've never seen before
and for a moment to find yourself doubting who's one and
who's the other, I'm sure, at least at first sight, that even you
wouldn't be able to tell which of the two was your son, and
if you got it right, it would be pure chance, Even if they
brought me ten men identical to you, all dressed the same,
and you were stuck in the middle of them, I would point
straight to my son, maternal instinct never fails, There's nothing in the world that can properly be called maternal instinct,
I mean, say we'd been separated when I was born and didn't
meet until twenty years later, are you sure you'd still be able
to recognize me, Well, I don't know about recognize, because
the little wrinkled face of a newborn baby is not the same as
the face of a young man of twenty, but I bet you anything

you like that something inside me would make me look at you twice, And the third time, perhaps, you might look the other way, Yes, possibly, but from that moment on, I might feel a kind of ache in my heart, And what about me, would I look at you twice, asked Tertuliano Máximo Afonso, Probably not, said his mother, but that's because children are all such ungrateful creatures. They both laughed, and she asked, And is this why you've been so worried, Yes, it was such a shock, it's hard to believe that anything like it can ever have happened before, even genetics itself, I imagine, would deny it, to start with I had nightmares about it, it was like an obsession, And how are things now, Fortunately, common sense stepped in to lend a hand and made us realize that, having lived this long in ignorance of each other's existence, that was all the more reason to remain apart now that we had met, you see we couldn't even bear to be together, we could never be friends, Enemies more like, There was a point when I thought that might happen, but the days passed, things returned to normal, and now, all that's left is like the vague recollection of a bad dream that time will gradually erase from my memory, Let's hope so. Tomarctus was lying at Dona Carolina's feet, his neck outstretched so that his head was resting on his folded paws, as if he were asleep. Tertuliano Máximo Afonso looked at him for a few moments and said, I wonder what the dog would do if he was confronted by me and by that man, which of us he would see as his master, He'd know you by your smell, That's assuming we don't both smell the same, and I can't be sure of that, There must be some differences, Possibly, People's faces might look very similar, but not their bodies, I mean, I don't suppose you both stood naked in front of a mirror, comparing everything, down to your toenails, No, of course not, Mama, Tertuliano Máximo Afonso said quickly, and it wasn't really a lie, because he and António Claro hadn't actually stood in front of a mirror together. The dog opened his eyes, closed them, then opened them again, he must have thought it was time he got up and went out into the yard to see if the geraniums and the rosemary had grown since last he looked. He stretched, first his front legs and then his back legs, extending his spine as much as he could, then he walked over to the door. Where are you off to, Tomarctus, asked the master who only appeared from time to time. The dog paused on the threshold, turned his head in expectation of some intelligible order, and when this was not forthcoming, went out. And what about Maria da Paz, have you told her what's been going on, asked Dona Carolina, No, I didn't want to burden her with worries that even I have found hard to bear, Well, I can understand that, but I would equally well have understood if you had told her, It seemed best not to, And will you tell her now, now that it's all over, It's not worth it, one day when she could see how worried I was, I did promise to tell her what was going on, I said I couldn't tell her then but that one day I would, And now it looks like that day will never come, It's best to leave things as they are, In some situations, the worst thing you can do is leave things as they are, it just makes them stronger, It can also serve to let them rest and make them leave us in peace, If you cared about Maria da Paz, you'd tell her, But I do care about her, Not enough, though, if you sleep in the same bed as a woman who loves you but you're not open with her, what business have you to be there, You defend her as if you knew her, Even though I've never seen her, I do know her, You only know what I've told you, and that can't be much, The two letters in which you mentioned her, a few remarks you've made over the phone, that's all I needed, To know that she's the right woman for me, Well, I could have put it like that if I could also say that you were the right man for her, And you don't think I was, or that I am, Possibly not, The best solution, then, the simplest, would be to end the relationship, You said it, I didn't, Let's be logical, Mama, if she's right for me but I'm not right for her, why would you be so keen for us to get married, So that she's still there when you wake up, But I'm not asleep, I'm not a sleepwalker, I have my life, my work, There's a part of you that has been asleep ever since you were born, and my fear is that one day you'll be in for a nasty awakening, You've got the makings of a Cassandra, Mama, What's that, The question isn't what, but who, Teach me then because, as I understand it, teaching someone who doesn't know something is an act of charity, All right then, Cassandra was the daughter of Priam, the king of Troy, and when the Greeks placed a wooden horse outside the gates of the city, she began crying out that the city would be destroyed if the horse was brought inside, it's explained in detail in Homer's *Iliad*, the *Iliad*'s a poem, Yes, I've heard of it, but what happened next, The Trojans thought she was mad and ignored her prophecies, And then, The city was attacked, looted, and reduced to ashes, So this Cassandra woman was right, History has taught me that Cassandra is always right, And you said I had the makings of a Cassandra, Yes, I did and I'll say it again, as lovingly as a son who has a witch for a mother can, So you're one of those unbelieving Trojans whose fault it was that Troy was burned, In this case, there is no Troy to be burned, How many Troys with other names and in other places were burned after that, Too many to count, You don't want to be another one, do you, There's no wooden horse standing outside the door of my apartment, But if ever there is one, heed the voice of this old Cassandra, and don't let it in, All right,

I'll be sure to listen for any neighing, The only thing I ask is that you don't meet that man again, will you promise, Yes, I promise. Tomarctus the dog felt it was time to rejoin them, he had been sniffing around the rosemary and the geraniums in the yard, but these had not been his last port of call. He had gone into Tertuliano Máximo Afonso's bedroom, seen the open suitcase on the bed, and had been a dog for long enough to know what this meant, which is why he did not lie down at the feet of his mistress, who never goes away, but at the feet of this other person who is about to leave.

After all the doubts as to the most prudent way to tell his mother about the thorny problem of his absolute twin, or to use a more popular and somewhat vulgar expression, his spitting image, Tertuliano Máximo Afonso was now reasonably convinced that he had managed to get around the difficulty without leaving behind him too many anxieties. He had been unable to prevent the subject of Maria da Paz from resurfacing, but he was surprised when he remembered something that had happened during the conversation, at the point where he had said that it would be best to finish the relationship once and for all, for, precisely at that moment, when he had uttered that apparently irremissible sentence, he had felt a kind of inner lassitude, a half-conscious longing for abdication, as if a voice in his head were trying to make him see that his obstinacy was nothing but the last redoubt behind which he was still struggling with a repressed desire to raise the white flag of unconditional surrender. If that's true, he thought, I'm under a strict obligation to reflect seriously on the matter, to analyze this fear and indecision that is probably just left over from my first marriage, and to resolve once and for all, for my own sake, what it means to care about a person so much that you want to live with her, because the truth is I didn't even think about it when I got married, and the same truth requires me to confess that, deep down, what frightens me is the possibility of failing again. These praiseworthy resolutions occupied Tertuliano Máximo Afonso's journey, alternating with fleeting images of António Claro, whom his thoughts, oddly enough, refused to represent as being as identical as he actually was, as if, against all the evidence of the facts, they were refusing to accept his existence. He also remembered fragments of the conversations he had had with him, especially the conversation in the house in the country, but with a strange sense of distance and indifference, as if none of it had anything to do with him, as if it were a story he had read once in a book of which all that remained were a few loose pages. He had promised his mother he would never meet António Claro again and so it would be, no one would be able to accuse him tomorrow of having taken a single step in that direction. His life is going to change. He will phone Maria da Paz as soon as he gets home. I should have called her while I was away, an unforgivable lack of consideration on my part, even if only to find out how her mother was, that was the very least I could have done, especially when she might well be about to become my mother-in-law. Tertuliano Máximo Afonso smiled at a prospect that, only twenty-four hours before, would have set his nerves jangling, the holiday has clearly been good for mind and body, it has clarified his ideas, he's a new man. He arrived in the late afternoon, parked the car outside the door of the apartment building, and then, nimble, lithe, and in the best of moods, as if he had not just driven more than four hundred kilometers nonstop, he walked up the stairs as lightly as an adolescent, not even noticing the weight of his suitcase, which, as is only natural, was heavier returning than it had been going, and he very nearly danced into his apartment. In accordance with the traditional conventions of the literary genre known in Portuguese as the *romance*, or novel, and which will continue to be called thus until someone comes up with a term more in keeping with its current configuration, this cheery description, organized as a simple sequence of narrative events in which, quite deliberately, not a single negative note was struck, would be cunningly placed there in preparation for a complete contrast, which, depending on the writer's intentions, could be dramatic, brutal, or terrifying, for example, a murder victim lying on the floor in a pool of blood, a convention of souls from the next world, a swarm of furious drones in heat who mistake the history teacher for the queen bee, or, worse still, all of this combined into a single nightmare, for, as has been demonstrated ad nauseam, the imagination of the Western novelist knows no limits, or, rather, it hasn't since the days of the aforementioned Homer, who, when one thinks about it, was the very first novelist. Tertuliano Máximo Afonso's apartment opened its arms to him like a second mother, and with the voice of the air it murmured, Come, my son, here I am waiting for you, I am your castle and your fortress, no power can prevail over me, because I am yours even when you are absent, and even if I lay in ruins, I would still be the place that once was yours. Tertuliano Máximo Afonso put his suitcase down on the floor and turned on the overhead light. The living room was tidy, there wasn't a speck of dust on the furniture, it is a great and solemn truth that men, even those who live alone, never manage to separate themselves entirely from women, and we are not thinking now of Maria da Paz, who, for her own personal and dubious reasons would, despite everything, agree, but the upstairs neighbor, who spent all morning yesterday here cleaning, with as much care and attention as if the apartment were hers, or with more care, probably. The light on the answering machine is blinking. Tertuliano Máximo Afonso sits down to listen. The first call to leap out at him was from the headmaster, hoping that he was enjoying the holidays and wanting to know how the proposal for the ministry was getting on, Not, of course, that this should in any way affect your legitimate right to a rest after such a hard school year, the second brought him the slow, paternal voice of the mathematics teacher, nothing important, just to ask how his depression was faring and suggesting that a long, leisurely trip around the country, in good company, would perhaps be the best therapy for what ailed him, the third call was the one that António Claro had left the other day, the one that began, Hello, it's António Claro here, I don't suppose you were expecting a call from me, it was enough for his voice to ring out around that previously tranquil living room for it to become clear that the traditional conventions of the novel we mentioned above are not, after all, merely a hackneyed solution used by unimaginative narrators, but a literary resultant of the great cosmic equilibrium, because the universe, which, ever since it began, has been a system entirely lacking any form of organizing intelligence, has, nevertheless, had more than enough time to learn through its own infinitely multiplying experiences, and, as is evident from the endless spectacle of life, has produced an infallible compensatory mechanism that will require only a little more time to prove that any slight delay in the functioning of its gears has not the slightest impact on what really matters, for it makes no odds whether one has to wait a minute or an hour, a year or a century. Let us remember the excellent mood in which Tertuliano Máximo Afonso arrived home, let us remember, again, that in accordance with the traditional conventions of the novel, backed up by the clear existence of that universal compensatory mechanism to which we have just made such well-founded reference, he should have come face-to-face with something that would simultaneously destroy his happiness and plunge him into the depths of despair, pain, fear, of everything that we know one can meet when turning a corner or putting a key in a door. The monstrous terrors we described earlier were mere examples, it could have been those terrors or it could have been something far worse, and yet it was none of them, the apartment opened its maternal arms to the owner, said a few pleasing words, of the kind all houses are capable of saying, but which, mostly, their inhabitants do not know how to hear, in short, let us waste no more words, it seemed that nothing could spoil Tertuliano Máximo Afonso's happy return home. Pure illusion, pure confusion, pure fantasy. The wheels of the cosmic machinery had been transported into the electronic workings of the answering machine, waiting for a finger to come and press the button that would open the door of the cage of the last and most terrible of monsters, not the bloody corpse on the floor, not the incorporeal convention of ghosts, not the buzzing, libidinous cloud of drones, but the studied, persuasive voice of António Claro, his urgent entreaties, please, can we meet again, please, we have lots of things to say to each other, when we, here, on this side, are witnesses to the fact that, only yesterday, at this very hour, Tertuliano Máximo Afonso was promising his mother never to have anything to do with the man, either by meeting him in person or by phoning him to tell him that what's done is done and asking him, please, to leave him in peace and quiet. We energetically applauded that decision, but let us for a moment, and to do so we have only to put ourselves in his shoes, let us feel compassion for the nervous state in which the phone message has left poor Tertuliano Máximo Afonso, his forehead once more bathed in sweat, his hands again shaking, and the entirely new feeling that the roof is about to fall in on him at any moment. The light on the answering machine is still blinking, a sign that there are still one or two more messages inside. Reeling from the shock of hearing António Claro's message, Tertuliano Máximo Afonso had stopped the tape and now trembles to know what other messages there might be, possibly that same voice, scornfully taking his agreement as read, arranging the day, hour, and place of another meeting. He got up from the chair, and from the dejected state into which he had fallen, he went into the bedroom to get some fresh clothes but then changed his mind, what he most needs is a cold shower that will shake him up and reinvigorate him, that will wash away down the drain the black clouds hanging over his head and so dimming his reason that it has not even occurred to him until now that the next message, or at least one of them, might be from Maria da Paz. The idea has just now occurred to him, and it was as if a long-delayed blessing had just descended from the shower, as if another purifying shower, not the one enjoyed by those three naked women on the balcony, but the one enjoyed by this man, shut up alone in the precarious safety of his apartment, were, with the flow of water and soap, compassionately freeing his body from grime and his soul from fear. He thought about Maria da Paz with a kind of nostalgic serenity, as a ship might think of its last port of call before it set out on its voyage around the world. Washed and dried, refreshed and dressed in clean clothes, he returned to the living room to hear the remaining messages. He began by erasing those left by the headmaster and the mathematics teacher, which were not worth preserving, then, frowning, he listened again to António Claro's, which he also removed with a sharp tap on the appropriate button, and, finally, he settled down to listen to what might follow. The fourth call was made by someone who chose not to speak, it lasted an eternity of thirty seconds, but from the other end came not a whisper, no music played in the background, there was not even the slightest inadvertent exhalation, far less any deliberate, heavy breathing, as deployed in the cinema to raise audience anxiety levels. Don't tell me it's that same guy again, thought Tertuliano Máximo Afonso angrily, while he waited for the person to hang up. It wasn't him, it couldn't be, anyone who had just left such a prolix message would clearly not make another, totally silent call. The fifth and final message was from Maria da Paz, It's me, she said, as if there were no other person in the world who could say, It's me, knowing they would be recognized, I assume you'll be coming home about now, I hope you've had a good rest, I did think you might phone me from your mother's house, but I should have known better than to expect such things from you, anyway, it doesn't matter, I just wanted to leave you a few friendly words of welcome, give me a call when you feel like it, whenever you want to, but not because you feel obliged to, that would be bad for you and for me, sometimes, I imagine how wonderful it would be if you were to phone me just because you felt like it, like someone who suddenly feels thirsty and goes and drinks a glass of water, but I know that would be asking too much of you, never pretend a thirst you don't feel, sorry, I didn't mean to say all this, I just wanted to say that I hoped you'd got home safely and were in good health, oh, and while we're on the subject, my mother is much better, she's started going to Mass again and does her own shopping, in a few days, she should be as good as new, I send you a kiss, and another, and another. Tertuliano Máximo Afonso rewound the tape and replayed the message, at first, with the smug smile of someone listening to praise and flattery which he appears to feel perfectly confident that he deserves, gradually, though, his face grew serious, then thoughtful, then worried, he had suddenly remembered what his mother had said, I just hope she's there when you wake up, and these words are echoing around in his mind now like the last warning of a Cassandra grown weary of being ignored. He looked at his watch, Maria da Paz should be back from the bank. He gave her another fifteen minutes and then rang. Hello, she said, It's me, he said, At last, Yes, I got back less than an hour ago, just time enough to have a shower and to be sure that I'd catch you at home, You heard the message I left you, Yes, Oh, dear, because I have the feeling I said things I shouldn't have said, For example, Well, I can't remember exactly what, but it was as if I were asking you for the nth time just to notice me, and however much I swear it won't happen again, I always end up saying the same humiliating things, Don't use that word, it's really not fair on you or even on me, Call it what you like, but I see clearly now that this situation can't go on, otherwise I'll end up losing the little self-respect I still have, It will go on, What, are you telling me that our misunderstandings will continue as they have until now, that there'll be no end to my pathetic conversations with a wall that doesn't even give back an echo, No, I'm telling you I love you, Look, I've heard you say those words before, especially in bed, before, during, but never afterward, But it's true, I do love you, Please, please, don't torment me anymore, Listen, All right, I'm listening, all I've ever wanted is to listen to you, Our life is going to change, I don't believe you, Believe me, you have to, And you take care what you say to me, don't give me hopes today that you can't or won't want to fulfill tomorrow, Neither of us knows what the future will bring, that's why I'm asking you now, on this particular day, to give me your trust, And why come to me today asking me for something you have already, Because I want to live with you, I want us to live together, It can't be true what I've just heard, I must be dreaming, Well, I'm quite happy to say it again if you want me to, On condition that you use exactly the same words, Because I want to live with you, I want us to live together, This is just not possible, people don't change from one hour to the next, what's been going on in that head and heart of yours for you to be asking me to come and live with you, when up until now your one concern has been to make it absolutely clear that nothing could be further from your thoughts and that I shouldn't get my hopes up, People can change from one hour to the next but still be the same person, So you really do want us to live together, Yes, And you love Maria da Paz enough to want to live with her, Yes, Tell me again, Yes, yes, yes, That's enough, you're making me breathless, I might explode, Be careful, please, I want you in one piece, Do you mind if I tell my mother, she's spent her whole life waiting for this happy moment, Of course I don't mind, although she's not exactly crazy about me, The poor thing had her reasons, you kept stalling, you wouldn't make a decision, she wanted her daughter to be happy, and I didn't show much evidence of that, mothers are all the same, Do you want to know what my mother said yesterday when we were talking about you, What, She said I just hope she's still there when you wake up, Presumably those were the words you needed to hear, They were, You woke up and I was still here, I don't know for how much longer, but I was, Tell your mother she can sleep easy from now on, But I won't be able to sleep a wink, When can we see each other, Tomorrow, as soon as I leave work, I'll take a taxi and come straight there, You will hurry, Yes, right into your arms. Tertuliano Máximo Afonso put down the phone, closed his eyes, and heard Maria da Paz laughing and shouting, Mama, Mama, then saw the two women embracing and instead of shouts there were murmurs, instead of laughter, tears, sometimes we ask ourselves why happiness took so long to arrive, why it didn't come sooner, but appears suddenly, as now, when we've given up hope of it ever arriving, it's likely then that we won't know what to do, and rather than it being a question of choosing between laughter and tears, we will be filled by a secret anxiety to which we might not know how to respond at all. As if returning to forgotten habits, Tertuliano Máximo Afonso went into the kitchen to see if he could find something to eat. The eternal cans, he thought. Stuck to the fridge was a note that said in large letters, in red so that they wouldn't be missed, THERE'S SOUP IN THE FRIDGE, it was from his upstairs neighbor, bless her, for once the cans could wait. Exhausted by the journey, worn out by emotion, Tertuliano Máximo Afonso went to bed before eleven o'clock. He tried to read a page about Mesopotamian civilizations, but twice the book fell from his hands, in the end, he turned out the light and settled down to sleep. He was just drifting slowly off when Maria da Paz came and whispered in his ear, How wonderful it would be if you were to phone me just because you felt like it. She would probably have said the rest of the sentence too, but he had already got out of bed, pulled on his dressing gown over his pajamas, and was dialing her number. Maria da Paz asked, Is that you, and he replied, Yes, it's me, I was thirsty and I've come to ask for a glass of water.

CONTRARY TO WHAT MOST PEOPLE THINK, MAKING A DECISION is one of the easiest decisions in the world, as is more than proved by the fact that we make decision upon decision throughout the day, there, however, we run straight into the heart of the matter, for these decisions always come to us afterward with their particular little problems or, to make ourselves quite clear, with their rough edges needing to be smoothed, the first of these problems being our capacity for sticking to a decision and the second our willingness to follow it through. Not that either one or the other is lacking in Tertuliano Máximo Afonso as regards his relationship with Maria da Paz, we were witnesses to the fact that, in recent hours, this has undergone a huge qualitative change, as people say nowadays. He has decided to live with her and is absolutely sure about that, and if this decision has not yet taken concrete shape, or been actioned, which is another thing people say nowadays, it is because the shift from word to action also has its difficulties, its rough edges, it is vital, for example, for the spirit to summon up sufficient strength to push the indolent body into fulfilling its duty, not to mention the prosaic matter of logistics, which cannot be resolved from one moment to the next, for example, who should live in whose apartment, if Maria da Paz should move into her beloved's modest home or if Tertuliano Máximo Afonso should move into his beloved's more ample abode. Cuddled up on the sofa or lying in bed, the engaged couple's latest thinking on the subject, despite the natural resistance each one feels when it comes to abandoning the domestic shell to which they are accustomed, has led them to opt for the second alternative, given that there would be plenty of space in Maria da Paz's apartment for Tertuliano Máximo Afonso's books, but not enough space in Tertuliano Máximo Afonso's apartment for Maria da Paz's mother. On this front, things could not be going better. The trouble is that while Tertuliano Máximo Afonso, after pondering all the advantages and dangers, did finally tell his mother about the extraordinary case of the duplicate men, albeit smoothing some of the rougher, more jagged edges, there is no sign of his keeping the promise he made to Maria da Paz when, having admitted that he had lied to her about his reasons for writing the letter to the production company, he had postponed revealing to her the information that would make his half confession full, sincere, and conclusive. He did not mention it, and she did not ask, and the few words that would open that final door, Do you remember, my love, when I lied to you, Do you remember, my love, when you lied to me, could not be spoken, and had this man or this woman been given ample time to bring the whole painful business to a close, they would probably both have justified their silence by saying that they did not wish to spoil the happiness of these hours with a tale of cruelty and genetic perversity. It will not be long before we discover the tragic consequences of leaving unexcavated a second-world-war bomb in the belief that it was too old ever to explode. Cassandra was right, the Greeks will burn Troy.

For two days now, determined to finish once and for all the proposal that the headmaster had asked him to write for the ministry of education, Tertuliano Máximo Afonso has barely looked up from his desk. Although no date has yet been set for his move to Maria da Paz's apartment, he wants to be free of the task as soon as possible so that there are no complications when he moves to his new home, he will have quite enough to do, what with sifting through papers and imposing order on his many books. So as not to distract him, Maria da Paz has not phoned him, and he prefers it like that, in a way it is as if he were saying good-bye to his previous life, to the solitude, peace, and privacy of his apartment, which, oddly enough, the noise of the typewriter does not disturb. He had lunch at his usual restaurant and came straight back, another few days and he should finish, all he will have to do then is correct it and type it out again, yes, retype the whole thing, one thing is sure, sooner rather than later, he will have to do as most of his colleagues have already done and buy a computer and a printer, it's embarrassing to be still digging with a spade when the very latest in plows and plowshares are the norm. Maria da Paz will initiate him into the mysteries of computers, she has studied the subject and understands them, in the bank where she works, every desk has a computer on it, it isn't like it used to be in the old-fashioned registry offices. The doorbell rang. Who can it be at this hour, he wondered, annoyed at the interruption, it isn't his upstairs neighbor's day to come in and clean, the postman leaves any mail in the box downstairs, and only a few days ago, the men from the water, gas, and electric companies called to read their respective meters, perhaps it's one of those young men trying to sell him an encyclopedia that describes the habits of the monkfish. The doorbell rang again. Tertuliano Máximo Afonso opened the door, before him stood a bearded man, and this man said, It's me, although I may not look like me, What do you want, asked Tertuliano Máximo Afonso in a low, tense voice, I just want to talk to you, replied António Claro, I asked you to phone me when you got back from holiday and you didn't, Anything we had to say to one another has already been said, Possibly, but I still have something to say to you, Sorry, I don't understand, That's only natural, but you can't expect me to say it here on the landing, outside your front door, with the risk that the neighbors might hear, Whatever it is, I'm not interested, On the contrary, I think you'll be very interested indeed, it's about your lady friend, Maria da Paz is her name I believe, What's happened, Nothing as yet, but that's precisely what we have to talk about, If nothing has happened, then there's nothing to be said, Nothing's happened yet, I said. Tertuliano Máximo Afonso opened the door wider and stood to one side, Come in, he said. António Claro entered the apartment and, since the other man seemed reluctant to move from where he was standing, asked, Aren't you going to offer me a chair, I think we would talk better sitting down. Tertuliano Máximo Afonso looked distinctly irritated and, without a word, went into the living room that also served as his study. António Claro followed, looked around as if choosing the best place, and decided on the armchair, then, as he carefully removed the false beard, said, I suppose this is where you were sitting when you saw me for the first time. Tertuliano Máximo Afonso did not reply. He remained standing, his stiff posture a clear protest, Say what you have to say and then get out of my sight, but António

Claro was in no hurry, If you don't sit down, he said, I'll have to stand up and I'd really rather not. He looked serenely about himself, taking in the books, the engravings on the walls, the typewriter, the scattered papers on the desk, the phone, then he said, I see you were working, I've obviously chosen a bad moment to come and talk to you, but, given the urgency of the matter that brings me here, I had no option, And what was it that brought you here uninvited, As I said at the front door, it's about your lady friend, What have you got to do with Maria da Paz, More than you might imagine, but before I explain how, why, and to what extent, let me show you this. From his inside jacket pocket he took a piece of paper folded in four, which he unfolded and offered to Tertuliano Máximo Afonso, holding it with the very tips of his fingers as if about to drop it, I would urge you to take this letter and read it, he said, unless you want to force me to be rude and throw it on the floor, besides, it won't be new to you, you must surely remember mentioning it to me when we met at my house in the country, the only difference was that, at the time, you said that you yourself had written it, when, in fact, the signature is that of your friend. Tertuliano Máximo Afonso glanced at the piece of paper and returned it, How did you get this, he asked, sitting down, It took quite a bit of work, but it was worth it, replied António Claro, adding, In every sense, Why, Well, I have to admit that, initially, I was prompted to consult the production company's filing system by a rather base emotion, namely, a little touch of vanity, narcissism I think it's called, in short, I wanted to see what you had written about supporting actors in a letter of which I was the subject, But that was just a pretext, a way of finding out your real name, that's all, And you succeeded, It would have been better if they had never replied, Too late, my friend, too late, you've opened Pandora's box and now you have to live with the consequences, you have no alternative, There are no consequences, the matter is dead and buried, That's what you think, What do you mean, You're forgetting your friend's signature, Oh, I can explain that, How, It just seemed to me that it would be best if I remained out of sight, Now it's my turn to ask you what you mean, Just that I wanted to remain in the shadows until the last moment, and then make a surprise appearance, You certainly did that, Helena hasn't been the same since, it really shook her up, knowing that there's another man in the city exactly like her husband has left her nerves in shreds, although now, with the help of tranquilizers, she's feeling a little better, but only a little, Look, I'm sorry, I didn't mean to upset her, You should have foreseen that, all you had to do was put yourself in my place, But I didn't know you were married, Even so, imagine, just as an example, that I was to leave here and go and tell your friend Maria da Paz that you, Tertuliano Máximo Afonso, and I, António Claro, are alike, exactly alike, even down to the size of our penises, think of the shock to the poor woman, Don't you dare, Oh, don't worry, I haven't told her and I won't either. Tertuliano Máximo Afonso leaped to his feet, What does that mean, I haven't told her and I won't either, what do those words mean, That's a futile question, a rhetorical question, a question intended to gain time or because you don't know what else to say, Just cut the crap and answer my question, You can keep your violent tendencies for later, but just for your own good, I should tell you that I know enough karate to be able to knock you down in five seconds, admittedly, I've rather neglected my training lately, but I'm more than a match for someone like you, just because we're identical and have the same-size penis doesn't mean we're equal in strength, Get out of here right now, or

I'll call the police, Why not call the television, the photographers, the press, in a matter of minutes we'll be a worldwide sensation, Let me just remind you that if this got out, your career would be ruined, said Tertuliano Máximo Afonso in warning tones, Possibly, but the career of a supporting actor is of no importance to anyone but himself, That's enough of a reason for putting a stop to this right now, just go away, forget what happened, and I'll try and do the same, All right, but this operation, let's call it Operation Oblivion, will only start in twenty-four hours' time, Why's that, The name of the reason is Maria da Paz, the same Maria da Paz you got so worked up about just now and whom you seem to want to sweep under the carpet to stop her name from being mentioned again, Look, Maria da Paz has nothing to do with all this, So much so that I would bet anything you like she doesn't even know of my existence, How can you be sure, Well, I can't, it's a supposition, but you're not denying it, It seemed best, I didn't want the same thing to happen to her as happened to your wife, Oh, you're all heart, well, it's in your hands to prevent that from happening, Sorry, I don't understand, Let's stop beating about the bush, shall we, you asked me a question and since then you've been going around and around in order not to hear the answer I gave you, Go away, Believe me, I have no intention of staying, Go away now, at once, Fine, I'll go and present myself to your lady friend in the flesh and tell her what you didn't tell her either because you lacked the courage or for some other reason known only to you, If I had a gun here, I'd kill you, Maybe you would, but this isn't the cinema, my friend, in life, things are much simpler, even when it comes to murderers and murder victims, Just say what you've got to say, will you, have you spoken to her, tell me, Yes, I have, on the phone, And what did you say, Oh, I invited her to go for a drive with me today to look at a house in the country that's for rent, Your house in the country, Exactly, my house in the country, but don't worry, the person who talked to your friend Maria da Paz wasn't António Claro but Tertuliano Máximo Afonso, You're mad, what diabolical plot is this, what do you want, Do you really want me to tell you, Yes, I demand that you do, All right, I intend spending the night with her, that's all. Tertuliano Máximo Afonso advanced on António Claro, his fists clenched, but he tripped over the coffee table between them and would have fallen if the other man had not caught him at the last moment. He flailed and struggled, but António Claro nimbly immobilized him with an armlock, Get this into your head before you get hurt, he said, you're no match for me. He pushed him onto the sofa and sat down again. Tertuliano Máximo Afonso eyed him resentfully, at the same time rubbing his sore arm. I didn't mean to hurt you, said António Claro, but it was the only way to avoid a repetition of that ridiculous old cliché, two men fighting over a woman, Look, Maria da Paz and I are going to be married, Tertuliano Máximo Afonso said, as if this were an argument of irrefutable authority, That doesn't surprise me, when I spoke to her, I got the impression that you were really serious about each other, in fact, I had to use all my experience as an actor to hit just the right tone, but I can assure you that at no point did she doubt she was talking to you, and I see now why she was so excited about my invitation to go and look at the house, she was already imagining herself living there, Her mother's been ill and I doubt very much she would leave her on her own, Yes, she mentioned that, but it didn't take me long to persuade her, after all, a night passes quickly enough. Tertuliano Máximo Afonso fidgeted about on the sofa, furious with himself for apparently having admitted in so many words that António Claro might actually carry out his intentions. Why are you doing this, he asked, realizing, again too late, that he had just taken another step along the road to resignation, It's hard to explain really, but I'll try, replied António Claro, perhaps it's revenge for the disruption your appearance has caused in my married life and which you can't even begin to imagine, perhaps it's the whim of a Don Juan, of a serial philanderer, perhaps, and this is certainly the most likely reason, it's pure rancor, Rancor, Yes, rancor, you said only minutes ago that if you had a gun, you would kill me, that was your way of saying that there is one too many of us in the world, and I entirely agree, there is one too many of us in the world, and I can't really stress that enough, the matter would be resolved already if that pistol I took with me to our meeting had been loaded and I had had the courage to fire it, but, of course, we're decent folk, we're afraid of prison, and so, since I wasn't capable of killing you, I'll kill you another way, by screwing your girlfriend, the sad thing is she'll never know, she's going to think all the time that she's making love with you, all the tender, passionate words she speaks will be addressed to Tertuliano Máximo Afonso and not to António Claro, let that be some consolation to you. Tertuliano Máximo Afonso did not reply, he quickly lowered his eyes so that the other man would not be able to read the thought that had just crossed his brain from side to side. He had suddenly felt as if he were playing a game of chess, waiting for António Claro's next move. He seemed to have allowed his shoulders to slump, as if vanquished, when the other man said, glancing at his watch, It's time I was going, I still have to drop by Maria da Paz's house to collect her, but he straightened up with renewed energy when he heard the man add, Obviously, I can't go as I am, I need your clothes and your car, if I'm going to wear your face, I'll have to wear everything else of yours as well, Sorry, I don't understand, said Tertuliano Máximo Afonso, adopting an air of perplexity, then, Ah, yes, of course, you can't risk her thinking it odd that you should be wearing that suit or asking where you got the money to buy a car like that, Exactly, So you want me to lend you my clothes and my car, That's what I said, And what would you do if I refused, Something very simple, I would pick up the phone and tell Maria da Paz everything, and if you had the unfortunate idea of trying to stop me, you can be quite sure that I could put you to sleep in less time than it takes to say knife, so be careful, we've managed to avoid violence so far, but if it becomes necessary, I won't hesitate, All right, said Tertuliano Máximo Afonso, what clothes will you need, a suit and tie or something similar to what you have on now, summer wear, Something casual, like this. Tertuliano Máximo Afonso left the room, went into his bedroom, opened the wardrobe, opened drawers, and in less than five minutes he was back with everything the other man would need, a shirt, trousers, a sweater, socks and shoes. Get dressed in the bathroom, he said. When António Claro returned, he saw on the coffee table a wristwatch, a wallet, and his identity papers, The documentation for the car is in the glove compartment, said Tertuliano Máximo Afonso, and here are the keys, and the house keys too, just in case I'm not in when you come back to change your clothes, because I assume you will want to change your clothes, Yes, I'll be back by midmorning, I promised my wife I wouldn't be home later than midday, replied António Claro, Presumably you've given her a good reason for spending the night away from home, Work commitments, it's not the first time, and António Claro, suddenly confused, was asking himself why the hell he was giving all these explanations when, ever since he first entered this apartment, he had been the authoritative one, the one in perfect control of the situation. Tertuliano Máximo Afonso said, You shouldn't take your documents with you, or your watch, or the keys to your apartment or the car, you shouldn't have any personal items on you, nothing that can identify you, women, as well as being naturally curious, or so people say, always notice details, What about the keys to your apartment, you're bound to need them, No, take them, don't worry, my upstairs neighbor has duplicates, or copies, if you prefer that word, she does my cleaning for me, Ah, I see. António Claro could not shake off the feeling of disquiet that had replaced the unshakable coolness with which he had guided the tortuous dialogue in the direction that interested him. He had done this, but now it seemed to him that he had got diverted at some point in the discussion or that he had been pushed off the path by a subtle lateral touch which he had failed even to notice. The moment when he had to pick up Maria da Paz was approaching, but apart from that pressing matter, on which the clock, so to speak, was ticking, there is another, still more urgent private matter that is closing on him, Go on, get out of here, one should know how to make a timely withdrawal even from the greatest victories. António Claro hurriedly set down on the coffee table, side by side, his identity papers, the keys to his apartment and those to his car, his wristwatch, his wedding ring, a handkerchief bearing his initials, a comb, adding, unnecessarily, that the documentation for the car was in the glove compartment, then he asked, Do you know my car, I left it parked very close to the door downstairs, and Tertuliano Máximo Afonso said that he did, I saw it parked outside your house in the country, And where's yours, You'll find it on the corner of the street, on your left when you leave the building, it's a blue two-door sedan, said Tertuliano Máximo Afonso, completing this information with the make of the car and the registration number, just in case there should be any confusion. The false beard lay on the arm of the chair in which António Claro was sitting. Aren't you going to take it with you, asked Tertuliano Máximo Afonso, You were the one who bought it, you keep it, the face I'm leaving with now is the same one I'll have to return with tomorrow when I come here to change my clothes, replied António Claro, recovering a little of his previous authority and adding sarcastically, Until then, I will be Tertuliano Máximo Afonso, history teacher. They looked at each other for a few seconds, yes, now the words with which Tertuliano Máximo Afonso received António Claro when he arrived were true, and would be forever, Anything we had to say to one another has already been said. Tertuliano Máximo Afonso noiselessly opened the front door and stood aside to allow his visitor to leave, then slowly, and equally carefully, he closed it again. One would naturally assume that he did this in order not to arouse the malicious curiosity of his neighbors, but if Cassandra had been here, she would have reminded us that it is precisely in this way that one lowers the lid on a coffin. Tertuliano Máximo Afonso went back into the living room, sat down on the sofa, closed his eyes, and leaned back. For a whole hour, he did not move, but, contrary to what you might think, he was not asleep, he was simply allowing time for his old car to leave the city. He thought about Maria da Paz without pain, merely as someone who was slowly disappearing off in the distance, he thought about António Claro as an enemy who had won the first battle, but who, if there is any justice left in this world, will lose the second. The afternoon light was fading, his car would already have left the main road, they would probably take the shortcut that avoids going through the village, now they are stopping outside the house in the country, António Claro has taken a key out of his pocket, this was one key he could not have left at Tertuliano Máximo Afonso's apartment, he will tell Maria da Paz that it was given to him by the owner, except, of course, he doesn't know that we're going to spend the night here, He's a fellow teacher, completely trustworthy, but I still wouldn't confide my private affairs to him, wait here a moment, and I'll go and check that everything's as it should be. Maria da Paz was about to wonder to herself what could possibly not be as it should be in a country house for rent, but a kiss from Tertuliano Máximo Afonso, one of those deep, overwhelming kisses, distracted her, and afterward, during the minutes while he was not there, she was drawn to the beauty of the countryside, the valley, the dark line of poplars and ash trees that follows the course of the river, the hills in the background, the sun almost touching the highest ridge. Tertuliano Máximo Afonso, the one who has just got up from the sofa, can guess what António Claro is doing inside, coolly looking for anything that might give him away, a few film posters, but there's no danger in those, he will leave them where they are, after all, a teacher might well be a movie buff, the worst culprit was that photo of him and Helena that stood on a table in the hallway. At last, he reappeared at the front door and called to her, You can come in now, there were some old curtains on the floor which made the house look really shabby. She got out of the car, ran happily up the steps, and the door slammed shut behind her, at first sight, this could seem to show a regrettable lack of consideration, but one must bear in mind that the house is isolated, there are no neighbors near or far, and besides, it is our duty to be understanding, the two people who have just gone into the house have far more interesting matters to deal with than worrying about the noise a door might make as it closes.

Tertuliano Máximo Afonso picked up from the floor, where it had fallen, the photocopy of the letter that António Claro had brought with him, then he opened the drawer in his desk in which he had kept the reply from the production company and, with those two pieces of paper in his hand, plus the photograph of himself wearing the false beard, went into the kitchen. He put them in the sink, held a lighted match to them, and observed the swift work of the fire, the flame chewing and swallowing the papers, then vomiting them up in the form of ash, the rapid scintillations that kept nibbling at them even when the flame, still rising up here and there, appeared to have gone out. He turned the charred remnants this way and that until they were entirely consumed, then he turned on the tap and washed every last bit of ash down the drain. Afterward, he went into his bedroom, took the videos out of the wardrobe where he had hidden them, and returned to the living room. António Claro's clothes, which he had brought from the bathroom, were piled on the seat of the armchair. Tertuliano Máximo Afonso got undressed. He wrinkled his nose in disgust as he pulled on the underpants worn by the other man, but there was no alternative, he was driven by necessity, which is one of the names adopted by fate when it suits it to go in disguise. Now that he had become the double of Tertuliano Máximo Afonso, he had no option but to become the António Claro that António Claro had left behind. When, in his turn, he comes back tomorrow to recover his clothes, António Claro will be able to go out into the street only as Tertuliano Máximo Afonso, and will have to remain Tertuliano Máximo Afonso until his own clothes, the ones he left here or others else-where, restore to him his identity as António Claro. Whether he likes it or not, clothes do indeed make the man. Tertuliano Máximo Afonso went over to the table on which António Claro had left his personal belongings and methodically con-cluded his work of transformation. He began with the wrist-watch, slipped the wedding ring onto his ring finger, put the comb and the handkerchief bearing the initials AC into one trouser pocket, the keys to his apartment and to his car in the other, and, in his back pocket, the identity papers that, in case of doubt, will provide indisputable proof that he is António Claro. He is ready to leave, all that's lacking is the final touch, the false beard that António Claro was wearing when he en-tered the apartment, it's almost as if he knew it would be needed, but no, the beard was just waiting there for a coinci-dence, because sometimes coincidences take years to arrive and, at others, come running along in Indian file, one after the other. Tertuliano Máximo Afonso went to the bathroom to complete his disguise, what with all the putting on and taking off, and being passed from one face to another, the beard no longer sticks very well, it threatens to arouse the sus-picions of the first lynx-eyed glance from some agent of au-thority or the systematic distrust of some fearful citizen. It finally stuck more or less to his skin, now it just has to last until Tertuliano Máximo Afonso finds a rubbish bin in some reasonably deserted place. There the false beard will end its brief but agitated history, and there in the darkness, among the fetid remains, the videos will find their rest. Tertuliano Máximo Afonso walked back into the living room, looked around to see if he had forgotten anything he might need, then went into the bedroom, on the bedside table is the book about ancient Mesopotamian civilizations, there is no reason why he should keep it with him, but, nevertheless, he picks it up, why should Tertuliano Máximo Afonso feel the need for the company of the Amorites and the Assyrians if in less than twenty-four hours he will be home again. *Alea jacta est,* he murmured to himself, there is nothing more to discuss, what will be will be, there's no escape. The Rubicon is this door that is closing, these stairs he is going down, these footsteps leading to that car, this key opening the door, this engine carrying it smoothly out into the street, the die is cast, it's in the hands of the gods. The month is August, the day is Friday, there isn't much traffic or people around, the street he is heading for was so far away and is now suddenly near. It has been dark for more than half an hour. Tertuliano Máximo Afonso parked the car outside the building. Before getting out, he looked up at the windows and saw not a single light. He hesitated, asked himself, Now what do I do, to which reason responded, I really don't understand this indecision, if you are, as you hoped to appear to be, António Claro, what you have to do is go calmly upstairs to your apartment, and if the lights are out, there must be some reason for it, after all, none of the other windows are lit either, and since you're not a cat and can't see in the dark, you'll simply have to turn them on, always supposing that, for some unknown reason, there isn't someone waiting for you, or, rather, since we all know the reason, just remember you told your wife that work commitments meant you had to spend tonight away from home, so now you just have to get on with it. Tertuliano Máximo Afonso crossed the street, with the book on the Mesopotamians under his arm, opened the street door, got into the lift, and saw that he had company, Good evening, I was expecting you, said common sense, Oh, I should have known you'd turn up, What's the idea of coming here, Don't act the innocent, you know as well as I do, To take vengeance, to hit back, to sleep with your enemy's wife, now that yours is in bed with him, Exactly, And then what, Nothing, it will never occur to Maria da Paz that she's slept with the wrong man, And what about these people, They're going to get the rough end of this tragicomedy, Why, You're common sense, you should know, Well, I lose some of my qualities in lifts, When António Claro comes home tomorrow he's going to have great difficulty explaining to his wife how it is he managed to sleep with her and, at the same time, be away working outside the city, Well, I had no idea you were capable of such a diabolical plan, Human, my friend, just human, the devil doesn't make plans, anyway, if men were good, he wouldn't even exist, And tomorrow, Oh, I'll think up an excuse to leave early, And that book, What this, I'm not sure really, perhaps I'll leave it here as a souvenir. The lift stopped on the fifth floor, Tertuliano Máximo Afonso asked, Are you coming with me, No, I'm common sense, there's no place for me in there, See you later, Oh, I very much doubt that.

Tertuliano Máximo Afonso pressed his ear to the door. Not a sound came from within. He should behave naturally, as if he were the man of the house, but his heart was beating so violently it was shaking his whole body. He wasn't going to have the courage to go on. Suddenly the lift started to descend, Who can that be, he thought, frightened, and, without further hesitation, put the key in the door and went in. The house was in darkness, but the vague, tenuous luminosity, presumably coming in through the windows, began slowly to pick out contours, to give form to objects. Tertuliano Máximo Afonso felt the wall by the door for a light switch. Nothing stirred in the apartment, There's no one here, he thought, I can have a proper look around, yes, it's vital he gets to know the apartment that will be his for one night, perhaps all alone, what if, for example, Helena has family in the city and, taking advantage of her husband's absence, has gone to visit them, what if she will only be back tomorrow, then the plan that common sense termed diabolical will fall flat, like the most banal of mental pranks, like a house of cards blown down by a child. Life has its ironies, they say, when the truth is that life is the most obtuse of all known things, one day someone must have said to it, Keep straight on, straight ahead, don't leave the path, and ever since then, foolish and incapable of learning the lessons it boasts of teaching us, it has done nothing but blindly follow the orders it was given, knocking down everything in its path, not even stopping to see the damage it has caused or to ask our forgiveness, not even once. Tertuliano Máximo Afonso searched the apartment from end to end, turned on and switched off lights, opened and closed doors, wardrobes, drawers, in which he encountered men's clothes, the troubling sight of women's underwear, the pistol, but he touched nothing, he just wanted to know where he was, what relation there is between the rooms in the house and what he can see of its inhabitants, exactly as happens with maps, they tell you where you should go but don't guarantee you'll arrive. When he had finished his inspection, when he could find his way around the whole apartment with his eyes shut, he went and sat down on what must be António Claro's sofa and waited. All he asks is for Helena to come, let Helena come through that door and see me, so that someone can bear witness to the fact that I had the courage to come here, that's all I want basically, a witness. It was just past eleven when she arrived. Alarmed to find all the lights on, she called from the front door, Is that you, Yes, it's me, said Tertuliano Máximo Afonso, his throat dry. The next moment she walked into the living room, What happened, I wasn't expecting you home until tomorrow, they exchanged a brief kiss between question and answer, The work was postponed, said Tertuliano Máximo Afonso and immediately had to sit down again because his legs were trembling, possibly out of nerves, possibly because of that kiss. He barely heard the woman say to him, I went to see my parents, How are they, he managed to ask, Fine, came the reply, and then, Have you had supper, Yes, don't worry, Well, I'm tired, I'm going to bed, what's this book, Oh, I bought it because of a historical film I'm going to be in, It's been used, someone's written notes in it, Yes, I found it in a secondhand bookstore. Helena left the room, and a few minutes later there was silence again. It was late when Tertuliano Máximo Afonso went into the bedroom. Helena was asleep. On the pillow were the pajamas he must put on. Two hours later, he was still awake. His penis lay inert. Then the woman opened her eyes, Can't you sleep, she asked, No, Why, I don't know. Then she turned to him and put her arms around him.

THE FIRST TO WAKE IN THE MORNING WAS TERTULIANO MÁX-imo Afonso. He was naked. The bedspread and the sheet had slipped onto the floor on his side of the bed, leaving one of Helena's breasts exposed. She appeared to be sleeping deeply. The morning light, barely tempered by the thick curtains, filled the whole room with a glittering penumbra. It must be hot outside. Tertuliano Máximo Afonso felt his penis grow hard, unsatisfied again. That was when he thought of Maria da Paz. He imagined another room, another bed, her prone body, of which he knew every inch, and António Claro's prone body, identical to his, and suddenly it seemed to him that he had reached the end of the road, that ahead of him, blocking the way, was a wall with a sign on it saying, STOP, ABYSS, and then he saw that he could not go back, that the road he had traveled had disappeared, and all that remained was the little space on which his feet were standing. He was dreaming and he did not know it. An anxiety that immediately became terror made him start violently awake just as the wall was shattering, and its arms, for worse things have been seen than a wall growing arms, were dragging him toward the precipice. Helena was clutching his hand, trying to calm him,

It's all right, it was a nightmare, it's over, you're here now. He was panting, gasping for breath, as if the fall had suddenly emptied his lungs of air. That's it, calm down, said Helena again. She was leaning on one elbow, her breasts exposed, the thin bedspread outlining the curve of her waist, her thigh, and the words she was saying fell on the body of this suffering man like fine rain, the kind that touches the skin like a caress or a watery kiss. Gradually, like a cloud of steam flowing back to its place of origin, Tertuliano Máximo Afonso's terrified spirit returned to his exhausted mind, and when Helena asked, So what was this bad dream about, tell me, this confused man, this builder of labyrinths in which he himself is lost, who is lying now beside a woman who, although known to him in the sexual sense, is otherwise entirely unknown, spoke of a road that had ceased to have a beginning, as if his own steps as they were taken had devoured the very substances, whatever they might be, that give or lend duration to time and dimension to space, of the wall, which in cutting across time, cut across both, of the place where his feet had stood, those two small islands, that minuscule human archipelago, one here, the other there, and of the sign on which was written STOP, ABYSS, remember, who warns you is your enemy, as Hamlet could have said to his uncle and stepfather, Claudius. She had listened to him surprised, slightly perplexed, she was not used to hearing her husband express such thoughts, still less in the tone in which they had been spoken, as if each word were accompanied by its double, like an echo in an inhabited cave, in which it is impossible to know who is breathing, who has just spoken in a murmur, who has just sighed. She liked the idea that her feet were also two small islands, and that very close to hers rested another two, and that the four together could constitute, did constitute, had constituted a perfect archipelago, if there is such a thing as perfection in this world and if these sheets are the ocean where it chose to be anchored. Are you feeling calmer now, she asked, Yes, he said, I don't think there could be anything better than this, It's odd, last night you came to me as you never have before, you entered me with a tenderness that I thought afterward was mingled with desire and tears, and joy too, a moan of pain, a plea for forgiveness, Well, if that's what you felt, that's how it must have been, Unfortunately, some things happen and are never repeated, Others are repeated over and over, Do you think so, someone once said that if you give a person roses, then you can never again give them anything else but roses, Perhaps we should try, Now, Yes, seeing that we're naked, That's a good reason, Good enough, although probably not the best. The four islands joined together, the archipelago re-formed, the sea beat wildly against the cliffs, if there were shouts up above, they came from the mermaids riding the waves, if there were moans none were moans of pain, if someone asked forgiveness, may they be forgiven now and ever after. They rested briefly in each other's arms, then, with one last kiss, she slipped out of the bed, Don't get up, sleep for a while longer, I'll make breakfast.

Tertuliano Máximo Afonso did not sleep. He had to leave that apartment quickly, he couldn't risk António Claro coming home earlier than he had said, before midday had been his actual words, what if things at the house in the country had not gone as he expected and he was already racing back here, angry with himself, eager to bury his frustration in the peace of his own home, where he will tell his wife about his work, inventing, to justify his bad mood, setbacks that did not exist, arguments that did not take place, agreements that were not made. Tertuliano Máximo Afonso's difficulty lies in not being able to leave just like that, he has to give Helena an excuse that will not arouse her distrust, remember that up until now she has had no reason to think that the man with whom she slept and took pleasure last night is not her husband, and where is he going to find the nerve to tell her now, having concealed the information until the last moment, that he has urgent business to deal with on a morning like this, a summer Saturday, when the logical thing, bearing in mind the sublime heights of harmony reached by this couple, and to which we were witness, would be to stay in bed to continue their interrupted conversation, along with anything more interesting that might occur. Helena will soon appear with the breakfast, it's been such an age since they had breakfast together like this, in the intimacy of a bed still redolent of love's particular fragrances, that it would be unforgivable to waste an opportunity that, in all probability, at least all the probabilities we know about, is clearly conspiring to be the last. Tertuliano Máximo Afonso thinks and thinks and thinks, and, as he thinks and thinks, because what we would term the paradoxical energy of the human soul can reach such extremes, the need to leave grows fainter and fainter, less urgent, and, at the same time, imprudently brushing aside all foreseeable risks, a wild desire to be an eyewitness to his definitive triumph over António Claro is growing in strength inside him. To be there in the flesh and prepared to face whatever the consequences might be. Let him come and find him here, let him rant, let him rage, let him use violence, whatever he does, nothing will be able to lessen the extent of his defeat. He knows that Tertuliano Máximo Afonso wields the ultimate weapon, it will be enough for that thousand-times-cursed history teacher to ask him where he has been and for Helena, finally, to know the sordid side of the prodigious adventure of these two men identical down to the moles on their arms, the scars on their knees, and the size of their penises, and from this day forward, identical too in their couplings. An ambulance may have to come and collect Tertuliano Máximo Afonso's battered body, but his aggressor's wound, that will never heal. These base thoughts of revenge produced by the brain of this man lying in bed waiting for his breakfast might have gone no further, were it not for the aforementioned paradoxical energy of the human soul, or, to give it another name, the possible emergence of feelings of an unusual nobility, of a gentlemanly nature all-the-more-worthy of applause given their otherwise entirely deplorable personal antecedents. Incredible though it may seem, the man who, out of moral cowardice, out of fear that the truth would be revealed, allowed Maria da Paz to fall into the arms of António Claro, is the same man who not only is prepared to carry out the most difficult task of his entire life, but has also realized that it is his strict duty not to leave Helena alone in the delicate situation of having one husband by her side and seeing another walk in through the front door. The human soul is a box out of which a clown is always ready to spring, making faces and sticking out his tongue, but there are times when that same clown merely peers at us over the edge of the box, and if he sees that, by chance, we are behaving in a just and honest fashion, he merely nods approvingly and disappears, thinking that we are not yet an entirely lost cause. Thanks to the decision he has just made, Tertuliano Máximo Afonso has removed from his record a few of his minor faults, but he will have to suffer greatly before the ink in which the others were written begins to fade from the brown paper of memory. People often say, Let time do its work, but what we always forget to ask is if there will ever be enough time. Helena came in carrying the breakfast just as Tertuliano Máximo Afonso was getting up, Don't you want to have breakfast in bed, she asked, and he said no, he would prefer to be seated comfortably on a chair rather than constantly having to keep one eye cocked for the slithering tray, the sliding cup, the smears left behind by the melting butter, and the crumbs that creep into the folds of the sheets and always end up in the skin's most delicate crevices. He tried to make this speech sound as comical and good-humored as he could, but its sole objective was to disguise Tertuliano Máximo Afonso's new and pressing preoccupation, which is this, that if António Claro does turn up, at least he won't find us in the marriage bed nibbling sinfully on scones and toast, that if António Claro does turn up, at least he will find his bed made and his room aired, that if António Claro does turn up, at least he will find us properly washed, combed, and dressed, because as with appearances so it is with vice, since we're walking hand in hand with it, and there seems no way of avoiding this or any real advantage in doing so, we might as well make vice pay occasional homage to virtue, even if only in form, besides, it's highly unlikely it would be worth asking any more of it than that.

It's getting late, it's gone half past ten. Helena has left to do some shopping, she said, Bye, and gave him a kiss, a warm and still consoling remnant of the bonfire of passion that had, in recent hours, illicitly joined and inflamed this man and this woman. Now, sitting on the sofa, with the book about ancient Mesopotamian civilizations open on his lap, Tertuliano Máximo Afonso is waiting for António Claro to arrive, and, being someone whose imagination frequently throws off the fetters, he imagined that the said António Claro and his wife might have met in the street and come up the stairs to sort out this tangle once and for all, Helena protesting, You're not my husband, my husband's at home, that's him sitting over there, you're the history teacher who has been trying to ruin our lives, and António Claro assuring her, No, I'm your husband, he's the history teacher, look at the book he's reading, he's the biggest impostor in the world he is, and she, cutting and ironic, Oh, yes, so perhaps you can explain why it is that he's the one wearing the wedding ring and not you. Helena has just come back alone with the shopping and it's now eleven o'clock. In a while, she will ask, Are you worried about something, and he'll deny it, No, whatever gave you that idea, and she'll say, Well, in that case, I don't understand why you keep looking at the clock, and he will reply that he doesn't know why either, it's just a tic, perhaps he's nervous about something, If they gave me the role of King Hammurabi, my career as an actor would really take off. Half past eleven came, a quarter to twelve, and still no António Claro. Tertuliano Máximo Afonso's heart is like a furious horse dealing kicks in every direction, panic tightens his throat and screams at him that there's still time, Look, while she's in the other room, seize your opportunity and make your escape, you've still got nearly ten minutes, but be careful, don't use the lift, take the stairs and look both ways before you set foot in the street. It's midday, the clock in the living room slowly counted out the beats as if wanting to give António Claro one last chance to appear, to keep his promise, even if he did so only at the very last second, although there's no point in Tertuliano Máximo Afonso trying to deceive himself, If he hasn't come now, he won't be coming at all. Anyone can be late, the car can break down, you can get a puncture, these are things that happen every day and from which no one is exempt. From now on, every minute will be an agony, then it will be the turn of puzzlement, perplexity, and, inevitably, the thought, All right, he's been delayed, seriously delayed, but what are phones for, why doesn't he phone to say that the differential has broken, or the gearbox, or the fan belt, which are all things that can happen to a worn-out old car like his. Another hour passed and not a sign of António Claro, and when Helena came to announce that lunch was on the table, Tertuliano Máximo Afonso said he wasn't hungry, she should eat alone, and, anyway, he needed to go out. She wanted to know why, and he could have retorted that they weren't married and that he was therefore under no obligation to tell her what he was or wasn't going to do, but the moment to place all his cards on the table and begin to play fairly had not yet arrived, and so he merely said that he would explain everything later, a promise that Tertuliano Máximo Afonso always has on the tip of his tongue and which he keeps, when he does keep it, only partially and late, ask his mother, ask Maria da Paz, from whom we also have no news. Helena asked if he thought perhaps he should change his clothes, and he said yes, what he was wearing really wasn't suitable for what he had to do, a suit, jacket, and trousers would be more appropriate, after all, I'm not a tourist and I'm not off to spend the summer in the country. Fifteen minutes later, he left, Helena accompanied him to the lift, in her eyes was the warning glimmer of tears to come, and before Tertuliano Máximo Afonso had even had time to reach the street, she was sobbing, repeating over and over that question as yet unanswered, What's wrong, what's wrong.

As Tertuliano Máximo Afonso climbed into the car, his first thought was to get away from there, to go and park in some quiet spot where he could reflect seriously on the situation, impose order on the confusion that has been jostling about in his mind for the last twenty-four hours, and decide what to do. He started the engine and only had to turn the corner to understand that he did not need to reflect at all, all he had to do was phone Maria da Paz, why on earth didn't I think of it before, presumably because I was shut up in that apartment and therefore unable to make a phone call. A couple hundred meters farther on he found a telephone booth. He stopped the car, hurriedly entered the booth, and dialed the number. It was suffocatingly hot inside. The female voice at the other end asking, Who is it, was not her familiar voice, I wanted to speak to Maria da Paz, he said, Yes, but who is it, I'm a colleague of hers, from the bank where she works, Maria da Paz is dead, she died this morning in a car accident, she was with her fiancé and they both died, it's a tragedy, a real tragedy. In an instant, Tertuliano Máximo Afonso's whole body, from head to toe, was bathed in sweat. He babbled some words the woman could not understand, What did you say, yes, what had he said, a few words that he no longer remembers or ever will remember, that he has forgotten forever, and, without realizing what he was doing, like an automaton whose power supply has suddenly been turned off, he dropped the receiver. Standing utterly still inside the furnace of the telephone booth, he could hear one word, just one, echoing in his ears, Dead, but other words soon came to take its place, and these screamed, You killed her. António Claro didn't kill her with his reckless driving, always supposing that was the cause of the accident, he, Tertuliano Máximo Afonso, killed her, his moral weakness killed her, the will that made him blind to everything but revenge killed her, it was said that one of them, either the actor or the history teacher, was superfluous in this world, but you weren't, you weren't superfluous, there is no duplicate of you to come and replace you at your mother's side, you were unique, just as every ordinary person is unique, truly unique. They say you can hate someone only if you hate yourself, but the worst of all hatreds must be the hatred that cannot bear another person to be the same, worse still if that sameness should ever become total. Tertuliano Máximo Afonso staggered like a drunkard out of the booth, got into the car as if he were hurling himself inside, and sat there, staring blankly ahead, until he could stand it no longer and tears and sobs shook his chest. At this moment, he loves Maria da Paz as he had never loved her nor ever would love her in the future. The grief he feels is for her newborn absence, but an awareness of his guilt is creating a suppurating wound that will secrete pus and filth forever after. Some people looked at him with the gratuitous, impotent curiosity that does neither good nor ill in the world, but one person did come over and ask if he could help in any way, but he said no, thank you, and, having thanked him, wept still more bitterly, it was as if someone had come and placed a hand on his shoulder and said, Be patient, in time your sorrow will pass, it's true, in time everything does pass, but there are cases when time takes time to let the grief abate, and there have been and will be cases, fortunately few, in which the grief never abated and time did not pass. He sat on like this until he had no more tears to shed, until time decided to start moving again and to ask, And now what, where will you go, and it was then that Tertuliano Máximo Afonso, in all probability transformed into António Claro for the rest of his life, realized that he had nowhere to go. In the first place, the apartment he used to call his own belonged to Tertuliano Máximo Afonso, and Tertuliano Máximo Afonso is dead, in the second place, he can't drive from here to the apartment that was António Claro's and tell Helena that her husband is dead because, as far as she is concerned, he is António Claro, and finally, there is Maria da Paz's apartment, to which he had never even been invited, he could go there only to offer his useless sympathies to a poor mother bereft of her daughter. The natural thing at this point would be for Tertuliano Máximo Afonso to think of another mother, who, already informed of the sad news, will likewise be weeping the inconsolable tears of maternal orphanhood, but the unshakable consciousness that, as far as he is concerned, he is and always will be Tertuliano Máximo Afonso and that he is, therefore, alive, must have temporarily blocked out what, in other circumstances, would certainly have been his first impulse. Meanwhile, he will still have to find an answer to the question that has been left hanging, And now what, where will you go, one of the easier difficulties to resolve in any city, whether a vast metropolis like this or not, with hotels and boardinghouses to suit all tastes and purses. That is where he will have to go, and not just for a few hours to find shelter from the heat and to be free to weep. It was one thing to have spent the previous night with Helena, when doing so was just a move in the game, if you're going to sleep with my wife, then I'll sleep with yours, an eye for an eye and a tooth for a tooth, as demanded by the law of talion, never applied more appropriately than in this case, for our present-day word "identical" means the same as the Latin etymon *talis*, from which the term "talion" comes, for not only were the crimes committed identical, those who committed them were identical too. It was one thing, then, if you will allow us to return to the beginning of the sentence, to have spent the night with Helena when no one could possibly have guessed that death was about to enter the game and declare checkmate, it would be quite another thing, knowing as he does that António Claro is dead, even if tomorrow's newspapers say that the dead man's name was Tertuliano Máximo Afonso, to spend a second night with her, thus compounding one deceit with a still-worse deceit. We human beings, although we are still animals, some of us more than others, do have a few decent feelings, sometimes even a remnant or a beginning of self-respect, and this Tertuliano Máximo Afonso, who, on so many occasions, has behaved in ways that justified our severest criticism, will not dare to take the step that, in our eyes, would condemn him forever. He will, therefore, go in search of a hotel and see what tomorrow brings. He started the car and drove toward the center, where he will have more choices, all he needs is a modest, two-star hotel, it's only for one night, And who can say that it will only be for one night, he thought, where will I sleep tomorrow, and after that, and after that, and after that, for the first time, the future seemed to him a place in which there will definitely still be a need for history teachers, but not this one, in which the actor Daniel Santa-Clara will have no option but to give up his promising career, and in which it will be necessary to find some point of equilibrium between having been and continuing to be, it is doubtless comforting to have our consciousness tell us, I know who you are, but our own consciousness might start to doubt both us and its own words if it were to notice, all around, people asking each other the awkward question, Who's he. The first person to have the opportunity to display this public curiosity was the clerk at the hotel reception when he asked Tertuliano Máximo Afonso for some proof of identity, thank heavens he didn't ask him his name first, because Tertuliano Máximo Afonso could easily have said, out of sheer force of habit, the name that has been his for the last thirty-eight years and which now belongs to a mangled corpse waiting in a cold morgue somewhere for the autopsy that no accident victim can escape. The identity card he handed to the clerk bears the name of António Claro, the face in the photograph is the same as the face the receptionist has before him and which he would scrupulously examine were there any reason to go to such lengths. There isn't, Tertuliano Máximo Afonso has signed the guest book, in these cases all that's required is a scrawl that bears some resemblance to the proper signature, he has the key to the room in his hand, he has already said that he has no luggage with him, and to support a truth that no one has asked him to justify, he explained how he had missed his plane and left his suitcases at the airport, which is why he is staying only one night. Tertuliano Máximo Afonso may have changed his name, but he continues to be the same person whom we accompanied to the video shop, who always talks more than is necessary, who does not know how to be natural, fortunately, the receptionist has other things to think about, the telephone ringing, a few foreigners who have just arrived weighed down with suitcases and travel bags. Tertuliano Máximo Afonso went up to his room, made himself comfortable, and went to the bathroom to relieve his bladder, apart from having missed his plane, as he had told the receptionist, he appeared to have no other worries, but that was before he lay down on the bed, intending to rest a little, for his imagination immediately placed before him a car reduced to a pile of scrap metal and, inside it, wretchedly bleeding, two mangled bodies. The tears returned, the sobs returned, and who knows how long he would have gone on like this if, suddenly, the shocking thought of his mother had not irrupted into his disoriented brain. He sat bolt upright, placed his hand on the phone, at the same time heaping insults on himself, I'm a fool, a half-wit, an idiot, an imbecile, an utter cretin, how could it not have occurred to me that the police were bound to go to my apartment, that they would ask the neighbors if I had any relatives, that my upstairs neighbor would give them my mother's address and telephone number, how could something so very obvious not have crossed my mind, how was it possible. No one answered. The telephone rang and rang, but no one came to ask, Who is it, so that Tertuliano Máximo Afonso could at last say, It's me, I'm alive, the police made a mistake, I'll explain later. His mother wasn't at home, and this fact, unusual in any other circumstances, could mean only one thing, that she was on her way to the city, that she had hired a taxi and was on her way, she might even have arrived, in which case, she would have gone to ask the upstairs neighbor for the key and will now be weeping out her grief, my poor mother, how right you were to warn me. Tertuliano Máximo Afonso dialed his own phone number, and again no one answered. He tried to think calmly, to clarify his muddled mind, even if the police had been exceptionally diligent, they would need time to carry out and conclude their investigations, one must remember that this city is a seething mass of five million restless inhabitants, that there are many accidents and even more victims of accidents, that it is necessary to identify them, to go in search of their families, no easy task when there are negligent people who go about the streets without so much as a piece of paper on them warning, In case of accident, call so-and-so. Fortunately, Tertuliano Máximo Afonso is not such a person, nor, it would seem, was Maria da Paz, in their respective address books, on the page reserved for personal information, was everything necessary for a perfect identification, at least as regards any initial requirements, which almost always end up being the last requirements too. No one, apart from a criminal, would be wandering around with false documents or documents stolen from another person, and so it is legitimate to conclude, with respect to the present case, that what the police took to be the truth was the truth, and since there was no reason to doubt the identity of one of the victims, why on earth should there be any doubts about the other one. Tertuliano Máximo Afonso rang again, and again there was no reply. He is no longer thinking about Maria da Paz, now he just wants to know where Carolina Máximo is, taxis these days are powerful machines, not like the old clunkers of yesteryear, and, in a dramatic situation like this, there would be no need to bribe the driver with the promise of a tip if he put his foot down, in four hours she should be here, and given that it's a Saturday and everyone's away on holiday, with the traffic on the roads reduced to a minimum, she should have arrived at his apartment already, so that she could ease her son's disquiet. He rang again, and this time, unexpectedly, the answering machine came on, This is Tertuliano Máximo Afonso, please leave a message, it was a terrible shock, he had been in such a state of nerves before that he hadn't noticed the machine had not come on, and now it was as if he had suddenly heard a voice not his own, the voice of a dead stranger that, tomorrow, so as not to upset the sensitive, will have to be replaced by the voice of someone living, an operation of removal and replacement that happens every day in thousands and thousands of places all over the world, although we may prefer not to think about it. Tertuliano Máximo Afonso needed a few seconds to calm himself and recover his own voice, then, tremulously, he said, Mama, it's not true what they've told you, I'm alive and well, I'll tell you later what happened, but I repeat, I'm alive and well, I'm going to give you the name of the hotel I'm staying at, the room number, and the telephone number, call me as soon as you get there and don't cry anymore, don't cry, Tertuliano Máximo Afonso might have said these last words a third time, if he himself had not burst into tears, tears for his mother, for Maria da Paz, whose memory was back with him again, and tears of pity for himself too. Exhausted, he fell back on the bed, he felt weak, as helpless as a sick child, he remembered that he had not had any lunch, and the idea, instead of arousing his appetite, made him feel so violently sick that he had to get up and run to the bathroom, where his retchings summoned up from his stomach nothing but a little bitter foam. He went back into the room, sat down on the bed with his head in his hands, allowing his thoughts to drift like a small cork boat heading downstream and which, now and again, when it bumps against a rock, changes direction for a moment. It was thanks to this half-conscious daydreaming that he remembered something important he should have told his mother. He rang his own number, fearing that the machine would again play tricks on him and refuse to work, and he gave a great sigh of relief when the answering machine, after a few seconds' hesitation, whirred into life. He left only a short message, he said, Don't forget, the name is António Claro, and then, as if he had just discovered a weighty bit of evidence that would contribute to a definitive elucidation of the shifting, unstable identities under discussion, he added the following information, The dog's name is Tomarctus. When his mother arrives, he won't need to recite to her the names of his father and of his grandparents, of his aunts and uncles on both sides, he won't have to mention the arm he broke when he fell out of the fig tree, or his first girlfriend, or the bolt of lightning that demolished the chimney when he was ten years old. In order for Carolina Máximo Afonso to be absolutely sure that the child of her heart is there before her, there will be no need for that marvelous maternal instinct of hers or for any scientific, confirmatory DNA tests, the name of the dog will be enough.

It was nearly an hour before the phone rang. Startled, Tertuliano Máximo Afonso leaped up, hoping to hear his mother's voice, but the voice he heard was that of the clerk at the reception desk, Senhora Carolina Claro is here to speak to you, Oh, it's my mother, he stammered, I'll be right down, I'll be right down. He ran out of the room, at the same time telling himself, I must get a grip on myself, I mustn't be overly affectionate, the less fuss we make the better. The slowness of the lift helped to moderate the rush of emotions, and it was a fairly acceptable Tertuliano Máximo Afonso who appeared in the foyer and embraced the elderly lady, who, either instinctively or after long reflection in the taxi that had brought her there, prudently returned these displays of filial affection without any of the vulgar, passionate exuberance that finds expression in phrases such as, Oh, my sweet boy, although in the present drama, Oh, my poor boy would be more suited to the situation. The embraces, tears, and sobs had to wait until they got to the room, until the door had closed and the son risen from the dead could say, Mama, and she had no words to say other than those that managed to emerge from her grateful heart, It's you, it's you. This woman, however, is not the easily pleased type, for whom a hug is enough to make her forget an offense, an offense, in this case, not against her, but against reason, respect, and common sense too, lest it be said that we have forgotten how much the latter had tried to do to prevent the story of the duplicate men from ending in tragedy. Carolina Máximo will not use that term, she will say only, There are two people dead, now tell me from the beginning how all this happened, and without concealing anything, please, the time for half-truths is over, and that applies to half-lies too. Tertuliano Máximo Afonso drew up a chair for his mother to sit on, sat down on the edge of the bed, and began his story. From the beginning, as she had requested. She didn't interrrupt him, and only twice did she look shocked, once when António Claro was saying that he was going to take Maria da Paz to the house in the country in order to make love with her, and again when her son explained how and why he had gone to Helena's apartment and what had happened there. She moved her lips as if to say, Madness, but the word did not come out. Night had fallen, darkness covered the features of both. When Tertuliano Máximo Afonso stopped speaking, his mother asked the inevitable question, And now what, Now, Mama, the Tertuliano Máximo Afonso I was is dead, and the other one, if he wants to continue to be part of life, will have no option but to be António Claro, And why not just tell the truth, why not say what happened, why not put everything back in its rightful place, You've heard what happened, Yes, so, Do you really think, Mama, that those four people, the dead and the living, should be brought out into the public gaze for the pleasure and amusement of the world's fierce curiosity, and what would we gain with that, the dead wouldn't come back to life and the living would start to die there and then, So what shall we do, You will go to the funeral of the false Tertuliano Máximo Afonso and you'll mourn for him as if he were your son, and Helena will go too, but no one must know why she is there, And you, As I said, I'm António Claro, when I turn on the light, the face you will see will be his, not mine, But you're my son, Yes, I'm your son, but I won't be able to be your son in the town where I was born, as far as the people there are concerned, I'm dead, and when you and I want to meet, it will have to be in a place where no one even knows of the existence of a history teacher called Tertuliano Máximo Afonso, And Helena, Tomorrow I'll go and ask her forgiveness and give her back this watch and this wedding ring, And for this two people had to die, Yes, people I killed, and one of them an innocent victim, entirely innocent. Tertuliano Máximo Afonso got up and turned on the light. His mother was crying. For a few minutes they remained silent, avoiding each other's gaze. Then, dabbing at her eyes with a damp handkerchief, his mother murmured, Old Cassandra was right, you should never have let the wooden horse in, There's nothing to be done about it now, No, there's nothing to be done about it, and there'll be nothing to be done about it in the future either, we'll all be dead. After a brief silence, Tertuliano Máximo Afonso asked, Did the police give you any details about the accident, They said that the car left its lane and drove straight into a truck coming in the opposite direction, they also told me that they would have died instantly, That's odd, What is, Well, I had the impression he was a good driver, Something must have happened, They might have skidded, there could have been oil on the road, They didn't say anything about that, just that the car left its lane and drove straight into the truck. Tertuliano Máximo Afonso sat down again on the edge of the bed, looked at his watch, and said, I'm going to ask reception to get a room for you, we'll have supper and you can stay here tonight, No, I'd rather go back to your place, after we've eaten, you can call a taxi, But I can take you, no one will see me, And how are you going to take me when you have no car, I've got his car, his mother shook her head sadly and said, His car, his wife, all that's lacking now is for you to have his life too, Well, I'll have to find a better life for myself, but now, please, let's go and eat something, and let the tragedy rest for a while. He held out his hands to help her up, then he put his arms around her and said, Remember to erase the messages I left on the answering machine, we can't be too careful, not like cats that hide in a box but forget to put their tail in. When they had finished supper, his mother said again, Call me a taxi, No, I'll take you home, You can't risk being seen, besides, just the thought of getting in that car makes me shudder, All right, but I'll come with you in the taxi and then come back here, Look, I'm old enough to go alone, don't insist. When she left, Tertuliano Máximo Afonso said, Try to get some rest, Mama, you need it, Probably neither of us will be able to sleep, neither you nor I, she replied.

She was right. Tertuliano Máximo Afonso, at least, did not close his eyes for hours and hours, he kept seeing the car leaving its lane and hurtling toward the truck's huge snout, Why, he asked himself, why did he lose control like that, perhaps a tire blew, no, that can't be it, the police would have mentioned it, true, the car has been in constant use for a good few years, but I took it in for a full service only three months ago and they found nothing wrong with it, either mechanical or electrical. He fell asleep toward dawn, but his sleep was short-lived, just after seven o'clock he was startled awake by the thought of something urgent he had to do, the visit to Helena presumably, but it was still too early for that, what could it be then, a light suddenly went on in his head, the newspaper, he needed to see what was in the newspaper, an accident like that, just outside the city, was news. He leaped out of bed, pulled on his clothes, and rushed down to reception. The night porter, not the receptionist who had attended him the previous day, eyed him suspiciously, and Tertuliano Máximo Afonso had to say, I'm just going to buy a newspaper, in case the man thought that this agitated guest was trying to leave without paying. He did not have to go far, there was a newspaper kiosk on the corner. He bought three papers, there must be something about the accident in one of them, and strode back to the hotel. He went up to his room and started leafing through them anxiously, looking for the section on road accidents. It was reported only in the third newspaper. There was a photograph showing the car's ruinous state. With his whole body shaking, Tertuliano Máximo Afonso read the article, skipping over the details to get to the essential facts, Yesterday, at around 9:30 A.M., on the outskirts of the city, there was a head-on collision between a car and a truck. The car's two occupants, So-and-So and So-and-So, immediately identifiable from the papers they had on them, were dead by the time the ambulance arrived. The driver of the truck suffered only minor injuries to his face and hands. Questioned by the police, who do not hold him in any way responsible for the accident, he stated that when the car was still some distance from him, before it left its lane, it had seemed to him that the two occupants were grappling with each other, although he could not be entirely sure because of the glare on the windscreen. Information acquired later on by our reporter revealed that the two unfortunate travelers were engaged to be married. Tertuliano Máximo Afonso read the item again, at the time that it happened, he thought, he was still in bed with Helena, and then, inevitably, he connected António Claro's early-morning drive back with what the truck driver had said. What went on between them, he wondered, what could have happened at the house in the country for them still to be arguing in the car, no, more than arguing, grappling, as the sole eyewitness to the accident had said with such vivid exactitude. Tertuliano Máximo Afonso looked at his watch. It was a few minutes to eight, Helena would already be up, Or perhaps not, she probably took a sleeping pill so as to be able to sleep, or, more accurately, to escape, poor

Helena, as innocent as Maria da Paz had been, little does she know what awaits her. It was nine o'clock when Tertuliano Máximo Afonso left the hotel. He had asked reception to supply him with shaving equipment, he has had breakfast and is now on his way to say to Helena the word that is still needed for the incredible story of the duplicate men to come to an end once and for all and for normal life to resume its course, leaving, as usual, its victims behind it. If Tertuliano Máximo Afonso were fully aware of what he is about to do, of the blow he is about to deliver, he might well run away without a word of explanation or justification, perhaps leave things in their current state to rot, but his mind is somehow fogged, under the influence of a kind of anesthesia that dulls the pain and is now pushing him beyond his own will. He parked the car opposite the building, crossed the road, and got into the lift. He is carrying the newspaper rolled up under his arm, the bringer of tragic news, the voice and word of fate, he is the worst of Cassandras, the one whose sole duty is to say, It happened. He did not want to open the front door with the key he has in his pocket, there is no room now for vengeance, revenge, retribution. He rang the bell like that seller of books boasting of the sublime cultural virtues of the encyclopedia in which the habits of the monkfish are so minutely described, but what he wants now, with every fiber of his being, is for the person who opens the door to him to say, even if she's lying, No, thank you, I've already got one. The door opened and Helena appeared in the half dark of the corridor. She looked at him in astonishment, as if she had lost all hope of ever seeing him again, she showed him her poor, drawn face, the dark circles under her eyes, clearly the pill she had taken to escape from herself had failed. Where have you been, she stammered, what happened, I've been in utter torment since yesterday, since you left. She stepped forward into his arms, which did not open, but which, purely out of pity, did not repel her, and then they went in together, she still clinging to him, and he, awkward, gauche, like a clumsy puppet. He did not speak, he will not utter a word until she is sitting on the sofa, and what he has to say will appear to be the innocuous statement of someone who has gone out into the street to buy a newspaper and now, with no apparent hidden motive, says only, I've brought you the news, and he will show her the open page, will point out the place where the tragedy occurred, Here it is, and she will not notice his coldness, she will carefully read what is written, will look away from the photo of the crushed car and mutter sadly when she has done, How awful, but she said this only because she is a woman with a kind heart, the misfortune does not really touch her directly, indeed, in contradiction to the apparent solidarity of her words, there was something like relief, clearly involuntary, but to which the words spoken afterward give intelligible expression, That's terrible, it brings me no joy at all, on the contrary, but at least it puts an end to the confusion. Tertuliano Máximo Afonso had not sat down, he was standing before her, the way messengers always stand when still on duty, because there is more news to give, the very worst news. For Helena, the newspaper is already a thing of the past. the concrete present, the palpable present is this, her husband returned to her, António Claro is his name, he is going to tell her what he did yesterday afternoon and night, what important matters could have made him leave her without a word from him for so many hours. Tertuliano Máximo Afonso realizes that he cannot wait a minute longer, if he does, he will have to remain silent forever. He said, The man who died was not Tertuliano Máximo Afonso. She looked at him with troubled eyes, then uttered five words that would prove of little use to her, What, what did you say, and he said again, without looking at her, The man who died was not Tertuliano Máximo Afonso. Helena's disquiet was suddenly transformed into outright fear, Who was it then, Your husband. There was no other way of telling her, there was not a single preparatory speech in the world that would have helped, it was pointless and cruel trying to apply a bandage before there was a wound to bind up. Wild with despair, Helena was still trying to fend off the catastrophe breaking over her head, But the documents the newspaper mentioned belonged to that awful man, Tertuliano Máximo Afonso. Tertuliano Máximo Afonso took his wallet out of his jacket pocket, opened it, removed António Claro's identity card and held it out to her. She took it, looked at the photograph, looked at the man in front of her, and understood everything. The evidence of the facts took shape in her mind like a rush of harsh light, the monstrousness of the situation overwhelmed her, for one brief moment she seemed about to lose consciousness. Tertuliano Máximo Afonso stepped forward, grasped her hands, and she, opening eyes that were like one vast teardrop, drew back abruptly, then, all strength gone, left them there, convulsive weeping saved her from fainting, sobs were now pitilessly shaking her chest, This is just how I cried, he thought, this is how we all cry when faced by a situation about which we can do nothing. Now what, she asked from the depths of the pool in which she was drowning, I'll disappear from your life forever, he said, you'll never see me again, I'd like to ask your forgiveness, but I daren't, it would be adding insult to injury, You weren't the only guilty one, No, but I bear most responsibility, I'm guilty of cowardice and because of that two people are dead, Was Maria da Paz really your fiancée, Yes,

Did you love her, Yes, I cared about her deeply, we were going to be married, And yet you allowed her to go with him, As I said, out of cowardice, out of weakness, And you came here to have your revenge, Yes. Tertuliano Máximo Afonso straightened up and took a step back. Repeating the same movements that António Claro had performed forty-eight hours before, he took off the wristwatch, which he placed on the table, then he put the wedding ring down beside it. He said, I'll return the suit I'm wearing by post. Helena picked up the ring and looked at it as if for the first time. Distractedly, as though trying to remove the invisible mark left behind, Tertuliano Máximo Afonso rubbed the ring finger on his left hand with the index finger and thumb of his right hand. Neither of them thought, neither of them will ever think that the lack of that ring on António Claro's finger could have been the direct cause of two deaths, and yet that is how it was. Yesterday morning, at the house in the country, António Claro was still asleep when Maria da Paz woke up. He was lying on his right side, with his left hand resting at eye level on her pillow. Maria da Paz's thoughts were confused, oscillating between a sense of languid physical well-being and a spiritual unease for which she could find no explanation. The light, steadily growing in intensity and seeping in through the gaps in the rustic window shutters, was gradually filling the room. Maria da Paz sighed and turned to look at Tertuliano Máximo Afonso. His left hand almost covered his face. On his ring finger was the round white mark that wedding rings leave on the skin after years of wear. Maria da Paz shuddered, her eyes must be deceiving her, or else she was having the worst of nightmares, this man identical to Tertuliano Máximo Afonso is not Tertuliano Máximo Afonso, Tertuliano Máximo Afonso has not worn a ring since his divorce, the mark on his finger has long since faded. The man is sleeping placidly. Maria da Paz slipped gingerly from the bed, picked up her scattered clothes, and left the room. She got dressed in the hallway, still too stunned to think clearly, incapable of coming up with an answer to the question going around and around in her head, Am I mad. The man who had brought her here and with whom she had spent the night was not Tertuliano Máximo Afonso, of that she was sure, but if it wasn't him, who could it be, and how could there possibly be two people in the world so exactly alike that they could be mistaken for each other, in their body, in their gestures, in their voice. Little by little, like someone looking for and finding the right pieces for a jigsaw puzzle, she began to relate events and actions, she remembered Tertuliano Máximo Afonso's equivocal words, his evasive answers, the letter from the production company, the promise he had made to her that, one day, he would tell her everything. She could go no further, she would still not know who this man was, unless he told her. Tertuliano Máximo Afonso's voice came from the bedroom, Maria da Paz. She did not reply, and the voice insisted, insinuating, caressing, It's still early, come back to bed. She got up from the chair in which she had been slumped and went toward the bedroom. She went no farther than the door. He said, What's the idea of getting dressed, come on, take your clothes off and jump in, the party's not over yet, Who are you, asked Maria da Paz, and before he could reply, Where did you get that mark on your ring finger. António Claro looked at his hand and said, Oh, that, Yes, that, you're not Tertuliano, No, I'm not, I'm not Tertuliano, Who are you then, For the moment, you'll have to make do with knowing who I'm not, but when you see your friend again, you can ask him, Oh, I will, I need to know just who I've been deceived by, By me, in the first place, but he helped, or, rather, the poor man had no option, your fiancé is not exactly a hero. António Claro got out of bed completely naked and came toward Maria da Paz, smiling, What does it matter which one I am, stop asking questions and come to bed. In despair, Maria da Paz screamed, You bastard, and fled into the living room. António Claro appeared shortly afterward, dressed and ready to leave. He said coolly, I've no patience with hysterical women, I'll drop you off at your house and that'll be that. Thirty minutes later, at high speed, the car collided with the truck. There was no oil on the road. The one eyewitness told the police that, although he couldn't be absolutely sure because of the glare on the windscreen, it seemed to him that the car's two occupants were grappling with each other.

At last, Tertuliano Máximo Afonso said, I hope there comes a time when you can forgive me, and Helena replied, Forgive is just a word, Words are all we have, Where are you going now, Somewhere or other, to pick up the pieces and try and hide the scars, As António Claro, Yes, the other one is dead. Helena said nothing, her right hand was resting on the newspaper, her wedding ring glinted on her left hand, the same hand that was still holding in the tips of its fingers the ring that had been her husband's. Then she said, There's one person who can still call you Tertuliano Máximo Afonso, Yes, my mother, Is she here in the city, Yes, There's another person too, Who, Me, You won't be able to, we'll never see each other again, That depends on you, Sorry, I don't understand, I'm telling you to stay with me, to take the place of my husband, to be for all intents and purposes António Claro, to continue his life, since you were the one who took it from him, You mean I should stay here, that we should live together, Yes, But we don't love each other, Possibly not, You might come to hate me, Possibly, Or I might come to hate you, It's a risk I'm willing to take, it would be another unique case in the world, a widow divorcing her husband, But your husband must have family, parents, siblings, how can I pretend to be him, That's all right, I'll help you, But he was an actor, I'm a history teacher, Those are some of the pieces you're going to have to put back together, but there's a time for everything, We might grow to love each other, Possibly, Because I don't think I could hate you, Nor I you. Helena got up and went over to Tertuliano Máximo Afonso. It seemed that she was about to kiss him, but no, the very idea, a little respect, please, there is, after all, a time for everything. She took his left hand and slowly, very slowly, to allow time for time to arrive, she slipped the ring onto his finger. Tertuliano Máximo Afonso drew her gently to him and they stood like that, almost embracing, almost together, on the edge of time.

ANTÓNIO CLARO'S FUNERAL TOOK PLACE THREE DAYS LATER. Helena and Tertuliano Máximo Afonso's mother had gone to play their respective parts, one to mourn a son who was not hers, the other to pretend that the dead man was a stranger. He had stayed at home, reading the book about ancient Mesopotamian civilizations, the chapter on the Aramaeans. The telephone rang. Without even thinking that it could be one of his new parents or siblings, Tertuliano Máximo Afonso picked up the receiver and said, Hello. At the other end, a voice identical to his exclaimed, At last. Tertuliano Máximo Afonso shuddered, António Claro must have been sitting in this same chair on the night when he, Tertuliano, had phoned him. Now the conversation is going to repeat itself, time has changed its mind and turned back. Is that Senhor Daniel Santa-Clara, asked the voice, Yes, speaking, Good, I've been looking for you for weeks, and I've finally found you, How may I help you, Well, I'd like to meet you, Why, You have doubtless already noticed that our voices are identical, They do seem to be rather similar, No, not similar, identical, As you wish, It isn't only our voices that are identical, What do you mean, Anyone seeing us together would swear that we were twins, Twins, More than twins, identical, In what way identical, Identical, quite simply identical, Let's just stop this conversation right here, I have things to do, So you don't believe me, No, I don't believe in impossibilities, Do you have two moles on your right forearm, beside each other, Yes, I do, So do I, That doesn't prove anything, Do you have a scar under your left kneecap, Yes, So do I. Tertuliano Máximo Afonso took a deep breath, then asked, Where are you, In a telephone booth not far from your apartment building, And where can I meet you, It will have to be in some isolated spot, where there will be no witnesses, Of course, after all, we're not circus freaks. The voice at the other end suggested meeting in a park on the outskirts of the city and Tertuliano Máximo Afonso agreed, But you can't drive into the park, he remarked, All the better, said the voice, Yes, that's my view too, There's a wooded part just beyond the third lake, I'll wait for you there, Unless I get there first, When, Now, in an hour or so, Good, Good, repeated Tertuliano Máximo Afonso, putting down the receiver. He grabbed a bit of paper and scribbled, I'll be back, but did not sign it. Then he went into the bedroom and opened the drawer containing the pistol. He put the clip into the stock of the gun and transferred a cartridge into the chamber. He changed his clothes, clean shirt, tie, trousers, jacket, his best shoes. He stuck the pistol in his belt and left.

ACKNOWLEDGMENTS

The translator would like to thank José Saramago,
Tânia Ganho, Maria Manuel Lisboa, and Ben Sherriff
for all their help and advice.